# Barren Vows

# Barren Vows

WREN WESTON

TOPSY-TURVY PUBLISHING

Topsy-Turvy Publishing
512 West MLK Jr. Blvd, Suite 264
Austin, Texas 78701

ISBN 978-1-68381-026-1 (print)
ISBN 978-1-68381-027-8 (epub)

Visit Topsy-Turvy Publishing on the World Wide Web at
www.topsyturvypublishing.com.

Visit Wren Weston at www.wrenweston.com.

# 1

Lila hoped it would be one of *those* mornings.

She yawned under the covers in the dim room, lit by a neon-blue *Vacancy* sign several buildings over. The chill of mid-November coursed over her bare shoulders. The whirl of the space heater hung in the air, far too loud for the meager heat it offered. Glints of steel twinkled around her like stars, the light reflecting off a dozen knives, a tranq gun, and a mace pegged to the wall. A string of bottle caps hung silently in the window.

She turned to her companion and snuggled deeper in his arms.

"Stay," Tristan mumbled sleepily, his grip tightening around her. His brown eyes opened, and his long eyelashes fluttered against her cheek, tickling her skin.

"I am. I have no intention of getting out bed. Ever."

"Oh, really?" Tristan offered a deep, satisfied *mmm* and rolled atop her, his purring growl transferring from his chest to hers. Soft fingers brushed a few stray brown locks from her face while his arm snaked under her back. Closing his eyes, he dipped his head. His mouth worked at hers, lazily sucking upon her lips as his hand drifted southward.

She tasted whiskey.

He probably tasted her wine.

She breathed in the scent of his shampoo and thumbed his cheek, exploring his mouth. Stubble brushed her palm, a palm broken by pink, healing scars.

Velvet tongues tangled.

Tristan broke away first.

He moved to her neck and nibbled the spot that made her jump and giggle, chuckling when she did. "I claim this spot for Tristonia."

"Last night, it was Tristopolis."

"It was?" he asked, pulling away. "Damn the natives. They're too fickle."

He tugged her closer, grasping her thigh firmly, sparking an ache and an itch for more. "I like another spot, too. I like it so much that I'll have to visit it again."

The bed shook under his shifting weight. Feather kisses brushed her skin, their trail snaking lower and lower across her belly.

Oh, thank the gods!

It would be one of *those* mornings.

She needed it after the dream she'd just had. She needed his arms, his promises, his closeness.

She needed to forget.

Lila sucked in a breath as his mouth drifted ever lower, as she arched her back and reached for the headboard.

The spark he started grew into a fire, catching, swelling, waking every cell in her body from her toes to her fingertips.

She heard a pop as Tristan's breath warmed her skin.

As he stopped.

"Damn it, Lila, you broke the headboard again."

Lila looked back, wincing at the pinkie-thin dowel rods he'd cut and stained to look as though they belonged.

The dowel rods she'd just broken.

Again.

"Stop trying to fix them. I'll buy you a new headboard, a stronger one. One that can take our tugging and pulling. One that's Lila and Tristan proof."

"That's not the point."

"What is the point?"

"Dixon laughs at it enough already. If I carry it to the dumpster and bring up a new one, do you know how many of my people will drop to the floor in fits?"

"They'll drop to the floor weeping. We're getting quality sex, and they aren't." Lila grinned smugly and sat up. She threw a leg over Tristan's waist and straddled him. "By the way, you broke it the first time."

"I did not break it the first time," he muttered.

"Did too."

"Did not."

"Did too."

"Did not."

"Did too."

"Did not." He intertwined their fingers. "You're not going anywhere, Lila Randolph, you know that? I intend to stay near Tristanville for a while. I enjoy its scenic paths and—"

"I thought it was Tristonia."

"You're right. Damn those fickle natives. Something really must be done."

Her palm computer vibrated on the bedside table, the thin, flexible sheet of plastic and circuits traveling across the scuffed wood.

"Don't answer it," he said, squeezing her fingers, not letting them go.

"It might be work."

"You're on vacation, and I have work for you here." He sat up and kissed her deeply, wrapping his arms around her like a vise. "I have lots and lots of work."

"I'm sure you do." Lila wiggled from his arms and snatched up her palm, the bright screen bathing the room in light and shadow. A name blinked on and off.

*Beatrice Randolph.*

Lila sighed at the interruption. The chairwoman of Wolf Industries had left her a message. The matron of the Randolph family. Her boss.

Her mother.

She tapped the screen, and the light grew brighter.

*Breakfast at eight.*

Lila fell back onto her pillow, dropping the cold device between her breasts. She hadn't seen her mother in a week and a half, and not just because she was on a forced vacation.

She had screwed up. A hacker had found out that she'd snuck into a government network and taken data, writing up the event as though it were a newspaper article. After the hacker sent it to her matron, her mother had summoned her immediately to explain.

Lila had not done well. Though the story was true, the details had been far more complicated. She had paid one hundred thousand credits for a temporary silence, all so that she would have more time to trace the hacker's location. After all, she was the Randolph militia chief, charged with protecting every Randolph family compound. It wouldn't do for some half-wit to bribe her, just as it wouldn't do for Bullstow to arrest her.

Of course, she couldn't tell her matron that Bullstow had given their permission for the hack, just so she could find and plug a leak in their system. Bullstow didn't hire highborn militia chiefs as consults, and a matron wouldn't have allowed it. No chairwoman would risk the press and a scandal.

"What were you thinking?" her mother had snapped after Lila fumbled her excuse. The chairwoman had paced restlessly through the parlor, her silver-dyed hair spiraling around her silken robe of the same hue, both messy in their disarray. Her mother had always been put together in times of crisis, but not that evening. That evening, she was as frantic as she was angry. "Why on earth did you need access to the BIRD?"

"There was a situation."

"A situation?"

"A security situation." Lila had refused to explain any further. It wasn't her situation, after all. Someone had laid a trap in the Birth Identity Records Database, also known as the BIRD, ensnaring all who tried to barge in and look around. Her father, the prime minister, had seen one too many highborn blackmailed to believe it was a coincidence. When Bullstow failed to find the culprit, he and the chief of the Saxon militia had hired Lila to investigate.

She'd thought that she'd found the hacker, Tristan's associate, but she knew the man had a partner. That partner continued the ruse after Reaper's death, blackmailing her, treating her like another nosy, corrupt highborn.

She hadn't the time to deal with it then, for she had been busy with other things. So she had paid, and the blackmailer had squealed to her matron.

And Lila couldn't explain any of it.

"You and your little secrets," her mother had said after a long silence. "Fix it, Elizabeth. Don't you dare come back to this estate until you have. I mean it. Not one toe!"

Lila had bowed, packed a bag, and left the compound for Tristan's shop. Unfortunately, she hadn't fixed it, not yet, and not for lack of trying.

But at least the blackmailer had not contacted her since.

"What does your mother want now?" Tristan stroked her belly with his thumb. His head tilted to the side as he studied her face.

"How'd you know it was her?"

"How could I not?" He pointed between her eyes. "You only get this furrow when you mention her."

"She wants me to have breakfast with her in an hour. No reason given. Cryptic, isn't it?"

"Your vacation doesn't end until Monday."

"Perhaps she wants an update. And when I don't have my blackmailer's identity, she'll kick me out of the Randolph compound for good. I'll be exiled like Natalie Holguín. I'm guessing that's why my father messaged me last night."

Her father had cleared his schedule, all so he could return early to New Bristol, the capital of the southern state of Saxony. He wouldn't say why, but she could guess. Prime ministers didn't do such things days before the legislative session closed, not unless they had a damn good reason.

"You think he came back because of you?"

"The timing is awfully convenient, don't you think? He made a point of making lunch plans with me for this afternoon. He knows what my mother has in store for me, and he'll try to soften the blow."

"Maybe he wants to hire you for another job."

"Doubtful. I was less than cooperative the last time we spoke."

"He'd gone behind your back to put you on a forced vacation, and you were trying to protect secrets that weren't yours to tell. You were exhausted, angry, and you still had a blackmailer to find."

"I still do."

"What if he asks you to find Oskar and Maria?"

"Then I'll say no," she said, sitting up and scratching at her tangled hair. "He won't ask me, though. He and Chief Shaw still believe that the Holguíns set up the hit on Natalie and sold Oskar and Maria Kruger to the Germans. So does the Allied press."

"Maybe the family will fall."

"They won't fall. They're handling it, despite the protests. They've cooperated with Bullstow and proven the deal they had set up, a perfectly legal deal with a family in England, if what I saw in Shaw's files is correct. One of my spies informed me yesterday that Chairwoman Holguín might even volunteer to go under the truth serum to prove it. If she's reached that level of desperation, then she might demand every highborn and servant in her compound submit to the serum. She won't let her family fall over this."

He stroked her back. "Do you think your father found out about the warehouse?"

Lila shook him off.

They hadn't talked about what happened at the warehouse since the day it happened, the day they recovered Oskar and entrusted him and his sister to the oracles for safekeeping, the day she helped kill a dozen Italian mercenaries, the day the oracle had taken the survivors to her compound so that she might gain more information about the empire's plans.

Tristan did not cause the silence. Lila merely walked out of the room whenever he brought it up.

If only she could pull the same trick with her memories. If only she could wake before the dreams started, long before the bullets flew and the blood pooled upon the ground. If only she could slam that door behind her for good, keeping it shut and locked and forgotten.

But the door would not stay closed, and it would not stay forgotten. Like a monster beating its club upon the heavy wood, it demanded attention.

It demanded again, but Lila ignored it.

The club struck once more.

"The oracle has kept silent," Lila said at last. "Your people too. From what I can tell, no one knows."

"Lila—"

She stood up, but he lunged, caught her hand, and tugged her back to the bed.

Lila tensed, wanting to bolt.

"Do you really you think your mother might kick you out of your family?"

"She caught me hacking a government database, Tristan. I'm surprised she gave me time to fix it. If she can't use my vacation to explain away my absence, she'll be forced to do damage control, separating the cancer from the rest of the family. She can't have a member of her militia, much less its chief, hacking into government databases, and she can't allow Bullstow to hang me for treason while I'm part of the family. People will talk."

Lila shivered. Perhaps the thought of exile triggered it. She wouldn't just lose her home and her job. She'd lose everyone she loved, everyone she cared about, every friend and relation.

She'd be dead to them all.

A third of all highborn exiles killed themselves within five years. The rest survived as workborn or lowborn, usually moving far away to escape the shadow of their family's tower.

And Wolf Tower stood so very tall.

"You only hacked into the BIRD because your father asked you to. Even Chief Shaw gave his permission. Surely that—"

"Would put both their heads in the hangman's noose. At best, it would ruin my father's political career, and Bullstow would cast Shaw from the militia. They won't save me from my mother's wrath, Tristan. It would give her too much ammo. Besides, she'd likely exile me anyway."

"Why?"

"It would affect our family's stock price too much if I was dragged before the press. The only way that doesn't happen is if the chairwoman of Wolf Industries has already restored her family's honor by culling the problem before the story goes public. It sends a message that the Randolphs don't tolerate that nonsense among its own members, that they police themselves."

"I can't believe she'd exile her own daughter just to make a little extra money."

"It's not just a little extra money, and it's not even the highborn who would be most affected. We have thousands upon thousands of workborn who hold contracts with us. Would you rather see our workforce slashed and jobless just because I made a mistake? Do you know how many people that would affect?"

"She's your mother, Lila."

"She's a matron first. Those are the sorts of decisions you have to make when you take the job. Now you know why I didn't want it."

Tristan sat up behind her put his chin on her shoulder, pulling her body to his. "You should reconsider my suggestion. We'll go to Bullstow tonight and break in. This time for real, not as a favor to Shaw and not to test their defenses. We'll see what else Reaper and his little friend did in BullNet. You'll have all the data you need to figure it out. They can't have just laid traps in the BIRD."

Lila thumbed her palm. Every day, Tristan and his half-brother Dixon suggested breaking into BullNet. Every day, Lila said no. She didn't want to risk waking the blackmailer without good reason.

"No," she said again.

Tristan tightened his arms. "If she kicks you out, you'll always have a place here. No matter what. You don't have to share my bed, though I wouldn't complain if you did. I'd even put a few pegs on the wall for your Colt and boot knife."

Tristan had said as much before. With the exception of one dinner party she'd attended at the Masson winery and a visit to Randolph General to have her stitches removed, she'd spent most of the last two weeks in Tristan's apartment, too busy studying the data from the BIRD to do much else. She'd also dug through a few wiped computers and star drives from Reaper's apartment, as well as a few devices he'd left behind at the shop.

But no matter how hard she'd looked, she hadn't found any leads.

While she worked, Tristan pulled her away for breakfast, for lunch, and for dinner. At night, he pulled her away for eight hours of sleep and a prelude to dreams.

And nightmares.

Lila squeezed her eyes shut.

"Did you call the oracle back?" Tristan asked.

"No." Lila had no desire for the lilac-robed woman to mess with her mind again. The oracle had an entire compound full of private militia. She and her purplecoats could deal with whatever crisis had come upon them.

They could reap the nightmares that followed.

Damn the gods and damn the oracles. Lila didn't even know what she believed about them anymore, and she had grown tired of thinking about the question and its implications.

"I've seen her name on your palm nearly every day," Tristan pressed. "She's even started calling me now."

"So block her ID."

"She wants to see you. I think she wants to help."

"I don't need her help." Lila stood and slipped into Tristan's shirt from the night before.

"Maybe you do. Maybe you should consider it."

"When she has one of her so-called visions about Reaper's partner, then I'll consider it. That's the only useful thing she can offer me right now."

"I don't think that's the kind of help she's offering."

"I told you. I don't need help, not from her."

"Lila—"

"I need a shower."

Lila turned to go. The bed creaked. Tristan grabbed her arm once more. "If you don't want that kind of help, fine. But if something happens at breakfast, if your mother tries anything, I want you to go to the oracle's compound. I don't care if you're an outsider. That woman owes you. She owes both of us."

Lila slipped from his grasp. "My mother won't send her blood squad after me, Tristan. I didn't mess up that badly."

She left the bedroom, easing into the dark apartment beyond before sliding into the bathroom and switching on the light. The sudden, apathetic brightness burned her eyes, and the tile chilled the soles of her feet. She closed the door with a quick little snick, careful not to wake Dixon in the room next door. She strode quickly to the shower and turned on the water. A loud growl thundered down the pipes, then faded as the plumbing shuddered to life.

As the water rushed and warmed, Lila bent over the cracked sink and stared at her image in the mirror. Her vacation had taken away the dark circles under her eyes, but her dreams had left their mark upon them. They'd grown darker, grown harder, grown…

Different.

She turned away from the mirror and ran her fingers through her curls. Stepping into the shower, she warmed herself underneath the water and reached for her shampoo, perched beside Tristan's as if it had lived there all along.

As if she had lived there all along.

A month ago, she wouldn't have believed that a bottle of shampoo could freak her out so completely. But highborns didn't live with one another, and they never focused on one lover.

Being with Tristan in the shop?

Only the poorer classes did such things.

At some point, she'd stopped caring, only understanding that she didn't want to slip into anyone else's bed. Tristan had gotten under her skin, and she didn't know what to do about it. Maybe she didn't even want to do anything about it. It didn't help that she'd enjoyed every minute of her time with Tristan, at least when she wasn't panicking. Panicking about him, her blackmailer, the eventual loss of her job and place among the highborn, about everything she'd worked for her entire life turning to shit.

She stepped out of the shower and blew her hair dry quickly. Then she returned to Tristan's room, dropping her damp towel before his watchful eyes. She pulled on a pair of scratchy black trousers, a long-sleeved gray t-shirt, and a black sweater—servant's clothes, for colors weren't allowed among the workborn unless you had a contract with a highborn family. A pair of cheap, worn boots completed the look. She tucked her boot knife into a sheath near her calf.

She shoved her mesh hood in her front pocket, something she'd need as soon as she stepped outside the apartment, for few of Tristan's people knew her face or her identity. So far they'd stayed quiet, but Lila didn't want to risk any more of them finding out.

Just another risk. Just one more thing that could result in exile.

She stared at her canvas bag in the corner of Tristan's bedroom, filled with a few other similar outfits and toiletries. She wondered if she should even bother taking it along.

Where would she go after her mother kicked her out?

Would she flee to Burgundy like so many exiled highborns, just in case her blackmailer leaked her story? The country refused extradition orders. She'd be safe there. Then again, perhaps she'd stay in New Bristol, continuing this thing with Tristan until it eventually faded, staying until her blackmailer got her arrested.

She deserved the arrest, didn't she?

Perhaps not for her hack, but what had happened in the warehouse.

"Leave it," Tristan said, following her gaze. His fingers trailed down her back, soft against the knit of her sweater. His arms closed around her waist.

She snuggled back into his warmth, stealing a few more precious moments. "I should take it with me."

"*Should* is one of the most insidious and hateful words in the English language," he said, kissing her neck. "You can always take it back to the compound later. It will be fine here."

"I have to go."

"I know."

She gave him a long kiss. Then she picked up her satchel and left the damn bag behind.

# 2

Lila plopped into the driver's seat of her Cruz sedan and shoved a pair of false license plates into her satchel. They'd kept her off her matron's radar for the last two weeks. She'd known her mother's spies would be out, looking for the hole she'd crawled into.

But no one had found it, nor had they found the car she'd taken.

She turned the heater up to full blast, a balm against the chill, then twirled the radio dial to a jazz station. A mournful trumpet called out in long, solemn notes as she backed from her spot in the parking garage and drove away from Shippers Lane. Dirt and mud and cigarette butts filled the gutters. The occasional plastic bag and scrap of paper flitted across the streets in the dim, waking morning.

Smoky diners, pawn shops, and cracked apartments soon merged into the well-lit cafés, bookstores, and boutiques of the better sort of poorer classes. Lowborns, those citizens of New Bristol who ran at least one business, owned many of them. Perhaps more than one, cramming each store into a little complex, mimicking the highborn estates.

Lila rushed through a green light and lifted her eyes to the skyline. Above the grit of the workborn and the lowborn loomed the twelve highborn estates with their sprawling mansions and skyscrapers, far taller than any lowborn would ever be allowed to build, no matter how rich they'd become over the generations.

Now that the Wilson family had fallen to the Randolphs, their tower would topple. It watched over the city like a scornful monarch, gripping her crumbling throne while the peasants swung axes at her door.

New Bristol had swung harder and harder with every passing day. Celeste Wilson and her son would soon hang, serving as an example to anyone who might do business with the Holy Roman Empire, the twin kingdoms of Italy and Germany. The pair's arrests had cast the rest of the Wilson family to the poorer classes. Those who could not afford to purchase their marks from the Randolph family would work as slaves. Those who could pay would take jobs as workborn wherever they could find them, even if it meant traveling out of state.

At season's end, the New Bristol High Council of Judges would announce Suji Park as the next highborn matron. The family would then wall itself off from the poorer classes, erect a similar tower in their compound, and replace the Wilsons as highborn.

Such was the newest verse of the same old song.

Lila stopped before the southern gate of her family's compound, her engine running as a saxophone trilled on. The mansions of the fifteen heirs peeked over the stone wall of the estate, dwarfed by a crowd of maples. Toward the center, Wolf Tower loomed tallest of all the buildings in New Bristol, a glass marvel that glittered as the sun rose. Other skyscrapers and office buildings surrounded it, containing the executive offices, administration personnel, and management for all Randolph holdings throughout Saxony.

A lone saxophone drifted into an announcer's smooth baritone. "That, of course, was the Robby Walsh classic 'Rainy Moon.' In the studio this morning, we have General Ancrum and General De Silva to discuss the Slave Freedom Bill, a piece of legislation rumored to be bouncing around the halls of Bullstow. Ladies, good—"

Lila switched off the radio as Sergeant Nolan knocked upon her window, her blackcoat waving in the chilly wind. Behind Nolan, the door to the gatehouse hung ajar. Her rookie leaned against the glass with curious eyes. The surface steamed with every breath.

"Morning, chief," Nolan said, touching the brim of her cap. "Nice to see you back."

"Nice to be back, sergeant."

"We missed you in the security office. Commander Sutton ordered us to spend two hours at the gun range this week. I suspect Sergeant Jenkins has her ear."

"*Hrmmm…*" Lila replied. Commander Sutton had complete control over the New Bristol estate unless Lila overruled her decisions. But Lila rarely did that, for she had nearly a dozen other compounds to oversee throughout Saxony.

Sutton would have made the requirement even if Lila had not been on vacation. "Perhaps she should order something similar for the gym. As I recall, some of you barely passed your fitness tests last quarter. I'll be sure to pass on your suggestion."

Sergeant Nolan frowned as her rookie pressed the button to open the gate.

Lila hit the gas.

"Hey, pull-ups are hard!" Nolan shouted as Lila drove past, snaking down the asphalt lane that cut through the compound. She passed the lush lawns, the forest groves, and the gravel paths that crisscrossed the estate. The crimson roses had just begun to open, peeking over the fading summer blooms that lined each path.

Lila stopped at the end of Villanueva Lane and parked in front of a fountain. Four bronze wolves strained in each direction, threatening to bite and shred anyone who came near. The great house loomed behind it with a similar attitude, for the architect had built the neoclassical monstrosity for apprehension rather than wonder.

Lila disembarked and marched to the front door. A footman opened it as she approached, his crimson breeches and coat pressed to stiffness.

She pulled her motorcycle jacket more tightly around her, declining to take it off. He'd see too clearly what she wore beneath and report it to the chairwoman. Instead, she quickly jogged upstairs, past the silver Randolph coat of arms. Dozens of paintings surrounded it, all of the Randolph family over the last three centuries.

Fashion hadn't changed that much since then, at least for the highborn.

Lila pulled open the door to her bedroom, a bedroom filled with furniture carved in ebony: a massive desk with a dozen secret nooks, a bed with a thick headboard, a bedside table, a dresser, and a coffee table. Black leather covered her desk chair and a heavy couch. Bursts of Randolph crimson peeked from the pillows, bedclothes, and velvet drapes.

Quickly, she took off her servant's clothes and slid open the secret compartment in her closet with a muffled scrape. The clothes fit easily inside, and she shoved the panel closed again with a dull thunk.

Hangers scratched against the metal bar in her closet as she sifted through her casual highborn clothes. Tailors had cut them in Randolph crimson, stitching the family's coat of arms on the breast. She settled on a high-necked blouse and a pair of black woolen trousers, similar enough to her militia uniform for comfort, different enough to signal that she remained on vacation. Cramming her trouser legs into a pair of knee-high leather boots, Lila looked herself over in a mirror.

She was ready to meet her mother.

Or, at least, she looked like it.

The doorknob jiggled in the silence. Alex peeked in, her blonde hair twisted in a knot, her black skirt and white shirt pressed and unwrinkled. She seemed like a highborn pretending to be a slave, a highborn wearing a costume.

"Ms. Wilson?" Lila asked as her old friend hopped inside and closed the door quietly.

Alex bowed. "Chief Randolph."

Lila inclined her head at the awkward formality. She supposed she deserved it. After all, she'd helped Bullstow arrest Alex's mother and brother, and the pair would be executed soon.

Her friend had seethed before Lila left on vacation, and though they'd since talked, they'd likely never be friends again, at least not like before.

Alex's counseling sessions and anger management classes might help them get through the rough patch, a court-ordered consequence of her arrest for assault. At some point in the next six months, Alex would surely bring up Lila's name. Perhaps the counselor would remind Alex about how much they'd been through together and how much their friendship meant.

Of course, the therapist would more likely remind Alex that she was now a slave and would always be a slave, and that she should accept it and start acting like one.

Slaves did not presume friendship with the highborn.

"You didn't tell me that you were coming back this morning," Alex said, pursing her lips. "It's the middle of the week."

"My mother summoned me for breakfast."

Alex raised a brow. "Did she say why?"

"No, do you know something?"

Alex shook her head. "Not exactly, but Jewel stayed in her room all last night with Senator Dubois. I could hear her crying the whole time, and she paged Isabel every five seconds. Your mother drifted in and out as well. They all went to bed around two in the morning. I don't know what it was about. Ms. O'Malley wouldn't let me come upstairs."

Jewel's fiancé had stayed overnight in the great house, rather than Bullstow? That wasn't rare, nor was her sister's tears, but why would the chairwoman visit them so late?

"I thought you should know."

"Thanks." Perhaps the chairwoman hadn't called her back to discuss her blackmailer after all. Perhaps her sister was in trouble. How ironic that her mother might soon request Lila's services to save the family, the very same services that might get her exiled.

"I didn't even know you were going away, Lila. I missed you." Alex hugged her as though they hadn't seen one another in years.

The soft notes of perfume filled Lila's nose.

Honeysuckle.

Alex's scent had changed.

It felt like everything had changed. Lila had hoped things might be less weird between the two of them after some time apart, but it hadn't changed a thing.

Well, except for maybe one.

"I've missed you as well," Lila said as she finally pulled away. "Alex."

Her old friend smiled at the return of her first name. "I'd better go help Chef with breakfast."

Without another word, Alex peeked into the hallway, then slipped out the door.

Lila twirled her sapphire ring and gave one last look at her bedroom, wondering if it would still belong to her when she returned. She could pay a decorator to recreate it in a new house somewhere. She had plenty of money in her accounts. Perhaps she'd take Alex with her and run away to Burgundy.

Perhaps her friend would forgive her.

She'd taken one step closer, at least.

Lila shook her head at the beautiful, impractical dream and jogged downstairs. She found her mother in the morning room, a room surrounded on three sides by glass and the backyard gardens. Usually spectacular in the spring, much of the color now came from the crimson maple trees and evergreens surrounding the great house.

The chairwoman sat at a table laden with pancakes, eggs, bacon, and blackberries. Pewter pitchers of milk and orange juice loomed over the meal. An open bottle of Gregorie perched in the middle.

"Come, Lila," her mother said tiredly, beckoning her with one twitch of a finger. Her crimson dress and silvercoat flowed about her in a wispy pile of fabric. Matching boots completed the look. She'd arranged her silver hair so that it hung straight around her face, nearly hiding her crow's feet and the fine lines in her forehead, all made deeper by her pensive expression. Dark circles marred the skin under her eyes, a rare look for the chairwoman. "Do you know why I've summoned you here this morning?"

Lila stepped into the room and rested her hands upon a chair back, the seat upholstered in crimson and gold. "I suppose that Jewel needs my assistance with something."

Her mother stiffened at Jewel's name and sipped her orange juice. "You always seem to know more than you let on."

Two weeks ago the statement would have been true. Lila usually knew a great deal about what went on in the compound. Though her mother's spy network was impossible to best, Lila had learned from a master. She'd made an art of indulging the workborn on every Randolph compound throughout Saxony and bribing several key relations in each location. She also exploited WolfNet to her advantage.

She'd heard no news about Jewel, though, except from Alex.

The chairwoman cleared her throat. "Your sister has decided to marry."

"Marry the senator?"

"Senator Dubois. He has a name and a title. Do not be impolite."

"Yes, Senator Louis Oliver Masson-Dubois. I know his name and title," Lila said, finally falling into a seat beside her mother.

Lila rubbed at her eyes. All this time, she'd obsessed over taking other lovers, just so she wouldn't get too attached to Tristan, and Jewel had been thinking of marriage? "I can't believe you're worried about politeness at a time like this. Marriage, Mother? Are we workborn, or are we highborn?"

"Highborns marry," the chairwoman replied grumpily.

Lila shot her a look.

"Occasionally we marry. It's becoming more common."

Lila reached for a dish of blackberries and popped one in her mouth. "Surely you've counseled her against this. She's prime. She needs an heir. How will she do that if she couples exclusively with a man as unproven as Senator Dubois? I like him immensely, Mother, I really do, but he's had several seasons to get the job done. He's failed time and time again."

The chairwoman pursed her lips and cast her eyes down at the table.

"You told her the same thing, and she ignored you." Lila snatched the Gregorie and poured herself a generous glass. "Surely someone can get through to her. Prime or not, no one should tie themselves down to one person forever, much less bind themselves in a marriage contract. That's not love. That's a business arrangement, and a rather dumb one at that. She'll regret it entirely after they've drifted apart."

"She can always get a divorce."

"That will go over well at parties." Lila dumped several pancakes and a heaping spoonful of eggs onto her plate, then poured maple syrup over the lot. "When did Jewel make this decision?"

"The couple made it last night."

"The couple? Jewel is twenty-four years old. She's far too young to marry. She's always wanted a large family. She cannot mean to throw that away for a man who has not managed one child in four years. She'll be lucky to bear two or three at this rate. And what of the senator? His political career will be over before it's begun."

"He's thinking of love. They both are."

"Love?" Lila jabbed at a pancake. "Fools. Both of them are pretty, little fools."

The two women ate silently for several moments. As the initial shock of her mother's announcement wore off, Lila felt herself watched with far more intensity than she had in the last decade. Her mother might have been a starved cat eyeing a mouse hole.

And she hadn't even brought up her blackmailer.

"This isn't why you called me here so early."

"No, it's not. I'm guessing Ms. Wilson told you about Jewel's theatrics last night? Surely you don't think an engagement triggered your sister's hysteria?"

"I never quite know what will set Jewel off. However, I could give you a list of several topics that are sure to cause a meltdown."

"I think I know that list very well, thank you. Her fits are not her finest attribute. Tell me, Lila. With such a flaw, do you really believe she is fit to lead Wolf Industries? Does she possess the steadiness of character to bear the full responsibility of the company?"

Lila pushed her pancakes away. "With all due respect, Madam Chairwoman, that is no longer my problem. I abdicated my position over a decade ago. I am the chief of your militia, and Jewel is the prime heir of the Randolph family. If you wish to change that, then you would need to declare her unfit under the Inheritance Law and train the next heir in line. I'm sure Aunt Georgina would love the position. If that doesn't suit you, then choose another heir or try again for another daughter. I'm sure there are a thousand senators in Saxony who would—"

Her mother slapped the table. "This is no time for impertinence. Senator Dubois was tested by a fertility specialist. He received the results yesterday evening. Jewel spent last night calling his doctors because she didn't want to believe the results. The senator is seedless, Elizabeth. He will never have children, not even from a tube, and Jewel's far too in love with him to break off the union."

"That's impossible. Senators are screened before they begin their internships. If testing had revealed a fertility issue, Senator Dubois would have been directed into another occupation at Bullstow long before he saw the inside of High House."

Lila, as well as most highborn, had always approved of such a system. No senator had ever achieved a position of political significance without allying himself with multiple highborn families through fatherhood. Ever since Senator Benedict King betrayed the Allied Lands to the Holy Roman Empire over two hundred years ago, the nation was leery of bachelor politicians. It was generally thought that the more children a senator had, the more trustworthy and fair he would be in his deliberations, the more invested he would be with his legislation and the future of the country, the less likely he would be to accept bribes, and the less likely he would turn traitor and scamper away to another country with American or Allied secrets.

At least, that was the theory.

The High House in each city served as the proving ground of the young and the pasture of the old, with only a dozen cities prized among the chaff. Senator Dubois's brethren had elected him to New Bristol, the capital of Saxony, the most prized city of all. The man's exceptional charisma, unparalleled fairness, and ties to Jewel had allowed Bullstow to keep nominating him year after year. Since Dubois would soon seed an heir for the Randolph prime, everyone gave him a certain amount of leeway, for if the Randolphs had found him worthy, then Bullstow and New Bristol should as well. But that leeway would not last forever, no matter how much potential he might possess.

Lila drained her wine. "He needs a second—"

"That *was* the second opinion, Lila. The senator cannot have children, and since your sister is determined to marry him without exercising the right of *eyre-cleue*, neither will she. Jewel will bear no heirs for the Randolph family. As such, I have had to rethink several prior arrangements about Wolf Industries."

"We have a contract."

"A contract I can rescind any time I please," the chairwoman reminded her. "Regardless of your ill-timed and ill-thought-out foray into BullNet, I can no longer accept your abdication. Starting today, your contract is forfeit. You are once again prime, and you will be my legal and rightful heir, and as my heir you have certain responsibilities, responsibilities that you have dodged for long enough."

"I'm chief of your militia. I'm the best damn chief you've ever had, regardless of my current—"

"Not anymore. I will expect the name of a trustworthy and competent replacement by the end of the year. Commander Sutton can pick up the slack until then."

"You can't do this. She can't do this!" Lila hopped up from the table, quieting every impulse to overturn it. "She promised."

"This isn't a game, child. Jewel has never had any real responsibility to remain as prime. For oracle's sake, she was twelve when she made the vow!"

"How old was I?"

The chairwoman's fork dropped into her plate with a clink. She abandoned her orange juice and poured herself a glass of Gregorie.

Lila retreated to the corner, her eyes fastening on to the buildings outside the glass. On the drive in, the compound had seemed solid and secure. Her job had always been to protect it, to smooth out the infighting and plotting among the heirs and relations, to ensure that the whole structure did not crumble from within or become vulnerable to infiltration. Now her mother asked her to take on an altogether different responsibility, to war against the other families in Saxony. The compound seemed so much smaller and more fragile.

All except Wolf Tower. It caught her eye in the center of the estate, a shard of glass cutting through flesh, penetrating the sky. Her new office would be at the top, just down the hall from her mother's, both overlooking the compound.

Every structure on the estate contained members of the Randolph family, and every one of them needed someone competent in Wolf Tower.

But why did it have to be her?

Her mind strayed to the warehouse floor, to the rivers of blood pooling underneath torn necks and broken limbs.

The gods had seen fit to punish her at last.

Why not? Why did she deserve a happy ending after dealing so much death?

Remorse.

Compensation.

She had to pay, and the gods had given her just enough time with Tristan to make it hurt.

"Surely there are treatments for the senator," Lila said, somber, calm, and confused by the detour the morning had taken. She'd thought she be exiled, but now—

Now she was being promoted.

And punished.

Both at the same time.

"Be serious, child. There are few treatments for men in his condition. It's never been all that important when a man cannot conceive. Perhaps in twenty years, Grace Medical might discover some treatment for his case if we put all our resources into it, but it will be far too late for Jewel and Senator Dubois."

"How do you know?"

"Because I asked!" the chairwoman snapped. "Do you really think I want both of my children to be unhappy?"

Lila crossed her arms over her chest, stilling her impulsive answer. "Jewel isn't barren. She can easily keep the senator around while she takes other men on the side. Let her bed the whole damn High House one man at a time. She doesn't have to live with any of them."

"She only wants Senator Dubois."

"So let her marry the senator, then. Declaring *eyre-cleue* would completely absolve her of any charge of adultery or duty to compensate Senator Dubois while she—"

"Elizabeth Victoria Lemaire-Randolph, I said no. I have rescinded your abdication, and your contract is void. You are once again prime. You might have dodged your duty if your baby sister had been able to produce an heir, but we both know that she would have been incapable to run things after I'm gone. She's not woman enough to lead. You are. You would have had to take over, anyway. It's just sooner rather than later."

Lila peered through the glass-paneled wall. "I have no interest—"

"I don't really care what you have an interest in. You had your fun. Count yourself lucky to have had the last ten years and adapt quickly to the change."

"I would rather—"

"Yes, you'd rather gallivant around in the middle of the night stealing data from Bullstow, putting this entire family at risk."

"I'm handling it. You told me that I'd have two weeks to find—"

"I'm trying to protect you, you little—" Her mother broke off and took a long sip of wine. "You've had nearly two weeks to fix your mess, Elizabeth. Two weeks. It's my turn now. I need to know what Bullstow will find if your blackmailer forwards the story."

"I scrubbed the logs. Bullstow won't see me there, not even if they know what they're looking for. At best they'll find shadows." Lila cleared her throat, hoping she'd finished the job completely. "I'm not that worried about Bullstow, madam. I'm worried about what proof this blackmailer might have against me. I broke into Bullstow for the hack. If this blackmailer copied the logs before I took care of them, then my identity and intentions will be clear. Things could get complicated."

"Our lawyers can spin all sorts of confusion, Elizabeth, and I can pay them to weave the best. Any company that consults with Bullstow on your case is sure to have connections to our rivals, and our lawyers can highlight that. As for a trespassing charge, you've been sneaking into Bullstow to visit your father and Shiloh since you were a child; they can hardly complain about it now. All we need is doubt and enough votes on the senate disciplinary committee. I can make it all go away with enough money and favors."

"You'd ask Shiloh to lie for me?"

"No, you'll ask him to lie for you. Without proof, this story is nothing but tabloid twaddle. Is there anything they'll find? Did you profit from this hack?"

"Gods no."

"They can audit your accounts? Even the ones outside the country?"

"If they can find them."

"That's what I thought. It's the only reason why I gave you two weeks, you know. I should have summoned Commander Sutton to escort you out that night. It's what your great-great-grandmother would have done."

"No, she would have summoned her blood squad. She called them for her own son."

"Yes. It nearly killed her to do it, but she preserved the family's honor. Perhaps I should have done the same. Unfortunately, you're my heir, and you have put yourself and this family in a very difficult position. I either exile you and keep Jewel in your place, or I elevate you and fight your charges. A highborn, even an heir, might be hanged for your crime, but the standard of evidence is quite a bit higher for a prime. But if the truth comes out and our lawyers do not believe they can overturn the charges, I will exile you from this family, do you understand?"

Lila nodded.

"Best case, no one finds out what you've done. Slightly worse case, Bullstow arrests you, you go free, and we put this whole mess behind us. A cloud of mistrust will hang over the Randolphs for years. Half the highborn families will sever their ties with us out of protest. We will lose some of our lowborn partners, some of our accounts. Bullstow will audit our files. It will sour our relationships with High House, with the oracles, with the High Council of Judges. We will take a major hit, but—"

"Half our business would crumble."

"Yes, and it would be your doing. We would survive, though, and so would you. This blackmailer won't do anything as long as we pay him. So you will continue to pay him, Elizabeth, and you will fix it. If you can't, you risk harming several thousand in your care. At least you'll be alive, though. What's the alternative? You spend the rest of your life in Burgundy?"

"Yes," Lila said quietly.

"What happens when you get caught doing something equally stupid there? I can't help you in Burgundy, and once you leave, you can't return and take my place." Her mother shook her head. "Oracle's wrath, I thought you were smarter than this."

Lila clenched her jaw and took the hit.

"Do you think so little of yourself that you thought you had to cheat to get what you want?"

"It wasn't like that."

"How in the world would I know what it's like? You haven't told me. This sneaking into BullNet stops now. You've been much too careless with the Randolph name. This is why you hire out such work if you're going to do it."

"Maybe I should be exiled. Maybe I would prefer Burgundy."

"You'd be bored within a month. Burgundy is a very small country with very limited prospects. You'd be unhappy playing on such a tiny chessboard. No matter how much you resist our likeness, you are still my daughter. You could never be happy unless you controlled an army. How many people are under your command right now, spread over the compounds? Two thousand?"

Her mother waited for confirmation, but Lila refused to give it.

"Soon you'll control a great deal more. Every Randolph, every contracted workborn, every slave on every compound will bow to your authority, just as it should have been for the past ten years. You might have hidden from the cameras for the last decade, but everyone knows your name. Now they'll know your face."

Lila looked away. She hadn't even thought of that. Her precious anonymity would be stripped away as soon as she put on the whitecoat. "I'm not the only one who can take over. I can fix this and remain chief. Any one of your sisters could be the new prime. Aunt Georgina—"

"My little sister can barely handle her own businesses, profitable as they are. She may be able to throw the most lavish weddings in Saxony, but could you imagine her handling the oil rigs? She's never even seen them. You have. You've even earned the respect of those who work on them." Her mother sighed, clearly tired of the fight. "Georgina has the time to dawdle with brides and grooms because her eldest daughter has taken charge of the Beaulac compound. I'll not hand Wolf Industries to any of my sisters or their offspring. I won't see everything that I've worked for over the last thirty years run into the ground. None of them have what it takes to lead the family. You are the only one who has the mettle and the brains to run this place successfully. I should know. I designed you that way."

"I didn't know I was a new coat."

The chairwoman raised her glass. "It's an apt metaphor. I ensured that you had the correct education, that you had the proper experience. I even controlled how you played as an infant. You—"

"Don't want to lead, and I don't want children," Lila interrupted. "That was what Jewel was for."

"She can still be useful in that role. Have a few children and pass them off to your sister and her fiancé the day they are born. Senator Dubois aches to be a father. He spent too long at Bullstow taking care of all those boys while dreaming of his own. He'll mend what Jewel rips. I'll educate the heir. You wouldn't even have to see your children if you can't be bothered."

"I'm not that cold-hearted."

"Well, I'm glad to hear it," the chairwoman said. "Think of what will happen to the Randolphs should someone else become prime. Would your aunt or cousins do well by the family or would they line their own pockets first? Would they do well by your little brother? Would they show the same dedication and consideration for Randolph General? What about poor Ms. Wilson? Think of what you can do for her as prime. I am not completely ignorant of your plans."

"What plans?"

"Freeing her and letting her run Grace Medical after I die. You both will no doubt forget your stations and become what you were before she lost her mark. I'd be exceedingly angry if you gave it all back to her, but after I am dead there will be nothing I can do to stop it."

Lila rubbed her chin. Alex's fall had occurred long after Lila had abdicated as prime, so such a plan had never crossed her mind. The thought tempted her now, though, the idea that she could do this thing for her friend. Alex certainly desired her old world once more. She wouldn't be highborn, but she could be lowborn.

Lila certainly owed her that much.

The fact that her mother brought up the idea made Lila wary, though, for that and for hinting that her brother and her hospital might fall under someone else's careless hand. She was being bribed, and her mother did not even try to hide it.

"Lila, you had more time to indulge than I did."

The mild censure, said so quietly, kicked Lila in the gut. Her mother had become the chairwoman of Wolf Industries at the age of fourteen due to her own mother's early death. She'd survived intrigue and assassination attempts from several aunts as a teenager, then had Lila at seventeen, all to settle the chaos surrounding her and procure the stability of her family.

Luckily, a young, caring senator with a great deal of potential had made the job easier. Henri Lemaire, Lila's father, had become a close friend and confidant of the young chairwoman. A decade ago, she had repaid that kindness by helping him become the American prime minister.

Lila couldn't imagine becoming a mother at seventeen, nor could she imagine attending the execution of a few murderous aunts. But by the time her mother had become pregnant, she'd already run a company worth several billion credits. She'd done well for the family over the last thirty years, tripling their holdings and wealth. She'd also wormed her way onto the Saxony High Council of Judges, which made the Randolphs one of the most important families in the state. She'd even begun buying land in Unity, her eye already on the nation's capital.

"You might not like it, Lila, but this is the only way I can keep you safe and ensure the security of the family. I have thousands to think about, not just the whims of my eldest daughter, a daughter who has put herself in a very precarious position. A chief does what she must to protect the family. This is what you must do to protect us now. If you refuse to accept your new role, then you will no longer be a part of this family." The chairwoman refilled Lila's glass, then looked her daughter in the eye. "What will it be? Will you finally become the prime you were always meant to be, or will you choose exile instead?"

Lila felt the morning room close in around her. It would have been easier if her mother had fixed her with the same look she reserved for the boardroom, but that expression did not lurk behind her eyes.

Pity filled them instead.

Lila looked away first. She returned to the table and snatched up her abandoned wine.

The chairwoman nodded, taking it for assent. "I'm sorry, Lila. I did try to let you live your life the way you wanted, but for all I know, my time is growing short. I've already outlived my mother. I have to think of the family and its future."

"You're not dead yet."

"Much to your dismay, I'm sure. Your first act as prime is drawing near. You have an appointment at noon to have your birth control reversed."

"Oracle's light," Lila whispered. Her mother's demands had crystalized before her, like a fanged wolf, circling.

It growled, lunged, and snapped at her womb.

She clutched her belly, unnerved.

"Bullstow marks the end of legislative session on Friday, Lila. After the Closing Ceremony, the High Senate will throw their annual Closing Ball. You need to be ready."

Lila drained her wine in one long swallow. During the Closing Ball, women from highborn families and very prosperous lowborn families selected men for the season, that time when every local, regional, and national legislature closed its doors. From mid-November until April, senators expended all their efforts on making babies, rather than laws, all in order to tie themselves to the people.

That wasn't the only reason, of course. Men raised in Bullstow, especially senators, really loved having children. A senator didn't consider himself remotely finished with his family unless he had at least a dozen, and none would breathe easily until he had a son to raise. But only heirs gave up their firstborn sons to government service, handing them off to their fathers and Bullstow soon after birth.

As such, heirs without sons were mobbed in every ballroom by well-dressed senators trying their best to tempt the lady into a season. Lila avoided highborn events for that reason, even though her role as heir was fuzzy and unofficial. Senators became quite frustrated when an heir claimed she did not want any children. It usually ended up as some extended legislative session where small groups of men attempted to filibuster her into changing her mind.

And now she had Tristan to think about.

She didn't want another lover, not if she was honest with herself, but perhaps she needed one. She'd completely lost herself in the man. She was a highborn, for oracle's sake. She'd never let herself end up like Jewel, letting one man absorb all her attention. It was pathetic and clingy and...

Weird.

"It's not too late to find a good match," her mother said. "Many of the truly eligible men are rather coquettish until the last moment, holding out for precisely this sort of situation. Providing you with a daughter would make any senator's political career or his happiness should you bear a son. Both are valuable to a woman in your position. You'll have your pick of men. It will be the talk of the highborn and good for business."

"I'm to choose a partner for the season based only on one party?" Lila despaired at how ridiculous her life had become in an hour.

"Choose or don't choose, but Wolf Industries requires a new heir. At the very least, we need a firstborn son to send to Bullstow. It will signal to the rest of New Bristol that our family has settled at last. Our stock has declined over the last few years due to your sister's ill-placed constancy."

"Not just her constancy."

"Lila," her mother said gently. For the first time in her life, Lila saw a hint of desperation in the chairwoman's eyes. "Wear the whitecoat and commit to a child. It has always been your duty, just as it was Shiloh's duty to go to Bullstow. You've had your fun, and perhaps it's my fault for indulging you, but it is time to grow up. You must do this for the sake of the family and your own future, and you know it."

She had seen her mother's face as she gambled on a deal.

This wasn't it.

Lila stayed silent, hating her mother for her ultimatum, hating that she must choose between joining the family as prime or being an exile among the poorer classes, powerless to wield any influence to help the family at all.

When she finally spoke, her words came out thin and weak. "Not prime, Mother, not until I've chosen a senator for the season. I don't want the fuss at the Closing Ball. Besides, I still need to clean up my mess."

"I understand."

"Reschedule the appointment, too. I have a prior commitment."

"Fine, I'll change your appointment to five o'clock this evening. A car will pick you up in front of the house. For what it is worth, I am sorry. This is what happens when you are born with responsibility and duty and talent."

The chairwoman tinged the last few words with a sad half-smile.

Lila could not help but think that part of her mother in that moment was fourteen years old again, still at breakfast, told that she would begin running an empire as soon as she finished her meal.

# 3

Lila sat at her desk, her gaze focused on the silver coat of arms nailed above her couch. When her computer beeped, she logged into WolfNet as her sister, something she'd only ever done to protect the interests of the family. Perhaps curiosity had pushed her into the hack this time, coupled with the implications to her future. Or perhaps she only worried that Senator Dubois's condition might strike another senator.

A man like Dubois did not go sterile for no reason.

Scrolling through Jewel's inbox, she found half a dozen messages from several sets of doctors. She pulled Dubois's medical records from the emails and saved them to an empty star drive, taking care to redact the senator's name from the information. The records did not seem altered in any way, but Lila couldn't help but wonder again at Dubois's predicament. Doctors had only diagnosed a handful of senators with fertility problems since they'd begun testing the interns, and they could trace every case to illness, injury, or age.

As far as she knew, Dubois had not caught any illness, nor fallen to an injury.

Alex brought a kettle of tea. She questioned Lila with every glance, every bow of her head, every raised brow, but Lila was not ready to explain what had occurred in the morning room. The pair had known each other for a long time. Alex knew when to back away.

She left Lila to her thoughts.

Lila was glad for it. After she visited the clinic, rumors would spread. She just needed a chance to get used to the idea before that happened.

Would she really do this? Would she really abandon her career and take up one she had no interest in? Would she really have a child?

Her family needed her, didn't they? Thousands of Randolphs throughout Saxony waited for her to carry on her mother's reign.

She wanted to remain part of the family, didn't she?

Perhaps this was the only way to deserve them, after what she'd done at the warehouse.

Perhaps accepting her mother's demand would stop the dreams.

Lila put the thought out of her mind. She pulled the star drive from her desktop and thrust it into her coat pocket. Snatching up her teacup and kettle, she padded toward her sister's chamber next door, her boots muffled by a pastel rug near the entrance. A struggling fire lit the dim room, little more than embers glowing among ash.

Jewel's room always suffocated her. Her sister had chosen the paintings carefully from her most brilliant works, each one spared the accolades of its neighbor by perfect spacing. She'd imbued most with happy flourishes of blues, greens, and purples. Above the bed, a nude young woman wrapped herself around a bedpost, coyly waiting for her lover. Near the dresser, two young men in short breeches and nothing else grasped one another during a wrestling match, a match for fun rather than competition. Jewel had placed sadness in the corners. A bone-thin cat ran through the crumbling ruins of a castle, hidden by ivy. Above the fire, two demons wrapped around each side of a woman, pressing against her thighs and hips, whispering in her ears.

Lila didn't know what to make of that one. Jewel had asked her to sit for it the day she turned eighteen and officially abdicated as prime. Lila hadn't known what the painting would look like until her sister had finished. Though intended as a gift, Lila could not hang it. It unsettled her too much.

She wondered what Jewel would paint now, if she knew all that she'd done.

Perhaps the demons would have her face this time.

Her mother had not escaped her sister's work, either. Paintings hung in several New Bristol galleries with her face. The only comment she had made upon seeing them was that they did not contain enough red.

But Jewel never painted with the color, no matter the size of the commission.

The rest of the room was lux, elegant, and far more sophisticated than Lila's would ever be. Whereas Lila had abandoned her room to the care of a minimalist designer, Jewel had sent hers away and designed her room unaided. A canopied bed dominated the back, large enough for a ménage à trois or ménage à ten. Gossamer silk poured down the bedposts like the trailing wisp of a fairy's hem. Heavy tapestries hung over the windows to keep away the light. The other side of the space held two white love seats and a matching plush chair, forming a faux-parlor. Pale white dressers and tables made of spruce dotted the room. Several pedestals held small marble sculptures, twisted into the shapes of fantastical creatures.

Lila stood at the door awkwardly as though she was unworthy to enter the bedroom. When her gaze flicked to the lumps in bed, lumps that had not stirred at her entrance, she gritted her teeth and pushed inside.

Jewel's couch scraped against the floor as Lila plopped down.

She poured a cup of tea and sipped impatiently. Jewel did not wake early at the best of times. If she had stayed up all night, perhaps she had decided to take off work for the entire day and sleep in.

It must be nice to care so little.

Propping her boots upon the glass table before her, Lila leaned deeper into the couch. The wine from breakfast had set to work upon her, relaxing her muscles like a practiced masseuse. She nearly fell asleep. Her teacup tipped several times, nearly splattering her raw fingers with hot liquid as she waited for her sister and the senator to wake.

A not completely accidental banging of china betrayed her as she poured a second cup.

The lumps twitched.

Jewel woke with a start.

"What the— Who the—" she shrieked, snatching up a bedside lamp. Lila wondered what her sister intended to do with it from the leisure of her bed, especially since it was still plugged in.

Senator Dubois sat up. "Whuddadoear?" he mumbled groggily.

Lila thought about letting the scene play out. What would the pretty prime and the handsome senator do against an intruder? Ring for a workborn to deal with it? Perhaps yell at Alex to attack the shadow with her heels?

"Relax," Lila said as she stood up. She padded to a window and drew back the curtains, letting the sunlight stream into the room.

Jewel cursed and squinted against the brightness.

Dubois ducked his head under a pillow. The senator seemed to have a harder time with mornings than any Randolph. Jewel often joked that he only assented to their seasons together because the chairwoman gifted him with a steady supply of coffee, a brand flown in directly from Brazil. Lila had not known before how much the senator might need it every morning.

"What are you doing here so early?" Jewel groaned, pulling the covers over her naked breasts.

Lila ignored the question and continued her assault. She worked steadily around the room, throwing open the curtains at every window. "Senator Dubois, it's time for you to take a shower. I need to speak with my sister."

The senator finally removed his head from the pillows. He ran his fingers through his long blond hair, somehow not overly mussed from an entire night in bed, and rubbed sleepily at his hazel eyes. The man had a calming air about him that the most successful senators possessed, as well as a beauty that only grew when he woke without a shave or clothes.

They likely taught such things at Bullstow.

Perhaps it was an entire semester's class.

Dubois bowed his head at his future sister-in-law and stifled a yawn. He stripped off a sheet and wrapped it around his midsection, then stumbled toward the bathroom.

"Not here. Go home to Bullstow."

The senator raised an eyebrow and glanced back at Jewel, saying nothing of Lila's rudeness. Bullstow taught senators from a young age not to reproach anyone for anything but the most grievous offense. Diplomacy called for such patience.

"Louis, how about coffee?" Jewel asked. "Please ask Chef Ana for a cup while I speak with my sister. Ask her to make us something nice for breakfast, too. Whatever you want is fine with me."

"Yes, madam." Dubois snatched up his clothes and ducked behind an antique changing screen in the corner.

Jewel glared at her sister.

Lila resumed her perch on the couch and glared back. A silent battle loomed between two alley cats, fought with warring eyes instead of warring paws.

To his credit, the senator dressed quickly. He dashed out again a moment later, pausing only to offer his fiancée a kiss on the forehead.

Perhaps they practiced quick exits at Bullstow. Perhaps they had even tests.

"You didn't have to be so rude," Jewel snapped when the door closed, throwing on her robe and tying the belt around her waist angrily. Her brown hair tangled fetchingly around her neck, and even in anger, her sky-blue eyes were lively and doll-like, though rimmed in red. "He's to be your brother-in-law, and we talked until early this morning. He's still exhausted, as am I."

"I'm exhausted too. Mother recalled me from my vacation."

Jewel's mouth dropped open. Her pale cheeks reddened. She knelt before Lila on the rug and placed her head in her sister's lap. "I wanted to tell you first. I tried to contact you last night before we told—"

Lila shook her off. "Crying and carrying on at your age? Stand up and face me like a woman, not like a child."

"You don't have to be rude."

"Rude? Since when is telling the truth rude?" Lila stood up to pace from one end of the room to the other.

"Because you didn't mean it as the truth, you meant it to wound. You were being mean."

"Mean? What are you? Five?" Lila did not hold in her laugh this time, a laugh of pure frustration. Gods, Jewel hadn't changed at all. She really couldn't lead the family, not now, not ever. "I don't care if I sound rude or mean right now. You promised, Jewel. You promised that you would be prime. Ever since we were children, you promised. You told me how lucky you were to have an elder sister who would pass the honor onto you. Now you're taking back that vow as if it meant nothing."

"I was a child! I didn't know what it meant back then. You can't expect me to keep a promise I made when I was twelve."

"I never even got the chance to promise!"

Jewel shifted on the floor. "My life has changed a great deal since then."

"So has mine! I worked my way up from nothing in the security office. Do you think it mattered who my mother was in the barracks? I stayed up so many nights chasing intruders and finding boogeymen in WolfNet. I protected you when you messed up your office. I traded away my youth to make chief, and I did it all on my own. I earned it. Now it turns out that everything I worked for during the last ten years was for naught."

"I'm sorry."

"Don't you dare apologize. You didn't spill wine on my favorite coat, Jewel. You didn't wreck my car. You've taken away my life. I could have spent my twenties in bed like you, flat on my back in the arms of some senator, but I didn't because I had a job to—"

"Don't—"

"Oracle's wrath, Jewel, you gave me your word!"

Jewel pressed her lips together, the effort hardening the lines in her mouth. "Did I? Did I really promise it of my own free will, or was I endlessly talked into it by an older sister who never wanted to face her duty?"

"My duty? Why is it my duty? Just because I'm older?"

"Yes, just like Shiloh was sent to Bullstow because he was the firstborn son, whether he wanted to go or not. Do you think Pax should have taken his place just because Shiloh might not have wanted such a life?"

"All men want to be senators, even the workborn," Lila said, pausing in her pacing, annoyed that Jewel had brought up their brothers.

"All men?"

"Yes. Few are lucky enough to be the firstborn sons of a highborn family. They have the chance to become the most powerful men in all of Saxony."

"Not all men want such a life, just like not all women want to be heirs to a family. Ms. Wilson didn't. You didn't."

"It's not the same thing."

"It's not? Pax has never had designs for such a future, and you know it."

Lila leaned against the window. "This conversation is between you and me. Don't bring them into this."

"Why not?" Jewel said, standing up. She stepped closer, and her eyes darted to her closed bedroom door and the door beyond it. "Would you have sent Pax to Bullstow in Shiloh's place?" she asked quietly. "Even now, even knowing that he would fail, knowing that he would be miserable? For gods' sake, you would have stood by while Pax was forced to lie with women just so Shiloh could—"

"No one forces the men of Bullstow to do anything," Lila whispered, also casting a glance at the bedroom door. "There are plenty of things they can choose beside politics. The ones like Pax have children among the highborn anyway, at least until they find lovers or husbands. Others spend their days as educators or lawyers, happily coupled with one another from the start. They tend to the sons of Bullstow while their brothers dabble in politics. It's actually the best place for boys like—"

"You don't know that!"

"Actually, I do. I based my career on seeking out information and protecting it, a career you've tossed into the flames. Who shushed up your first year at Bokington before the papers caught wind? I haven't spent my adult years painting pictures and plucking fruit from High House. Some of us—"

"You shut your mouth right now," Jewel shouted, stabbing her finger at Lila's chest. "It is because I've done what I've done that you had the opportunity to become the chief of security, so don't you dare pretend that you're better than me now. I might have had my fun, but you're not the only one who has worked." Jewel's pupils shrank to pinpricks as she stepped into the light. "Grow up, Lila, and take your turn for the family."

Lila studied the woman before her, a woman who shrank a bit under her scrutiny.

"I think you just grew teeth, Jewel. Perhaps you aren't so hopeless after all."

Jewel took her finger back, surprised and disgusted by her own violence, then plopped down on the couch in exhaustion. "I'm sorry. I'm just so tired."

"Obviously. You were raised to think more intelligently about these things. Marriage, Jewel? Humans weren't made for one partner. You'll end up miserable. Go talk to Commander Sutton if you don't—"

"Commander Sutton isn't miserable. She and her husband enjoy fighting with one another. Sometimes people want more from life than a series of lovers."

"Why do you have to turn it into a contract, then?"

"You would get hung up on that. It's not a business contract. It's an emotional one. I get that you're upset, Lila, but—"

"Upset? You don't know the meaning of the word. My life is over, Jewel, don't you understand that? For what? A man? Your man?

A man you'll cast aside in a few years once you get bored, then use the angst as inspiration for a series of paintings? Of course, I shouldn't be upset at all."

Jewel laid her head against the cushions. "Sometimes I forget how selfish you can be. You think you're better than her, but you're not. At least Mother wept for me."

"Wept?" Lila snorted. It was harder to imagine her mother weeping than Jewel giving a competent speech before the High Council of Judges.

"I can see that even now you do not understand. I shouldn't have to point out what should be plain. You're not the only one whose life is ruined, but you're so full of your own problems that you don't see anyone else's. You didn't even stop to think about what I have lost, what my Louis has lost. Pardon me if I don't have any more tears to spare for you right now."

Lila licked her lips, her bluster gone. "I'm sorry."

Jewel straightened her shoulders, inclining her head.

"Your life isn't over, though. You could still have a house full of children. You're prime. Take other lovers. If you just found someone—"

"Don't say it," Jewel interrupted, putting her hand up in the air. "You wouldn't understand the rest of that sentence anyway, and I'll only get mad at you again."

"My apologies," Lila said, but only because her sister looked so miserable.

"What a fine pair we make. Neither of us got what we wanted in the end."

Lila had no idea how to respond. "It's not all bad. You'll get to spend more time in your studio now. Mother will likely goad me into having so many children that you'll move into an empty heir's home, just for the quiet. You'll have plenty of nieces and nephews to occupy your time."

Jewel gave a strange, strangled sort of sound, a cross between a laugh and a cry.

Lila squeezed her shoulder and took it as a cue to escape.

# 4

Lila settled into her seat at her father's table, shifting on the golden-upholstered cushion. The craftsman had fashioned the chair from pale ash, shaping the legs into curving stems and carving roses along the side. The table mirrored it, a beautiful antique that Bullstow had likely owned for at least a century.

A servant in a golden coat and breeches poured hot chocolate into china mugs. He placed a tray of chocolate chip cookies on the table, the crockery clinking as it touched. Leaving the kettle behind, he bowed himself from the room.

The suite door snicked from far away, audible in the silence.

Neither Lila nor her father touched the cookies.

Lemaire sat at the table like an aging warrior only recently returned from war, still muscular and full of life, filling out his white coat and breeches. The hue brought out the silver in his short beard and hair.

Lila ignored his stare. She looked over his shoulder through the large open window, turning away from the sweet scent of chocolate. Even at the center of Bullstow, she could hear the protestors chanting at the gate, shouting something incomprehensible about the Holguíns and Oskar Kruger. The men of Bullstow ignored them, walking to and fro several stories below, all dressed in their coats and breeches. Some wore the black of the Saxony Senate, others the burgundy of New Bristol. Others had donned the colors of their respective cities, early arrivals for the weekend's festivities. They swarmed in and out of various marble buildings in muted voices, trying to finish their senate business before the Closing Ceremony.

They only had two days left.

She only had two days left.

Her father's chair creaked. "Lila, about what you said last time we spoke—"

"Is that why you asked me to lunch?"

"No."

"Good, because I really don't want to talk about that right now."

"Fine. Perhaps you'd like to talk about the oracle instead," he said, interlacing his fingers.

Lila whipped her head from the window. "What?"

"You and the oracle. You both seem to be friends now."

"Friends with the oracle? Have you gone mad?"

"Oh, did you have a quarrel with her, too?" He took his palm from his coat pocket and laid it on the table with a dull rattle. "She's called me three times now."

"She called you?"

"She's requested that you come visit her in the temple. I'm to talk you into it."

"Why on earth would I go visit the temple?"

"I don't know. I thought you could tell me. She promised that she'd convince the Sioux Falls oracle to stop her assault in the press. The woman hasn't let up on me since you returned her daughter."

"You want me to go see the oracle so that she'll kill a story for you?"

"That's not what I meant." Her father tucked his palm back in his pocket. "I'm not even sure how she knew we'd be meeting today. I should be in Unity."

"There's still time to go back."

"Now I know how your mother feels," Lemaire muttered. "We've never fought before, Lila, and I didn't ask you here to fight again. That's not how we are together. I don't like it."

"I don't like it either."

"Good. I've had time to settle down and think in the last week. You always have a reason for what you do, and I understand that reason now. I pushed you too hard and too soon after all that business with Peter Kruger, and you did what you did because you saw yourself in those children. Chief Shaw and I have spoken. He's not happy about playing politics with the oracles, but he has his hands full with the Holguín investigation, so he's leaving them to me. I'm meeting with the oracles next month, unofficially, to discuss this business with hiding their young."

"They won't tolerate your interference."

"And I won't tolerate them wasting militia resources. We might have found Oskar and his sister if Chief Shaw had not been forced to divert his resource." He nudged the plate of cookies, bumping her arm. "Come on, Lila girl. Eat something. Chef Mathieu won't be finished with lunch for another two hours"

"I'm not hungry. I didn't even finish breakfast."

"You should eat something anyway," he said softly. "Your appointment is this evening."

"Don't tell me what to do. That's all anyone seems to do these days."

The prime minister searched her face. "For what it's worth, I'm sorry. Bea told me last night, but I wasn't allowed to warn you. Duty is not always what one desires."

"I was dutiful. I had a clear trajectory in my life. I protected the family as chief. I protected Bullstow and Saxony through our work together. Now I'm to make money for the Randolph family? Is that all that my life has become? It's bullshit, Father."

"It's not bullshit," he said, crinkling his nose as he cursed. "This is just a different way of protecting your family. Money equals power and privilege and security. You can't have those things without it."

He pushed the cookies forward again.

Lila shoved them away. "Happiness and security can be had without money."

"Tell it to the poorer classes."

"Chef Ana is happy."

"Yes, Chef Ana *is* happy. She's contracted with a very powerful family, and she's one of the highest paid chefs in the state. When her daughter was very ill, that powerful family pressed an entire team of doctors into service. It never would have happened if Bea hadn't gotten involved. If anyone in Chef Ana's family falls ill again, she can reasonably expect that your mother will marshal her resources once more. It's power and privilege and security by proxy."

"So it all goes back to that?"

"It always has. Chef Ana will always be at your mother's beck and call. How much would you enjoy the Randolphs laboring under the whims of the Holguíns or the Weberlys?"

"Gods, you're trying to talk me into it." Lila had thought he would help her find a loophole—not that she deserved one. "You want me to agree."

"I thought you already had. I'm sorry, Lila girl. I had hoped things might be different."

"You expected this all along, didn't you?"

Her father nodded, eyes heavy. "I knew how it would turn out. I'd hoped to stop it last night by offering your mother the Unity hospital contract in exchange for your chief's contract. She didn't go for it, though. She still thinks that she can get the job on her own merits, and she's probably correct."

"She has hundreds of Randolph women she could choose from, and yet she believes that I am the only one who can succeed her. It's madness. Others want it more. Others have more experience."

"It's how it has always worked, Lila, and there's never been any doubt that you're the best candidate for it."

"It's not how it always works. Many northern families don't tie everything up by birthright any longer. And why am I the best candidate? Because I succeeded with Randolph General? I was fourteen years old, Father. Nothing I did was my idea. Everything came from my advisors."

"From what I heard, you did have one or two novel ideas, but you're right. Most of it did come from your advisors. You rejected a fair number of their bad ideas and quite a few atrocious ones. Your mother insisted they give you the spectrum. In the end, you sifted through the lot and picked the most profitable course of action, better than what Bea would have picked herself. You dared where she would not."

He rubbed his chin, his beard raking against his nails in the quiet. "Lila, do you think it's any different with me and your mother? She's not a successful chairwoman because she has good ideas on her own. She's successful because she surrounds herself with intelligent, savvy people and listens to what they have to say. She then sifts through the muck and selects the course she believes is right. It's what leaders do. It's what you did with Randolph General all those years ago, and it's what you've always done with your militia. You've been training as chairwoman this entire time. You just didn't know it."

"Fuck you." Lila hopped up from her place and paced around the table, her chair wobbling in place until it settled.

"Your mother didn't come up with the plan. After it became clear you'd never willingly take on the prime role, she employed a dozen psychologists to suggest possible ways to change your mind. You haven't been sparring against your mother all these years. You've been parrying blows from the best minds money can buy. I think you've done rather well, considering."

"You let me think I'd won?"

"Think?" Lemaire snorted, and sipped his hot chocolate. "I'd thought that you had. Perhaps not the prize you wanted, but a prize nonetheless."

"What's that?"

"A reprieve. A chance to live the life you wanted, at least for a time. A chance to know exactly what might have been, to know that you'd accomplished what you'd always wanted. That's what Bea did for you, Lila, whether you appreciate it or not. She never got that chance."

Lila turned away.

"Should I have told you that it wouldn't last forever, even though you knew deep down it wouldn't? Should I have taken the pleasure of your occupation away from you?"

"Yes."

"Getting mad at me isn't going to change a thing. Even if Jewel hadn't decided upon marriage, Bea would have pulled you from the security office eventually. We both know that. She hoped you'd get bored with the militia and come to the decision on your own. If Jewel hadn't given up her position for marriage, she would have let you continue for a little while longer. That was what she wanted for you, and that's what she claimed would happen eventually. She wanted it to be your idea."

"I'm not bored. I like being chief."

"Really? I rather thought you were a bit too interested whenever I called you for a job."

Lila did not rise to the bait. "Now your jobs will just go away? Just like that? Who will you call in my stead?"

"Chief Shaw will have to figure that out. I'm up for election in the Allied Council this season. Head Councilman Abbot is finally stepping down, and I have enough votes to take the empty slot. If all goes to plan, I'll be a councilman next session, crafting policy for the entire Allied Lands from the comfort of Paris."

"And then you'll make a play for head councilman in a few years?" Lila asked, unable to muster the energy to celebrate his achievement. "You'll have your legacy, and I've lost mine. I'm to spend the rest of my life, mulling over spreadsheets and mergers, playing tennis and having tea with the other matrons, all so we can close deals and approve legislation."

"You're to conquer, Lila. How you do it is up to you. Despite what you believe, you are the best woman for the job."

"Why?"

"Because you care," he snapped. "You care about everyone in Saxony, not just the Randolphs or the other highborn, but all of them. Why do you think the workborn and the slaves respect you? Do you think it's because of the blackcoat?"

He jammed his finger into the table. "It's something I've tried to instill in you since the day you were born, not so you would take these jobs I keep offering you, but so you would act reasonably when you became chairwoman. You're my legacy too, Lila. I didn't want you to be the sort of matron who mows down the poorer classes just to make a few extra credits. Bea didn't care about any of that until we met. I had to teach her to do so."

Lila paused in her pacing. "Jewel cares."

"No, she doesn't. Jewel cares about herself. She always has. Why else did she so easily give up her role as soon as she wanted something else? Today she wants to try marriage."

"Tomorrow she'll want to try divorce."

"I'll get her father involved if she tries that. Maybe he'll be able to make a dent."

"Where is he?"

"Off finishing a mural on some backwoods city council building. Jewel probably won't listen to him, anyway. She surpassed his talent when she turned fifteen, and that's all she's ever really respected. I pity Senator Dubois. I didn't know he'd fallen in love with her. I don't know what will become of him if she throws him away."

Lila shuffled back to the table and sat down, finally pouring herself a cup of hot chocolate. "I'll make sure he's not tossed out of the compound if Bullstow does not accept him back. I've always been fond of Louis."

"That eases my mind," he said, taking a cookie.

Lila pulled the plate away. "Your doctor, Father. You know what—"

"It's only one. And it goes without saying that you've done your last job for Bullstow and Chief Shaw. You can't be prime and do that sort of work too, not when you have the entire family depending on you. Things could get sticky if you were caught."

Lila fidgeted with the handle of her mug. "Things are sticky now," she said. "I've had some complications." She looked Lemaire in the eye as she told him about the blackmailer, about the messages, about the broken promise after she'd paid.

Her father crossed his arms over his chest, worry peeking from every line on his face. "Bea didn't tell me. This is a mess, Lila. You have to clean it up. You can't have this problem still in your lap. If your blackmailer comes forward, it will have repercussions for us all. Deadly repercussions."

"I know," Lila said, eyeing her father carefully. "That's why I need your permission to hack BullNet once more."

"Elizabeth—"

"Don't. I'm tired of being called that today. You asked me to find the hacker in BullNet. I haven't finished the job, and until I do, this blackmailer is a threat to us all. If you don't let me hack Bullstow again, you'll lose your council seat before the first session."

Her father scratched at his beard. "What do you need?"

"A day. I need to make sure I deleted everything from the logs that night. I also want to check the rest of BullNet for more traps. I peeked into the BIRD because we that's where the highborn had been caught, but every state database might be booby-trapped. I don't know what sort of partner this person was to Reaper. They might still have access to everything Reaper hacked. I need more data. We need more data."

"Lila, I don't know about this."

"I can do it from here."

"That would put me at risk," he warned, and sipped his hot chocolate. "You know exactly what will happen if the press thinks I gave you free rein in BullNet. I couldn't even blame them."

Lila nodded. She'd been against Tristan's plan to steal into Bullstow and hack the network without permission. Asking her father directly seemed the better course of action, playing on their sense of honor, on the desire to finish what they'd started, on the need to protect the state from the likes of Reaper and his partner.

On the need to protect her.

She hadn't counted on her father having second thoughts.

"You're already at risk, but if you have any better ideas, I'd love to hear them. For oracle's sake, you can always just say that you had no idea what I was doing anything on my laptop the entire time I visited you."

Lemaire put down his hot chocolate. "I'd have to bring Chief Shaw in on it."

"Of course, but he wouldn't want a gaping hole in his network either. Let me finish the job we started."

After a moment of silent contemplation, Lemaire snatched up his palm and trudged from the room, greeting Shaw over the quiet in his booming voice. While he spoke, Lila grabbed her satchel and slid out two brand-new laptops. As they booted up with a series of little beeps, she took off the star drive from around her neck and uploaded her snoop programs to each one.

Her father sighed from the doorway. "You've already started, haven't you? What if he'd said no? What if I'd changed my mind?"

"I would have figured out a way to do it anyway. We can't leave this asshole in the network. Too many people could be harmed, and I'm not just talking about the hackers or the ones who pay them. This asshole has access to everyone's data. Everyone's at risk."

Lemaire pulled up his coat sleeve and checked his watch. "I need to go. I couldn't dump all my meetings when I left Unity. I have a holo-conference at eleven, but I'll be back for lunch."

Lila waved him off. "Go. We'll eat when you get back."

"Without the laptops."

"No, around the laptops. I'm not wasting my time with food and conversation when I could be downloading data. My time is finite. I have an appoint at five for Helen to stick a few scalpels up my—"

"Don't finish that sentence." Her father frowned, raising his hand. "The less I know of that, the better."

With a graceful turn, her father exited the suite.

The door closed behind him with an echoing snick.

Her palm vibrated in her pocket. Tristan had sent her another message, the fifth since breakfast. She sipped her hot chocolate and cycled through the messages one by one.

*How did it go?*

*What happened?*

*Are you okay?*

*Do you need help?*

*Talk to me.*

She had no idea how to reply to any of them. What could she write that he'd understand? She wasn't even sure that she understood, and speaking with Tristan would only spin her head and make things worse.

Besides, he'd always hated the highborn. What would he say when he realized that she wouldn't just be a highborn or an heir, but that she would soon be in the thick of highborn intrigue once more?

He'd try to talk her out of it.

And what would happen when he found out about the Closing Ball? They had never talked about monogamy, but he'd press it now. He'd demand it. She'd have to choose, and she couldn't choose him.

She'd lose him the second she opened her mouth.

But for now, at least, while silence reigned between them, they still belonged to one another.

*Everything's fine*, she typed out before shoving her palm in her pocket.

She had other things to think about. Tristan and his reaction would have to wait.

She rang downstairs for a bottle of Sangre de las Flores, her favorite wine, and turned back to her work.

# 5

Lila reclined against the smooth leather seat in the back of the luxury sedan, trying to relax as a piano concerto pumped through the car's speakers. A small rip in the seat kept scratching against her thigh, an annoyance even through her thick woolen trousers. Other things also annoyed her, like the odor of oil and industry that lingered in the gray carpet. Someone had tried to cover it with a liberal application of something overly chemical and overly floral, but she had trouble judging which smelled worse.

Lila rolled down the window halfway and pressed her forehead against the glass. Sergeant Norwood drove the car through New Bristol, crawling past the parks and lowborn businesses, both clustering around the grandeur of the highborn estates like poor, begging relations. Blackcoats patrolled around the edges of each compound, with only the cut of their coats, the shape of the coat of arms, and the piping on their uniforms betraying their family's identity.

The militias waved off most of the traffic attempting to enter each compound as unsuitable or unwanted because the inhabitants did not have the proper paperwork. Few could slip inside a highborn compound, not unless they belonged to the family through blood, marriage, contract, or purchase. Only an appointment and grasping money—money ready to be spent on the businesses inside—might gain entry.

The clothes on the passersby never dipped in quality, all straining to match the highborn around them. At least, they didn't until the sedan took a turn to the east, sliding past Wilson Tower, the skeletal backbone of a haunted family estate. Her mother now owned it. Lila now owned it. No one lived inside any longer, for Bullstow had removed the Wilson family, ferrying them to workborn housing throughout the city. Only a few Randolph appraisers and a detachment of militia tarried inside the stone walls.

The detour was no accident. Her mother had willed it, had wanted Lila to gaze upon the fallen giant.

Lila rolled the window all the way down, not caring if the workborn children in the area peeked into the sedan to glimpse her.

She needed air.

It didn't help that Sergeant Norwood drove much too quickly. The car hurtled through the streets, promising to arrive at Randolph General far too soon. She stifled a laugh at the idea of her appointment, at the idea of Elizabeth Randolph becoming the heir to Wolf Industries, and a mother. Both seemed equally comical in their ridiculousness, and she did not know which one she looked forward to the least. But she supposed anything trumped Elizabeth Randolph, the exile, or Elizabeth Randolph, the felon and soon-to-be-executed heir.

Perhaps that made the entire situation even more ridiculous. Instead of digging through the mounds of data she'd just pilfered from BullNet, her mother had forced her to take an evening off to repair her broken womb. At least her snoop programs would still dig and search while she slept after the surgery.

Perhaps she would have answers by the next morning, not that she really believed it would be that simple.

Randolph General quickly came into view, a sprawling complex of a half-dozen buildings, each connected by a series of covered walkways. One could make a circuit through each building or pass into a courtyard in the middle. Lila had filled the space with the greenest grass in all of New Bristol, ensuring it remained so even during the height of a drought-marred summer, all to calm the patients, their families, and her staff.

She had not come up with the idea, regardless of what her father likely believed. Before her childhood best friend had died, she'd spent a great deal of time in the hospital. Holly had often lamented that the only flower or tree she ever got to see during those times had been made of plastic and jammed in a pot. It seemed like such a little thing to fix.

Lila had wanted to fix all of Holly's problems back then. That desire led to the chairwoman gifting Lila the hospital on her fourteenth birthday, along with a horse named Daisy. Lila had renamed the horse Captain Beauregard and the hospital Randolph General. The project had been meant to show Lila that her efforts would be well served as prime, to show her all the good she might do in the world.

Lila had taken the challenge seriously, not because it was a test, but because she either wanted the project to work as a tribute to Holly or fail so miserably that her mother would choose another as prime. After weeding through her group of advisors, ejecting as many flatterers and spies as she could, she made several key changes to the structure of the hospital. The most important change had to do with the staff. Though most employees were Randolph family members, Lila had taken steps to ensure that the best talent had been poached throughout all of Saxony. She had even used her fledging spy network among the servants and slaves of New Bristol to ferret out which doctors and specialists might be convinced to break from their families and work at the hospital. A decade later, medical professionals from all over Saxony aspired to work among the best at Randolph General.

Family be damned.

Class be damned.

It had not been easy to remake the hospital. Lila had taken advantage of her tenure on the High Council, exchanging favor after favor among senators and other highborn heirs to achieve her aims. She'd also endured her mother's criticisms, the endless complaints that she'd put sentiment above profits. Her birthdays had flown by, straddled between the hospital, classes at Bokington, and High Council meetings.

The chairwoman had stopped complaining about Lila's methods when her daughter's promises rang true. Money had poured in from all over Saxony after the highborn realized what level of care could be expected at Randolph General. It had become the highest-rated trauma center in all of Saxony, perhaps the entire country, and had already doubled in size. Even the less affluent lowborn in the region saved their money and traveled to the hospital to seek treatment. The cancer center was particularly accomplished and lucrative. For although it did accept those who could pay very little, those family members still needed to eat and sleep while in town. As such, the surrounding hotels rarely had vacancies, and the restaurants, florists, and toy stores nearby were always busy.

She'd impressed her mother with that, for the Randolph family owned those businesses outright. The hospital added prestige and money to Randolph coffers, and even if the servant class could rarely pay their entire hospital bill, it all balanced far in the black at the end.

Unfortunately, Lila had surrendered the day-to-day operations of the hospital to the care of another after becoming a militia officer, for she had little time to run it. Over the years, she'd backed off more and more. Indeed, her schedule had become so busy lately that she had not visited the hospital in almost a month. Before her appointment, Lila abandoned Sergeant Norwood in the lobby and checked in with the harried Ms. Fredericks, who looked even more harried than usual at her arrival.

After a quick chat, the director of the women's clinic found her. The affable woman escorted Lila to the fifth floor, mouth continually flapping with pleasantries, and held open the door to the clinic.

But Lila did not step through.

She brushed her belly, knowing she couldn't put off the decision any longer. She either walked through the door and continued along her mother's path or she dove for the exit and…

Did what, exactly?

Turned her back on everyone and everything she'd ever known? Ran away to spend the rest of her life in the city or in Burgundy, tarnishing her reputation?

She'd already ruined it, hadn't she? Not in Bullstow, but in the warehouse.

The gods had seen it.

The gods now asked for compensation for her actions.

Perhaps it didn't matter if she believed in them or not.

Lila fixed her gaze on the engraved plaque next to the entrance. The Sophia Randolph Women's Care Clinic had been named after her grandmother, who had died in childbirth with her mother's younger sister, Katrina. Sometimes Lila wondered if the chair-woman and her mother had ever clashed so much. Judging by the chairwoman's reddened eyes when she found out about Lila's small gesture, she guessed that they had not.

Two peas in a pod, Aunt Georgina had told her later.

"Is there a problem?" the director asked her, clutching a file.

"No," Lila said, stepping inside the clinic at last. She'd chosen a dusty orange hue for the walls, matching it with brown moldings and trim. The doctors, nurses, and assistants that should have bustled about inside had vanished, save one. Not a strand of gray hair stuck out amid the blonde to prove her experience.

"I'm Dr. Cristina Rubio, madam," the young woman said, bowing, clad in scrubs of the same orange hue as the walls. "If you'll follow me, we'll get started."

Lila cocked her head, surprised that her usual doctor, the squat, steel-haired Dr. Helen Hardwicke-Randolph had not been waiting. Lila trusted Helen, and only Helen, to provide all her medical care, despite her specialty. Not only had she proven herself a brilliant and capable doctor, but she also stood thirtieth in line to the chairwoman, as Edith Randolph's only daughter by blood.

In contrast, Dr. Rubio looked barely older than Jewel. She was not even a Randolph, nor was she a highborn, judging by her name. The silver caduceus around her neck got Lila's attention, though, for on the same chain she wore a tiny Randolph coat of arms. Only members of the Randolph family could wear such a pendant, and no one joined the family unless they married a Randolph daughter. Who had Rubio married to earn that pendant? Few women in the Randolph line favored other women. Fewer still favored marriage, and Lila could not remember any taking a wife recently.

She fingered her palm. It would only take a few minutes to seek out the woman's identity.

"Your mother has made all the arrangements," Rubio assured her, escorting Lila to an operating room that had been prepped for surgery, painted in the same dusty hue. A bed sat in the middle, covered with wax paper, waiting.

"This room is not necessary, of course," the doctor said. "The chance of complication is extremely low for this procedure, but we like to be on the safe side, especially with the chairwoman's firstborn daughter."

"Where is Dr. Helen Randolph? I always see her," Lila asked cautiously from the doorway, nose crinkling at the smell of cinnamon cleanser.

Rubio stared at the floor. "Dr. Randolph is out sick, and even your mother could not make her fit for surgery."

That got Lila's attention. A trap lurked somewhere. She just couldn't see it.

Or perhaps she could. The chairwoman had wanted Lila to reverse her CUT since the day she got it, all so she could have an heir. But Helen knew exactly how Lila felt about children. She would have refused to do the procedure until Lila had a few days to consider her choices, especially if she knew her mother had scheduled the last-minute appointment.

Rubio would do it, though. She wouldn't even question it.

"You can choose another doctor if you wish. I can get the numbers from—"

"That won't be necessary. I was just curious." Lila slipped her palm into her pocket. In this one instance, she agreed with her mother.

Delaying the CUT procedure would only delay the inevitable. This was her birthright. Her duty. Her punishment. Her compensation for the lives she'd ended. It was the place she'd always end up eventually, no matter how much she fought against it.

Even her father had said as much.

If she waited, the rumor mill would only grind louder and louder. A crowd of senators would encircle her at the ball.

"I'm here to reverse my birth control," Lila said. "Nothing more."

"Of course, chief."

A nurse entered the room, carrying a clipboard. After Rubio performed a quick physical on Lila, she started an IV. The pair injected the line with a shot of clear fluid, which made Lila terribly sleepy, sleepier than it should have because of the Sangre she'd drunk in her father's suite. If she hadn't been half naked, with her feet stuck in cold stirrups, she might have actually slept through the entire procedure. Instead, she faded in and out of consciousness, annoyed at the dull tugging and pinching.

All at once, Lila opened her eyes with a start. At some point, Rubio had switched off the overhead light and worked her legs free from the stirrups. A blanket now covered her body, tucked under her chin.

Rubio looked up from her computer beside the bed. "You're awake. Everything went well," the young doctor assured her with a smile. "I did make a notation in your file about the anesthesia. It hit you a little hard."

"It was likely all the wine I had earlier," Lila said, yawning.

Rubio gaped at her, then typed something into the computer. Lila might have been a student again, receiving a note home from her tutor about some bit of bad behavior. "I feel the need to remind you that drinking before surgery, even a minor surgery, can be dangerous. As is not telling your doctor when you have consumed alcohol—"

"Next time," Lila promised with another yawn. "How long was I out?"

"Fifteen, twenty minutes. Not long." Rubio gathered up three needles, apologized quietly to Lila for the stick, and gave her a large injection in the side before her brain could spin into gear once more.

"What on earth was that for?" Lila cried out, fully awake after Rubio jammed the second needle into her hip. "I already had my STI vaccines!"

"Those weren't STI vaccines, Chief Randolph. They were fertility shots. This last one is to hold off the pain after surgery."

"Fertility shots?" Lila asked in alarm, surprised into silence when the last needle burrowed into her side, a sharper pinch than the others. "I told you not do anything but reverse… Who authorized you to give me fertility shots?"

"Your mother… I thought… I thought that you were aware of all aspects of today's procedure. I would have explained in detail if—"

"Cut the crap, doctor. My mother has been pulling this shit for decades. This is why I wanted Helen today." Lila rubbed her side. "I knew she was up to something! I should have known she had more up her sleeve than keeping Helen away."

Rubio backed up.

"How potent is this stuff? Will I end up with multiples?" Lila wasn't sure which way she wanted the doctor to answer. She didn't want to bear a litter of children, but she could not deny her mother's practicality on the matter. It might not be a terrible idea to birth an heir, a spare, and an eldest son for Bullstow all at once.

A womb sale. Three kids for the price of nine months.

"It's possible."

"My mother did the same when she was chairwoman," Lila confessed, her brain thickening from the pain injection. "It took her only a few weeks to conceive, every time."

"The drugs have improved quite a bit since then."

"Drugs I didn't need and that you didn't tell me about. You realize I could turn you into the ethics board for this? I own you now."

Rubio whimpered. Her back smacked into the wall.

"I hope she paid you well."

"I don't know what—"

Lila waved off the doctor and slipped off the bed onto the cold tile floor. The air chilled her through the backless gown. She searched her clothes for her star drive. She'd intended to ask Helen about Dubois's records, but a compromised Rubio would suffice. "Look at this for me," Lila said, passing her the drive. "There's only one folder."

Rubio shoved the drive into her computer and scanned the data. "Chief, I can't—"

"Have you forgotten my words so quickly? Who controls this hospital? I would hate for your recent mistake to affect your employment."

The doctor gulped and turned back to the screen. After several seconds of studying the file, she cocked her head. "I don't specialize in men's fertility."

"I don't care." Lila longed to lie back down on the hospital bed. She grew more tired with every passing second, for her brain had wrapped itself in fluff.

She stood anyway.

"Whose files are these? Where did you get them?"

"That's none of your concern."

Rubio looked as though she might protest, then thought better of it. While Lila dressed, Rubio scrolled all the way through the file twice, squinting at the doctor's notes. "This patient cannot conceive. There is almost no sperm in the samples."

"So I read. What could cause that?"

"Genetics." Rubio ejected the star drive.

Lila snatched it from the doctor's hand. Senator Dubois had passed his testing as an intern. He had not been infertile then. Genetics did not seem likely. "What about other causes?"

"It could be any number of things. Chemotherapy, cancer, diabetes, kidney or liver failure, age. Any of those could cause it. Is this a friend of yours?"

"Perhaps."

Rubio frowned. "Has he had any serious illnesses?"

"No, he's been perfectly healthy."

"Drug use?" the doctor pressed.

"No."

"Are you sure?"

Lila's annoyed expression silenced the doctor's protest.

"How old is he?"

"Far too young for this."

"It could be a blockage caused by a prior infection, but that seems unlikely from his physical exams. Like I told you before, it's most likely genetic. Sometimes men just shoot blanks."

"It's not genetic."

"Then if it's not age, it's idiopathic. Sometimes such a condition develops for no reason—at least no reason we can detect."

Lila didn't believe it for a second. It had never happened in the history of High House.

"I apologize. I suspect you want a different answer."

Lila put on her coat, grasping the wall when she nearly over-balanced. "Tell no one about my questions, and I might not have a conversation with the ethics board."

"Of course, Chief Randolph," the doctor promised, wringing her hands as she watched Lila struggle with her clothes. "It's likely that you'll feel a bit of nausea over the next twenty-four hours. You should take care to stay in bed until it passes."

The doctor retrieved a bulging shopping bag from a cabinet. The hospital's name stretched across the front in glossy letters. "Supplies for the coming weeks," she explained.

Lila snatched up the bag as Rubio called for the nurse to escort her to the lobby. It bothered Lila's pride to accept the help, but the shot still clouded her mind, making her groggy. So did the anesthesia, the wine, and the abbreviated nap. She knew it would better if people saw her escorted by a nurse, rather than passed out and drooling in a hallway.

Once the pair reached the elevator, Lila finally peeked inside the bag. It contained several pregnancy tests, prenatal vitamins, and various pamphlets on pregnancy care.

"She's insane," Lila murmured. "My mother is completely, certifiably insane."

The nurse raised an eyebrow. Her mouth opened and closed as if she were unsure how to answer, or if she should even acknowledge Lila's statement at all.

Choosing selective amnesia, the nurse thumbed the down button on the elevator, hitting it repeatedly as though she might prevent an apocalypse if only she pressed quickly enough. "The elevator is so slow sometimes," she muttered before returning to her rabid button pushing.

Lila leaned against the wall and watched the nurse work. Many from the poorer classes had no idea how to act around heirs, for they rarely met one, even an unofficial one. Their behavior usually hovered somewhere between uncomfortable and awkward.

As soon as Lila became prime, it would only get worse.

The elevator dinged, and the pair stepped inside. The nurse stared at her shoes while the car descended. When it reached the ground floor, Lila dismissed the nurse, resolving to escape the woman's unease as soon as possible and find Sergeant Norwood on her own. The lobby was large, but not so large that he would go unnoticed.

Her palm vibrated.

Tristan had sent her another message. *What did she want? Call me.*

Lila slipped the device into her pocket. She had no intention of speaking to Tristan while drugged.

She soon spied Sergeant Norwood amid the squealing children and anxious parents. Ignoring the Muzak that pumped through the speakers, she dodged the pacing crowd, mostly men who had not shaved due to stress, fright, or too little time.

Sergeant Norwood helped her to the car, parked at the front of the building. Once Lila was safely ensconced inside, she cracked the window, needing more air to quiet her stomach.

As Sergeant Norwood backed out of the parking spot, the hospital bag fell over into her lap with a crinkled thud.

Lila shoved it as far away as possible.

# 6

By the time Sergeant Norwood drove through the south gate of the Randolph estate, Lila had shaken off her drowsiness, glad for the heavily tinted windows that kept her bleary eyes from the view of the crowds. She collected her things while Sergeant Norwood parked at the front of the great house. He helped her take a wobbly stroll up the steps, recently power-washed by the groundskeepers. Her crimson woolen coat felt damp in the chilly, humid air.

The blackcoat opened the front door, and she parted with him at the entryway. Luckily, the staff had been called away to other tasks, and no one met her as she climbed upstairs to her room. After dropping her pregnancy supplies in her closet and slamming the door, she caught her face in bathroom mirror.

Tired. Irritated. Pale. Slightly green.

Green or not, she had a meeting to attend. On the way home, she had messaged Commander Sutton. They had much to discuss.

She withdrew her star drive and quickly hid it in her desk. Her palm vibrated as she slid the secret compartment closed. For once, it wasn't Tristan.

"Chief, I just got a strange request that I thought you should know about," a familiar, musical voice said by way of greeting.

"Always a pleasure, Captain McKinley." The blackcoat handled network security for the estate and often called when she believed that Commander Sutton might not understand her report. Sometimes, she also called to remind Lila that she existed and enjoyed being promoted. Lila wondered which sort of call it would be this time.

"I assure you, the pleasure is all mine," McKinley said. "I heard you were on the compound once more. Are you back from vacation?"

"What did Sutton tell you?"

"Not to call you. But something weird happened this afternoon. Bullstow called. A man named Davies requested access to the family's net logins."

"Which logins?"

"All of them."

Lila gaped at the request. It was unheard of for Bullstow to request so much private information, and she could not believe that the officer had any reason for it.

Her mind spun with the possibilities. Chief Shaw had nearly fired Sergeant Davies less than a month before for being involved in questionable activities, activities linked to Reaper. She must have hit another of Reaper's traps during her hack that afternoon. Her blackmailer either knew or suspected that she'd been inside again and put Davies on it.

At least her fake ID wouldn't be so easy to decipher this time.

At least…

Lila squeezed her eyes shut. Her mind had fogged too thickly after the anesthesia. She needed sleep before she acted on the information.

"Are you sure it was Sergeant Davies?" she asked.

"Yes. I looked him up, chief. He's the son of Suji Park, owner of Toewon Research Group and the Eclipse chain of coffee houses. How he even got into Bullstow as a lowborn—"

Lila faded out as McKinley prattled on about the dangers of lowborn citizens buying their way into Bullstow. It was true, Toewon and Eclipse were lowborn businesses, but they were very prominent businesses on the rise, grossing more than many poorly performing highborn families, far more than the Wilsons ever had. Not only did Ms. Park sit on Saxony's Low Council of Judges, but she had managed to get two sons elected into New Bristol's Low House and another in Saxony's. Placing an eldest son in Bullstow was the next logical step, and proved that Ms. Park was a shrewd player, for it was exceedingly costly for the lowborn to buy their way inside. The first boy from a lowborn family never became a senator, but it was a sacrifice and a start into highborn society.

It had paid off for Ms. Park. The New Bristol High Council had confirmed the Parks as the next highborn family less than a month before.

It could harm the Parks' confirmation if Bullstow arrested Davies and tried him for impropriety now. The council still had time to deny the family and chose another.

"I found out who his partner is, too," McKinley said. "Officer Muller, from the Weberly family."

"Web Corp?" Lila asked, feigning ignorance.

"Yes, chief. Strange coincidence, huh?"

Lila rubbed her chin and made a noncommittal grunt. It was more than a coincidence, and Captain McKinley knew it. Web Corp was a highborn company based in New Bristol, though the bulk of their income came from oil fields several hundred kilometers away in Beaulac. As such, they were a direct rival of the Randolphs.

"I already told Commander Sutton about Sergeant Davies. I didn't find out about his partner or their matrons until just now. I thought I should tell you directly."

"Captain McKinley, you did not give Sergeant Davies the logins, did you?"

"Of course not. I told him to go through the proper channels and obtain the correct paperwork. He was pushy, though. Could be trouble."

"Keep the commander informed when she returns to the security office. I'll want to know about any further communication from Sergeant Muller and Sergeant Davies, whether I'm on vacation or not."

"Of course, chief," the captain answered before she broke the connection.

A knock sounded at the door.

"Come in," Lila said.

Her younger brother poked his head into the room. Loose brown waves touched his shoulders, and his blue eyes mirrored Jewel's. At sixteen, Pax Randolph-Blanc was well on his way to becoming a giant like his father, Senator Blanc. He already had the body of a man who could pick up a couch and fling it through the window, and his new fall coat already strained at the shoulders. In a few years, he would have to duck just to enter a room. In a few more, he might have to enter sideways.

"Hello, Lila," he said, calling out in a voice so rowdy and full that it dwarfed his entire body. He had still not gotten used to the change from high to deep, and his face screwed up in embarrassment at his own loud bellow.

"Hello, Pax."

"I kept the door open all afternoon. I didn't want you to slip past me when you returned home. Here you are, all drugged up, and you managed to get past. I didn't even notice until I heard the door close."

"It's my boots."

He nodded and picked at her wooden doorframe. "I'm sorry that you have to be prime. I know you don't want to."

"So you heard?"

"I heard it all last night and put it together. Jewel doesn't take bad news privately. It's all tears and snot with her, and damn the neighbors."

Lila chuckled.

"She's really upset."

"She's always upset about something, but it's hardly the end of the world that she claims. I guarantee you that she'll have children in a few years anyway. If it's not her own idea, then it will be at mother's urging. Jewel always wanted children too much to forbear now, regardless of her feelings about the senator. Knowing him, he might even press the issue."

Pax shrugged. It was the shrug of a younger brother who did not wish to contradict his elder sister.

"What do you think about it all?" Lila said, noting the impatience of his tutor, Ms. Beaumont, framed by the nursery doorway across the hall. The room had been converted after Pax refused to return to boarding school, for the boy needed some place to study. Though Lila enjoyed having him so close, she wondered how long it would be before he returned to school, especially since Ms. Beaumont annoyed her.

The feeling seemed to be mutual. The woman frowned at the interruption and eyed Lila as if she were a poisoned wound that might fester into educational necrosis if she did not intervene.

Naturally, Lila ignored her.

Ms. Beaumont returned to her work, too far away to eavesdrop.

"I think it's all terribly romantic." A goofy smile broke upon Pax's face. "The idea of giving up what you've always wanted most for love. What else could one hope for?"

"You would. You want to marry."

"Yes, I do want to marry. Lots of people marry, even lowborn and highborn, so don't act like I'm strange for it."

"Only the poorer classes can afford monogamy."

He shrugged again. "You're doing the same thing, you know, giving up what you want for love."

Lila peered at her brother. "What do you mean?"

"You could have easily refused her."

"Easily?"

"Well, not easily—nothing is ever easy with Mother, is it? But you could have refused and remained chief if you really wanted, or you could have bought back your mark and struck out on your own. You have the mind for it. Anyone who knew the history of Randolph General would know as much."

Lila appreciated the sentiment, but Pax was still a child, one who had no interest or skill in commerce. He didn't understand how difficult it was for a highborn to start a company after cutting ties with her family, how hard the highborn had made such a prospect by covering it with layers upon layers of rules and bureaucracy and terms like *conflict of interest.* He didn't understand the dirty games the highborn played with one another. For her to be successful, she would have to leave Saxony, if not the country.

She'd have to leave her family too.

The idea repelled her.

Besides, her mother would never sell her mark back to her, not unless she followed Alex's tactic and blackmailed her matron into it.

That was something she'd never do. She had a duty to her family. If she was of more use as the president of Wolf Industries rather than its chief of security, then perhaps that was her burden. The chairwoman had known exactly what buttons to push during breakfast.

"You could have forced mother to make Jewel keep her promise," Pax said. "She would have been forced. You can count on it. Mother wouldn't have approved of Aunt Georgina becoming heir. She's too bloodthirsty. I suspect it's from being around all those brides and grooms all day long. But you love Jewel and Mother even though you don't get along with either of them, so you'll become prime and make everyone happy even though it's not what you want."

"Is that so? I suspect you think too kindly of me, Pax."

"No, I just know you. Mother was right this morning. You would have gotten bored in the security office. You need more of a challenge. You need a bigger chessboard."

Lila narrowed her eyes. "How would you know what was talked about this morning?" She wasn't quite sure what annoyed her more: that he had clearly eavesdropped or that he was partly right. Because it was true that Lila had tired of the drudgery of her office soon after becoming chief. The only challenge, the only pleasure she had received over the last few years, had been working with Tristan and her father.

Perhaps Saxony had been a much bigger chessboard.

Perhaps the Randolph compounds were so much smaller in comparison.

"I have my ways."

"Yes, you do. You like games too, Pax. You dabble in intrigue too much for your own good. Perhaps you shouldn't choose medicine after all."

Her brother laughed. "Being prime isn't so bad, is it? You'll control everything after Mother retires. You can do whatever you want then."

Lila wanted to contradict Pax. She wanted to tell him that she didn't want to control everything, that she only wanted to make everyone safe.

"Think of what you can make of the hospital when you're prime. You could turn it into a whole system spread throughout Saxony." Pax's eyes shone, partly due to his youthful optimism and partly due to his calling. Lila wasn't sure if she had been the one to instill this drive toward medicine or if it had been Holly's death, but she was glad that the boy had found his purpose early. He already volunteered at Randolph Hospital several times a week, and would go more if he could fit it around his studies, which must have been why Ms. Beaumont tarried so late.

Lila had expressly forbidden Pax from doing more volunteer work. His interest in medicine had only increased since his best friend Trevor had died several months back. Trevor had been stabbed in front of him, murdered, though no one really understood why. None of Lila's private spies had turned up any answers.

Lila hadn't either.

Pax had retreated into himself immediately after. No one could get him to return to boarding school, for he was determined to become a trauma surgeon as soon as possible. He told everyone that the rest of the students slowed him down, but Lila knew the real reason. He simply couldn't walk down the halls without his friend, a friend that Lila knew had been far more than a friend.

She wondered if Pax had even realized it.

Lila had banned him from too much time at the hospital, hoping that he wouldn't use it as a crutch to retreat, but she didn't think it was helping. He rarely went out unless it was to visit the hospital or the library. He'd become something of a hermit.

Lila stood up and grabbed his chin affectionately. "That was a really good pep talk. Bullstow would have been lucky to have you," she said, and kissed his cheek.

He twisted his face in annoyance.

"What? Have you gotten too old for kisses from your sister?"

"No, I'm just glad I don't have to live in Bullstow. I couldn't imagine having to give speeches all day."

Lila nearly laughed at his horrified expression. It was true that Pax was not skilled in the masculine arts. He was neither witty nor skilled at diplomacy and public speaking. For all his rowdy bluster with family and friends, he sometimes still blushed when he greeted a stranger. Even if Pax practiced all his life, Lila doubted that he could make a speech before a room of ten friends, much less High House.

It had only gotten worse after Trevor died.

Pax would never be able to take a role with another highborn family, in politics or negotiations among the houses. Unfortunately, the only things masculine about her brother were his size and his skill in taking care of people. That, coupled with his rather prodigious brain, gave her hope for a successful marriage, for the pool of men who favored men among the highborn, at least enough to marry, was quite small, and she wanted him to have his pick.

Regardless of marriage, Lila knew that she would be able to find a use for him, either as a doctor at Randolph General if he could get over his difficulty speaking with strangers, or as a researcher at Grace Medical if he could not. The pay would not be enough for him to leave the family, not if he wanted to afford the life that he had grown accustomed to with his dividends, but Pax was not the sort who would leave.

Besides, he'd never have to leave his family. Any husband with any brains would agree to become a Randolph if given half a chance, highborn or not.

Lila gave Pax a last pat on the cheek. "Go study, you old gossip, or I'll have to pay a thousand bribes to get you into medical school."

Pax chuckled at his sister and returned to Ms. Beaumont and the large stack of books spread out on the table.

# 7

Commander Sutton hopped to her feet as soon as Lila entered the parlor. A stout woman in her mid-fifties, she wore her blackcoat as elegantly as an evening gown. She could also take down a man twice her size, not that she needed to rely on hand-to-hand. She'd been a sniper in the army, a sniper who had only gotten more and more experienced with her endless practice at the gun range. As Lila's mentor, she'd demanded the same relentlessness with her charge. Lila had become one of the best shots in all of Saxony under her and Sergeant Jenkins's tutelage.

Lila had never been worth much at hand-to-hand, though. Since she could bull's-eye a target at fifty meters in a fraction of a second, besting all but a few shooters in Saxony, she didn't see the problem with being horrible on the mat. She'd decided a long time ago that avoidance and distance were the best ways of handling herself.

Speak softly and carry a rather large gun.

It might not have helped her with Peter and Reaper, but it had saved her and her friends at the warehouse.

Lila sat across from the gray-haired commander, choosing a spot on a white leather sofa, large enough for Pax to stretch across. The commander plopped down in the thick armchair across from her.

"I apologize for keeping you from the security office," Lila said in greeting, glad that Alex had already put out a kettle of hot chocolate for their meeting.

"New scenery is always welcome, as is seeing the great house. But a woman in your condition should already be in bed. You're a fool for even having this meeting. It can all be discussed tomorrow."

"My condition?"

"Your mother messaged me this morning. She requested that I see to your security personally. She told me that you would be too weak after your doctor's appointment at the women's clinic to defend yourself should there be an attempt on your life."

Great, the chairwoman had basically informed her second-in-command that Lila would be reversing her birth control.

"With the exception of Peter Kruger last month, no one has attempted to assassinate an heir in the last thirty years, at least outside of a family compound," Sutton continued. "Still, it's best to be safe. I would have gone myself if I could have gotten away. I assigned Sergeant Norwood in my stead. He's discreet, and I figured you would prefer a man of few words."

"I appreciate it." Lila poured them both a mug of hot chocolate. The sweet smell turned her stomach, but she refused to show it.

Commander Sutton thanked her and swallowed heartily. "Husband never lets me have any these days. Says it makes me bitchy."

Lila hid a smirk. She was all too aware of her husband's ban.

"I always told you that you'd change your mind about having a kid. I just didn't think it'd be so soon. I can't stop wondering when we might expect a new baby in the great house."

Lila sighed, knowing her commander's words heralded the first of many such statements by well-meaning relations on the estate. It would only get worse once she wore the whitecoat.

She brushed at her sleeve as though she had found a bit of dust on the cuff.

"If you find the right senator at the Closing Ball on Friday night—"

"Commander," she warned.

"Lucia is a marvelous name."

"Is it now?"

"My mother thought so."

Lila took a very small sip from her mug, shirking from the sweetness. "I've missed nearly two weeks of updates, commander. A report, if you please."

For the next half-hour, Sutton broke down everything of importance that had happened, or was still happening, throughout the Randolph family holdings. A pipe had burst in Beaulac, but there was no evidence of foul play. A few employees had crashed a family truck in La Porte after a few beers, but the local commander had it well in hand. A manufacturing plant outside of New Bristol had been shut down for an hour due to a squirrel.

After several years at her job, Lila had come to one conclusion: squirrels were evil, costly, and prone to barbecuing themselves in electrical boxes at every opportunity.

"So nothing out of the ordinary, then?" Lila asked.

"Not much, chief. I did get a report from Captain McKinley a few hours ago. It seems there was a…" Sutton trailed off in an unbecoming huff after glimpsing Lila's face. "Let me guess—she called you. Infernal woman was supposed to leave you alone. You're still officially on vacation."

"She had more information. She found out the caller's full name and the name of his partner. Sergeant *Park*-Davies and Sergeant *Weberly*-Muller."

The commander's frustration vanished. "Toewon Research Group and Web Corp? Well, well, well, isn't that an interesting picture?"

"Yes. I find it very interesting that rival companies are involved. Leave them to me, commander. I'm going to look into it more thoroughly as soon as I wake in the morning."

"As you wish. I'm guessing they work the day shift. It's well after seven now. They won't pester us until tomorrow morning, whether they are on the clock or working well away from it."

Lila nodded and paged Isabel, calling for a bottle of champagne.

Commander Sutton eyed her suspiciously but said nothing while the drinks were poured.

"I know that expression, commander. I probably shouldn't be drinking so soon after anesthesia, but if you dare to use the phrase 'in your condition' one more time today, I will put you 'in a condition.'"

Sutton laughed, a bellowing laugh that started from the tips of her toes and ended with one hand flopped around her middle. "I'd like to see you try. Do you remember that day in hand-to-hand training when you—"

"I'm sure I do." Lila picked up one of the champagne flutes, and Sutton let the subject drop with a last delayed snicker. "Without going too far into the reasons, I find myself in need of a successor in the security office."

"You're leaving the militia?" Sutton said, nearly dropping her glass. "Why?"

"Personal reasons. They'll become clear in—"

"Oh my gods, you're finally taking over for Jewel." Sutton stood up and grasped her chair back, fumbling for words. "It's finally happening, isn't it?"

"You seem happy, commander."

"You're damn right I'm happy. You were born to be prime. You've made a damn good chief, don't get me wrong, but the family needs an able prime at the helm. Someone who will not only match your mother's reign but best it. The family ascended to Saxony because of her. You could take us to Unity. So, you're damn right I'm happy. The family has drifted over the last ten years. We've waited for too long."

Sutton drained her glass of champagne.

"Keep it to yourself. It's not official yet."

"What will be official?"

"At first, that I'm taking time away from the security office. Later, I'll reveal that I'll bear an heir for the family."

"You don't want to be mobbed at the Closing Ball?"

"That's the idea."

"It's probably for the best." Sutton sat back down and refilled her glass. "I'm guessing you'll need me to fill in as acting chief for a bit longer. I'd be happy to do so."

"Are you sure? It might take me a while to find a replacement. I need someone more than just competent. I need someone trustworthy, who will care for every person on every Randolph compound and all our holdings. I need someone who can lead a militia that's spread over the whole of Saxony. I need someone who might not mind a little time away from their husband."

Sutton perked up, finally realizing where Lila's thoughts had turned.

"Yes, you idiot. I want you to be that woman, *Chief* Sutton."

Lila raised her glass to the woman's new title and clinked her champagne flute against the one in Sutton's hand.

The commander had not moved at the announcement. Her forehead crinkled in a comical expression. "I don't know what to say, Ch— President?" She snorted and rubbed her face. "Gods, I don't even know what to call you."

"Stick with chief for now."

"Chief." She smiled, sipping her champagne at last. "I assumed I'd never be promoted past commander. My tech skills have never been all that good."

"I have a solution for that," Lila assured her, and took a very small sip of the champagne. Her stomach flopped in protest at the smell and taste of alcohol, but she ignored it. She studied the commander over the rim, knowing that her next words would knock some of the smile off Sutton's face. "I believe that Commander McKinley will be an invaluable asset to you in your new position."

"*Commander* McKinley?" Sutton repeated, and drained her glass. Lila poured another for her, knowing Sutton might have to finish the whole bottle before speaking again.

"Look at it this way, chief. If I don't promote her, you'll be subject to every suck-up call she's likely to place. Besides, she is good at what she does, and she'll need all the data coming to her so that she can plug the gaps in your knowledge. She'll be an invaluable consult on any tech problem. You'll both have to find a way to make it work."

"I will endeavor to do just that," Sutton said, as though being led to the noose.

It was Lila's turn to laugh. "It could be worse. You could be working with your husband."

Sutton considered the thought. "I'm not sure which idea is worse."

"You should be the one to tell Commander McKinley. The news should come from her new superior. Later. Much later. I don't want this getting out before I'm ready. That means no husband. No children. No one knows."

The pair sipped champagne for several quiet moments. "You're awfully thoughtful," Sutton said. "Anything else you want to run past me? You didn't promote me because I'm not one to be trusted."

Lila tapped her fingers on her armrest. "It's this thing with Senator Dubois," she began, before bringing the commander up to speed. "I find it odd that a senator would suddenly become seedless at his age, don't you?"

"So that's what happened." The commander reclined into her seat. "It's highly irregular. When do they go through testing? Eighteen?"

"Yes. Shiloh was just tested this summer."

"I bet that went over well."

"I was at Randolph General when they brought the interns in. Poor kid. He was extremely embarrassed about the whole thing, came out red-faced. I'm not sure that I made it any better. Father and I took him shopping afterward to get his mind off it."

"I think anyone would be embarrassed. Testing is necessary, though. The kids need to find out before they devote two years to an internship that might prove fruitless in the end, as does the senate."

"I agree. Senator Dubois passed before he became an intern. It's difficult for me to believe that his situation could have changed so completely between then and now."

"He either passed, or someone paid good money to make it look like he passed," Sutton conceded. "Those are the only two options."

"Paying off the senate doctors doesn't really make sense. Even if you could accomplish it, which you can't. The doctors might spend some time at Randolph General, but they are still men of Bullstow. They cannot be bribed. The cost is far too high. It would be treason to falsify a report like that. Besides, the Masson family is comfortably highborn. His mother is only the sixth heir, and Senator Dubois is far from the only Masson son in the New Bristol and Saxony High Houses. There is absolutely no reason for the Masson family to waste the money, the resources, or the effort in getting him into the senate. Not when he'd be found out in two or three years anyway, which he would have, if Jewel hadn't become enamored with him and muddied the waters."

"True. People talk, but everyone has assumed that it's a love match and that Jewel hasn't been ready to conceive, especially since she hasn't given him up."

"It's worked in his favor."

Sutton crossed her legs. "The Massons are a computer family. Consoles, software, and the like?"

"Toys and computer games, mostly. They also have their vineyards, but that's more of a hobby for Chairwoman Masson than a business."

"Well, I'm not sure I see the use of having another senator either. They don't have to outvote the damn environmentalists every time they want to add a new well or an oil rig along the Costa Sur. It would be a big risk for little in return."

"Judging from how much he wants to marry my sister, a political career has never been all that important to him. If it was, I'd expect him to draw things out with Jewel for a while longer. He could have wormed his way into another year or two at High House, but he's about to throw it all away. From what I can tell, no one seems that bothered by it."

"No one except you."

"Because it's weird. If the Masson family knew he was infertile or that such a malady ran in his line, they could have pushed him toward another career at Bullstow. He could have gone into law, social services, education, the militia. He could have been happy doing something else."

"Yeah, but there's much less canoodling with highborn women."

"Commander, Senator Dubois is very pretty. He could do plenty of that year round in another occupation. If he wanted to marry, he could have done so. Men are allowed to leave government service for that. Bullstow is far too conservative to ever get in the way. He's beautiful enough to have found a wife among the highborn, and he could have had his pick among the lowborn elite. Even if he couldn't have children, someone, somewhere, wouldn't have minded."

"Perhaps he wanted better. Perhaps he wanted the Randolphs," Sutton suggested. But the blackcoat offered a quick shake of her head immediately after. "I can't even suggest that in good conscience. I've been around the man for years now. I see no deception in him."

"Neither do I, and I looked hard. Do you think there is something weird about the whole thing?"

"It does seem a little odd." She nodded. "I've learned to look deeper when I come upon things that don't quite add up. It's a consequence of being a security officer, and it's what makes you a good one. If you think something weird is going on, you might be right."

"Might be?"

"It could also be that you don't want this new future of yours."

Lila looked away from her mentor, not able to refute her.

"Investigate if you need to. Satisfy your curiosity, but don't obsess, and be prepared to accept what you find."

# 8

Lila surveyed the city from atop Wolf Tower, a cold burst of wind catching her blackcoat. It mussed her hair and shoved her away from the roof's edge. She flexed her thighs and stood her ground, listening for any noise below. She heard nothing but the cawing of grackles in the maples. The people in the compound below moved to and fro like ants while the sun dipped below the horizon. The sky burned in orange and pink. Darkness would follow soon.

"You have not done as I asked."

Lila spun around, hand on her tranq.

A woman stalked forward, ignoring Lila's weapon. Her long blonde hair shifted in the wind, and her blue eyes traveled over the lawns. She wore leather armor, somewhat faded from the sun and the battlefield, just beginning to crack and show its age. Fur-lined boots covered her feet and calves, the toes marked with flecks of blood. A leather cord drooped at her neck with the weight of two large pearls. The bow and sword that peeked over her shoulder had both seen battle, just like the ancient oracle who wore them.

"What did you ask?"

"We spoke only a few hours ago, yet you do not remember. I suppose the healer made you forget."

"The healer?" Lila frowned, barely remembering her CUT procedure. "It's called anesthesia."

"It's called an annoyance."

"Did you just make a joke?"

The woman turned, nary a smile line on her face. "Lila of New Bristol, you have become problematic."

"How so?"

"You do not listen. You bring me to look at scenery instead of battlefields."

"What battlefields?"

"You know exactly what battlefield I speak of. You finally take up arms against our enemies, then you turn away from your victory. You should be celebrating. You should be drinking and feasting and recounting the story with those who stood at your side. A tale spinner should have written a—"

"I don't want to talk about it."

"I do not care. You killed for the glory of the gods. You protected future oracles. You won a great victory."

"I killed eight human beings."

"You killed eight enemies of the gods, and that is only the beginning. More will die. You will be a part of it, yet your stomach turns at the thought." She leaned into Lila's face. Her breath smelled of honey. "I could take you there again."

Lila stepped away.

"But that would not help you, would it? You'd run from the sight like you run from your thoughts. You would have preferred it if those men had taken the oracle daughters."

"No, I wouldn't."

"You would rather have spent this time tracking the kidnappers back to their homeland?"

"No."

"You would rather have brought back three small corpses?"

"Four."

"Four, and yet you still you turn away. If you cannot cheer your victory, then at least put it behind you."

"Just like that?"

"Yes. Stop wasting your time on remorse. There is no time for it."

"Fuck you."

The woman reached for her sword. Her hand lingered on the hilt, but she did not draw. "Sileas' daughters have much work ahead of them. They neglected you for too long."

"Sileas' daughters? You mean the oracles?"

"At least you know the old names," the woman said, dropping her hand at last. She rolled her shoulders and sighed. "The world has become soft and deaf over the centuries."

"We've become civilized."

"At some point, civilized people must rise up, their words spent, and pick up a weapon. Otherwise, they won't have a civilization left to defend. That is what you did, Lila of New Bristol. You rose up. You did what must be done. Now you must continue on your path."

"I am *continuing on my path.*"

"How so? You make merry with your lover. You hold on to this place," she said, her chin jerking to the compound. "You cling to what you must abandon."

"I'll never abandon my family."

"You sacrifice yourself, not because you think it is right, but because you think you deserve it. Punishment? Compensation? Do not twist the old ways and the words of the gods. You are the victor, Lila of New Bristol. You are the punishment."

"I was born to—"

"That life is forfeit," the woman insisted. "None of this matters. The oracle in your village summons you. Attend her, or I will return. I won't speak so politely next time."

"Why should—"

A knock sounded on Lila's bedroom door.

She flinched, startling at the noise. Her breath hitched as her sore belly protested the sudden movement.

Sinking into her covers, she ignored the next knock, her mind spiraling to the day before. She hadn't spent too long in the gym or gotten into a fight. Her future had changed. Rubio had reversed her CUT. Bullstow would hold the Closing Ceremony the next evening before the ball. She would attend and stand among the heirs. She'd take a senator. She'd accept the prime role soon after.

She'd have a child, an heir for the family.

It didn't matter how many odd dreams her mind produced. Nothing would change her duty and her new future.

The knock came again.

Alex did not wait any longer to be invited. She wordlessly flipped on half the lights in the room rather than firing every cannon at once. Lila hid her face underneath the covers, but the sound of casters rolling on the hardwood floor garnered her attention, as did the smell of food. She poked an eyeball from under her blankets.

"Wake up, lazy bones," her old friend whispered over the clattering of silver trays and china. "Surgery or not, it wouldn't do for the new Randolph prime to wallow in bed all day."

"Jewel's been doing it wrong, then." Lila inclined her head toward the cart, sniffing eggs, bacon, pancakes, and maple syrup. In a little bowl, she spied blackberries. "How'd you find out?"

"I have my ways."

Lila raised a brow.

"I guessed," Alex admitted.

"What's with the pancakes?"

"Chef," Alex said, setting the breakfast on a tray so Lila could eat in bed. Given the amount of food, Chef apparently believed that Lila was already eating for two, or perhaps ten. "After the chairwoman asked her to cook all your favorite foods yesterday, Chef naturally assumed that you'd need it today as well. She's still in the dark about the consequences of your meeting. As far as I can tell, everyone is. The family is talking, though. The chairwoman summoned you back from vacation early, and everyone knows it."

"Great." Lila winced as she sat up, holding her stomach.

"Perhaps you should lie down."

"Not when there are pancakes on the line. Chef will take them away and send up oatmeal. I hate oatmeal. I'm just sore, and there's nothing wrong with my appetite."

"Are you sure?"

"Positive. I just sat up too fast."

The slave nodded, and her fingers lingered on a second plate. "I thought you might want to have breakfast with an old friend, given everything that's happened. Am I an old friend?" She waited uncertainly next to the dinner cart, her ankles bending like an awkward child. She wouldn't meet Lila's eyes.

"Of course you are. You'll always be."

Alex gave a little smile and put her plate next to Lila's, both barely fitting on the shared tray. She picked up a pitcher of orange juice. It clinked against their glasses as she poured. "I didn't know if it would be too forward given my position, especially with my behavior a few weeks ago. Chef said I shouldn't ask."

A month ago, Alex wouldn't have cared what Chef thought. Then again, a month ago Alex hadn't smacked her around in front of the High Council of Judges. Lila hadn't yet put her friend's mother and little brother in a holding cell, either.

They'd both done things they regretted.

"We've had breakfast many times."

"You've never been prime while I've been a slave." Alex sat down across from her, her movement slow enough to barely disturb the bed.

The mattress barely wobbled. Orange juice sloshed in their cups.

"Things will be different when it's official. I won't be having breakfast with Chief Randolph. I'll be having breakfast with President Randolph. Truth be told, I think everyone has always assumed I was a snitch, and that it couldn't be helped since we'd been friends for so long. Things will be different now."

"Is that what you think?"

"Yes. I could never have imagined sharing a meal with a slave when I was prime. It just isn't done. You know that. Stop pretending we're both something we're not."

"I'm not—"

"You don't know what it's like among the workborn when the highborn aren't around. They get jealous and gossip about the strangest things. Others are the sweetest and kindest of souls. Chef, for one. If you pout around her long enough, she might make pancakes all week."

"She almost does that now," Lila said, trying to stifle a yawn.

She failed in her attempt.

"If I had known you'd be this tired, I would have let you sleep."

"What time is it?"

"Six, just as you asked. You slept for ten hours, Lila, but I'm not sure it was enough." She placed a few utensils before Lila so that she could sort out her breakfast. "What did your doctor say?"

"Nothing about staying in bed."

"Maybe you should anyway. You just had surgery."

"A CUT reversal is not surgery."

"Is too."

"Barely. And ten hours is plenty of rest." Lila dumped several pancakes onto her plate. Yesterday's nausea had disappeared, and now that she had food in front of her, she was ravenous. She hadn't eaten much the day before, and planned to make up for it. "I have work."

"What work? You have no job right now."

Lila's fork paused over her eggs. "Why don't you twist that knife a little harder?"

"I just meant—"

"I know what you meant, but I have a great deal to do before I leave the security office."

"You'll take a nap later if you need it?" Alex hinted, pushing the maple syrup toward her.

"I don't need a nap. I'm not a toddler."

Alex wrinkled her nose. "You're fussy enough for one."

"Yeah, well, you look like one."

"You smell like one."

"You sound like one."

Her friend clucked her tongue. "You eat like one."

Lila frowned at her breakfast. She'd once again poured maple syrup over everything.

"It's good. You should try it sometime." She snatched up the syrup and poised the spout over Alex's eggs.

"Don't you dare!"

Lila grinned evilly but put down the syrup.

"So how are you really doing with all this prime business?"

Lila forked a bite of pancake and chewed thoughtfully before answering. She didn't want to think about it, just like she didn't want to think about the warehouse, just like she didn't want to think about the stupid dream she'd had the night before.

Apparently, some deep, dark part of her felt pride in what she'd done. It also wanted her to visit the New Bristol oracle, probably so she could whine about her stupid feelings and move on like nothing had happened.

That part of her was a murdering sociopath.

"I don't want to talk about it."

"So you'll stick your head under the pillows until Saturday morning?"

"Something like that."

"At least someone will be in your bed with you when you wake up. Maybe you'll be biting that pillow instead of hiding under it."

Lila dropped her fork.

"Oh, you should be so lucky! I could give you the name of a senator or two who will give you a good time. Just give me the word. They'll fuck you so well that you won't care if you're prime or not. You won't even remember your name for days."

Lila had to admit, the offer tempted her—at least until she thought of Tristan, naked and sweaty atop her, his eyes and mouth set on Tristanville. "Maybe later."

Alex nodded. "Are you going to the execution?"

Lila choked on her pancake.

"I'm sorry. I have to ask."

"No, I'm not going."

Alex put down her fork. "I need you to go, and I need you to take me. I can't go unless my masters give me permission, and your mother has denied it. I need you to change her mind. I need you to come with me. I couldn't go alone even if I didn't need anyone's permission. I can't watch it without..."

Lila wiped her hands on her napkin, partly to stall, mostly because she had no idea how to answer. The last thing she wanted to do was attend the execution. She'd seen enough death lately, especially death that she had caused. Watching Patrick and Celeste Wilson hang would only add to her dreams.

Two more bodies would appear in the warehouse.

And what of Alex? She'd never get it out of her mind either.

"I don't think you should go."

Alex's face fell. "Don't do this to me. I know what I want, and I want to go. I have to go. You owe me this much. You know you do."

Lila couldn't dispute her words. She did owe her friend, but what was the best way to *be* a friend? Should she keep Alex from witnessing the executions because it was for the best? Or should she go with her and let her make a mistake?

Watching the executions would haunt Alex.

"Please, Lila. It's my decision."

"As you wish," Lila said at last.

After a few moments of awkwardness, the pair resumed their earlier good humor. They enjoyed a pleasant breakfast, both chuckling as they rehashed childhood memories. For a while, it felt as though they had become shadows of those girls again, promising they'd strike out on paths that their mothers had not laid out for them, blind to the knowledge that life is a product of choices that do not belong solely to oneself.

Memories soon gave way to the present, and by seven o'clock, Lila had finished her meal. While Alex cleared the dishes and carried them away, Lila briefly thought of hitting the obstacle course for her morning workout, then realized the stupidity of that idea.

Her belly was still sore. It might be days before she could go for a jog.

Even if she was well enough to work out, she no longer belonged in the security office anyway. The entire building stood as her gravestone. Perhaps she'd run along the estate's gravel paths from now on, or perhaps she'd use the executive gym in Wolf Tower like her mother and sister.

Lila groaned at the thought. Now that she was prime, she'd never be able to get away from the chairwoman. She'd see her every single day of every single week of every single year for the rest of her life.

She nearly crawled back into bed and hid under her blankets. No one would fault her for it. She could always say that she needed time to recover after her surgery.

The bed did look so very cozy.

Instead of succumbing to temptation, she trudged to her desk and plopped down in her chair, peeking at her palm with long sigh. Tristan had called at least a dozen times during the night. She nearly typed out his name, but stopped after her eyes strayed to the window. It was still a bit early. She'd let him sleep and call him later. After all, she still had no idea what to tell him, much less how to tell him. She had no desire to start the day with a fight, especially one that would end in a breakup.

She would lose him the moment she told him. She already knew it.

Turning to her desktop, she pulled up the crimson logon page for Randolph General. She entered a user ID and password from one of her dummy accounts so that what she searched for would not get back to anyone. After typing in Dubois's name on the patient search screen, she pored over the results, hoping the senator had done his initial fertility testing at Randolph General. Most interns did.

Lila was rewarded with a hit. Though Dubois's test results did not mean much to her in detail, it did confirm that his doctors had ruled him fertile several years before. From what Lila could tell, the records had not been altered, not unless the original doctor had lied in his report. In addition, Dubois had not been seen for any major illnesses at the hospital.

That didn't mean he hadn't been treated elsewhere, though.

She retrieved her star drive from her secret compartment with Dubois's most current test results, then redacted Dubois's name from the files and saved his past fertility test.

After sneaking into BullNet and downloading his medical files from the onsite health clinic, she pulled up her snoop programs. Once she and Sutton had concluded their meeting the night before, she'd checked her search results on the stolen Bullstow data. Unfortunately, she'd gotten no hits. In a drowsy haze, she'd written a quick but very general search to run during the night, all in the hopes of finding more traps in the code.

Her search hadn't revealed anything.

Lila drummed her fingers upon her knee as she contemplated her search parameters. She'd looked for a similar trap to the one she'd found in the BIRD. Unfortunately, she had no idea if the BIRD had been Reaper's first hack in BullNet or his last.

Lila hoped it was his last. The BIRD trap had not been that sophisticated. It would be easier for her to find something cruder.

But the fact that she had not found anything in her first two searches didn't bode well.

After she set up a new search, Lila took a quick shower and dressed in a dark sweater, dark trousers, and her heavy motorcycle jacket. Then she grabbed her star drive and a scarf and padded downstairs.

A footman opened the front door of the great house with a flourish, his boots shining as the sun peered over the horizon, reflecting off the polished leather.

Lila shivered as she stepped out into the morning and adjusted her scarf.

A sharp whistle caught her attention.

Sutton jogged past the fountain toward her. Streams of water sprayed into the air, gurgling and bubbling as they dove and hit the surface.

"You're up early," Lila called out.

"I could say the same for you. Figured you'd be up and about, though. I hoped I might have a word," Sutton said as soon as she reached the door.

"Always." Lila tugged her jacket around herself, hoping Sutton didn't notice the servant's garb underneath. The commander would complain that she was too ill to meet with spies today.

Fortunately, the commander's mind had traveled elsewhere.

The pair walked down the gravel path between the great house and the garage, their feet crunching the rocks, the wind rattling the leaves of each shrub and rose as they prowled past. At last, Sutton paused and sat upon one of the stone benches, a wordless request for a moment's conference.

Lila joined her, the cold seeping through her woolen trousers. She was reminded of her perch on the senate building's ledge the month before, right after she'd downloaded the BIRD. Things had gotten so much more complicated since then. Her life had drifted so far off track.

A cold wind seeped through her scarf.

"Sergeant Davies contacted the security office early this morning," Sutton said, her fingers thumping on the bench.

"Again? What did he want?"

"The same thing. I told *Commander* McKinley that I'd speak to you personally. I wanted to make sure you were awake and well before I told you."

Lila crossed her legs against the cold and watched the trees bend in the wind. Knuckle-sized golden leaves fell in her hair, tangling amid the strands. "Did he have a warrant?"

"No. I tried to pump him for more information, but he was tight-lipped. He wanted to know if the Randolph security office had reconsidered cooperation with Bullstow, and he hoped that his messages were being passed along to those who would more carefully weigh the implications of refusal. The asshole is threatening the family."

"Wouldn't be the first time. I'll handle it."

"No, it's part of my duties. I'll—"

"You can take the next one. You'll take them all soon enough."

Sutton handed over a piece of paper with Sergeant Davies's contact information scribbled upon it. "I figured you'd say something like that."

Lila retied her scarf around her neck more tightly. "Is that all?"

When Sutton nodded, Lila stood and gestured for the commander to follow. The pair walked toward the great house garage.

"So how are your ovaries?"

Lila cringed. "Oracle's light! Never ask me that again."

"When my daughter Chloe had her CUT reversed, she said it felt like a mule kicked her for days. It hurt to stand up, to sit, to pee, to eat. It hurt worse when she threw up what she ate. They never tell you that before you get them."

"I'm fine."

"You look it. I'll tell Chloe. She'll hate you for it." Sutton clasped her hands behind her back. "You're barred from the gym for a week, just so you know."

"I'm barred from it forever. Members only."

"You'll always be part of the militia. You'll always be welcome."

"It'd be weird."

Sutton nudged her shoulder. "Work out with me as my guest."

"Because you do so love to work out?"

"I might develop a taste for it, given the right partner."

Lila eyed her.

"I might."

"And the chairwoman might turn into a pretty little fairy and frolic in the fountain," Lila muttered.

Sutton let out a snort before composing herself.

"How's being chief treating you so far?"

"It'll go better when I can tell *Commander* McKinley to go jump in the—"

"She's practically your new partner. You have to coexist peacefully with your partner even when they're a pain in the ass."

"Was I a pain the ass?"

Lila winked. "I'll be along this weekend to clean out my office. I'll have to leave it boxed up for a bit until it's official."

"One office is as good as another. Take your time, madam."

"Madam?" Lila grumbled, stopping before the garage. "Has it really come to that? I'm to be madamed to death?"

"Literally. You'll be on your deathbed at eighty years old, and some young doctor—"

"Eighty? I'm to die at eighty?"

"Eighty is respectable."

"So is ninety!"

"So is a hundred." Sutton gave an overly exaggerated bow, her blackcoat rustling and fluttering in the wind. "I will message you if Bullstow calls again."

The commander gave a stiff nod, turned, and headed toward the security office.

Lila wished she could follow.

Instead, she pulled out the slip of paper as Sutton's footsteps receded on the gravel. The calls from Davies could have been a coincidence. Bullstow's tech department might have asked him to do them a favor. They might have asked him to fetch some small piece of information before they informed Chief Shaw of her hack. But Lila didn't believe in coincidences, and it didn't seem likely that they would have asked a man outside their department for assistance.

Another explanation seemed far more plausible, now that her mind had cleared from the fog of wine and anesthesia. She had rattled the blackmailer by stealing into BullNet again. She had been seen. And Sergeant Davies had found himself a new employer, only a few weeks after being disciplined by his superiors for the very same thing.

Or perhaps he and Muller had worked for Reaper's partner all along, rather than Reaper. Whoever had found her in the BIRD that night had gone by the name Zephyr. But what if she'd been wrong in assuming that Reaper and Zephyr had been the same person? Reaper had boasted he was Zephyr, but only after she'd pressed him.

Just because he'd claimed to be Zephyr, didn't mean he was.

Reaper had never been that great a hacker, anyway. What if the real hacker still lurked in New Bristol?

Lila punched Davies's contact information into her palm.

"Sergeant Davies," he answered, voice honeyed with the high-born drawl.

Bullstow had served the lowborn well.

"This is Chief Randolph. My commander informs me that you have twice demanded a list of my family's logins."

"That is correct," he said with barely contained amusement.

"Do you understand how irregular that is?"

"Bullstow has asked such things before."

"Asking and receiving are two different things, sergeant. Would you mind telling me why you'd like the list?"

"Yes, I would mind."

There was a pause. Lila expected him to offer up something besides smug arrogance, but she received nothing but silence. "How many other families have assented to this highly illegal and evasive demand?"

"We're not looking at other families. We're looking at yours. I assumed that as chief, you would be concerned about illegal activity within the Randolph household. I assumed you would want Bullstow to resolve the matter quickly and quietly."

"What matter? What illegal activity?"

The officer quieted on the other end of the line.

"No comment, sergeant? Fine. Here's mine. The only thing I'm concerned about this morning is keeping my family's rights protected from very vague accusations. You'll not get any logins from me without a damn good reason."

"Your rights are not at risk," Sergeant Davies grumbled, his veneer of professionalism slipping. "We can get a judge's order.

I was extending the opportunity as a professional courtesy. War-rants tend to be intercepted and misinterpreted by the media so easily these days. Ask the Holguíns how much a scandal can cost a family."

"You let me worry about that. Bring me a warrant and a reason for wanting the list before you trouble me again."

"As you wish," he said curtly, and disconnected.

Acting on instinct, Lila searched for his contact information in Bullstow's official directory. As a member of the government militia, he should have given Sutton his office line.

The hit she received did not surprise her. The number hadn't come from Bullstow.

# 9

The garage door opened with a creaking rumble in the quiet morning. At least a dozen cars had been parked in two rows, half classics, half new. Lila ignored them and slipped her leg over a silver motorcycle parked on the end. Her Firefly glinted in the beams of the early morning light. Drawing out her palm, she pulled up her snoop programs and waved the device over the bike. It beeped, signaling that a GPS chip had been tucked away in the seat cowl. It beeped again as she waved it over the front fairing, alerting her to an audio bug.

Lila picked them both from her Firefly as if they were chunks of vomit, her face crinkling in disgust, and thumped them across the garage. Her mother's spies had been at it again.

Once Lila judged her bike to be free of bugs and GPS, she popped her helmet over her head, tugged on a pair of riding gloves, flexed her mostly healed fingers, and sped out of the compound, dodging the few early risers on their way to the bullet train or their offices in the northern half of the estate.

Nodding to Sergeant Hill at the gatehouse, she zipped through the southern entrance and turned toward downtown. The streets were thankfully free of fog, and few people were out so early in the morning. It made Lila feel more confident on the motorcycle. Though she loved the Firefly and enjoyed how powerful it made her feel to ride it, the one embarrassing consequence of riding the bike was when she occasionally tipped the damn behemoth on the street and needed help righting it before she could go farther.

Crowds tended to laugh at heirs in distress, even unofficial ones, and they rarely did anything to alleviate the problem. The only balm was a few well-placed bribes, which Lila had waiting in her pocket.

Resolving not to tip the motorcycle when few people were around to take her cash, Lila flexed her legs and rode on to her destination, squirming a bit on the seat as it roughly vibrated the soreness between her legs and her belly.

Perhaps she should have taken her Adessi roadster instead.

As she was already halfway to her destination, Lila stubbornly rode on. She had never visited her doctor outside of the hospital. Helen did not live on the family estate like nearly every other Randolph in New Bristol. Instead, she chose to live among the poorer classes in a condo near the hospital. It was close enough to be convenient, but far enough away not to be chained to her work. She claimed that she needed to live downtown because the hospital called her out of bed at all hours to tend to patients, but Lila saw it for what it was—a bid for freedom away from the family and the hospital.

Lila respected it, and her, immensely.

As such, she would traverse the city without complaint. There were too many eyes and ears at the hospital, and since Helen's workday did not begin until ten o'clock, they would have plenty of time to talk without interruption. Even if she asked questions the doctor did not want to answer, Lila trusted Helen to point her in the right direction. If there was one thing the doctor hated, it was subterfuge, which was why Lila's mother would never control her.

It was also why Lila would never try.

She entered the condo's parking lot and stopped in front of a building neither gleaming with its tidiness nor particularly grimy in its disarray. No trash littered the grounds or crumpled under her wheels, and the grass had not grown over the sidewalk. That was about all that the place had going for it. It must have been quite an adjustment for Helen after growing up inside the pristine walls of the Randolph estate.

Lila settled the Firefly quickly, giving herself plenty of room to turn the bike around again. She had barely stretched her leg over the seat when she heard furious barking in one of the condos, echoing off the windows. The beast made such a fuss that Lila feared it might wake the neighbors.

Certainly, Helen could not sleep through such an announcement.

Thin fingers pulled down the blinds on the first floor, then quickly snapped closed as Lila passed by, a shadow startled by her nearness. The barking only intensified when Lila climbed the stairs, and when she raised her hand to knock, she realized that the dog was on the other side of the door.

Lovely.

There was nothing like trying to have a conversation while being slobbered upon.

Helen answered the door in sweats and a robe that were both several sizes too large for her frame. Her natural gray hair was mussed. She possessed the oft-coveted silver hue that colorists promised their clients all over the commonwealth, even though the doctor was only a dozen years Lila's senior. Even unbrushed, it moved like silk across her face.

A black Labrador sat next to the doctor and licked his nose with a short sigh, well behaved now that he had run out of any argument against Lila's presence. His tail swung back and forth, mouth thankfully free of drool.

Helen took one look at her visitor and shook her head. "I should have expected to see someone like you today."

"I'm sorry. I know you're not well, but it is important."

"Come in, come in," Helen said with a yawn, stepping away from the door. "Would you like some hot chocolate?"

"Always."

Lila entered the condo as the doctor turned on a few lamps with a tinny snap, then parked herself on the sofa out of the doctor's way. The room was comfortably furnished, far more practical than frilly, and Lila spied no piece of furniture that did not serve some purpose. It was not neat, nor overly large, but it felt like more of a home than the Randolph great house.

Lila liked it immensely.

Helen bustled into the kitchen, preparing two mugs of hot chocolate with a clatter of cheap porcelain rather than china. The dog remained uncertain of where to go. He answered the confusion by plopping himself in the center of the room so that he could watch both women with his large brown eyes.

Helen reentered the room and handed Lila a mug, then excused herself to find clothes befitting an audience with the Randolph militia.

"Are you feeling better today?" Lila asked when Helen reappeared, dressed in slim trousers and a crimson sweater.

The doctor cocked her head to the side. "Was I sick?"

"You weren't at the clinic yesterday."

"I'm guessing you were, and you weren't there for a simple walk-through. I presume your mother struck again. Have I missed some bit of mischief?"

"Yes. Unfortunately, I didn't figure out her scheme until after it was over. I blame the wine." Lila took a sip of the hot chocolate, letting the warm sweetness coat her tongue.

Helen settled on the opposite side of the sofa and lifted her mug. "They told me that Dr. Carver needed to swap his schedule, and they hoped I might help him out. I figured Scout would not mind the imposition too much." She scratched behind the dog's ears while he nosed at her thigh. "What was the real reason they wanted me away from the hospital?"

"I had an emergency appointment to reverse my CUT."

The doctor's face twisted in confusion. "I thought you didn't want children."

"I don't, but I will be prime soon. It requires a functioning womb."

Helen nearly dropped her mug onto Scout's head, frightening the dog so much that he retreated into the corner. His collar and tags rattled as he rushed away.

"That information is not to be shared with anyone, not until it's official."

"Of course," Helen said, her mouth still gaping. "Who performed the procedure?"

"Dr. Cristina Rubio."

Helen nodded. "I was on her hiring committee. She wasn't my first choice, but our candidates are the best of the best. I'd wager she took good care of you. I don't understand why your mother didn't want me to perform the procedure, though. I have far more experience."

"It wasn't a slight against your abilities. My mother chose Dr. Rubio so that she could pump me full of fertility drugs afterward without my knowledge and consent. Not only does my mother want Jewel replaced as prime, she also wants a grandchild quickly. Our stock price is dipping."

Helen leaned back in the cushions, her face strained and furious. "Fertility drugs? No wonder she kept me away. I never would have done that even if you had asked. I refused to give them to your mother, too, not that it stopped her. Those drugs are not to be abused and shouldn't be given so soon after surgery. It's all very hard on your body. You should be resting. You didn't ride here on your motorcycle this morning, did you?"

"Of course not."

"Leave it here. Take a cab home."

"I'll manage."

"Stubborn fool. At least take a nap when you get a chance. You'll need it," the doctor said. "Will you go to the Closing Ball tomorrow?"

Lila sipped her hot chocolate.

"I recommended against spending the night with a man so soon after surgery. You might not be in pain tomorrow night, but your body has been through an ordeal. We've made a great deal of progress in women's fertility since the days of tubal ligations, Lila, but your womb isn't a light switch you can just turn on and off whenever you feel like it."

"You sound like one of those damn Catholics from the empire," Lila muttered. If she was supposed to take a man for a whole season, she wanted to try him out before committing. She couldn't think of anything worse than being forced to spend an entire season with a senator who couldn't bed her properly. It was rare, but there were a few out there, mostly among the younger senators. She didn't have the time or desire to train a bedmate. "What if it's in my best interest for the lights to be on?"

Helen refilled Lila's cup. "I'll not give you permission to go against medical advice, child."

"Child?"

"Yes, I'll call you a child when you're acting like one. Are you so starved that you can't wait for a few days?"

Lila thought guiltily of Tristan. She definitely wasn't starved.

"There are other concerns," she said.

"There always are. There always will be."

"So, what you're saying is that if I spend the night with someone on the night of the ball, then I will spontaneously combust. I understand now, doctor. You've been very helpful."

"Don't be flippant. There is a risk of infection."

"Is that all?"

"Lila, stay away from the senators on Friday night unless you really do want a child. Those drugs are far superior to what your mother used, and the surgery forces you to ovulate. If a senator so much as looks at you with an erection, you will get pregnant."

"Is that how it works now?"

"Child," the doctor snapped. She whistled at Scout across the room, and the dog's ears rose at the sound. "At least you're keeping the hot chocolate down. How's your appetite?"

"I ate breakfast for five," Lila answered, shifting in her seat as Scout hopped up on the sofa, fear of falling mugs forgotten. He curled up between them and rested his chin on the doctor's thigh. "The surgery wasn't the only reason why I came here. I have something I need you to look at."

"It's not a mole, is it? Everyone always wants me to look at their moles, even at parties."

Lila shook her head. She explained why her mother had declared her prime in the first place, and pressed the star drive into the doctor's hand.

Or at least she tried, for Helen refused to take it. "If that's Senator Dubois's medical files, then no. I can't look at the medical records of a patient who is not assigned to me. It's a violation of patient privacy."

"It's medical malpractice and treason if a Bullstow doctor is falsifying medical files on Randolph property. I need to know if we have a doctor working at Randolph General who can be bribed."

"He's a Bullstow doctor, Lila. Not one of ours. They rarely practice at the hospital unless it's during the interns' fertility testing. This isn't our problem."

"Do you trust the media and the public to see the difference?"

"Don't insult my intelligence. That's not the reason you want me to look at it."

"No, it's not, but it's a reason you should care about."

Helen took the star drive from Lila, cursing under her breath as she trudged to her desktop computer. She pored over the records while sipping her hot chocolate. A wagging tail dully thumped against the rug at her feet. "These first results look pretty standard. He wasn't infertile at eighteen, that's for sure. He shouldn't have any problems getting a woman pregnant, assuming normal rates of intercourse."

"Are you sure?"

"Yes. Like most senators, he's more fertile than average. I'm surprised Jewel doesn't have a few kids by now."

"Could someone else's test results have been included in Senator Dubois's file accidentally, or could the doctor have faked this result and lied about his conclusions?"

"Anything is possible, but it's highly improbable that anything happened by accident or design. There are too many safeguards for that to happen, too many checks in the process for one sample to end up in the wrong file, much less two. Besides, I know the doctor attached to Senator Dubois's results. He's thorough. Dr. Vasquez would not stand for any impropriety to touch his work."

"So the file is honest."

"I'd count on it. The lab matches each intern's sample to the DNA stored on file. Still, it's strange that he could go from healthy to infertile in only a few years. Where's his most current record?"

Lila pointed out the folder. Helen became quiet while she studied the new information. "If he had an illness or an injury..."

"I've seen the man at least once a week for the last few years. He's never had more than a cold. His only records at the hospital and the clinic consist of yearly physicals and mild illnesses. He isn't the sort of man to do any drugs, either. He doesn't even smoke cigars."

Helen opened his physicals and studied the data, then returned to Senator Dubois's latest round of testing. After several moments, she chuckled.

"What?"

"It's nothing. I just had an image of the pretty senator in a set of muddy overalls and a straw hat. Could you imagine?"

"No. Why are you?"

"Because exposure to NAT could do this."

"NAT?"

Helen clucked her tongue. "I forget sometimes how young you are. NAT was a very popular insecticide several decades ago. It's nasty stuff. A lot of the farms in Saxony and La Verde didn't know the risks when they first started using it. They just knew that it was cheap and worked very, very well. It wasn't too long before reports flooded into the government regulators. It turned out that NAT triggers fertility issues in men. It also causes high rates of birth defects in pregnant women, asthma problems in children, breathing problems in the elderly, and a slew of other unpleasantness.

"You can imagine the outcry when the Saxony and La Verde senates engaged scientists to study the problem. The High and Low Council of Judges in Unity banned every farm in the country from using NAT a few years later. That was years ago, of course.

I was still at university when it hit the press, but I remember the highborn farming families didn't argue the issue. Too many of them had seen the effects firsthand. Most of them had already ditched it for what they knew to be safe, either because they were moral enough not to use it or because it was too expensive to pay their slaves' medical bills. I doubt anyone would touch it these days, since there are safer insecticides that won't bring the Farmers' Bureau down on your head for interclass abuse."

"Where would someone get a hold of NAT today?"

Helen shrugged. "A university? A research center? I'm sure that someone, somewhere, is trying to design a safer alternative. Dr. Rubio would know. She worked with Dr. Ana Rodriguez, the biochemist who first recognized how NAT interacts in the body. Dr. Rubio was part of her team until she switched from grad school to med school. When we interviewed her for the clinic, she told us all about the work she did in Dr. Rodriguez's lab. Apparently, it prompted her to go into reproductive health. She even brought along several of her journal articles."

"What were the articles about?"

"Standard stuff. Mouse models. Finding the pathways NAT triggers when it's absorbed in the body. Logging the frequency of different outcomes on reproductive health. Most of Dr. Rubio's work was with mice. I bet that girl can perform a rodent autopsy in her sleep." She chuckled, then glanced at Lila's face. "Although I doubt that's the sort of thing you want to hear about a person after they've had their hands inside you."

Lila ignored the mental image, or at least she tried. "I did ask Dr. Rubio about the senator's file. She was strangely silent about NAT."

Helen pursed her lips. "Well, who would think that a senator had been exposed to an insecticide?"

"The Massons own a vineyard."

"Yes, but even if they used NAT illegally, Senator Dubois would have had to work in it for at least a year or two before it affected his fertility. Worked, mind you, not just visited."

"I didn't tell Dr. Rubio the file belonged to a senator."

The doctor ejected the star drive from her computer. "It's not NAT, Lila. If it was, other symptoms would have shown up in his physical."

Lila tucked the star drive into her pocket. "What do you think about Dr. Rubio?"

"If you're referring to her earlier behavior, I find it odd, yet unsurprising, that she followed your mother's instructions with the fertility shots. It goes against basic medical ethics. There's no reason to give fertility injections to a woman on the same day that she's had her CUT reversed, and plenty of reasons not to. Even if Dr. Rubio believed your mother about your supposed fertility issues, then she would be required to do a full workup on you beforehand. I don't care if she thought her job was on the line—"

"Dr. Rubio is working for my mother. Just say it."

Helen rubbed at her eyes and nodded. "It's likely, especially since she was the one to call me about switching shifts. I intend to lodge a formal complaint with the ethics board about your case."

"Highborn intrigue is not worth the trouble. I should have paid better attention and not put myself in that—"

"She abused her calling, Lila. I won't stand for it."

"So you'll let the press embarrass Senator Dubois?"

Helen drummed her fingers on the table. "Fine. I'll let you handle it. Find a reason to fire her. I don't want her working in my clinic."

"Your clinic?" Lila grinned. "I'll have to look into her financials to ensure the hospital is not liable for any risk. Her wife's records too. Who did she marry to get into the family?"

"Emily. They eloped last year. That's why you don't remember a wedding. I think Emily did it just to spite Georgina."

Lila's jaw dropped, which was something she prided herself on rarely happening. "But she's—"

"Don't say old. I swear to the oracles, if you say old, I will punch your nose, prime or not," Helen promised without taking a breath.

"She is my age. She's mature. She's experienced, regardless of how silly and vapid she might be, but she's not old. There is merely an age disparity between the pair that highlights Emily's maturity."

"Tell me what you really think." Lila smirked.

"I think that Dr. Rubio is the ambitious sort. It could be love, or it could be that she found a way into highborn society by playing on Emily's vanity. Add in her position at the hospital, and you have someone highly intelligent who's willing to do whatever the chairwoman asks, either for a bit of coin or because she's in too weak of a position to refuse. Never see her again, child. Not even to treat a splinter."

Lila could not disagree with Helen's logic.

# 10

Lila sped down the streets of New Bristol on her Firefly, annoyed at the motorcycle in her rearview. A navy Barracuda had been tailing her since she left Helen's condo. As Lila was alone, she had decided against provoking a meeting. She also dismissed the idea of returning immediately to the Randolph estate. If she led a stalker back to Sutton and her mother, she might not be allowed to leave the compound without an escort for months.

She'd not allow herself to fall under house arrest, not on top of everything else going on in her life.

Lila escaped the exhaust and fumes of the clogged downtown streets and headed toward the loop. As soon as her tires hit the interstate, she increased her speed to over a hundred and seventy kilometers per hour, then threaded through the spotty traffic. The freezing winds cut through her trousers. She barely felt her fingers inside her gloves.

Green fields and bluebonnets flashed in her peripheral. Scattered lowborn diners, cheap hotels, and shabby gas stations fled from view. Even the cars on the road whipped behind her as she passed, but not the Barracuda. Every time she checked her mirror, the rider hung on behind her, stubbornly chasing. Lila didn't care whether it was friendly or aggressive. She only wanted it gone.

But it kept following.

Soon Lila gave up, not willing to press her speed or her luck any further. She took the Twelfth Street exit, mindful of the slower cars and trucks that populated the lanes, then zipped through the sluggish traffic. She kept much of her speed, but the cars flowed closer and closer as she progressed, making such movements more and more difficult.

She approached the first intersection, planning to blast through the yellow light and leave the Barracuda far behind. Unfortunately, the light switched to red earlier than expected, and a fleet of three delivery trucks hit the gas, ready to cross.

She would have to stop. Lila only hoped that the rider would not take the opportunity to abandon his bike and approach her.

Lila squeezed the right-hand brake.

It smacked against the grip, offering no resistance at all.

Lila took her eyes off the road. Her frozen fingers shaking, Lila pumped the brake again, her mouth slackening when it didn't catch.

Her foot brake didn't, either.

Lila looked up at the delivery trucks accelerating toward the intersection, a moving wall of rubber and steel. The second driver saw that she had failed to slow down, understanding quickly that she would run the red. He beat on his steering wheel, honking in loud squawks, his mouth full of angry threats trapped behind thick glass.

But he braked.

So did the driver next to him. The woman's curls twisted around her face, and she shook her head in fright as Lila skated before them.

Lila nearly clipped the rear bumper of an oblivious sedan as it sped across in the opposite direction.

The Barracuda followed her across.

It was at that moment that Lila understood the obvious. The Barracuda's rider had done something to her brakes. It had been following her the entire time just to watch the aftermath. Perhaps the rider had a helmet camera trained on her, all to capture her last bloody moments.

It wouldn't be the first time that a death tape was leaked to the media. Her stomach dropped as she realized that Pax might see it, re-watching her last few minutes, immortalized in cold pixels. Knowing him, he would watch the morbid scene play out over and over again, obsessing over it, just as he had done with Trevor's memory.

He couldn't handle it. Not so soon after losing his friend.

Lila shook her head against the thought. She wouldn't leave him so unhappy, weeping over a polished casket that no one could open.

Gathering her wits, Lila thumbed the kill switch, her hand shaking so badly that it nearly slid off the handle. She was frightened now of the vibrating beast between her legs as though it might turn its head and strike like Grendel's dragon. The cold dropped away around her, and her palms began to sweat inside her gloves.

When the motor died, she downshifted into fifth gear, panicked at the thought that the clutch might not function either.

She grinned stupidly when it did.

The motorcycle cruised forward, inertia still pushing her along.

Her speed wasn't dropping fast enough, though, not for the traffic around her, not enough for the next intersection just a few shops down. The cars might have been slaloms built to hinder her progress, and she knew her luck would soon run out. A wreck loomed with every vehicle she approached.

She dodged the slow-moving cars, her breath coming in hurried gasps.

The green light ahead switched to yellow, a red beacon of death to follow after.

Lila would not be able to speed through the intersection again, but she still zipped forward too quickly to stop.

Thinking quickly, Lila crossed several lanes of traffic and swung to the right-hand lane, turning sharply. She cut off a skittish car, and her knee almost tapped the asphalt in front of it.

She nearly lost control.

She gripped the handlebar all that much tighter when she did not.

Merging with traffic, Lila downshifted into fourth, her speed still too fast for the cars around her, too fast for the intersections spaced far too close. Unfortunately, the street she had been forced onto was not built for much beyond a slow crawl at such a late hour of the morning.

Threading in between the vehicles, Lila yelped as her rearview mirror shattered and flew off, decapitated by a car's side mirror. Both smacked against her hand, leaving her bones throbbing, glass and metal shards ricocheting off her jacket and helmet with a few dull plinks. The handlebar wrenched to the left and almost twisted her off course with the impact.

Correcting her course, she vainly searched for a side street, one without an interaction so soon after the last. She endured a half-dozen honks and a dozen middle fingers, as well the catcalls of the workborn on the sidewalk. The women and men wore cheap, puffy coats in bright colors, laughing and calling out to their friends. They pulled out their palms, those who had enough money to own them, for all had the same idea.

Film her when she crashes.

Sell it to the media.

Cash out on the net.

It would serve the rich bitch right.

Up ahead, a line of cars braked before the next intersection, ready to turn.

Lila was still going too fast. Thinking quickly, she rode her Firefly up a handicapped ramp and zoomed over the sidewalk, taking the corner.

Pedestrians shouted and cursed. Their palms and shopping bags flew into the air as they scrambled to get away from the speeding bike.

Her body jostled harshly as she landed on the next street.

Lila downshifted once more, too frightened to laugh at their confusion, her hand throbbing harder and harder. Her bike joined traffic toward the downtown bridge. Brakes squealed as cars crawled forward, impatient drivers cycling constantly between stop and go.

She had to stop too, but she was trapped in a sea of guardrails and cars and brick storefronts, all threatening to crush her. They were her only options, though, not unless she wanted to launch herself from the bridge and go for a swim fifty meters below.

The water's impact might break her neck.

Thinking quickly, she downshifted again, slowing her bike as much as possible, dodging what traffic she could.

Then she turned her bike toward a lowborn business, stamped her boots against the asphalt, and slammed her beloved Firefly into solid brick.

# 11

Lila lay on the ground in shock.

The Firefly lay a few meters away, the wheel bent at an odd angle, the frame dented. Her body felt as though it had been through a particularly tough workout, overseen by the most torturous of trainers.

But she was alive.

Lila wiggled her arms and legs, wincing as she tried to clench the hand that been hit by the rearview mirrors. It throbbed almost as much as her hip and shoulder, which had absorbed much of the impact when she hit the sidewalk and rolled away. The bones in her hand still worked. She made a fist and moved on, turning her head from side to side, then gripped the bottom of her helmet and pulled it off.

"No, no, no," the mystery rider shouted, downing the Barracuda on the sidewalk with a clutter. The rider sprinted toward Lila and ripped off his helmet, letting it drop and thunk dully beside her. "Lie back down," he ordered.

Lila's eyes widened as Tristan crouched beside her.

"Don't ever move after a crash, you hear me? Not ever!" He cupped her cheeks and tilted her face upward, squinting into her eyes. "Why were you driving so fast?"

"I thought you were trying to kill me."

"What?" Not waiting for an answer, Tristan yanked his palm from a jacket pocket and jabbed at the screen for several seconds. Then he put his palm away and knelt on the street next to her, pulling at her arms and legs as though searching for hidden contraband. She tried to push him away, wincing as her injured hand made contact, but he ignored it. Now that her adrenaline was fading, his poking and prodding began to hurt. When he brushed her belly, Lila cried out, for her soreness had increased after the tumble.

"Oh shit, don't move. Don't move," he pleaded.

"I'm okay, Tristan. Just stop poking me."

He fell back on his ankles, his frown deepening. "I sent a message to Doc. He'll be here in five minutes. Lie down until he gets here."

"I don't want to lie down." In truth, Lila desperately wanted to lie down; she just didn't want to lie down in the middle of the sidewalk.

"What happened?"

Lila opened her mouth and tried to answer, but she didn't know what to say.

What had happened?

Both sets of brakes had failed somehow, and Pax had almost mourned a sister.

It all had happened so quickly, out of nowhere. Her death would have been stupid and commonplace and no one would have been surprised. A motorcycle accident in downtown New Bristol. Chief Randolph dead. Film at eleven.

This time, none of the regrets she'd gotten so used to had flashed through her head, and not because she didn't have any. She'd just been too busy trying to live to regret anything. She had felt only panic.

Bone-clenching, pee-in-your-pants panic.

It slowly drained away, but it had nowhere to go.

Tristan touched her face at the wrong time. She gasped, and it was that small noise that broke something inside her. Tears spilled over her cheeks, and she gulped in air, struggling to breathe, still terrified, still in shock that she had managed to survive at all. She bowed her head, resting it on Tristan's shoulder.

She didn't just cry.

She fell apart, and she hated herself for it.

It was worse than how she'd cried after her mother had kicked her out. Lila had gotten hold of herself almost immediately, like a true highborn should, but she wasn't sure she'd be able to do the same this time. Tristan's nearness only made it worse. His strong arms enveloped her, trying so very hard not to squeeze too tightly.

He rested his chin on her forehead and stroked her back. The weight rubbed up and down against her leather jacket, warming her.

Occasionally, people leaned out of their cars to offer assistance, but Tristan waved them on. "Help is coming," he assured them, and they moved on without another word.

Soon, a large truck filled with Tristan's people stopped before them, half on the sidewalk to avoid traffic. Lila dug her face into Tristan's neck, hiding her face while they loaded up her bike with stamping boots and quick shouts of "One, two, three, lift!"

All the while, she focused on her breathing. It was an attempt to settle her nerves and stop the flood of tears. Every time she drew breath, Tristan's scent flooded her nose. He smelled of soap, a bit like whiskey, and a little like engine grease from the shop. It calmed her, and she drew his scent in deeper.

A pair of boots stopped beside her. She heard a rustle of fabric and a popping knee. A hand clasped Lila's shoulder. "I'm a doctor, madam. Let me have a look at you."

"I'm fine," Lila said, glad to have her voice back at last.

"She's not okay, Doc. She was crying."

"It was only a little," Lila said, her cheeks growing hot against Tristan's neck.

"Now she's grouchy. Forget everything, Doc, she must be better now if she's grouchy."

"I'm not grouchy."

Doc chuckled, his deep voice rich and warm. "I'd be grouchy too if I just crashed into a brick wall. Let me check you out, madam. It will only take a moment."

Lila shook her head. "I wasn't going that fast. I'm okay."

"You were going fast enough." Tristan tried to gently pry Lila's fingers off his neck. "Let the doctor check you out."

Lila hid her face and refused to face the doctor. She'd only met him when she had a hood on. She didn't know if he could be trusted.

"I know your voice well, Hood. The others have returned to the truck, and none of them can see you. Let me assure you, I may be a lot of things, but I've never broken the confidentiality of my patients. I'm not about to start now."

"It's either him, or I'm taking you to Randolph General whether you want to go or not," Tristan vowed.

At that, Lila finally let go. She had no intention of spending the day in the emergency room while scores of doctors ordered unnecessary tests because their boss had been brought in. Nor did she relish the thought of her mother finding out she'd wrecked her bike.

Again.

As she turned around, she came face to face with the older man, dressed in the garb of a workborn, his hair carefully styled. His work boots had been polished to a shine befitting a highborn, and a stethoscope peeked out from under his green tartan scarf.

The doctor's eyes did not light up when they looked at one another. If he recognized her, he covered it well.

When Lila did not speak, Doc took it as permission. After helping her out of her jacket, he pressed the stethoscope into her chest and checked her breathing. He noted her pulse, tracked her eyes with a light that popped out of his thumb ring, and squeezed her hands.

Lila yelped at that, and he removed her gloves. One hand had turned angry and pink across the back.

"It's not swollen. That's a very good sign," he said calmly, marveling at the crisscross of scratches across her palms.

"That happened a few weeks ago," Lila said, pulling her hand away. "I'm fine. A rearview mirror just bounced off it. I've broken bones before, and this isn't broken."

"Bet it smarts, though." Doc grinned slightly. "Do you feel cold, or at least colder than you should?"

Lila shook her head.

"Does anything hurt?"

"No."

"Her belly," Tristan answered for her.

Lila's hand shot out and held the doctor back. "It's something else entirely. I'm fine, really."

The doctor nodded. "You'll likely be sore tomorrow, but if anything changes, you go to the emergency room immediately. Sometimes it takes a few hours for the shock to wear off, then people realize they were hurt worse than they thought."

Lila nodded.

"I think she'll be fine," Doc explained to Tristan before getting to his feet with a grunt. He whipped the stethoscope over his head, hid it under his scarf, and marched back to the truck.

Tristan's people drove away with her Firefly, and Lila realized that she didn't care where it might end up.

"Is he even a doctor?"

"He was once, and a damn fine one at that. The drink took him. Sometimes people won't let you come back after so many mistakes."

"Did you?"

Tristan nodded. "Doc's sober now, and he helped me once when I needed it. I gave him a job. Now he patches up my people."

"I'm not your people."

"Now you've become ornery." He rose and helped Lila to her feet, brushing a lock of hair away from her face. "It's a shame, you know. That was an expensive bike."

"I have expensive tastes."

"Me too." Tristan grinned. He clasped her good hand tightly and dragged her toward his navy Barracuda. Lila did not know whether to laugh or scowl.

"Why aren't you on your Amazon? I didn't recognize you. You scared me half to death on this old thing."

"Shirley's making a few upgrades on mine. I wasn't sure if you'd stop for me, anyway. You've been avoiding my calls. You go back to your family for one meal, and you forget all about me."

"I didn't forget."

Tristan pushed his toe into the sidewalk. "Don't worry about your bike. Shirley will work her magic on it, just wait and see. It will be good as new in a few hours. If you give us a few days, we could even repaint it."

"That's not necessary."

"It doesn't have to be necessary. What happened back there?"

"The brakes failed. Both sets."

"It's almost impossible for both sets to fail. Are you sure?"

"No, Tristan, I'm not sure. I decided to take a dive into a brick wall just for grins."

He held up his hands. "Sorry. Shirley will find the problem." Slipping his palm from his pocket, he typed out a message. "I'm telling her about your brakes. If both sets failed, someone might have tampered with them. She'll find proof."

Lila scooped up her helmet on the sidewalk. "Look, if you could just ask your people to drive it to… I don't care where. I'll have someone pick it up. My family has our own mechanics. I—"

"No. I want to know what happened to your bike, and I want to know now. I trust my people. I don't trust yours."

Lila fiddled with the strap of her helmet. There was more truth in Tristan's words than she wanted to admit. Being prime was dangerous, and if someone knew already, then they might have just tried to assassinate her. Even her family's mechanics might have been in on it.

If they'd tried once, they might try again.

It wasn't like it hadn't happened before. The first time someone had tried to assassinate her, she'd only been six months old. Her mother had held the poisoned bottle, tainted by her own cousin. She'd rushed Lila to the hospital soon after.

In the end, Lila had been lucky. She'd recovered, and her doctors had declared it a miracle.

Perhaps she'd just won a second reprieve.

Perhaps she wouldn't next time.

"How'd you even find me?" she asked, not wanting to dwell too long on the thought.

"You wouldn't pick up, so I had Toxic trace your palm. I didn't get to the condos before you'd taken off again, though, so I tailed you."

Lila frowned. Her snoop programs hadn't caught Toxic. Either the girl was getting better, or Lila was slipping. She'd have to be more aware, perhaps more paranoid to survive life as a prime.

"What was the chief of security doing in that neighborhood? You visiting your dealer?" Tristan tugged open the top of her coat as though looking for drugs.

Lila batted his hand away.

"Come on, let's go home," he said, climbing on the back of his Barracuda.

"Your shop is not my home," she muttered, climbing on behind him.

# 12

Tristan gently pushed Lila back onto his bed, his weight heavy against her sore belly. In between stolen kisses, he pulled off his sweater, his hair a mess as the collar tugged at his ears. "I was so scared," he whispered as a trail of kisses poured down her neck, brushing her skin. "I thought I was going to lose you."

Lila's hands fumbled at the hem of her sweater, her back arching as he hit the place on her neck that always triggered a giggle, a deep arousal, a wetness between her legs, a need for Tristan in her arms, thrusting as he took her mouth. Her fingers stilled, sweater half off, half on. She turned her head, and Tristan grinned against her, nibbling upon her ear.

"Stop making me worry so much."

Lila nodded, willing to say anything as long as he didn't stop. Tristan shifted on her belly again, and she sucked in a breath, biting her tongue against a grunt of pain.

She didn't want to call out.

She didn't want to tell him to stop.

She barely remembered why her belly hurt at all. Her only thought was of Tristan's body against hers, his cock between her legs, his clever lips and clever fingers and soft skin enveloping her, sweating against her.

Perhaps for the last time.

Lila pulled at his waistband, and he was all too happy to oblige.

She tugged off his clothes while he did the same with her, both chuckling when their limbs got tangled. Within seconds they were naked, hands groping and sliding upon warm skin.

"I missed you," Tristan said as he sucked at her lips, his thumb brushing against her cheek. "I've grown used to having you here with me all day."

A straining cock pushed at her. Before she could say a word, he pumped inside her, too eager to wait for their usual foreplay.

Lila's mouth opened, and she arched her back.

A burst of pain hit her all at once. A river of fire and tightness started between her legs and rushed up her spine to her shoulders.

Tristan pulled out at the third thrust and knelt beside her, his face a mass of confusion. "Lila, what's wrong?" His hands went to her face, gripping both sides.

"Lila, you're scaring me. Talk to me."

"I'm okay," she said with some effort.

But she wasn't okay. The pain remained, though it had dulled. She twisted away from him and curled on her side, panting from the fire that had wrenched at her.

"Damn it, I'm taking you to the—"

"No, I'm okay."

Lila squeezed her eyes shut. Gods, she was an idiot. Helen had told her not to have sex so soon after surgery, and she'd gotten caught up in the moment.

They both had.

And they'd never have a last time.

The bed wobbled as Tristan lay behind her, snaking his arm around her chest. He kissed her bare shoulder, a small breath across her skin. "Are you really okay?"

Lila nodded, then regretted it instantly. Even that small movement triggered a wave of nausea.

"You don't look okay. I—"

"Just lie quiet," she said, burying her head in the pillow. "Please."

Tristan closed his mouth and stilled.

The silence stretched on, awkward and strange. Tristan's bedroom had rarely been quiet. It was usually filled with moans or whispers or the sounds of deep breathing as they fell asleep.

Or the popping of a headboard.

It wasn't used to quiet.

They weren't used to quiet.

When the pain eased, Lila sat up. Her hand drifted to her belly, and her thumb stroked back and forth.

Tristan's arm wrenched back as though he worried of hurting her. His face had paled. He opened his mouth opened to say something, but then thought better of it, clamping down on his tongue once more.

"I'm fine," she assured him.

"You keep saying that, but I don't believe you. I'll get Doc to come up and check you out. He should—"

Lila grabbed his chin. "I'm fine, Tristan. It had nothing to do with the accident. Just let it go."

"No, I won't let it go. You're not okay. You need to see a doctor."

She slid off the bed and fumbled for her clothes, fingers aching, stomach sinking into guilt. She'd let Tristan start something without revealing that her birth control had changed.

Fuck.

She was a lousy excuse for a lover.

She slipped her tank back over head, her sweater far too warm in the heat. Dixon must have come back to the apartment while they tarried in the bedroom.

Tristan quickly dressed. "I'm going to get Doc. It will only take a moment. He's right downstairs, and he'll check you out properly this time."

"I said no."

Tristan paused at the door, clearly debating whether he should listen.

"I'm fine, really."

His fingers worked at the doorknob. "I think I heard Dixon in the other room."

Lila finished dressing, and they peeked inside the apartment's main room. The purple walls shone brightly in the afternoon sun.

The light glinted off the kitchen counter and coffee tables, made with wine barrels that had been stained to a deep shine.

Sure enough, Tristan's brother had returned at some point. He wore nothing but indigo boxer briefs and a shamrock bracelet. His legs rested on the coffee table, ankles crossed as he stretched in a plush chair near the couch. He had a body similar to Tristan's, a swimmer's build, slightly muscular and rangy at the same time. He'd shaved his head close to the skull, highlighting the elegant planes of his face. Gauze wrapped around one of this thighs, a consequence of their shooting match with the Italian mercs less than two weeks before. A darkly stained cane leaned against his chair.

A sandwich sat on the coffee table next to a stack of books about the oracles and the gods. He pointed a remote toward the screen.

He retracted it as soon as they entered, his blue eyes holding amusement as Lila smoothed her hair. Both plopped down upon the couch beside him.

"Did Shirley tell you about Lila's bike?" Tristan asked.

The tongueless man snatched up his notepad on the coffee table. *No, what happened?* he wrote.

Tristan absently intertwined his fingers with Lila's as he explained about the accident, giving the back of her good hand a kiss as he explained about the motorcycle's failed brakes.

Dixon worried the notepad in his lap, his pencil trapped and forgotten in the wire spiral along the top. As the son of a Holguín mother, Dixon had grown up as a highborn, rather than a slave. He knew exactly what had happened, for he had grown up in Lila's world.

He didn't need her to connect the dots, but Tristan did.

*Tell him why someone would do that to an heir.*

Tristan looked back at her, his eyes searching.

"There could be any number of reasons. May I have some Sangre?"

Tristan walked to a little locker in the back of the room. He took out a bottle of Sangre and a couple of black Jolly Roger mugs and poured Lila a glass.

The locker closed in the quiet.

Dixon whistled and pointed to his notepad once again.

"What is he on about?" Tristan said as he handed her a mug.

Lila shrugged and reclined into the couch. She dropped her boots on the scuffed coffee table and gave one last look to the apartment and the friends who occupied it. Tristan had called it home, as though it had belonged to both of them, but the moment she opened her mouth, it would all be gone.

Dixon whistled again.

The Sangre soured on her tongue. Her mother had banned the wine from her compound years before, some silly dispute between the Randolphs and the Holguíns. She shouldn't have been drinking it at all. She was overreaching. She wanted things she couldn't have. Perhaps Jewel and her mother were both right. She needed to grow up. A grownup Elizabeth Randolph couldn't have Sangre.

She couldn't have Tristan DeLauncey, either.

She didn't deserve a happy ending anyway. She'd killed. Punishment and compensation had always been the price for such acts, if not death.

She didn't feel like she deserved death.

But this?

She deserved this.

Lila put down the mug, drew herself up, and recounted the conversation she'd had with her mother the previous morning.

Dixon's eyes flicked back to his brother, but Tristan didn't say a word. Not when she admitted that she'd agreed to become prime, not when she spelled out the consequences. The brakes had been cut because another heir had wanted her spot.

Tristan crossed his arms at that.

As soon as Lila mentioned her purpose at the clinic, he hopped up from the couch and began prowling around the room, his scowl deepening. "So that's…" He pointed at her belly.

"I shouldn't have let you touch me without telling you first. I got carried away."

"I thought I hurt you." To his credit, he didn't seem to mind that they'd nearly had sex without birth control.

It was more than she deserved.

"This is utter bullshit," he said at last. "You've never wanted to become prime. You've never wanted a child. Now you're suddenly prepared to throw your entire life away for both? Why?"

"For my family's security, Tristan. The Randolphs need a competent prime. Duty is not always what one desires."

"That's a bunch of highborn twaddle, and you know it."

"I don't expect you to understand. I knew that you wouldn't."

"Is that some backward knock at me being workborn?"

"No, it was a very forward one. My family needs me."

"They've been saying they need you for years, yet you've always told your mother to find someone else. Why agree now?"

"Because my mother has always allowed for my disagreement. Now she's threatened to exile me if I don't accept my birthright."

"Then that's her loss. You don't need a family who would cast you aside if you don't agree to their whims."

Lila's eyes narrowed. "It would be my loss, actually. Some of us like our families even when they're a pain in the ass."

"This is a more than just being a pain in the ass. You're not thinking clearly right now."

"Maybe I'm finally thinking clearly. The Randolphs are legion, Tristan. Every single one of them is depending on me to—"

"I forgot. You are Lila, the Chosen One, the only Randolph who can lead her family to greatness. Gods, no wonder you're so arrogant. You believe your mother's bullshit. She's manipulating you, and you don't even see it. Call her bluff. She'd rather have you as chief than not have you at all."

Dixon held up his notepad. *Matrons have no need for highborn who refuse their duty. Her mother would exile her as an example, daughter or not. She'd have to.*

"No, she wouldn't. But even if she did, who cares? If your mother doesn't want you as chief, then join me. I'll take you on as a hacker.

We've done a lot of good together, Lila. We can keep doing good together." His eyes pleaded with her, and she knew his frustration wasn't only about the prime role.

"I don't want to leave my family."

"Family? Family doesn't force you to be what you're not."

*There are worse things than doing what others want.*

"Well, it's pretty far down on the list. A real family doesn't do that to one another."

Lila pushed her mug around the coffee table. The scraping filled the silence. "Real families aren't neat and tidy, Tristan. Just because you ran out on yours when it wasn't perfect, doesn't mean I should do the same."

"You'd rather have sex at your mother's command, Chosen One? Dixon left his family, and he's okay."

*That was different,* his brother wrote. Lila thought back to the countless times she'd seen Dixon's back. Dozens of white scars slashed it. Someone had done that to him, tortured him, though she'd never found out why.

She'd always suspected it had been his highborn family, but he'd never explained.

*I was half dead when we got away. I had to go. That's not what Lila is facing. Being exiled is being cast out from your home, cast away from everything and everyone you've ever known.*

Tristan's feet stilled upon the wooden floor. "Not everyone you've ever known. I'm your brother. I'm here, aren't I? Do you actually miss those assholes?"

*Sometimes. Some of them, at least. They were my family. That was my home.*

"I'm your family. This is your home. I'm the only one who gave a damn about saving you from that place. Doesn't that count for anything?"

*Is this my home, or is it a cause?*

"Is that how you feel?"

Dixon closed his notepad and dropped it on the coffee table.

"Maybe you should leave, then," Tristan said, retreating to the window. "Maybe both of you should. For oracle's sake, why am I never good enough for either of you?"

"Becoming prime has nothing to do with you."

"Doesn't it? You're going to attend that ball tomorrow night, and some highborn asshole is going to climb into your bed. You're going to spread your legs and fuck him, and you think that has nothing to do with me?"

Dixon stood up and squeezed Lila's shoulder. He pulled on a pair of pants abandoned on the floor and slipped on a sweater. His cane smacked against the floor as he retreated from the apartment.

Tristan watched him go.

"None of this has anything to do with you," she said after the door snicked behind Dixon. "You're not my husband. You're my lover, and I have my family to think about. There is truth in what my mother said and in what she asks of me, whether you want to admit it or not."

Tristan lowered himself into Dixon's spot. The plush chair scraped against the wooden floor as he sat. "Gods, it really is that easy for you. You see nothing wrong with slipping out of my bed and climbing into someone else's."

"You knew what you were getting into. Don't act like this is a surprise."

"A surprise? I thought you were—"

Different.

Lila knew exactly what he would say. He'd said it over and over again as though trying to shape her behavior, as though she were a wayward puppy to be molded. If what she had done was on the list of things he liked, he'd say it with a smile. If it was on the list of things he hated, he'd say it with a sneer.

A sneer crossed his face this time.

"If you say different one more time, I swear to the gods that I'm going to walk out that door and I will never, ever come back," Lila said, the phrase awakening something inside her, some fear she'd had since they'd begun seeing one another. "Gods, Tristan, do you even see me at all? Do you even know who I am, or am I just some woman you dreamt up because your idea of me was more palatable than the real thing? I have never once snubbed you because you were a slave or because you're a workborn. I have never once called the workborn inferior. Yet you've done as much to me every day we've been together. Who's the snob now?"

"It doesn't make me a snob. It makes me observant."

"Observant? How observant can you be? I am a highborn, Tristan. This is who we are. I never hid myself with you. Highborns sacrifice the wants of the individual for the needs of the family."

"For years, you didn't do that."

"Because I thought I was needed in the security office. Because I believed that my mother could pluck another heir to become prime. I was wrong."

"Now the needs of the family dictate sleeping around?"

"We have a great many children because it preserves us. We take a great many lovers to do that."

"Because it binds your kind with one another and earns you more and more money. That's all your kind cares about."

Lila clenched her hands into fists, her injured knuckles crying out. It was like she'd bent time to several weeks before and now stood in front of the old Tristan. "You don't give two shits about the money or that I'm going to become prime, so stop arguing about it like you do."

"I do care about that, actually. I care about that an awful lot. Apparently, I care about it more than you do."

"No, you don't. You're pissed because in your mind, you have some special claim on me. This is why I resisted us being together. I knew you wouldn't be able to handle a relationship with a highborn. People aren't meant to have only one lover, just as they aren't meant to have only one friend. We're not meant to be monogamous, Tristan."

"Yes, we are."

"So workborn don't cheat on one another?"

"Don't do this, Lila."

"I'm not the one running, Tristan. I know I should, but I'm too invested in this." She waved her hand vaguely, unable to explain her feelings any more than that.

It was far more than she should have said, but Tristan didn't seem to care. "I'm not going to be your toy on the side, Lila. I watched my mother do that all her life. I have more respect for myself than that."

"How is it a question of respect? Does Shirley get angry that you're friends with Doc? Does Doc get angry that you're friends with Shirley?"

"That's different."

"No, it's not."

"Yes, it is. For oracle's sake, Lila, I'm in love with you!" He looked away and sank his head into his hands. "Is that all this has ever been for you? Are we just friends who sleep together? I thought I meant more to you than that."

Lila played with her sweater. Tristan had never said *love* before, though Dixon had hinted at his brother's feelings more than once. Love implied marriage for the highborn, which was a great deal more than it implied for workborn. What particular shade of gray did Tristan even mean? "There's a difference between lovers and friends."

"Not much of one. Not for you."

"Tristan—"

Tristan hopped up from the chair and slipped into his room. He came back seconds later, carrying the bag she'd left the day before. He dropped it next to her with a loud thump and backed away. "I guess the oracle's prophecy has come true after all."

"Tristan—"

"Just go, Lila, and take this with you. You won't need it here any longer."

The room went silent. He stared at her, daring her to say or do something.

Lila didn't know what he expected. She snatched up the bag with her good hand, slinging it over her shoulder, then gave him one last look before she turned and walked out the door.

He didn't call out for her to return.

# 13

Lila ducked into her bedroom, the straps of her bag cutting into her good hand. She dropped it and changed into a much more expensive version of her outfit, a sweater marked by her family's coat of arms and a pair of woolen trousers. Then she stuffed her old clothes into the bag and shoved it in her closet's secret compartment.

Just like that, all evidence of her time with Tristan had disappeared.

It was for the best. They didn't work. They never had, and they never would.

At least no one in her family had found out where she'd been on vacation. It hadn't helped that she'd been forced to take a cab back to the great house. Shirley had refused to abandon her broken Firefly into her care when she'd tried to leave the shop. "I'm still looking into it, Hood," Shirley had said, her shrewd eyes meeting Lila's behind the mesh hood. "Take a cab today, then steal a new car as soon as you can. A Nostaru Y-class if you can swing it. It might not look like much, but they're hard to tamper with and they're full of airbags. It'll take a beating, and it'll protect you."

"I'll be fine."

Shirley shook her head. "I'm not sure that you will. Only luck got you out of this today. Someone wants you dead. Someone smart. I don't like the look of this at all."

Lila hadn't liked it either, not when her eyes slid to Shirley's workbench. Two plastic cubes had been melted into the brake lines, but the mechanic had refused to hand them over. "They were rigged to blow from some signal. There was another one on your kill switch that never went off. Like I said, Hood, you were lucky. I'm looking into it, though."

She had said no more.

Lila didn't like the confused looks that Sergeant Hill and his rookie had given her, either. She'd walked several blocks from where the cab had dropped her off and ducked under the southern gate on the Randolph compound.

They'd eyed her bag curiously, a bag she'd need to unpack.

But not today.

Lila sat down at her desk and pulled up her search results.

A knock sounded on the door.

"Commander Sutton is downstairs waiting for you," Alex said, peeking inside. "Also your mother requests your presence at dinner this evening."

"Who else—"

"Everyone else will be suffering with you, including Senator Dubois," the slave replied, rolling her eyes.

"Well, in that case, the chairwoman will have many targets. Please tell Sutton to come up."

"Up here?"

"Yes. Leave the door open."

Alex bowed. Her clicking heels retreated down the corridor.

While Lila waited for Sutton, she scanned through the latest search results on the BullNet data. This time, she'd received a hit.

She looked up as the new chief entered the room, her leather blackcoat duller than the polished ebony furniture. Lila's heart stuttered at the uniform she'd never be allowed to wear again, at the position she'd worked so hard for, now slipping through her fingers. If she'd known two weeks ago that she'd never wear the uniform again, she might have tried to enjoy it more on her last day.

Alex put down a kettle of hot chocolate and two mugs, then closed the door behind her.

"I haven't been here since you were a rookie." Sutton smirked, running her finger over the silver coat of arms. "It looks exactly the same. It looks just like your office, actually, except for this on the wall."

"That was the point."

Sutton nodded and tucked her arms behind her back. "So when does your new position become official, madam? The militia looks at me like they already know."

"They might. Someone might have spotted me at the clinic yesterday." Lila picked up a little pin molded into the shape of a star from her desk. She ushered Sutton to the couch, plopping down on one end while Sutton sat on the other. "It might come out tomorrow night at the Closing Ball, no matter what my mother has promised. She's not always subtle in these matters."

"In that case, I suppose we should make plans to address the militia."

"You're probably right. Sometime early next week, perhaps. And on that day, you'll need another star for your collar." Lila pressed the little pin into Sutton's palm. "I thought you might like one of mine. I could get you a new one, if—"

Her former mentor shook her head, squeezing the pin in her fist. "No, I'd be honored to wear Her Madam's pin." She opened her palm, her finger brushing the star as though it were a diamond.

Lila nodded and poured them both a mug of hot chocolate. "We'll hold a ceremony next week. Dress uniforms, speeches, toasts, champagne." The commander's face fell. "I know you don't like to make a fuss, but it's a necessary ritual, especially for the people under your command. I'm sure there's some psychological term for it, but I'll be damned if I know what it is."

Sutton chuckled at that, still turning the silver pin over and over in her fingers. "I suspect so. You never make it easy on me, do you?"

"I'm like a rose, always pricking."

Sutton carefully put the pin into her pocket. "Ms. Nancy Randolph from accounting has run into a bit of trouble. Her son Anthony was arrested last night for another bit of mischief."

Lila raised an eyebrow.

"That's why I came to talk to you. The kid was in the process of reprogramming his building's security system. Instead of emitting a beep when someone entered the wrong code, it was rewired to give off a mild electric shock. He was in the process of changing the code when we arrived."

"The forced-entry program notified us?"

"Yes, Chief—President Randolph. Your program worked perfectly."

Lila's face fell with the change of her title, but she was getting more and more used to it as the days wore on. Forcing a smile, she leaned back into the couch, her mug of hot chocolate forgotten. "It only worked because Anthony didn't know about it. I almost admire the kid. Most twelve-year-olds have trouble with algebra and basic programming. Meanwhile, he's scrambling security systems."

"Nostalgia makes fools of us all. It was only a condo this time, but an internship with one of the R&D departments might put his energies to better use. It might also save us the trouble of dealing with him yet again."

"I should have done it sooner. Is he still at the security office?"

"Yes, in a holding cell. He thinks he's going to court next week and might lose his mark. Ms. Randolph is encouraging our play-acting. She's at her wits' end. She's willing to try anything at this point. When she visited this morning, she told him that if we pressed charges and sent him to Bullstow, then she wouldn't get him a lawyer. She claimed that if he's sent to auction, then she'll pack his lunch and wave him off to live with whatever family buys him. It shut the boy up fast. He hasn't eaten a thing since. Perhaps it's made a dent this time."

"I'll call around to the labs and find him a spot. He'll be out of your hair before dinner."

"Tomorrow morning," Sutton countered.

"Fine. You can offer the deal, then."

"A deal? How very film noir of you. I'll tell him it's only good if he keeps his nose clean from now on, or we'll toss him in the lake. Is that the standard line?"

"How would I know? I haven't had time for a movie in years. Are you sure you still want the job?"

Sutton straightened her shoulders instantly. "I've never cared much for the cinema, madam. I won't miss it."

"What about your husband?"

"I've never cared much for him either," she said, her lips twitching. "I care a great deal about you, though. I hope that when I'm chief we can still talk as we have over the years. At least sometimes. I've always considered you something of a friend. I should have said that this morning instead of razzing you. It's been bugging me all day."

Lila nodded quickly, her eyes beginning to water.

Sutton knew her too well. She stood up quickly and clasped Lila's injured hand, not spying its red hue.

Lila didn't say a word. The throbbing returned as Sutton crushed it affectionately, and Lila had to stop herself from crying out in an altogether different manner.

But at least she hadn't started blubbering in front of the woman.

After Sutton left, Lila snatched up her palm. It took only a few moments to call one of the R&D labs about Anthony. After a brief conversation, she managed to find the boy a place with a take-no-shit lab director who didn't seem too put off by having the boy in her lab. Lila sent the details to Sutton and plopped down at her desk, finally able to pull up her search results.

Smiling, she scanned the data. Her search had found several cruder versions of the same trap from the BIRD. The least sophisticated had been melded into the state's mental health registry almost four years before.

Reaper hadn't even lived in New Bristol back then.

Her hunch had been correct, then. Reaper and Zephyr were not the same person. Reaper had likely been a pawn, just another hacker her blackmailer had turned.

More to the point, Zephyr had chosen a difficult database to infect for a first attempt.

The hacker was either impatient or arrogant, or both.

Lila dug into the trap, pulling back each strand of the web until she located the hacker's ID. It did not belong to Zephyr. It was someone called the Baron.

Lila snorted at the obviously fake ID, an ID predicated on aristocratic German nobility. What was the hacker trying to say with that? It couldn't be a German who'd infected BullNet. It wasn't the empire's style. The empire was a loaded gun, pointed at your head. Zephyr and the Baron, on the other hand, led you with a plume of perfume, tempting you to fall obliviously onto a pile of spikes.

No, the ID didn't belong to an enemy merc.

Lila set up an exhaustive search for the Baron's ID and let it run, wondering where else the hacker's sticky little fingers might have been, but she had no idea if the search was pointless or not. Reaper, Zephyr, and now the Baron? How many more IDs might she find?

Would they lead to her blackmailer or to more questions?

Her eyes lit onto the scrap of paper with Sergeant Davies's palm ID. While she waited for the search to run, she hacked into Davies's account data at Bullstow Financial and cycled through his current statement.

She found no new transactions.

Unconvinced that he'd suddenly become a good boy, Lila hacked deeper. The Park family owned a chain of banks, a chain that Lila had hacked into on the previous case with her father. It wasn't unreasonable to assume that Davies had set up an alternate account.

It took less than half an hour to prove her instinct right. Davies had opened an account only three weeks before. Nothing had graced it but one deposit that very morning. One payment from a Liberté bank account that she'd never seen. One payment for the exact amount he'd received the month before.

Whoever had been pulling Davies's strings had found another way to pull them.

What was the purpose of the payment? To stir up trouble by asking for the family's logins? To pay for the assassination of a prime who had gotten far too close for comfort?

The amount was too high for a few calls, but it damn sure seemed too low for an assassination attempt.

Then again, perhaps she valued her own neck more than the account holder did.

Lila pushed the implications out of her mind and turned the investigation back to her assassination. She poked into WolfNet and pulled up the garage's security footage from the night before, syncing each camera perfectly and setting them to run simultaneously on her screen. They played in reverse from the moment she picked up her motorcycle that morning.

It didn't take too long to find it. There were no cuts in the footage. The cameras hadn't been damaged, nor had they gone out or been sprayed over. They hadn't been looped or hacked, either.

Whoever had done the job was too smart for that, likely knowing that someone always watched the cameras in the security office. Usually several someones, not to mention Lila's programs. The latter would detect many anomalies too subtle for a pair of bored militia eyes.

The break-in had occurred at four o'clock that morning while she slept off the effects of her surgery. A figure clothed in a short black coat had crept into the garage and wheeled Lila's Firefly into the back of the garage behind her silver Adessi roadster. Five minutes later, the motorcycle had been wheeled back into place.

She could hardly blame her people for not spotting the intruder. The footage was so dark that you could barely make anything out. The snoop had used night-vision goggles and deactivated the motion sensors in the garage, for the lights should have turned on the moment anyone walked inside or stepped near the building. The change in brightness would have triggered her programs to increase the camera's priority, demanding that someone in the security office look immediately.

The snoop had bested Lila's system by going low tech, rather than high.

Instead of stopping the cameras, Lila let them run back further, watching every view, waiting to see the intruder loiter in the garage during the daytime. Judging by the form's shape and size, it had to have been a teenage boy or a petite woman.

It didn't take long to find the figure again. At around eight o'clock, a figure in the same black coat darted into the garage behind Jewel and Senator Dubois, crawling along the perimeter while the couple laughed and stole a kiss, their bodies pressing against one another and the chairwoman's Blanc roadster.

Lila reversed the footage and squinted at her monitor. The intruder had added something on the motion sensor's plugs. If she had to guess, it was some sort of switch that turned them on and off remotely.

The snoop then slinked around the wall, waiting to dart out once more as soon as Jewel and Senator Dubois left the garage in a sedan.

It had only taken five minutes to get the job done, and Jewel and Senator Dubois had never even realized they'd been accomplices.

Lila followed the figure through the compound's security footage, watching as the snoop dodged a militia patrol after leaving the garage, nearly getting caught in the process. Long red hair peeked from a skull cap, but the intruder managed to avoid the cameras well enough to stay hidden. The trail ended ten blocks away when the snoop ducked into an alley on the north side of the complex and did not come out again.

Whoever wanted to kill Lila knew the positions of the security cameras, or at least knew them enough to get away.

That seemed to rule out Sergeant Davies, and increased the likelihood that someone in her own family was trying to kill her.

Lila snatched up her palm, ready to order an extra patrol near the garage. The only thing that stopped her was Sutton. The new chief would want to know why she'd ordered the change.

Not only that, but there was a reason why patrols didn't pass by the garage so often.

Lila liked slipping out of the compound with as few eyes upon her as possible.

She sent Sutton and McKinley a message anyway, attaching the camera footage and asking for a discreet investigation. Between the pair of them, they had plenty of knowledge and experience to ferret out the culprit.

Unfortunately, she had a compromised doctor to investigate.

Logging onto Randolph General's network with her own ID, she searched for copies of Rubio's pay history. The hospital would have the doctor's bank account information, which would make hacking into her accounts much more straightforward. She'd dig into Rubio's financials and her personal accounts, finding out exactly what relationship the doctor had with the chairwoman in the process.

Lila sucked in her breath when Rubio's pay history came up. Somehow, the young doctor received a bonus paycheck every month, marked as overtime in the system. After reviewing the clinic's schedule, the hours billed for each doctor, and the budget, Lila could not locate the reason or the source for her overtime pay. When she looked further at the payment itself, she found that it was paid out of the Randolph family's discretionary account.

Lila paced around the room, her boots stamping on the floor as she turned, her sore fingers thumping against her thigh. She spent several weeks wrangling donations every year from the highborn for that money. She used the extra cash for equipment or supplies that department budgets couldn't quite cover. Occasionally, she even treated departments by stocking their lounge with free food and other gifts as a reward for exceptional service.

Someone had diverted a precious chunk of that money for the last ten months. Not only had Rubio been paid off since her very first day at the hospital, but someone had used the hospital's own funds to do it.

What had Rubio been doing in the clinic for that extra money, and why had the chairwoman been particularly generous this year with her donation?

Lila returned to her desk, her toe tapping against her chair. She'd always known everything that went on at Randolph General and on every family estate. How could something like this escape her attention? Sure, she'd been stretched thin lately, especially in the last month, but that was no excuse. Very few people even knew about the discretionary account. Only a handful had access to it.

Her mother was at the top of the list.

Lila dismissed that thought immediately. Her mother wouldn't have bribed Rubio with money, especially from the hospital's account. Money left a trail that could be traced by other spies. It was sloppy. She would have traded opportunity for favors, especially opportunities that could be taken away on a whim. The chairwoman would have offered Rubio the job, not added bonus payments to it.

So what had happened ten months ago to start the payments? Why would the doctor keep receiving them month after month?

An unpleasant thought struck Lila.

Had Rubio blackmailed her mother?

That was silly, wasn't it? The chairwoman would not allow herself to be blackmailed, not by a workborn. She'd consider it an insult. She would have summoned her chief the second she received a blackmailer's demand.

On the other hand, Rubio could be doing something useful for the chairwoman.

Lila squinted at the screen, her mind pinwheeling. Perhaps the reason did not matter much in the short term. What did matter was that her mother had hired Rubio as a spy, and not just a few days ago, either. With such a history, the doctor would certainly tell the chairwoman that she'd asked about Dubois's medical records. Lila should never have attempted to gain information from someone she had not thoroughly vetted beforehand.

What had she been thinking?

"Wine, anesthesia, pain medication." Lila ticked off the reasons on her fingers. Clearly, thought had not entered into her decision-making at all.

Following her last lead, Lila sat back at her desk and pulled up the most current list of businesses for the Randolph family, as well as the records for her R&D departments. She knew what she'd find, though. The family did not operate or partner with any agriculture enterprises, nor had the family been pursuing research into NAT or other fertilizers.

Lila turned off her monitor and left her computer searching for the Baron's ID, the hum of the tower quiet in the room. Wandering over to the closet, she checked the time, which glowed back on the apathetic display, signaling she was already late for dinner.

Lila didn't care. Her fingers strayed over her beloved militia uniforms and settled on her blackcoat. She brushed the silver stars on her collar and the tiny pinprick hole where one had gone astray. It would now live in Sutton's pocket, waiting for the day when it would be reattached to a new uniform, for the day that Sutton would take command of the militia.

Her militia.

Lila stamped her foot against the floor, like a spoiled child. It wasn't fair. She'd worked so hard and given up so much, and now it was all being taken away.

Even Tristan.

She'd never even gotten a chance to say goodbye to her old life properly. All her blackcoats and uniforms would be destroyed in a matter of days, all to make room for the dresses and whitecoats of a prime.

She laid her forehead against her bedroom mirror, wondering if they'd come for them while she was at the Closing Ball. Would they leave any uniforms behind for her to treasure? Just one to remember her old life by? The day she'd arrived at Bullstow for militia training and been fitted for her first blackcoat. The day she'd run after her first intruder in the Randolph compound, hoping he didn't have a tranq gun or knife or worse. The day she'd received her first militia commission and had to learn how to manage a group who considered themselves different from the other highborn on the property.

All those days had been just as sweet as the day she'd been made chief.

All those days couldn't be erased by taking away her old things.

But her mother would order it anyway. Her uniforms would be thrown out without a care, just as her mother had thrown out everything she had worked for, just as she might throw out the childhood toys of a teenage girl. Toys she had clung to, rather than growing apart from.

Lila sniffled, feeling very foolish for letting such sentimentality strike her right before she must face her mother. A mother who would be looking for weakness before the ball.

Lila stood up straighter, determined not to fall apart again. She'd done enough crying.

But when she caught her face in the bedroom mirror, she didn't see a face full of resolve. She saw a face full of misery, eyes half-laden with tears.

Instead of triggering more waterworks, it pissed her off.

Screw her mother. She wasn't prime yet.

She'd have her one last goodbye, no matter what.

She'd earned it.

Putting on one of her formal militia uniforms, she dressed in her blackcoat for the last time, adding her Colt and officer's short sword to her holster. Then she brushed her hair and marched downstairs, head held high.

# 14

Chairwoman Randolph raised her wine glass as Lila entered the parlor, silver fabric fluttering around her thin form. Her eyes paused on her daughter's blackcoat but did not linger. "We awaited our prime before entering the dining room, as is custom. It would help for you remember that from now on. Otherwise, we might all die of hunger."

"I'm not prime yet," mumbled Lila, nodding toward Jewel's whitecoat. It wrapped around her figure like a pool of velvet, all aflutter, gauze thin on the air. Senator Dubois held his lover's hand on the couch, his elegant burgundy jacket settled around him. They'd been talking of the wedding, no doubt, for Pax sat forward in a chair beside his mother, listening with a large smile. He'd worn a wrinkled crimson jacket, one cuff smudged with ink.

Her mother shifted the folds of her silver coat and stood. "Details, Lila." She led the little group into the dining room with Jewel following immediately after, Senator Dubois at the former prime's side.

Pax lingered in the parlor, offering his elder sister a bow. A mischievous glint lurked in his eyes. "Jewel will have to get used following behind you soon. As well as the new seating arrangement."

"I couldn't care less."

"You don't care, but Jewel does." He winked before bounding away, keen not to miss any wedding plans.

Lila followed them all, taking a place next to Pax and across from Senator Dubois, in the table's lowest position. She'd never considered it low, though. Since it was far away from her matron, she'd always considered it a perk.

Alex gave her a little wink as she circled the table, settling the first course of the evening in front of them, bowls of creamy asparagus soup that turned the air salty.

"Did you really have to wear that ugly thing tonight?" Jewel asked, crinkling her nose at Lila's blackcoat.

Lila unfolded her napkin and set it in her lap. "As I've said many times before, regulations state that when in the presence of the chairwoman and her family, the chief of security should—"

"We know, but that hardly matters now."

"Regulations always matter to the chief of security."

"You aren't—"

The chairwoman put her wine down on the table, clinking it against the side of her plate with purposeful clumsiness. Jewel closed her mouth immediately.

"Will you excuse us, Ms. Wilson?" Chairwoman Randolph said, raising her voice.

Alex bowed, abandoning the soup cart and filing out of the room.

As Lila had not yet received her wine, she stood up and poured a glass of Gregorie herself. Manners be damned.

It was going to be a long night.

Chairwoman Randolph leaned over the table, her eyes burning into Jewel's. "Child, you will act as a prime should until Lila's place is official. If you cannot discharge this last breath of your duties, then I will be forced to reconsider your chosen employment afterwards. The art gallery isn't yours yet."

"I don't understand why any of this is necessary, Mother. Everyone suspects. They knew the moment you sent Lila to the clinic. Just because it isn't in the common press yet, doesn't mean it isn't on the lips of the highborn on the estate. It will have spread throughout the compound and the rest of the city after the Closing Ball."

"Perhaps no one would suspect Lila's business if you hadn't spent the entire night caterwauling about yours. There's only so much damage control that I can do, and our staff has ears. So, as I said, I suggest you act with care."

"Don't blame the staff, Mother," Lila said. "Everyone knows because you've begun to leak it, at least my intention to take a lover at the Closing Ball. Mother's playing her little games again," she said as she sat at her place, wine in hand.

"Leaked it? Why would I do that?"

"So that the senators attending the Closing Ball don't commit for the season, at least not until they receive an answer from me. I suspect Senator Dubois has already been busy today, shuttling the information to choice prospects."

Dubois's gentle expression turned to a frown, and he stared intently at his plate.

"It's okay, Senator Dubois, you'll be a Randolph soon. You should get used to being my mother's puppet. Sometimes you might even get paid for it." Lila stared at her mother. "Who else has been your puppet recently?"

As expected, her mother's gaze did not waver. "I am often a spectator to those who ill-use people in silly schemes. I do not believe that Senator Dubois feels ill-used on this occasion. Do you, senator?"

Jewel fiddled with her spoon.

Dubois sensed her unease and rubbed her back soothingly. "Of course I don't. Why would I? If your mother had not given me her blessing, then my friends would have felt slighted and betrayed. Should I have kept such information from my very best friends, from my brothers and cousins?"

"What did you tell them about my situation?"

"Only what you said before, that you were in the mood to take a suitor for the season."

"So none of them know that I will be prime?"

Dubois shook his head. "I would never betray you like that. I consider you a dear friend, madam. We are to be a family soon."

Pax's stomach growled, and he glanced up in embarrassment.

"Well then, shall we call Ms. Wilson back and eat as a civilized family?" the chairwoman asked, her gaze landing on Jewel. "You should take care with your behavior, child. You'll scare away your beloved if you aren't careful, and then poor Lila will be free to run the security office once again. Where would that leave you in the end?"

"Jewel couldn't scare me away." Dubois chuckled. "I love everything about her even when she lets her passions rule."

Jewel gave a hard little smile and said nothing more for the rest of the meal.

Lila didn't either. She listened as Pax described two difficult operations that he had observed earlier in the day. Both patients had required surgery for heart problems. One had been his own age.

Dubois encouraged every detail. "Pax, you should join one of my mother's focus groups," he said during a lull. "She'll be testing some new games at the start of the next quarter. They're designed for slightly younger teens, but she wants to release a few titles for an older crowd next year. You could sit in, perhaps help the developers plan their work after. I've told her that you would make a valuable resource, and there would be boys your age observing."

Now that Lila knew that Dubois would never be a father, it was difficult to watch how easily he maneuvered Pax into leaving the house, into interacting with other boys his age. He would be—would have been—a great father. It seemed criminal for him to lose the chance at a child so early.

Senator Dubois's loss was still on her mind as she trudged back upstairs.

Lila peeked inside her closet anxiously, but her uniforms still hung inside, just as she'd left them, the neat row of toy soldiers waiting for a battle that would never come. Erring on the side of caution, she took off her formal uniform and unpinned the remaining stars on her collar. She fished out one of the many informal uniforms, as well as another she wore for physical training, and folded them into a thick stack. Then she tucked the folded clothes and her blackcoat into her canvas bag and stuffed it into her secret compartment.

She had no more room for remembrances.

Lila sat in front of her desktop and pulled up the results of her search for the Baron. Her snoop programs had not found the ID anywhere, even after digging into all the dusty crooks of the net. As far Lila knew, the Baron did not exist, not until the snoop had slipped into BullNet and laid the first faltering trap. The Baron might have practiced stealing into Bullstow under a different ID, but she had no other ideas for how to find it.

Lila drummed her fingers upon her desktop. The only avenue she had left to explore was the Liberté bank account, the same account that connected Sergeant Davies to his latest bribe. Perhaps the account holder would lead her to Xavier Masson, a long-dead teen from the Masson family whose ID had been stolen by her blackmailer. The article the hacker had sent to her mother had been sent from it, leaving no trace of the culprit's identity.

It was infuriatingly competent.

Lila pulled open the secret compartment once again, carefully donning her workborn clothes. She withdrew a laptop from a bottom drawer of her desk and loaded it into a satchel, then stuck a few star drives into her pocket.

Her fingers had already typed in Tristan's ID on her palm before she realized what she was doing. Though he'd helped her the last time she hacked the Liberté, he wouldn't help her again. He likely wouldn't help her with anything anymore.

And Dixon?

He was Tristan's brother. He'd have his allegiances.

She'd have to do it alone this time, just as she had done everything alone before she met Tristan, just as she'd always do things from now on.

Sliding her palm back into her pocket, she slipped downstairs and left the great house, entering the family's garage only a few moments later.

A small pool of oil now stood as a monument to her broken Firefly, the only evidence that anything had ever sat there at all.

The space seemed much too wide and much too empty to contain her bike.

Jewel's red Firefly leaned nearby as though it were a bored teenager, wanting a night out with a side of trouble. It tempted Lila greatly. Jewel would never even know she'd taken it, not that her sister would care a whit one way or another. Each part, each wire, each tube seemed the same as her beloved bike, only in Randolph red instead of silver.

Perhaps the danger was the same as well. Lila knelt beside it, squinting at the brakes. She didn't see any plastic cubes on the brake lines, but what if the intruder had done something else to Jewel's bike, hoping to knock out two primes in a row through different means? The assassin might not know that Jewel never rode hers.

But Lila had no idea what to look for.

Shirley had said that only luck had saved her, that luck was the only reason why she still lived and breathed. Luck was only reason why Pax sat upstairs studying, rather than grieving for his elder sister.

If she had died, what would have happened to Jewel? Would her mother have demanded that her sister invoke the right of *eyre-cleue* and produce children with other senators, marriage and love be damned?

Probably.

Lila swept off the pile of GPS and audio bugs she'd laid atop the seat and called up her snoop programs. If something had been planted on Jewel's Firefly, she'd find it. It took only a moment to pass the device over Jewel's bike, but the computer did not beep once. She shook it pointlessly and tried again.

She found nothing.

It had to be safe, though. Jewel might not have ridden it recently, but the mechanics that tended the family's garage surely had, all under the guise of keeping it roadworthy. Jewel's bike likely had more kilometers on it than her own, even though the odometer never ventured above five hundred. Indeed, the few times that Lila had snuck out of the estate on it, her added kilometers had magically disappeared only a few days later.

Janice, her family's lead mechanic, could probably give Shirley a run for her money.

Had Janice been the one who messed with her bike?

Lila thumbed her palm and restarted the programs, peering at the brakes. Nothing alarmed her, though nothing had alarmed her about her own bike that morning.

Was this what the intruder wanted? Did the assassin want her to be afraid?

No, the assassin probably wanted her dead.

Lila trudged to a black Cruz sedan nearby and passed her palm over the frame. Within seconds, the computer beeped. She found two GPS chips hidden behind the bumper and a small audio bug attached to a crook in the front dash.

Lila dropped the devices to the ground and crushed them under her heel, then passed her palm computer over Jewel's Firefly a third time. Then a fourth time, assuring herself that she was only being cautious.

She aborted her fifth attempt as paranoia and shoved her palm back into her trouser pocket. Hopping up, Lila retrieved Jewel's key on a peg near the door and started the bike with a thundering roar. She'd be damned if she gave up riding just because some crazy person wanted her dead.

Gingerly climbing on the purring beast, she pulled from the garage.

Moments later, she passed through the southern gate, riding slowly through downtown New Bristol. She needed a safe spot to stage her assault against the Liberté. Chances were high that the Wilson estate still had a good net connection, since her mother's people had been on site for weeks, making plans for what would be torn down and what would be remodeled.

Chaucer's Ghost might not be a bad idea. She and Tristan's people had nearly been caught there, but the Wilson militia now worked security jobs for the lowborn or other highborn families in the region. Few even lived in New Bristol any longer, and none would linger near their old home.

Lila could relate. She'd likely never stroll inside the security office again after she became prime, regardless of Sutton's offer.

The Randolph militia wouldn't pass by Chaucer's Ghost, either. She'd been the one to approve the patrols around the Wilson compound.

Chief Shaw's blackcoats might, though. The city owned the blocks around the compound. They'd refused to sell them to Chairwoman Randolph, or rather, they'd delayed the sale until other families might get involved in the bidding. Now that the Randolphs owned the Wilson compound, those blocks had become much more lucrative. Her mother wouldn't snap them up cheaply.

Lila parked several blocks away from the restaurant, just on the off chance that Sutton had changed the patrols. The streets had not changed much in the last few weeks. Graffiti still covered the walls, especially the boarded-up windows. Old receipts and leaves and paper flyers had blown into the gutters, stamped into patches of hard-packed dirt and decomposing like mulch, their color leeched away in the autumn rain. It seemed everything had been leeched away, even the colors in the cars that slipped past. None slowed in the neighborhood, not for playing children and certainly not for the teens who stood around in groups. Not for the homeless who lived nearby, either, occasionally sticking out a fingerless, soiled glove for a bit of spare change.

Lila hitched her satchel higher on her shoulder and picked up her pace, the butt of her Colt a balm to the dangers around her. No one wanted to tangle with a tranq, not even for a twenty, and the people who tarried in this neighborhood recognized her boot knife bulging at her ankle.

The only thing they couldn't recognize was a woman who couldn't throw a punch to save her life.

Lila turned toward Chaucer's Ghost. She hacked into the terminal on the abandoned restaurant's side door and slipped inside.

Her breath caught at the change. No more pigeons cooed inside. Someone had cleared away the droppings that had littered the floor a month ago, as well as the smell of death from their fallen brethren. Only a whiff still lingered, a soft note amid the silence.

The city had hired cleaners to prep the property for sale.

Luckily, the cleaners didn't work at nine o'clock at night. She climbed upstairs and sat upon the floor in an empty room, reclining against the wall. Last time she'd been inside, Dixon had played lookout down the hall. Tristan had stayed at the window, his eyes fixed outside for any sign of movement. Toxic had helped research the results, straining to prove herself as a competent hacker.

They'd laughed together. They'd been nervous together. They'd nearly been caught together.

They'd run away together, all doing their part to get away.

This was what she'd give up to follow her mother's dictates. This was what she'd trade for family dinners and Randolph business and assassination attempts.

This was what must be given away, and given freely.

Tristan must be given away, for he refused to share.

Lila frowned and pulled her laptop from her bag, uploading her snoop programs. It wasn't her fault they'd broken up. She didn't want to end things. He wanted to end them because he couldn't agree to her terms.

He'd said he loved her.

Lila shook her head. She couldn't think about that now. She couldn't think about that ever. Love and monogamy were luxuries that only the poorer classes could afford.

They weren't for primes. Not ever.

Not unless you were Jewel Randolph.

Lila wiped away a tear and kicked away her satchel. She had to get hold of herself; all this blubbering at the slightest trouble was not how highborn handled their dismay.

They didn't cry. They conquered.

The hack shouldn't have taken long, but Lila refused to use her old exploit. Twirling her sapphire ring, she poked into the system, seeking another way inside, wanting her last hack to be her best, her injured fingers throbbing with every keystroke.

After an hour, she found a way in through a third party's door. Once inside the system, she created a new login, assigning herself as a new account manager. Then she stole into the strange account that had paid off Davies and Muller.

It wasn't new. Thousands upon thousands of transactions graced the account every month, stretching back for several years. Deposits and withdrawals shuttled to the far reaches of Saxony, some even traveling to the rest of the country.

Lila saved every piece of data. She'd piece together the entire operation and find out how far the blackmailer's influence spread. Earlier mistakes would show here, for the account had been dated to a few weeks before the Baron had laid the first trap in BullNet.

Lila scrolled back through the account, searching the contact information for a name.

Freiherr. More German.

She did a quick translation search and found exactly what she had expected.

Baron.

Why would her blackmailer have a German name? Were Germans behind the hacks in BullNet? Were Germans paying off Muller and Davies? Had a German merc played Celeste and Patrick Wilson as puppets?

Had German mercs hired two Bullstow militiamen to poke at her? To assassinate her?

Perhaps both?

Perhaps it wasn't the Germans. Perhaps it was the Italians again, setting up their German kinsmen to take the fall.

After all that had happened to Lila recently, it wasn't unlikely that an Italian would want to kill her.

But Roman mercs and Bullstow militiamen would still have to scale the walls of the Randolph compound and sneak into her family's garage. They'd still have to dodge Randolph patrols and avoid all the cameras.

On the other hand, Sergeant Davies was a rather small man.

Put a red wig on him…

Lila saved the data to a star drive and shoved her laptop into her satchel, ready to get rid of it at her first opportunity.

She had work to do.

# 15

Lila woke at six o'clock the next morning, belly still tender from the surgery, muscles stiff and sore from the accident, hip bruised where she'd struck the pavement and rolled. Banned or not, she wasn't in any shape to tackle the obstacle course, much less a few laps at the track. She couldn't even muster up the energy for a quick walk around the compound, leaving her body weak and her mind groggy from the lack of exercise.

Lack of sleep hadn't helped, either. She hadn't avoided her bed because of more dreams of the oracles or nightmares about the warehouse. She'd been too busy, spending most of the night poring over the Liberté data, not able to tear herself away after seeing how many highborn the Baron had bribed.

Senators, too.

Especially senators.

She'd given up the hunt after several hours, too tired to hack cleanly, her fingers too sore to continue.

She'd have another long day of it ahead of her, a day cut short by the damn Closing Ball.

Reluctantly Lila forced herself out from under her warm blankets. She trotted through the drafty room, easing herself into a hot bath. Steam rose as she slid in, and she scented the water with apple, scrubbing her hair in slow strokes. She could have stayed in the bath quite happily all morning, all afternoon, and all night, lingering until her skin shriveled into pink prunes, the water passing from hot to warm to tepid to cold. She could have skipped the Closing Ball altogether if only everyone would leave her alone.

But no one left anyone alone in the great house.

Certainly not her mother.

Certainly not when that someone was prime.

Lila stepped out of tub with a great deal of effort and admonished herself for lingering. At least something good would come out of the Closing Ball. She hadn't danced at one in ages, since an unmatched and childless heir caused too much of a stir.

Dancing was the only thing she actually enjoyed at balls, so long as her partner closed his mouth and stopped talking about children, either the ones he already had or the ones he inevitably promised to help her create.

How many senators controlled by the Baron would be at the ball tonight?

How many reasons did she have for not wanting to go? Not wanting to be prime, not wanting to dance with compromised souls, not wanting to waste an evening better spent researching the Baron...

Not wanting to drift further away from Tristan.

She hunched over the countertop, trying not to smack her head against the mirror. "I don't want to go tonight," she moaned, feeling like a teenager and knowing she was acting like one.

She promised herself another five minutes, and only five minutes, of sulking.

Ten minutes later, she finally pushed herself out of the bathroom and padded to her closet. She dressed in casual highborn clothing and sat for a quick breakfast in the morning room, consisting of tea, buttered toast, and an orange.

Thankfully, the rest of her family had not woken up yet.

Most wouldn't, not for a while. The day of the Closing Ball was a holiday throughout the Allied Lands. She donned a thick woolen coat and sent a message to Sutton, then slipped from the great house doors.

Gray clouds threatened overhead. Mist pooled around her. Little golden leaves dropped onto her hair, damp with fog.

She strolled down Villanueva Lane toward the south gate, recognizing Sergeant Nolan and his rookie inside the gatehouse. The rookie peered over the instrument panel as his superior pointed out different buttons.

Lila approved. Today was an excellent time for a lesson, for no traffic waited to be waved inside the compound. In fact, most business owners around the estate had shuttered their doors for the holiday. Only the most stubborn ran a skeleton crew on the day of the ball.

Only the highest of the highborn heirs throughout Saxony would attend the ball at the capitol, some traveling hundreds of kilometers to attend. The same would happen in the other three states: Bellevue, in the western state of Bordeaux; Andalusia, in the northern state of La Verde; and Westminster, in the eastern state of Victoria. A few wealthy and lucky lowborn families, like the Parks, managed to buy their way into an invitation. A lowborn could bring a couple of her daughters, though neither might be spoken to, except by the most gracious or youngest or desperate of senators.

Most everyone else in the country declared it a holiday. Many glued themselves to the screen, watching the arrival of each heir at their state's capitol, or more correctly, squint at the dress the heir had arrived in. The rest would flip through the channels, pretend not to care, claiming only to be interested in the novel, expensive commercials shown during the breaks. They would find themselves unable to look away, though. Gossip would be created, repeated, and amended over the course of the night by journalists who had lost their integrity years before.

Everyone took the day as an opportunity to feast and drink and find partners of their own.

Even criminals.

Indeed, the Closing Ball signaled a holiday for the militia as well. Despite a few drunken arguments between family members and new lovers, the day and night tended to be fairly quiet for the blackcoats.

Too many people were too busy making babies.

And next August, every doctor would be busy in every delivery room.

"Happy Closing Day," Sutton said behind Lila, startling her as she turned down another gravel path. "That might be the first time in a very long time I've surprised you."

"I was just coming to see you."

Sutton joined her in her walk. Their boots crunched the gravel underfoot.

"Tell me how."

"How?" Lila asked.

"How you knew that someone had broken into the family garage. As well as why you'd ask for an investigation the same day you returned home without your beloved Firefly."

"My bike is in the shop. I'm having some work done."

"Captain McKinley and I watched the footage. Someone did something to your bike. I also watched the footage from last night, thinking the culprit might return. I saw a great deal of hesitation on your part to borrow your sister's Firefly."

The commander paused in their walk, her shoulders tensing. "You're making it very difficult for me to do my job and keep you safe. Let me give you a rundown of my evening. No prints. No visual on the suspect except for red—"

"Tell me something I don't already know."

"McKinley and I recovered a set of plugs wired into the lights. Someone used them to remotely switch off the motion sensors. They weren't homemade, so McKinley's going to track that angle and hope for the best."

Lila wondered if Shirley had been doing the same with the devices that she'd pulled from her motorcycle. Perhaps Tristan had stopped her. Perhaps he didn't care any longer, not even about her safety.

Her chest tightened as she recalled the pained way he'd looked at her the day before, waiting for her to say something after returning her bag.

Lila put those thoughts away.

She didn't have time for them.

Instead, she slid her thoughts back to Sutton and back to work. Always back to work.

"That sounds like a promising lead," Lila said.

"It's all we have. Until then, the garage is under surveillance. All vehicles will be checked before they leave the garage for tampering."

Lila tried not to groan as they stopped in front of the security office, the glass and steel rising above them. "Update me when you have some—"

A cracking *ping* sounded in the foggy morning. A glass panel above Lila's head cracked, leaving behind a spider's web and a pinkie-sized hole.

Sutton shoved her to the ground, and the pair flattened themselves on the sidewalk.

A second bullet tore at a chunk of cement near Lila's fingers.

Lila yanked her hand back, her gaze spinning around the compound. She caught sight of a group of slaves who'd frozen, bags of mulch still propped on their shoulders. A hundred meters away, a group of highborn had stopped mid-chuckle, the wind still carrying their mirth. Another group raced toward a building nearby, one young intern squealing in fright with every step. A passing militia patrol had sunk down at the first bullet, knees bent, ready to sprint toward the unseen intruder.

The warehouse suddenly seemed like a distant, pleasant memory. She'd had a gun in her hand then, pointed at those who might hurt her and her friends. She had a way to end the threat and a visual on those who would do them harm.

For the first time in two weeks, she desperately wanted a weapon.

She wanted bullets and a target, too.

She'd shoot, for oracle's sake. She'd shoot again, and damn what dreams might come.

The asshole deserved it.

"Security office! Now!" Sutton ordered.

Lila shook her head. "No, too many people—"

"The militia exists to keep you and your mother safe, you idiot!" Sutton hopped to her feet and grabbed Lila's arm.

The pair ran toward the security office's front door.

Another glass pane shattered into webs.

A fourth shot rang out and hit the coat of arms on the front door. The metal wolf's head exploded as Sutton reached for it.

The commander did not shrink back even as metal shards sliced her fingers.

The pair burst inside.

Sutton turned quickly once they reached the lobby. "You hit?"

Lila looked down at her torso, patting her body as if she'd lost something. "I don't think so. You?"

"No, just a few paper cuts. The shooter can't hit the broadside of a barn."

Sutton stalked toward the front desk, rolling her eyes at a few curious militia members who crowded the glass walls and peered through the panes. She leaned over the desk with a grunt and snatched up the receptionist's headset, slamming the *all* button with an angry, bloody palm. "This is Commander Sutton. There is a shooter on the compound. I repeat, there is a shooter on the compound. Emergency teams get suited up and meet me at the back door. Two minutes. This is not a drill. I repeat, this is not a drill. And for gods' sake, everybody, get your asses away from the walls, or I'll shoot you myself."

A few embarrassed blackcoats, mostly office personnel, slinked away from the glass.

Sutton tossed the headset back to the trembling receptionist. "I want a full lockdown throughout the compound. Contact the great house first. Have the guards shuttle the matron and her family to the vault."

As if Sutton had reminded everyone that two plus two did equal four, the blackcoats hopped into action. Only their panicked eyes revealed it wasn't a monthly drill.

Lila started off with Sutton for the ground-floor armory, but the commander shoved her back. "Where do you think you're going?"

"With you!"

Sutton cocked her head to the side. Whatever she wanted to say, she didn't. "You're not going anywhere. Get upstairs, where it's safe. Don't make me tranq you." Sutton snapped her fingers at a passing sergeant. Judging by his stubble and the creases in his uniform, he'd been on patrol all night. "Assemble what's left of your patrol shift and escort the chief to her office. Shooter's targeting her. You know what to do."

The man did not seem surprised at the order. He turned immediately, calling out on his radio as he jogged back toward the cafeteria to fetch his squad.

Boots thudded on the granite. Leather swished. Cotton rustled. People brushed past Lila en route to the armory or their positions around the building. Annoyed by the jostling, Lila planted herself beside the elevator, waiting for the sergeant to return.

She did not have to wait long. The squad assembled quickly, still wiping away crumbs and drawing their weapons.

Lila swiped her keycard through the slot as the dozen blackcoats swarmed the elevator.

The doors closed. The glass chamber rose. Lila watched her bustling people grow smaller and smaller below.

Not her people. Not anymore.

The elevator dinged, and the doors opened. The militia poured into the waiting area. The receptionist gave the patrol a stiff nod and joined them, her rifle pointed toward the ground. A careful finger stroked the trigger guard.

The woman had not been chosen to work in the chief's office for her filing skills.

Neither had Sergeant Jenkins. He twirled his wheelchair, leading Lila back toward her office. They left the others behind, all crowded in the lobby, their tranqs pointed toward the elevator.

"Awful lot of fuss," Sergeant Jenkins said as the pair passed through his office and entered hers. He wheeled to the window and closed the blinds and curtains.

Lila locked the door. "It is, isn't it?"

"Someone's come for you."

She shrugged.

Jenkins parked his chair beside her desk and laid his gun in his lap. Lila knew what filled the chamber. Like her receptionist, Jenkins carried live ammo, precisely for this reason.

The oracle had taken Lila's guns at the warehouse. She'd been glad for it at the time, but now she regretted handing them over.

How had her switch been flipped so completely?

She drew her tranq for lack of anything better to do. Shoving her inbox aside, she sat on her desk, feet swinging.

"Stand up, chief. At least pretend you're worried."

"I'm not worried. I should be out there—"

"Getting shot?"

"Finding the shooter. Defending the family. That's what I'm here for."

"I think Commander Sutton can do just fine without her boss looking over her shoulder and drawing fire."

Lila looked at her bookshelf.

When had her books gotten so out of order?

Lila hopped up. Instead of fixing her books, she opened her top desk drawer and rummaged inside. Pens and notepads rattled together.

"What are you looking for?"

Lila withdrew a box of cookies.

"You can't be serious."

Lila popped a cookie into her mouth and pointed the package at Sergeant Jenkins.

Reluctantly, he took a few. "How'd they die, Commander Sutton?" he muttered. "Oh, the assassin just walked in and killed them both while they had a snack."

"We're not going to die. No one is going to die."

"No, they probably won't. Commander Sutton took away the target. Shooter's probably long gone now."

"Did you hear the shots?"

Jenkins nodded. "Shooter was close. Didn't have to be, you know."

"I know."

"I never liked the sound of those damn rifles much myself. The commander hates it worse than me. She's probably on the roof, hunting, just like when she was on the front lines."

Lila chewed on her cookie. "Never understood why she joined the military. She's a highborn."

"Did you ask her?"

"Yes, during my first week on patrol. She told me she wanted an adventure."

"Adventure my ass. She went because of her mother."

"Ms. Edith Randolph? What does she have to do with—"

"I meant her biological mother."

Lila frowned. "The woman died when Commander Sutton was a baby. That's how she became a Randolph."

"Yes, and she has no memory of her. Joining the military and becoming a sniper? It was the only way she could get to know her mother."

"By getting killed in action, too?"

"By following in her footsteps." Jenkins brushed crumbs from his lap and stared at the door.

Lila did the same. She perched on her desk again, boots still swinging back and forth.

The pair waited.

No sounds came from outside the building.

No sounds came from Jenkins's office.

No sounds came from Lila's as well. They might have been aboard an elevator, awkwardly avoiding eye contact and small talk.

The minutes stretched on.

Jenkins heard it before Lila. The elevator dinged from far away. One pair of boots stalked across the wooden floor in the next room.

Lila cocked her ear, listening for conversation.

She heard none.

She hopped from the desk, planted her feet, and raised her tranq.

Jenkins raised his gun too.

They listened for a voice and the password that all militia should use in such a situation.

Neither came.

The doorknob turned.

# 16

A blast ripped through Lila's door. Splinters and sawdust burst from the hole. The smell of gunpowder wafted across the room.

Two more shots followed.

Something soft and large thunked against the wall beside the door.

"Chocolate pancakes! Chocolate pancakes! Oracle's light, stop shooting!"

Jenkins lowered his weapon. "Commander Sutton?"

Lila aimed her Colt at the floor as well. "We have got to change the code word. It's embarrassing."

The door opened, creaking softly. Sutton entered, her officer's uniform replaced by a black tactical suit, the zippers jingling back and forth across her chest and legs. Her helmet hung askew, and a bullet trail skittered across the top, leaving a shallow groove. Her eyes cut to the tight grouping near her head.

"I never liked that door anyway," Lila said.

Over a dozen boots thudded across Jenkins's office. The militia froze. Their gazes shifted among the commander, the chief, and the admin.

Jenkins holstered his weapon. "If you were a little taller, you'd have a bullet through your brain. Why didn't you use the code phrase?"

"I forgot." Sutton stepped into the room and closed the door.

The squad lifted their heels, peeking through the bullet holes.

"Good work," the commander barked at the group. "Now go downstairs and finish your breakfast."

Boots clomped across the room.

The elevator dinged, taking the squad away.

Sutton took off her ruined helmet, then tore open the top Velcro strap of her bulletproof vest. "Shooter's gone. We found the sniper rifle, though. I have a team processing the scene. I'll let you know if we find anything."

"Who's running the investigation?" Lila asked.

"Me, and don't you dare say that I don't have time for it. I only left the scene so that I could walk you back to the great house. You, the chairwoman, and your sister are to remain inside until you leave for the Closing Ball, do you hear me?"

"Commander—"

"Don't *commander* me. Once upon a time, I used a rifle like the one we found. In the hands of someone halfway competent, it could have shot the stars off my collar from four times the distance. The only reason you weren't hit is because the scope wasn't calibrated."

"Good, my would-be assassin is incompetent."

"This time. Count yourself lucky, embrace fate, and let me do my job."

"I don't—"

"I don't care. Damn it, Lila, don't make me pull rank."

Jenkins eyed the pair.

Lila raised her arms in surrender. "I have work to do anyway."

"Good. I'll take you to the great house myself."

"Myself" ended up being Sutton and two teams of armored patrols. She forced Lila to don armor just in case, borrowing the helmet and vest and uniform from a rookie who was close to her size and hair color.

The slender rookie dressed in her clothes and a hat, then marched among the group as they set off for the great house. "Commander Sutton," he called out, "tell the militia I'm off tonight, so I can wander around the compound, shouting 'Boo!' at all the slackers."

He turned in a circle, waggling his fingers at everyone in the squad, even Lila.

Then he winked, fluffed his curls, and spun around to face the front.

"You know, those pants sure do look good on you, Bernard," someone called out. "Maybe chief should let you keep them."

"Maybe she should. They really accentuate my ass." He swished his hips. "Look at my ass cheeks, mortals, for mine will launch five thousand ships!"

"I don't think it was Helen's ass that launched all those ships," another said. "I think it was her vulva."

"Nah, her breasts," someone chimed in. "Never underestimate a pair of perfect breasts."

"Perfect breasts?" Bernard snorted. "Give me breasts with character. I like it when one nipple looks off to the side and follows me around the bedroom."

"That's enough, Bernard," his mentor called out from the back. The harried man scratched his beard.

"Everyone else said—"

"Everyone else already has a title or a nickname. Do you want Ass Cheeks to be yours?"

Bernard spun and walked backward. "Is that an option?"

His mentor sighed. "Why couldn't I get a normal rookie like everyone else?"

"Come on, sergeant, you know you love me."

"Can I tranq him, chief?"

"No, you cannot tranq your rookie. Use your words," Lila grunted. "I can't believe he fits into my trousers."

"I can't believe I fit into your bra." Bernard grabbed at his breasts and squeezed. "It sounded better before I put it on. The wire bit hurts, and rolled-up socks don't feel the same."

"You're saying you touched the chief's tits?" someone called out.

"Not yet." He winked.

"Damn it, Bernard!" his mentor cried out. "If you don't shut up, I'll make you wear one of those for the rest of shift!"

"Take him to the weight room instead," Sutton advised. "The cafeteria, too. He needs to spend the next year in both."

"I work out and eat loads!"

"Whatever you're doing, double it."

"I'll see to it personally," his mentor vowed, a vengeful glint in his eyes.

Bernard gulped and finally turned around. He said nothing for the rest of the march.

The group finally reached the end of the lane. Instead of leaving, they spread themselves around the great house's perimeter, adding to the patrols stationed outside the gate. Bernard joined them as soon as he and Lila swapped clothes.

"Ass Cheeks has returned," he shouted from the door, adjusting his chin strap as he jogged down the front steps.

Ms. O'Malley slammed the door shut behind him.

Lila returned to her bedroom and checked for snoops. Her palm vibrated as soon as she finished. Dixon's name appeared on the screen.

*Let's meet somewhere and talk.*

It was likely Tristan who'd sent it, thinking she wouldn't read or listen to any message he sent from his palm.

*I can't leave the great house right now,* she wrote back.

*Why?*

Lila drummed her fingers upon her desk, wondering if she should tell him the truth. A small part of her wondered if Tristan would even care.

That part won.

*We're on lockdown. Someone fired at me with a sniper rifle.*

She settled her palm on her desk. It stared back at her, unmoved.

It was official, then. Tristan didn't care, not even enough to ask if she was all right.

Instead of dwelling, she turned back to her desktop and pulled up her data. She wanted to find the Baron's identity before she left for the ball. She needed to have the situation well in hand before her mother announced her new position.

She'd only made a few hours' progress before a knock sounded upon the door. "Come in," she said, expecting to see Alex.

Instead, she saw Tristan. He slipped inside her bedroom, his face pale. "What do you mean someone fired at you?" he hissed.

"My would-be assassin fired a few bullets at my head, but they hit the security office." She noted his long brown coat. "How in the world did you get in here?"

"I have my ways." His gaze traveled across her face, a miserable expression in his eyes. "Your bike is parked in front of that restaurant a block from the southern gate. Simone's, is it?"

Lila nodded. "Did Shirley find anything new?"

"Not much. Your brakes were rigged to blow from afar, some complicated mess that likely received a signal from a palm. You never should have been able to slow your bike. You could have died." He pulled a baggie with cords from his coat pocket. "Shirley wore gloves. You should have these tested for prints."

"The assassin wore gloves, too."

"You already found them?"

"No, I just saw the security footage. My people are doing an investigation. This will help, though." She dropped the cords onto her desk.

Tristan peered at her computer, noting a familiar sheen to the data. "You hacked Liberté without us?"

Lila turned off her monitor. "What did you expect me to do, Tristan? I have a case to solve, and you made it clear you wanted nothing more to do with me."

Tristan sat down on the edge of her bed. The mattress creaked. "That's not what I said."

"You told me to go."

"I said a lot of things. That's the only thing you heard." He ran a hand through his hair. "Don't go there tonight, Lila."

"Go where?"

"You know where. Don't spend the night with one of those men."

"One of those senators," she corrected. "I don't want to have this argument again. We'll only yell at one another."

"Maybe we need to yell."

"To what end?"

He looked up and cleared his throat. "You want a child? Fine. I'll provide you with an heir if that's what you want. You wouldn't—"

"Do you even want a child?"

"Do you?" Tristan rubbed his scalp. "I need you. You need a child. Why are you making this more complicated than—"

"It's not about a baby, Tristan."

"Then what is it about? What do they have that you need? What do they have that someone else couldn't—"

"That you couldn't?"

"I would rather have seen you with Dixon for the rest of my life than to know you spent one night with one of those highborn—"

"So you're going to go back to insulting the highborn again, is that it?"

"I love you, Lila. I don't know what I'm supposed to do here."

"You can still have me. I just have to take a partner for the season, or at least until I get pregnant."

Tristan looked away. "I'm not going to stand by while you fuck some other man."

"Then you want too much. I'm not the chief anymore. I'm prime. There's just no time for us anymore, not in the way that you want."

Tristan stood up and pulled her out of her chair. He slipped his arms around her, and his mouth landed on hers hungrily. Their tongues intertwined. She tasted whiskey, quite a bit more whiskey than usual.

At some point, her kiss changed. Her lips stilled, and her thumb lingered on his cheek. Passion fled where goodbye lingered.

"Why do you kiss me like that? Why do you kiss me like that if you don't have feelings for me? If you can just run away and have feelings for someone else?"

"None of this is about feelings. I'm not taking a lover. I'm making an heir."

"You couldn't do that with me?" He blinked back tears. "Mine works just as good as theirs. Why am I not enough for you?"

"What would have me do, Tristan? Would you have me seal the child's birth record? Even accepting for the moment that your breeding does nothing for my family's prospects, what would I tell the child when it grows up? That she can't see her daddy because he'll be working in the mines for the rest of his life? That he's a slave who got caught doing something stupid? Or maybe I should say that she can't see her daddy because he hates everything she stands for. It's hard enough for me to put up with, and I'm a grown woman. How's a child supposed to deal with all your backhanded slaps? I won't put a child through that."

Tristan pulled away.

"I won't have a child who can't rely on her father for help. Look at Alex and Simon. Look how it worked for them."

"Get it from a jar."

Lila sighed. "That's not how this works, Tristan, and you know it. I'm prime—"

"If it's only too late if you become prime, then don't become prime. Live with me."

"I can't, and I'm sorry if you don't understand why I can't choose to be with you in the way that you want. I'm trying to meet you halfway, and I don't know why you won't do the same for me. I can't turn my back on my family, and you shouldn't ask me to."

"I wouldn't ask if you really wanted to be the prime. I'd let you go. But this doesn't suit you, Lila. None of it does. Not being prime, not having a child, not sleeping around with other men. Fine, maybe some people, some highborn, can do this, but you aren't like them. Dixon wasn't either. Don't you get that? Why must you go along with this?"

Lila swallowed. That morning she would have said she deserved it. She had killed people, and part of the compensation for that involved this life she had never wanted.

But her mind had changed since then. She no longer regretted her actions, not since the shooter took aim that morning. The Italian mercs had sealed their fate in the warehouse the moment they took her and her friends hostage. Were she in that place again, she'd draw her gun and shoot. No tears would fall upon her cheek. No remorse would cloud the aftermath. She'd shoot again, just as she would have shot the sniper that morning.

The monster in her mind vanished, along with his club.

For the first time in weeks, her mind quietened, but what remained surprised her. "I'm going along with it because I love my family, because I can handle the office, and because I can do more good as prime than I ever did in the security office. Pick one, Tristan. My mother needs me. My sister needs me. My family needs me. I was never meant to be anything but the next chairwoman. I'm tired of running from that. It's exhausting."

"No, you're just running from us. Again."

"It's not about us."

"So becoming prime is just fate?"

"I call it life. I call it duty and responsibility. I call it growing up."

Tristan scowled, shaking his head. "You could do more good by my side in a week than an entire lifetime as prime."

"Really? Where's your Randolph General?"

"Don't be an ass. That's not fair, and you know it. There are more ways to do go good than with money. Join me. We could do good things together."

"So long as I leave my family first? I'm supposed to leave everyone I know behind just because a man says he loves me? For a relationship I've only had for a few weeks? Do you understand how crazy you sound?"

Tristan licked his lips. "Don't do it for me, then. Do it for yourself. Buy your mark from your mother. You don't belong here."

"She's not going to sell it to me, Tristan."

"Then leave. You're not a prisoner, and you don't need your mark to live. Dixon lost his, and he hasn't missed it. I haven't missed mine. There are worse things."

"Yes, like being thrown into a holding cell the first time a militia patrol hauls you in, even for the smallest of things, because the chairwoman has put a bounty on my mark? I can't even work without it."

"You think too much like the highborn. There are other ways to work. I worked for you, didn't I? You're rich. Take your money and leave. I'd take care of you even if you had nothing."

"So, best-case scenario, I become some sort of kept woman? Like some daughter of the empire? Kept by a former slave who can't go more than five minutes without yelling at me?"

"You're the one who can't go five minutes without yelling at me!"

"Fine, we can't go five minutes without yelling at each other," she said. "Do you think that's going to stop just because we're fucking? How long before you realize that I'm just some stupid mistake?"

Tristan's face fell. "Is that what you think we are? Some mistake?"

"Maybe you need to take another lover as well."

"Gods, you're serious." Tristan backed away.

"What if we aren't a mistake? What am I supposed to do if something…when something happens to you after I've thrown away my mark and my family?"

"Why can't you just jump into anything? Why do you always overthink—"

"That's what I was trained to do. It's what I was born for, and it's what will make me a good chairwoman. And if I'm really lucky, I'll be half as good as my mother one day. People depend on me, Tristan. Perhaps you don't care about them, perhaps you even hate them, but they are people nonetheless. They deserve my care, just as much as Dixon deserves yours."

He stepped toward her, wrapped his arms around her, and rested his forehead against hers. "Be the prime heir, then, but don't go to that party tonight. Stay with me."

His body, his warmth, tempted her.

"This is all very easy for you to say. You're asking me give up everything while you lose nothing. Neither does your family. Dixon said once that you have trouble asking for what you want. I have the opposite problem. I have trouble wanting what I've got. Perhaps I don't want to be prime, but this is my life. I have to learn to want it."

"Lila, don't."

"I'm sorry, Tristan. You want too much."

"If you do this, if you go tonight and sleep with one of them, then I'll never forgive you for it. I'll never speak to you again."

"I didn't think you would."

Tristan turned on his heel and opened the door.

He didn't look back.

# 17

Lila did not hear the knock, nor did she notice the door open after. Instead, the casters woke her as they rolled against the hardwood floor. A rack of clothing glided across her bedroom. The crimson fabric blurred as Alex swiveled it into position.

Heels clacked.

The bathroom lights switched on.

Water crashed against the bathtub.

Lila's eyes burned at the light. She looked away, her eyes puffy and sore from crying. She'd kept the tears at bay while searching for the Baron, abandoning her swath through his highborn victims in favor of digging into the name Freiherr.

She'd found millions of hits. It turned out that Freiherr was the name of a German pop singer in the empire. A recording company had launched his first single five years before. The hacker had opened his bank account a year later.

Her blackmailer had concealed himself in a crowded room.

Lila had given up the search to take a nap, or more correctly, she'd given up because thoughts of Tristan had finally overwhelmed her.

"Rise and shine," Alex said gently as she reentered, straightening the distance between the hangers.

Lila thrust her head underneath a pillow. In the past, she hadn't wanted to go to balls because they were an annoyance, but this time was different. There'd be no coming back from her actions if she attended the ball.

Tristan wouldn't be coming back.

How on earth had she let herself get so wrapped in one person?

Lila pulled up her covers. Every part of her was sore and stiff from the surgery and the wreck, and now she had a headache from her crying jag.

"You have a ball tonight," Alex reminded her. The mattress shifted as she sat. "I heard you earlier. I know you're upset."

"I'm not upset," Lila mumbled, hating that someone knew she'd cried. Heirs didn't do such things, or at least they weren't supposed to do them, and lately it felt like that was all she did.

"This is about the man who came into the great house earlier, isn't it? He's the man you've been seeing?"

Lila's head shot out of her covers. "What are you talking about?"

"How do you think he got up here? He came through the tunnels, found me, and asked me to help him the rest of the way up. I had no idea he'd be able to fit into a dinner cart."

"Someone tried to shoot me earlier, so you naturally thought it would be the perfect day to let a stranger into my bedroom?"

Alex shrugged. "He was hot. I gave him a Lila quiz, and he passed. I figured if he wasn't supposed to be up here, then you'd tranq him. He's your lover, isn't he?"

"So attractive people can't be—"

"Ha! You admit he's attractive? You're totally fucking him. Is he good in bed? A man flexible enough to fit in a dinner cart has to be good in bed."

Lila swallowed and turned her gaze to the floor. He had been good in bed. He'd been really, really good.

"Oh gods," Alex said, her face falling. "You really like him. You quarreled, didn't you?"

"It doesn't matter." Lila shrugged, pulling her covers back over her head. "We don't work. He wants more than I can give him. We're not together any longer."

Alex nodded slowly, taking Lila's cue. "Good. He wasn't worthy of you, anyway. He was attractive, but lots of senators are far more beautiful. You'll find someone new to take your mind off him. Someone worthy of a prime."

"I don't want to go."

"Tough." Alex slapped her ass with a loud *pop*. "Hop in the bath and be quick about it. You don't have much time left to get dressed, and you'll definitely need time to work on your eyes. They're a puffy mess."

Lila didn't move. "There's always time to get dressed later. I'll be fashionably late."

"Yes, there'll be plenty of time if you want to go to the most elegant ball of the year dressed in your pajamas."

"Depending on the pajamas, it might improve my chances considerably."

"Chances of what?"

"Of becoming pregnant due to an erection alone."

"I don't think it works like that, but I could perhaps find something." She ripped Lila's blanket off her body and tossed it onto the ground. "I suppose I'll have to. There's no erection in the world that could get through those."

She jerked her chin at Lila's torn militia tank and cargo pants. "Out of bed, now," she ordered.

"No one is going to fuck me tonight based on how I look. I'm a childless heir. I could go in a burlap sack and still get mobbed."

"Then get out of bed and put on your damn sack."

Lila didn't budge.

"Elizabeth Victoria Lemaire-Randolph," Alex crowed, her hands on her hips. "You will get out of bed this instant."

"I might be tempted out of bed if you brought me something to eat," Lila said, her stomach choosing that moment to growl. "Did you bring me something to eat?"

"No."

"Well, then go away until you do."

"Oracle's wrath! This is like rooming together at Bokington all over again. Who knew that four years as your college roommate would prepare me for my future life as a housemaid?"

Lila grunted in reply.

"Chef put aside a plate for you at lunch. I can bring it up while you're in the bath. Soak for a little while. Perhaps it will wash away your mood and all the red in your eyes. Go," Alex said, flipping through the rack full of crimson dresses and coats.

Lila trundled off into the bathroom. Pinning her hair, she sank into in the water, moaning as her muscles unclenched in the tub. She let her arms fall into the water and stared at the soap on the lip of the tub.

It was much too far away to bother.

Everything was too far away to bother.

Her bedroom door opened and closed several times.

Still she did not bother.

"Elizabeth Victoria Lemaire-Randolph, you get out of that tub this instant!" Alex shouted, smacking on the door much too soon. "You've been in there for twenty minutes!"

"All right, all right," Lila answered. She washed quickly and hopped out, grabbing a robe on her way back into her room.

Alex pointed at the plate on her desk.

Lila forked a few bites of chicken salad, surreptitiously making sure that all her Liberté data had been hidden away in her secret compartments between Alex's suggestions. Then she stepped forward to inspect the crimson coats and dresses, all stitched with the family coat of arms in white thread. Such garments had less to do with fashion and more to do with status, though no one had ever told the designers. "There won't be a single surprised eyebrow among the entire bunch when I show up in one of these."

"You suspect that they've been warned that you're attending?"

"Not all of them, just enough. Senator Dubois's political career might be finished after he marries Jewel, but it would still look bad for him not to warn his brethren against committing too early for the season. He would either be labeled a fool for not knowing or selfish for withholding it. Too many would be slighted. You know how it is."

"He won't be a senator much longer."

"Old habits die hard. I wouldn't be surprised if a few know that I'll be prime," Lila said, wondering about her own habits: hacking, snooping, and breaking into places she did not belong.

How would she manage those in a whitecoat?

The answer was simple.

She couldn't. It wasn't punishment from the gods. It was merely time to put away childish pastimes.

That would be her life, as soon as she wrapped up her father's case with the Baron.

"Senator Dubois will never have children," Lila said. "The only thing he has, will ever have, perhaps, is his reputation. He wouldn't want to ruin it."

"Your mother will make good use of him."

"So will I. He's far too good a politician to waste, and his connections in the senate cannot be ignored. It's too damn bad he never made it into the Saxony High House, but many of his cousins and friends are well placed. He even has a few in Unity. Jewel made a useful match."

Alex suddenly wrapped her arms around her friend and brought her in for a rare embrace. Lila did not pull away. "For what it's worth, I'm sorry. I know you didn't want this."

"I know you didn't want to end up here either." Lila held her friend tightly, her lips twitching in a smile. For the first time, she felt like Alex might forgive her someday. "I'm sorry I was a beast earlier. I'm throwing a tantrum, just like a child."

"Yes, you are." Alex nodded, giving her one last squeeze before pulling away. "But I remember what it's like to be suckered into doing what your mother wills. Our lives aren't that bad, are they? Neither of us lack for anything. Even though I'm a slave, I'll never have to sit in a nursing home at the end of my life, half senile, wondering what might have happened if I had just dared to strike out on my own. I'll know that I tried to break free and that I got what I wanted, at least for a little while. I'll smile to look back on it. You will too when you think of the security office."

"No regrets, then?"

"No. My mother might have done what she did anyway, without the excuse of producing an heir. Perhaps I'd be in a Bullstow holding cell right now because she made me do things against my will. If I do have a regret, it's that I wasn't a better businesswoman. Grace Medical might have survived its first few years if I'd just been smarter, if I had moved farther away, if my elder sisters hadn't died and painted a target on my back. I should have sold Grace Medical the second I heard the news. You offered to buy it and let me run it. I should have listened."

"Alex—"

"I didn't realize the scope of the game at that point. I was too young to understand, even though I'd watched my mother all my life. I'd seen what you did with Randolph General, what you were still doing, and I wanted to do the same. I thought I could. You always made it look so easy. I thought that if I was focused as you were, if I skipped all the parties that you had to skip, that it would all just happen somehow."

"I had a lot of help that you didn't have."

"I had help, too. I just didn't listen to anyone. I was too eager and impatient. I kept pushing. I wanted to show you up, to prove that I was worthy of your friendship. We could have done great things together, my medical research company paired with your hospital."

"We are doing great things. I kept the name."

"I know." A sad smile broke over Alex's face. "I took off at a run before I knew how to walk. There's some small part of me that's relieved about the whole thing, though. I wouldn't have been able to do it in the end, Lila. I wouldn't have been able to take over the family and bring it to prominence. Call it what you want, call it my own temperament, call it poor training on my mother's part. Whatever excuse you devise for me, I know that I would have been the reason that it all came tumbling down. I have some sympathy for Jewel in that respect. Try to remember that when you look at her. Cut her some slack now and again, will you?"

"I would have helped, you know. You could have come to me whenever you needed. The Wilson family and the Randolphs would have become better allies under your leadership."

"I know."

"The biggest mistake your mother ever made was driving you away. She was a fool for it. My mother and I might not get along, we might not understand each other, but she's never driven me away. Going to the security office never had anything to do with her or the heirdom," Lila said, turning back to the rack.

"You and your mother respect each other. She treats you as an equal because you are her equal. Perhaps her only equal."

Lila traced her fingers down a silken sleeve and shook her head. "That's not true, it's—"

"I won't ever forget what you did for me. I suspect if you hadn't convinced your mother about my uses, then I would be cleaning toilets or worse instead of helping you dress right now. It's what the other families would have done. They would have thought it a fitting punishment."

"My mother favors boldness, as do I. It did not take all that much convincing for her to see your potential. When it's in my power to decide, you won't be carrying trays anymore. One of the few good things to come out of this whole affair is that I'll have more of a voice now. I'll be able to offer you more, perhaps get your mark back even if the Slave Bill doesn't pass."

Lila could not read Alex's expression. Her friend stared at the floor with a small smile on her face as though she didn't dare say a word and spoil the promise.

"I'll be late," Lila said, nudging her friend after a time. "Help me pick a dress."

The two women turned back to the rack of clothes and stared at Lila's choices. It was as though they were back in the dorms at Bokington, getting ready for the first party of the school year. Alex shook her head at Lila's plain selections and dug back into the fray, managing to find a luxurious crimson dress that suggested it might not be too uncomfortable for Lila's pragmatic sensibilities, yet still seemed to be one of the most expensive of the bunch. "This one is far more elegant and fitting for a prime. You'll have to get used to leaving your militia clothes behind, Lila. You're not storming a rival's compound."

"Are you sure?"

"Okay, fine. You'll be doing a different sort of storming, then you'll tell me all about it later."

Lila donned the silk dress, a comfortable sheath that showed her arms and legs to good advantage and would not compete against any of the coats on the rack. She shimmied out of it a moment later so that Alex could put her hair into a loose, intricate bun and finish her makeup while she ate her salad.

Then Alex tried on a few dresses too.

When Lila had no more time left to dawdle, Lila donned the dress once more. She tried on several long crimson coats until Alex stopped her with a cartoonish whistle of approval. Lila laughed and spun in front of the mirror, agreeing on the heavily tailored coat. It was so beautiful and elegant that she could have buckled it and worn it alone. It actually didn't look that dissimilar from her blackcoat.

"Now for heels," Alex said, rummaging through Lila's collection of barely worn dress shoes.

"Heels, why heels? I want to wear boots so I can dance."

"Oh, Lila, we were doing so well. Don't you want to look your best?"

"I told you, no one is going to want to fuck me for my looks. Certainly not for the shoes I'm wearing."

"No, they'll want to fuck you for your giant and occasionally obnoxious brain," Alex grumbled, pulling out a pair of heels that matched Lila's dress and the style of her coat. "You're fit and not that bad to look at, Lila."

"Gee, thanks. You're not that stupid."

Alex dropped the heels in front of her. "Occasionally obnoxious might have been optimistic. Put on the damn shoes."

Lila did as she was bid and twirled around in the mirror, her shoulder and hip and knuckles still sore, but glad the woman in the mirror didn't look like it. Perhaps a glass or two of wine would relax her muscles.

She pulled on a pair of full-length kidskin gloves and slipped on her Randolph silver pendant. It dangled fetchingly above her breasts.

Alex brushed her fingers longingly over the coat. "It will be a shock tonight, regardless of Senator Dubois's warning to the others. People will gossip, believing you might formally accept your role as heir. Some will guess you'll be prime soon. I wish I could go and see their faces."

"It won't be that shocking. I've played at being an heir for a long time."

"Well, soon it will be official, with no confusion to cloud it. Pay heed to the Red Baron tonight," the slave warned with a chuckle.

Lila's face fell immediately, and she snatched up Alex's wrist.

Her friend cried out, looking startled.

"What did you just say?"

"Pay heed to the Red Baron tonight," Alex said, wincing. "Did I say something wrong?"

"Where did you hear that name?"

"Jewel left her palm on speaker while talking with Senator Dubois a few hours ago. I overheard the senator mention someone named the Red Baron. I never caught his real name, but apparently, he's expressed a great deal of interest in you over the last couple of weeks."

Lila let go of Alex's wrist, finally realizing how hard she'd gripped it. "You were lingering outside Jewel's door? Accidently?"

"Of course not. I wanted details to give you now so that I'd get details later." Alex's grin waned. "Did I do something wrong? I thought you'd be happy at the information. If he's an acceptable suitor, you'll know his interest level beforehand. Senator Dubois seemed to judge it quite high."

Lila's stomach turned at the implications. The name couldn't be a coincidence. It wasn't a hacker who had broken into the BullNet but a senator. Even worse, he had decided to intercept her at the Closing Ball. Perhaps he had leaked her activities to the chairwoman just so her mother would remove her from the security office and put her in his path.

If so, the chairwoman had played right into his hand.

How much did the Baron know about her already? How much had he told others?

Did Dubois know of the Baron's true nature? Had he helped him work?

Perhaps it was a good thing the Baron would seek her out at the ball. She wouldn't need to pore over Mr. Freiherr's information any longer. She'd have him right in front of her. Tonight.

She only had to draw him out.

Lila smiled at her friend warmly. "You did very well, as always. Thank you for the information."

# 18

The chairwoman nodded at Lila's dress and coat selection after she arrived downstairs and entered the front parlor, Alex trailing along behind. A portly woman stood beside Lila's mother in a purple tartan dress and clapped. "Marvelous choice," she said in a thick Parisian accent. "The dress and cut of the coat emphasize your militia past, and the heels give you the height to look down upon all other women. You will be a warrior."

"A coat is a coat is a coat," Lila grumbled. "Unless it's a blackcoat."

"You have your work cut out for you, Madame Thayer."

But the designer hadn't heard the chairwoman, for Thayer had already settled upon one of the white couches in the parlor, studying how Lila's dress and crimson coat fell. Her fingers worked quickly as she sketched on a tablet. Soon, Lila would have a closet full of dresses and whitecoats in similar styles.

At least she wouldn't be forced to tool around a tailor's shop, picking out fabrics and having conversations about zippers. She was now very glad that Alex had not talked her into wearing anything uncomfortable. Otherwise, she might have been stuck with several incarnations of it until the designer had time to create something more suited to her tastes.

"Jewel will come in a second car," the chairwoman explained, marching toward the door in her elegant silvercoat. Where Lila's cut was clean and tailored, her mother's was loose and flowing and regal, as was her dress underneath. Two pearls dangled from her ears. "She and Senator Dubois are attending a dinner at the Massons."

"Good, you and Pax ate together, then."

A footman opened the front door. The pair descended the front staircase, the sun setting below the clouds as they walked.

"I know he must have enjoyed it," Lila said.

"I wouldn't know. He spent most of his time talking about his studies and the hospital."

"His tutor has been pleased with his progress this year."

"Yes, Ms. Beaumont keeps me updated. If he continues to work hard and can get over his shyness, he'll be an asset to Wolf Industries. He might not be a senator, but if we can make a passable orator out of him, then I'm sure he'll be instrumental in smoothing out many partnerships in the coming years."

"It's not just shyness, Mother. It's grief. He doesn't want to be an asset, anyway. You know what he wants."

"Let's not argue about Pax tonight."

A crimson limo purred at the bottom of the steps.

One limo. Not two.

"Did Commander Sutton approve this?" Lila asked.

"She wanted us to go in separate limos," her mother scoffed as they approached the car. "Randolphs do not change plans because—"

"Do you want to get shot instead of me?"

"We would look weak and afraid, Lila. Highborn do not wilt. Commander Sutton has things well in hand. If she doesn't, she won't earn that promotion you're holding over her head."

"I'm not holding it over her head," Lila muttered, crawling into the limo. She had no intention of debating the issue while they stood out in the open, not with her mother so close.

"Why aren't you? It's a perfect opportunity to—"

"Not tonight, Mother. Get in the car."

Lila's clutch vibrated. She retrieved her palm and settled into her seat.

*Pick an intelligent senator,* her father had written. *I want my grandchild to be smart.*

The chairwoman watched her expression. "Commander Sutton wants to put a guard on you during the ball."

"I'm sure she does, and I'm sure she knows my reply. I have no interest in being followed by a looming shadow."

The chairwoman pursed her lips. "You are prime once more, Elizabeth. You have to take your safety more seriously—"

"Said the woman who refused to go in two limos."

"Don't be petulant. Contact Commander Sutton and tell her you have reconsidered."

"No, a guard would spoil my libido."

The chairwoman seemed poised to say more, but thankfully closed her mouth.

"Pax should return to school at some point," Lila said, wrangling the conversation back where it should have stayed. "If he's going to make himself into a doctor, he'll need the push to return. You wouldn't have let me linger in such a mood."

"Quite right, Lila," the chairwoman said, her gloved fingers clenched in her lap. She said nothing in response to the idea of her son becoming a doctor as the limo crawled toward the gates of Bullstow.

A hundred protestors in drab workborn coats surrounded both sides of the gate, pacing and chanting behind flimsy stanchions. They carried homemade signs and shouted "Where is the boy?" at each limo as it rolled past. Some had scrawled *Justice for Oskar* in fat block letters. Others had written *Bullstow? Bullshit!* or *Down with Highborn Slavers.* Quite a few had donned red bands around their upper arms.

Suddenly a hundred balloons filled with liquid pegged the black limo before them.

Chairwoman Holguín's limo, if Lila had to guess. Going to the ball incognito had not paid off for her.

"Couldn't they have done something about these people? It is the Closing Ball."

"It's a protest, Mother. I believe that was the point."

"What point? It's a national holiday, and this is everyone they could muster? It's not much of a protest, if you ask me."

Lila's clutch vibrated once again, and she checked her palm's screen. *Pick a handsome senator. There's a better chance of a cute baby that way.*

"I'll talk to Pax about school," Lila said, dropping her palm into her purse as they pulled up to Bullstow's ballroom. "I'll figure out a way to convince him that returning is his idea even if it means changing schools, but I need you to back me up. Trevor wouldn't have wanted this."

"No, he wouldn't have," the chairwoman agreed as they disembarked. The protestors grew louder now without the limo to mute their cries. "I have every confidence in you, Lila. As for returning to your own duties, I thought you might take half-days for the next few weeks. Spend your evenings relaxing with whatever new friend you make at the ball. It will give you some time to adjust to your new position."

Lila did not reply to the insinuation.

Bullstow's grand ballroom loomed before them, a freestanding building of marble before a long silver carpet. Dancing couples had been carved into the exterior walls by several masters, though some dancers had turned to other games, locked in various stages of undress. The lovers gripped their partners flesh so tightly that veins protruded from their forearms. Aroused skin bunched between their fingers.

They all looked so alive, their faces locked in ecstasy and passion. In truth, Lila had lost her virginity not too long after staring at the sculptures one summer afternoon. It hadn't been that difficult to find a willing Bullstow boy who was keen to experiment too.

Lila supposed that was the point.

Cameras flashed from across the street, a row of poorly dressed paparazzi and journalists shouting over one another. When the group saw her, the cameras stopped, but the shouting increased to a fervor.

"Have you accepted a role as heir?" one shouted.

"Did someone try to shoot you this morning?"

"Did you consider staying home rather than attending the ball?"

Her mother ignored them.

Lila followed her example, her eyes straying across the roofs across from the Bullstow compound. If her would-be assassin had managed to find one sniper rifle, another might not be too hard to locate.

She wouldn't be hard to find, either, not when she'd draped herself in crimson cloth.

But no shots rang out as she and her mother stepped onto the silver carpet, each side lined by young boys with close-cropped hair and well-tied cravats. All wore serious expressions and burgundy breeches and woolen coats, embroidered with a golden rose upon their breasts. The flower was the symbol of Bullstow, and the only coat of arms they'd ever known, for they belonged to no family and all families at once.

The boys hid their faces behind bouquets of burgundy and white roses, but from time to time, one of the boys would rush out at an heir or chairwoman and present a gift from his bouquet with a black-gloved hand. Even the youngest boys of seven and eight managed the task alone. Lila would have to offer a compliment to the senators later for the boys' behavior. She never could have been that still and serious for so long at that age.

No roses came for Lila and her mother.

The farther the pair advanced, the older the boys became, until they reached a section of young men dressed in golden coats, the recent graduates of Bullstow, now interning in their chosen professions. These young men held their bouquets at their chests, keeping their faces free of petals.

Lila finally spied a familiar face. Shiloh's brunette hair had been slicked back, and his blue eyes followed her movements. He had noticed her since the limo, had been waiting for the pair to reach them. His delicate mouth twisted when Lila turned toward him, and he bowed low, holding up his bouquet for the pair to choose a bud.

Lila ignored the roses. She kissed her little brother on the cheek, for she had not seen him in several weeks. "Are you having a good time tonight, spying on all the ladies?" she whispered, remembering how keen he was to attend his first Closing Ball. Occasionally younger heirs plucked a golden coat from the line and took them inside, sometimes going home with them thereafter.

She'd even done it once as a young heir, mostly to annoy her mother.

Shiloh blushed and cocked a worried brow.

"I'm fine. Don't you know I can handle myself by now?"

He nodded, then jerked his chin at her coat.

"Senator Dubois has filled you in?"

He grinned, nodded, and slipped a white rose into her fingers, then retreated back to his place. Another boy behind them darted out to present another heir with a rose.

"You're not to speak to them, Lila, you know that. You'll get him into trouble," the chairwoman murmured, fingering her own rose as they continued on their way.

"That's a myth."

Her mother turned a questioning brow to Lila. "Is that so? I've always wanted to know all the frivolous bits of trivia about Bullstow. Senators never answer direct questions about this place, and I can never get a good read about what goes on inside. It's maddening."

"You misunderstand Bullstow if you think any of this is frivolous."

"I suppose it's from all that sneaking about that you used to do. Still do."

Lila felt the tug of her palm. *Make sure he's kind and a good conversationalist. Funny too. Neither of us want to endure a jerk or an insufferable bore for the next...*

"Oracle's light!" Lila muttered.

"What is it?" The chairwoman read the palm's screen and barely restrained a chuckle. "Ah, how adorable. Your father thinks he's helping." She pulled out her own palm and tapped on her screen, far faster than Lila could ever hope to follow, then slipped it into her clutch.

Lila did the same.

The pair did not have to stand in line for very long at the ballroom's entrance. The valedictorian of last year's class at Bullstow, now a page for Senator Forrester, stood ramrod straight at the door, announcing each guest as they stepped forward. He was dressed in gray breeches and a finely tailored golden coat. A gray vest peeked from underneath, and a silken cravat completed the look. His brunette waves reached to his chin. He'd already started growing it out in preparation for his entrance into High House. All in all, it was a good showing for the boy, so long as he did not misspeak during his duties, for every chairwoman and her daughters would know his name before the night was out.

If he was lucky, he'd have a partner for the season if he caught the eye of one of those young daughters.

He had more of a chance than Shiloh, at least.

Lila shook her head at her mother before she could even say a word. A boy of nineteen was far too young for her.

The boy seemed to understand, though he still blushed charmingly. "Heir or chief?" he asked politely, confused that Lila had not worn her usual blackcoat and formal uniform.

"Neither."

The boy nodded and cleared his throat. "Chairwoman and CEO Beatrice Ophelia Masson-Randolph of Wolf Industries, and daughter, Elizabeth Victoria Lemaire-Randolph," the boy called out over the chatter. His voice filled the ballroom without a microphone and rang with perfect elocution.

Several New Bristol and Saxony senators turned at the announcement, likely wanting proof of the gossip that Chief Randolph had set aside her blackcoat for the season. The rest of the room stirred and turned toward the pair with shocked eyes and wide mouths. They were either so new to politics that they had few contacts who mattered, or they were slipping out of the senate due to the lack of them. The rest of the crowd was a different matter. The din hushed, and Lila tried not to laugh at how many important families had been thrown into a feverish whispering.

It made for quite a segregated ballroom.

Lila's eyes trailed across the groups of senators, their tailored coats and breeches in the color of their respective city senates. Silver medallions displayed the towns' symbols around their necks. Scattered among them were the black Saxony coats and gray vests of the state High House. Burnished antique silver roses dropped to their chests in place of city medallions.

The men hung apart from the women, but only because the latter clustered together into groups by hue. The ballroom was a field of color, dotted by an assortment of whitecoats and silvercoats, donned atop dresses that spanned the spectrum from red to yellow to green to violet, and every shade in between. The monochromatic coats of those who were neither chairwoman nor prime matched their family's color or complemented it.

Starlight filtered inside the ballroom from the glass ceiling. Waiters carried trays with crystal wine glasses and champagne flutes from group to group, and tables laden with pastries and fruit crowded in the back. Thousands of roses lent the air their scent, for bouquets had been stashed on every surface.

For once, roses could not outshine their surroundings. Artists had painted the walls inside the grand ballroom with the same motif as outside. The painted couples had forgone most of their clothes and, in some instances, beds. Even the balcony overlooking the dance floor had not escaped such treatment, though most of the lovers tarried there with no clothes at all.

It was all highly inspirational.

Lila ignored the art and the fevered whispering, for somewhere in the press of bodies and color lurked the Red Baron, the one man who would seek her out before the night was through.

And she had no idea which one he'd be.

The only thing she did know was that he'd be eager and impatient.

He wouldn't be the only one, though, especially if she added irritated into the mix. The New Bristol heirs stared at Lila as if she had betrayed them in some way. She focused on one particularly harsh expression, the new chairwoman of Web Corp.

Lila winked.

Joanna Weberly clenched her little sister's arm and bared her teeth.

Lila's mother had not noticed the exchange. She touched Lila's back and steered her deeper inside the ballroom. "Come, let us find some champagne."

Once drinks had been procured off the ubiquitous silver-trayed and tuxedoed servants, the chairwoman installed herself on a leather chair in a nook far away from the entrance. It was the first time Lila had ever seen her mother sit at a Closing Ball.

"I assumed you'd have us seated right before the entrance. That way you could offer your opinion of each man as he was announced," Lila said, sitting beside her mother. She laid her rose upon the armrest.

"How tedious. I have no interest in sitting through the introductions of so many heirs and senators who have no potential. Eligible men of quality will flutter around us, waiting to be introduced. I will let you know my opinions then."

"Not in front of them, I hope."

The chairwoman ignored her. "It's a pity that I did not force you to attend more of these. It would be easier if you knew more of the senators, but perhaps it's better that you aren't swayed by years of friendship and feelings. It's better to rely on practicality in these matters."

"Yes, sex and breeding through practicality," Lila said, and sipped her champagne, knowing she'd need another soon.

"At least you've retained your judge's position in New Bristol. Have you had your eye on a New Bristol senator, by any chance? Perhaps a promising young man who would benefit from your direction?"

Lila took another long drink. Every senator was well groomed, fashionable, and handsome, trained from a young age to attend to their dress and body as much as their minds. The New Bristol senators were among the best of the lot. Although she did enjoy looking at the pretty way they moved and spoke, she had only ever lumped them into two categories: those who could help her with the hospital and those who were massive pains in her backside. She had never wanted to confuse the two categories by making pains of her allies or turning her allies into pains. As such, she'd never entertained any sort of relationship with New Bristol senators at all, except as professional and platonic friends.

She did dabble occasionally with senators from Saxony or other large cities in the region, though usually off season and only to pacify her mother. She typically saved conquests for the occasional rake among the highborn. Once or twice a year, she chose a few particularly irresponsible highborn males, those with good humor and adventurous spirits, and spent a few months indulging, every single night. She was like a sexual camel, powering herself up for another trek across the desert.

That had been before Tristan, though. As she thought back, she realized it had been years since she'd dallied with anyone. She barely knew who had been elected to which city anymore.

Lila swallowed a lump in her throat and tried not to think of whom she'd rather be with, not that it mattered. Everything she'd said earlier had been correct. She and Tristan would never work, not even if she remained chief.

She bit her lip. Hard. She didn't have time to let her feelings dribble down her cheeks again, nor could she ever let anyone in this room see or suspect her feelings.

She'd already cried enough for him, far more than was proper.

"The time you spent as chief of security was not completely wasted," the chairwoman said. "Every woman here is trying to figure out what you and I are playing at tonight. Perhaps you're only here to take a lover, or perhaps there is more afoot. They've all wondered why you never formally accepted a role as heir."

"Perhaps they thought I was defective."

"Nonsense. You are a Randolph. Randolphs aren't defective."

Lila sipped her champagne and did not reply.

"The giant in the middle of the room is Senator Edward Serrano," her mother explained, inclining her head toward a large figure who neatly gripped the lapels of his coat. The senator surveyed the room with a lazy, confident eye.

He was not a panther in his hunt but a drunken boar.

"I know of him. He's a state senator and the eldest son of Chairwoman Blanc."

Her mother nodded. "He's fathered at least a dozen girls and seven boys throughout the highborn families of New Bristol; that's not even counting his lowborn children. His aim is to become the prime minister one day. Rumor is he'll be in Unity next year."

That didn't surprise Lila. City senators longed to serve in the capitol. Senators in New Bristol wanted to serve Saxony. Those working for Saxony strived for Unity, and those in Unity curried favor to become prime minister.

And the prime minister longed for a seat on the Allied Council.

"He's virile and well connected, but he's not a good match for us," her mother said.

"Don't you mean me?"

"I meant the family."

"I thought you wanted someone well connected for your grand-child's father. You wanted it for me. A well-connected senator has his uses, as does a prime minister."

"I made your father. He did not make me. You have lost your sense in the security office. What would such power do for us when the man's mind has already grown fat from the flattery of others?"

Lila nodded, realizing her mother wished to bend yet another fresh, young senator to her will, rather than capitalize on the diver-gent attentions of an established figure. The thought annoyed her. She'd rather not be beholden to anyone, and didn't want anyone beholden to her. At least, that had been her plan for a little while longer, at least. It hadn't struck her until then how terribly naïve that idea had been.

She'd been around Tristan too long.

"Senator Serrano has already produced three prime heirs already, though the first was practically among the lowborn. The mother was wealthy enough to prompt his nomination into the New Bristol Senate. The second pushed him to Saxony."

"Why hasn't he been nominated to Unity?" Lila asked.

"He has, but it's never been accepted. There are always better candidates to choose from. Senator Serrano doesn't have the tongue or the brains to back up his ambitions. What he possesses in charisma, he lacks in wit and intelligence. His speeches ramble, his legislation is full of unintended loopholes, and his alliances lack the necessary linchpins. He's a fool who doesn't understand when he's being led. He'll never make prime minister unless he gains some sense, and I suspect he has grown too proud to recognize his deficiencies and correct them. But if he bears another prime, they'll have no choice but to advance him, politics being what they are. He'll seek you out before the night is through, mark my words."

"Great. Can't wait."

"We'd be better served with a younger, smarter, more ambitious sort, which is why we should pay attention to whom approaches Senator Serrano. If we smooth a young senator's path to prime minister, he would have no choice but to favor Wolf Industries above all his other ties."

"Just like Father because of me and Shiloh?"

"You pushed him into Saxony. Your memory, as well as a few others, pushed him into Unity. Senators in my good graces helped nominate him again and again to prime minister, though your father likely had the potential to get there on his own. But a great many men have potential, and few have the connections to realize it."

"You would rather I selected someone ambitious enough to be useful."

The chairwoman shrugged and eyed Senator Serrano's assets.

"And here I thought that I could choose whomever I wanted. I do have to share a bed with the man for the next few months, Mother."

"Of course. Choose whomever you wish, but don't play coy with me. You like the game as much as I do, much more than the faces upon the players. You'll be annoyed with yourself later if your opening move is not a strong one. Take Senator Serrano to bed this season if you wish. I've heard he's a jovial sort. We can always find a more ambitious and interesting senator for next season. Let's just hope that if you are lucky enough to produce an heir, she does not inherent her father's intelligence. Or better yet, that the child is only a boy who you can send to Bullstow."

Lila plucked a fresh glass of champagne off a tray and refrained from comment. She had not wanted Serrano; she merely wanted to disagree with her mother.

Her palm shook in her purse. *I shouldn't have been meddling*, her father wrote, *though I'm sure your mother is doing the same. Don't pick who we want. Pick who you want. Be happy, Lila girl.*

Lila smiled and put her palm away.

"Who was that?"

"No one."

The chairwoman eyed her daughter's face, then turned back to the crowd. "The one in the middle who just shook the senator's hand is Senator Jasper Coupe."

Lila looked again at the senator and noticed quite a different sort of man on his right. His dark hair had been shaved close to his head, a style rare among the highborn, and his thick eyebrows showed off his brown eyes to good advantage. His coat had been cut tightly, and his face was young, daring, and angelic, so long as the angel had already fallen.

Lila sat up.

That was much more like it.

"Senator Coupe has seeded two heirs among the wealthy lowborn already, which has cleared his path to an advantageous placement next season. He's only twenty-one, and—"

"Twenty-one?" All thoughts of the young man flew from Lila's mind and other parts of her body. The age disparity was practically criminal. "What sort of conversation could we have, Mother? Perhaps he could braid my hair and we could talk about ponies."

"You're not picking a conversation partner, Lila."

"No, just someone to rut with all evening."

"Evening. Night. That one will stay up long after the job is done. Over and over…"

Lila choked on her champagne. "Excuse me?"

"I've heard rumors, child. Quite explicit ones. All for you, of course," the chairwoman said, squeezing Lila's arm.

Lila wondered how in the world she and her mother had come to have such blunt conversations about the senators of Bullstow, all while surrounded by them. She was glad that no one had approached them yet, happy for once that protocol kept her apart from nearly everyone else in the room, at least until they puzzled out who among them had the right to break the crowd's silence first.

Mostly likely, they all waited for Serrano, and Serrano knew it. He'd decided to take his damn sweet time with it, too. Perhaps he knew he'd be rejected and didn't want to do it so publicly.

Perhaps he wasn't as dumb and egotistical as everyone claimed.

"I remember my first Senate ball," her mother said. "I was sixteen and too excited to think carefully. I would have taken home a rather beautiful intern I'd seen on the silver carpet if I'd had my way. Luckily, your grandmother had appointed Chairwoman Lafayette of New Orleans as my advisor. She reined me in and kept me from making a very foolish choice. Your father wasn't nearly so handsome before he became so distinguished. But he was kind, smart, and had a great deal of potential. Chairwoman Lafayette and I both saw it."

At the front of the ballroom, the musicians snapped up to attention, hauled their instruments to their chins and shoulders, and began to play. Senators and chairwomen and heirs quickly paired off and whirled around the ballroom floor.

"I pity you for starting so late. I had you early while I was still young and healthy. I managed to attend meetings up to the hour I went into labor, and feedings—"

"A nursemaid managed the feedings for you," Lila reminded her as a couple swirled close and ricocheted back into the room's center.

"Perhaps, but it is indelicate for you to be so blunt about it. Jewel was more difficult. She kicked during every meeting of the Heston acquisition. Best deal I ever made. I should have known from that alone that she'd have poor business sense."

Lila gave a noncommittal *hmmm* and sipped her drink.

"Jewel took Senator Remington home after her first closing ball. That was a good match, regardless of whether or not they lasted through the season."

"I thought a good match was one that did last through the whole season, madam. As well as one that produces an heir."

"None of us knew that the man didn't favor…the season. I hear he's made a very fine diction professor at Bullstow. He and his husband have adopted three lowborn children, though I'm not sure how he managed to swing so many. Competition is fierce among those of his disposition, you know."

"Well, he was a senator. That had to have helped immensely."

"True. One might even think that he planned it that way."

The music stopped, and the crowd clapped in appreciation. A few latecomers were announced at the door before the dancing started again.

"Who's that?" Lila asked, pointing her champagne flute toward a man who had brushed in front of Serrano and Coupe. She meant only to redirect the conversation away from the awkward bend it had traveled down, but her attention had also been caught by the man's auburn hair. It was so dark that it might have been brown, and it brushed his shoulders with a slight wave. Lila spied the ranginess of his steps, the ease with which he slipped through the crowd, searching for someone he could not find.

Here was the panther.

Hunting.

The chairwoman's eyes twinkled. "Ah, Senator Dorian La Roux. You've heard of him already, I presume?"

"Should I have?"

"I would have thought Senator Dubois would have foisted him on you at some point. They're cousins on his mother's side. He wouldn't be a bad choice, come to think of it. Chairwoman Masson does not know how to make use of him in his current appointment, nor has she spent much thought upon him. He's the son of the fifteenth heir. He's hardly even on her radar. The man is hungry to prove himself and intelligent enough to be useful. He ranked second in his class, if I recall. He only has a few children scattered among our ranks, none of them prime or firstborn sons. It's been enough to earn him a prized slot in the Beaulac Senate, and he's carried himself well there. He's young, but unfortunately his seed is falling behind his legislation. He's spent as many seasons sitting out of the game as he has inside it. Senator La Roux doesn't lack for attention, he just lacks for the right attention and someone to guide him."

That piqued Lila's interest. "What does he do during those seasons when he sits out?"

"No one really knows. Senator Dubois said that he circles the New Bristol clubs and balls, gathering information and building alliances for his work in the senate. He's been trying to make Beaulac more than a city full of oil money. Perhaps he does not have the time to juggle that work and an heir."

Lila sipped her drink. "He's an idealist, then. Naïve. A man who doesn't understand the importance of having children spread among the families." It made her think of Tristan, yet another man who was naïve and shortsighted.

Oh gods, she had a type.

"Senator La Roux knows the words but not their meaning. I don't know why not. It's drilled into their pretty little heads enough at Bullstow. It's his one failing. You'd think that he'd understand by now that the highborn need to see him intertwined with the families before we can trust his judgment. If he's not vested in seeing his children safe and prosperous, how can we believe he'll do the same for all of us? Perhaps he's just beginning to understand."

"If he's managed to stay in the senate this long with few children, then perhaps he hasn't needed to learn the lesson yet."

"He'll need to learn soon," the chairwoman said. "He should have had more children by now, and everyone knows it. His place in the Beaulac Senate is not secure, not if enough senators have a better season this year."

"You think he'll be shipped off to some no-name city if he doesn't seed a child?"

The chairwoman sipped her champagne. "I suspect that his political career will end before it ever truly began, and he'll be forced to teach philosophy at Bullstow. This year, next year, it makes no difference. He'll lose again when he was so close, just as he always does. That's what coming in second all the time does to you. He's hungry, Lila."

"What of his politics?"

"Favorable enough." Her mother sat up, taking a closer look at Senator La Roux now that her daughter had shown an interest. "Not so disparate that we could not bend him more favorably to suit us. Senator Dubois has spoken well of him, has called him a potential ally on more than one occasion, has worked with him on our behalf a few times. A season with you would secure him a seat in New Bristol. Proof of an heir might catapult him to Saxony the year after. He'd be an attentive suitor, that's for sure."

Had circumstances been different, Lila might have taken the senator more seriously as a possible match for the season. He was certainly beautiful enough. There was even a mischievous twinkle in his eye that called to her. But in truth, she merely needed someone to stir up desperation in her target.

La Roux would serve as pretty bait.

In exchange, her fleeting attention would help the senator find his match for the season. He'd surely go home with an heir. It just wouldn't be her.

The chairwoman beckoned for fresh drinks, a desire that was promptly attended to by the servants milling along the edges of the ballroom. "A man like that is ripe. A man who always finishes second has a hunger to prove himself, to finish first for once. It makes him more willing to compromise."

"Or it makes him angry, bitter, and confusing," Lila said lazily, thinking what else the man might have in common with Tristan.

"He's a senator, Lila, not a workborn. He has better manners than that. If anything, he has always been described as exceedingly fair and affable."

"Well then, here's to ambition," Lila said, clinking her flute with her mother's before the chairwoman could respond. "Call Senator Dubois over to make the introduction. I'm tired of waiting for Senator Serrano to pull his head from his ass."

"Language, child." Her mother frowned, gesturing for Senator Dubois. He and Jewel had been twirling through the ballroom, but he halted mid-dance, eager to attend to the chairwoman's wishes.

Her mother chuckled suddenly as Dubois padded toward them. "I forgot. Senator La Roux has a nickname, some silly childhood lark among his cousins at Bullstow. Senator Dubois called him by it once. It was…" The chairwoman thought for a moment, her eyes glassy and unfocused while she thought. "Ah, I remember. The Red Baron. What a silly nickname for a child."

Lila fingered the stem of her flute and tried not to break it.

# 19

Chairwoman Randolph insisted that Senator Dubois take her seat as soon as he made his way through the crowded ballroom. Then she gathered up Jewel and vanished into the throng. Lila understood the message. Her mother considered her work on the matter finished. The heads of the most powerful families in Saxony lined the ballroom, and she would use the time for the betterment of Wolf Industries. It would not be the first time the chairwoman sought out new business during the Closing Ball, smoothed over a dispute, concluded a multimillion-credit contract, or stroked the ego or temper of a rival. She often said that a chairwoman who came to a ball to dance wasn't doing her job right.

Her mother rarely danced at balls. She would do that at the great house later, either with the prime minister or an eligible senator she picked up on her way out the door.

She had done it with only with a twitch of a finger once.

Senator Dubois plopped himself down in the chair beside Lila, a grin overwhelming his flushed face. Usually Dubois took every opportunity to dance with Jewel during balls, leaving his beloved too exhausted for an encore after they returned to the great house, but he seemed happy to sit next to Lila and preside over her match. Though he did seem surprised by Lila's scrutiny of her cousin, he did not mention La Roux's tandem interest.

He mentioned everything else about his cousin, though. According to Dubois, Senator La Roux was a proud man who had been backed into a corner this legislative session. Her mother had been correct. La Roux had fumbled his place in the senate. He'd mentioned to Dubois weeks ago that he would not neglect either of the two paths to security this season.

"Either by deed or by seed," Dubois explained. "It's a saying at Bullstow. It means that you can declare yourself worthy as a senator by tackling some tricky piece of legislation that will endear you to Bullstow, or you can—"

"I understand its meaning, Senator Dubois. It is as subtle as the Saxon winter is cold."

"Of course." He blushed.

"Do you have any idea what deed the senator has chosen?"

"I don't know exactly. I don't think he's told anyone because we're all asking ourselves the same question. I'd wager he's holding some secret. Dorian has many hobbies, chief among them gathering information." Dubois smiled, and his dimples made their first appearance for the evening. "It's no wonder he's piqued your interest. You have found a kindred soul, madam."

Lila hid her thoughts with an indulgent smile. It appeared that La Roux was much more slippery than anyone gave him credit for. Not only had he pilfered secrets and placed traps in BullNet, but he'd actively sought out gossip among the highborn crowd.

La Roux might hold more secrets than anyone in Saxony.

Lila was one of those secrets.

She wondered again what Dubois really knew about his cousin.

Perhaps La Roux was not the Baron after all. The nickname could have been a coincidence. The senator might have pressed his cousin only because he wanted to spend the season with her in the hopes of seeding an heir. If La Roux truly was the Baron, then he'd be feeling her out and working the angles, but an ambitious senator would do the same. Lila wished that she had a night or two to dig up more information on him before making first contact, for she didn't like going into an investigation or an interrogation blind. But out of all the boring, lacking men in the room, La Roux had just become the most complicated and intriguing choice.

"He's a great father, too. You've picked well. My cousin would do anything for his children and their mothers."

"Introduce us, then."

Dubois flashed his dimples at the chance to play matchmaker. Lila almost felt sorry for him. He would be so disappointed by the outcome.

"I must warn you. Dorian can be quite direct in conversation. I feel he might be even more direct if you approach him abruptly."

"I am not interested in prolonging things. Directness is not always a bad thing. It can be refreshing, especially when we highborn are often too busy to dance."

"There's always time for dancing."

He escorted Lila toward La Roux, who was engaged in conversation with Ms. Charlotte Weberly, Johanna's younger sister and the fourth heir to Web Corp.

The young woman briefly flashed an annoyed look when Lila approached. Perhaps it was Ms. Weberly's fear that Lila would steal away her senator's attention.

Perhaps Ms. Weberly was in love.

The senator's smile did not reach his eyes while he chatted with Ms. Weberly, and his laughter seemed a forced obligation of his office. No senator would bed a woman if he felt nothing for her. It would be immoral, no matter how desperate his political career might be. And Charlotte Weberly, as the fourth heir, would not help his career as much as others in the room. Not as much as Lila.

She almost felt sorry for her.

"Ms. Weberly, Senator Dorian Masson-La Roux," Dubois said, "may I present Chief Elizabeth Victoria Lemaire-Randolph." He acknowledged Ms. Weberly with a slight bow.

Senator La Roux's eyes widened at the sight of Lila. She knew that it was not every day that an heir to one of the richest families in all of Saxony sought him out and addressed him. He bowed low in deference, and his hair fell into his face. When he straightened, he pushed it back with a quick shake of his head.

Lila tried not to stare. His eyes were the most beautiful shade of light green, almost glowing like the lights Tristan had used during her Liberté hack.

He grinned at his cousin, more of a thank you than a hello.

Interesting. He had asked for the introduction; he just didn't think he would get it.

Perhaps Dubois knew nothing after all.

"Senator La Roux, your cousin told me that you need to discuss a matter of great urgency. I do apologize for taking you away from such pretty company in order to attend to the drudgery of business, but I suppose that it cannot be helped."

"I'm sure that it can," Ms. Weberly said with narrowed eyes. "After all, it is a ball."

"Chief Randolph," La Roux said, nodding slowly and playing along, "Louis has kept you well informed. I must talk to you about an important matter. It concerns your family's oil interests in Beaulac. If you'll excuse me, Ms. Weberly, business must come before pleasure." He bowed and kissed her hand, causing the young woman to blush scarlet.

"Well, how long can a bit of business really take? Find me later, senator, for I have a bit of business to discuss, too. Don't make any plans for the winter without me."

Ms. Weberly paused to give Lila another scathing look, then turned on her heel and left.

La Roux eyed Lila's coat. "Louis, I find myself at a loss for remembering any conversations where I begged you to speak with Chief Randolph on my behalf."

"Something tells me that you do not beg Senator Dubois for anything, or anyone else for that matter," Lila interjected, her flirting skills a bit rusty.

It didn't seem to bother La Roux. He stood up a little higher at the compliment. "Begging has nasty connotations. Highborn do not beg. We ally. Are you seeking an alliance this winter, Chief Randolph?"

A trace of a smirk lined the edges of Senator Dubois's lips, and his gaze passed to Lila. "You certainly do not waste time with pretty language," she replied.

"I have no idea what you mean. Dallying about with pleasantries is tiring, is it not?"

"Do you just strike to the heart of the matter in all things? Sometimes, dallying about with pleasantries is the mark of a skilled, experienced man, so long as he's knowledgeable about dallying and pleasantries."

"I'd say I'm knowledgeable about both, but I always believe there's more to learn. What some women find pleasant in dallying, others find—"

Senator Dubois held up his black-gloved hands. "I think that's the cue for me to find Jewel for some dallying of my own." He bowed and left their presence, raising a questioning eyebrow to Lila, who merely shrugged.

"Your cousin is hilarious," Lila said when they were alone.

"Quite. Keeps me in stitches whenever I return to Bullstow." La Roux's voice lacked a certain roll in the vowels that she'd begun to treasure, but it was deep and warm, far warmer than she would have liked.

"Do you return to Bullstow every season?"

"Yes, madam." He did a graceful quarter turn and took her arm. "Let us go for a stroll. I require air."

Lila assented to his suggestion, for she did not want Ms. Weberly to interrupt their conversation. The senator seemed to have the same idea, for he led her around the dancing couples in the ballroom and up the main staircase. The men glared at the senator for taking Lila away, while the women in the room stood on their tiptoes, eyeing Senator Dubois curiously.

The couple soon crossed through a set of double doors, ending up on an empty balcony that overlooked a park.

Lila sighed. She'd forgotten about the paintings in this part of the ballroom.

Penises, penises everywhere.

"So, you have taken off your blackcoat for an evening. You've finally decided to seek an heir, perhaps to become one."

"Perhaps I just wanted to dance."

"If you just wanted to dance, you wouldn't have visited the women's clinic two days ago. You're taking up the whitecoat soon. You just want to find a partner for the season before it's announced."

"What makes you say that?"

"I can put two and two together. My cousin told me this morning that your sister has chosen love over business."

"It's quite romantic, isn't it?"

"Liar." La Roux leaned into her side and pressed her back against the high stone balustrade. His breath tickled against her ear as he boxed her in. An unwelcome thrill went up her spine at his presumption, at his nearness, at his aggressiveness. It was odd to be touched by another so soon after Tristan, but she knew she'd have to get used to it. "I think you find it all very irritating and inconvenient, especially now that your mother has pressed you to bear a child. Pardon me for saying, Chief Randolph, but you don't seem the type."

Lila did not answer him. She did not worm herself free of his closeness, either. His palm bulged in his coat pocket only a few centimeters from her hand.

If he really was the Baron, then there'd be plenty on it to incriminate him. She just wasn't sure how to manage a peek.

"I find it exceedingly odd that two sisters, both heirs to one of the highest-grossing families in all of Saxony, would turn away from their birthright. You were the first to forsake it when you began working in for the Randolph militia. Now your little sister has stepped aside."

Lila considered the fact that Chief Shaw would soon toss La Roux into a holding cell. The man wouldn't have time to chat with his brethren about her new occupation.

"She's always copied me, the brat. You're quite knowledgeable about my affairs. Has anyone ever told you that women find that creepy?"

"I'm not any more or less knowledgeable than any other ambitious senator in this room, and you're avoiding the question. I understand why your sister would forsake her place and marry. My cousin is a good man and will be an excellent father, but why did you turn down the prime role for the militia all those years ago?"

"I liked the game of it, and I wanted the responsibility."

His eyebrows quirked. "If you wanted responsibility, why not remain as prime? As for games, you'd be hard-pressed to find better among the highborn. The president of Wolf Industries could snap her fingers and influence half the New Bristol senate. Your mother could do the same with the state senate, perhaps even Unity if she wished."

"You're examining my words in terms of power and influence. I should expect nothing more from a politician."

"How should I examine them?"

Lila drained the last sip of her champagne. "I enjoy the militia because I've always seen my mother's little queendom as something altogether different than she sees it—different than any other chairwoman too, I imagine."

"Different how?"

"I've always seen the people inside our gates as people to protect, rather than tools to be used. People, family especially, should be more than chess pieces."

"Now who is thinking like a politician?"

"What a horrible insult," Lila said, untangling herself from La Roux at last. She ventured back to the balcony overlooking the dance floor and lifted a fresh glass of champagne from a roving servant.

The pair peered over the wooden railing to spy on the dancers below. Chairwoman Weberly and Chairwoman Holguín listened intently to Senator Serrano on the side of the ballroom.

"What do you think of the Holguíns?" she asked. "I enjoy your candor."

"I think the family couldn't get any dirtier if they rolled around in mud all day. I'm amazed their matron has not been hanged. I bet that little cabal is twisting Serrano's ear right now, urging him to do something he won't understand the implications of."

"You don't think highly of the senator, do you?"

He leaned into her again, pressing his cheek against her ear, and gripped her hip. "Serrano is too dim for the Saxony Senate. If he makes it to Unity, he'll do so on nothing more than the twist of his pretty little cock."

"So you've seen it, then?"

"Seen what?"

"His pretty little cock?"

"Mine's nicer." Their cheeks brushed as he pulled back, his nose grazing hers. "Would you like to become familiar with it this winter?"

"You're very blunt and eager, aren't you?"

"There are plenty of places where I take my time. Research is one such place. As chief, you have often been described as bold, with a rather shocking sense of humor. You are not one to waste time in your work."

"Is this work?"

"I suspect it is for a woman like you, but I'm trying to make it fun for you." He chuckled and sipped his champagne. "You give as good as you get. I like it. I don't think you would have asked Louis to introduce us if you had not already culled me from the senate's herd. I'm happy to have made the cut."

"Do you believe yourself to be the only one culled?"

"Of course not, but you are here with me when there are a thousand other men in the ballroom you could be flirting with. Since I am enjoying myself very much, I intend to put forth my best effort. Is it working?"

The senator's grin reached his eyes this time. Lila was a good enough judge of character to note his happiness, though she didn't know if it was due to her position, her personality, or because he believed her trapped.

Although she wanted a peek at his palm, Lila grew distracted by a different sort of want altogether. Her body had been responding to him during their conversation, regardless of her feelings for Tristan.

Why did the Baron have to be so amusing?

"You're welcome, by the way," Lila said, ignoring his question.

"For what?"

"For rescuing you from Ms. Charlotte Weberly. I suspect she wanted to wrangle you into a season. Imagine that."

"Yes, imagine that. Is there any reason why I should not accept a season with her?"

"I suspect you might be wrangled elsewhere," Lila replied carefully, giving him absolutely no confirmation of her intentions.

The intentions were there, of course. She knew very well how she could take a peek at his palm. If La Roux was the Baron, she'd find out very soon.

The insinuation of a season seemed to be enough for La Roux. Less than an hour later, Lila engaged a limo to ferry them back to the great house.

As they climbed inside, she sent a quick message to her mother. *Ride back with Jewel.*

# 20

La Roux paced around Lila's bedroom and stopped before the miniature Randolph coat of arms hung above her couch, tracing the twin silver wolves that howled and lunged in opposite directions. "I've never been inside a finer home," he said, mouth quirking as he folded his hands behind his back. "I'd like to see more of it."

"Right now?" Lila asked. The only way she'd managed to sneak La Roux up the stairs was due to Ms. O'Malley, who had the good sense to keep her brood downstairs upon Lila's return. The old woman had manned the front door herself, had taken their coats, had offered to bring up wine and anything else they desired, promising that she would answer all pages herself for the evening. She had nodded specifically to her mistress, a vow of discretion etched in every line on her wrinkled face.

Lila had returned it, glad that she hadn't discovered Alex or Isabel peeking at her from behind a door. It was hard enough enduring such knowing glances and smirks the morning after a guest stayed the night; it would be even harder to endure them after she sent La Roux away within the hour, for the man would not be staying.

She only wanted evidence. She only wanted a look at his palm. After she managed that, she would put in a call to her father and Chief Shaw. Bullstow would make an arrest, and then she'd have to deal with an entirely different set of questions, for she still needed to go through the Liberté data and all the information she'd gathered from BullNet. The Baron had a very long reach.

"I don't believe I need a tour tonight," La Roux said, pouring them both a glass of Sangre. He'd seen her eyeing the off-limits wine during their conversations. Before they left, he had excused himself, whispered into the ear of a bartender, slipped a wad of cash into the man's pocket, and returned with the bottle tucked beneath his arm, with no one the wiser.

La Roux handed a glass to her, put an arm around her back, and kissed the top of her head. Her senses filled with the smell and taste of wine.

"It occurs to me that I never got a chance to dance with you tonight."

"I didn't know you liked to dance."

"I don't like it. I don't dislike it. But more to the point, I've heard that you enjoy it very much. Perhaps even as much as my cousin, which I didn't know was possible." He moved to her desk, put down his wine, and slipped his palm out of his pocket.

"Here. Use mine. My speakers are fussy." She withdrew her palm from her clutch and scrolled through a dozen screens, searching for a public music site. Then she handed over her palm. She couldn't very well steal his and search its contents if it was otherwise engaged, especially if it was busy making an awful lot of noise.

La Roux leaned against Lila's desk and scrolled through the public playlists, smirking occasionally at the choices available. After making his selections, he slid the palm into a slot near her computer. Seconds later, soft jazz pumped through the speakers.

La Roux bowed theatrically with all the grace and charm of Bullstow, ratcheted up to near silliness, and kissed her hand. "Ms. Elizabeth Victoria Lemaire-Randolph, would you do me the very great honor of a dance this evening?"

Lila giggled. "Very great honor?"

He shrugged and kissed her hand again with a loud, melodramatic smack. "Hush, woman, it's tradition. I do know how much you love tradition. You did rush to become prime, after all."

"I don't recall dancing to jazz in any ball I've ever attended."

"Ah, well, now you've seen my fatal flaw. My good humor only goes so far."

"I think it goes just far enough." Lila smiled, enjoying the man far too much for own good. It was the same with Tristan, enjoying a man she knew she shouldn't get involved with, a man she'd never get to keep because of circumstance.

Oh gods, she was *that* sort of woman.

When had that happened?

La Roux grinned, wiping a thumb over the little frown that crossed her face. "I could change the music if you wish, but I dislike all that fussy piano music. This is a public list I created. I put it on in my office sometimes."

"Just your office?"

"Sometimes other people's offices too. Jazz is so much more expressive and evocative than classical music, don't you think?"

Lila put down her glass. "I like anything I can dance to." She slipped off her heels and placed them by the door.

La Roux joined her, toeing his shoes to line up beside her heels. "Ah, now, don't they make a pair? At least for now?"

"They seem to," Lila agreed, tugging on the edge of his jacket, hinting. He removed it, taking care not to crease it as he laid it across the end of her couch beside her crimson coat.

"They make a pair as well." La Roux rested his hand on Lila's waist and clasped her fingers, leading her around the room song by song. He handled her knuckles so delicately that she barely felt any soreness. With every note, every bar, and every verse, his grasp closed tighter and tighter. Eventually she realized that she'd placed her head upon his shoulder.

Perhaps La Roux's good humor and charm had been behind it, or perhaps she was merely tired, due to a second attempt on her life and her fight with Tristan.

"Will you excuse me?" he said, jerking his head abruptly toward her bathroom.

As soon as the door closed behind the senator, Lila shook herself awake. She lunged at La Roux's abandoned jacket and cycled through his palm. She scanned his contacts and found no one questionable. She scanned his messages for the last several days and found no smoking gun. She even scanned his logs and found no evidence of mischief, definitely nothing linking him to the Baron, Reaper, Zephyr, or Sergeants Muller and Davies.

What she did find was far more telling that what she did not. Evidence of the deed that Senator Dubois had mentioned, in nearly every message he sent and page he visited. Rather than planting traps in the BullNet to snag hackers, rather than attempting to snag a potential heir in some scheme, Senator La Roux had busied himself with crafting a resolution for inclusion into next year's legislative session.

He only lacked a seat in the capitol.

La Roux was the anonymous scribe who had penned the Slave Bill. He wished to abolish slavery among the highborn, at least for those who had done nothing so criminal as plunge into bankruptcy due to a few business missteps. His claim was that it stifled innovation.

Though Lila only had time for a quick skim of La Roux's proposal, his idea seemed sound, though far too progressive to pass the High House. After all, the highborn typically did not trust theories of obscure lowborn economics professors, and La Roux's resolution had been built upon one. Even if his resolution passed, the High Council of Judges would never approve it.

La Roux had to know that.

Perhaps the man believed he could sway others to his cause if he crafted a good enough speech, if he managed to swing enough votes his way, if he depended upon the conscience of his brothers.

No wonder he'd never gotten out of Beaulac. La Roux really was an idealist. A rather naïve one if he thought the resolution would save his career. The only thing his resolution would do was make him a ripe target for any matrons who would balk at the idea of losing so many rebellious daughters to industry. Daughters less bold than Alexandra Wilson, who'd risked everything and lost in the end.

That wasn't the only resolution he'd crafted. He'd also crafted the Slave Freedom Bill. He wished to give freedom to any slave who fought against the empire, no matter their sentence, no matter their crime. A family member could fight in place of one not old enough, strong enough, or healthy enough to carry the burden themselves.

He believed war was coming. He believed they'd need far more soldiers to win.

La Roux was probably right about that. The oracle had said as much. She and her sisters had been having the visions for too long.

Or so they claimed.

That didn't mean his idea was sound, though. Any matron who heard about La Roux's work might find it worth their time to get rid of him, for the amount of coverage both resolutions would generate in the press might destabilize all workborn throughout the commonwealth, generating a ripple of frustration among the masses.

The mere rumor of such bills had done enough already.

The fact of them might sound the death knell for all slavery in the Allied Lands.

Implicating La Roux in some sort of criminal activity would be one way to end the threat. Would her mother have found such sabotage worth her time? Would she have devoted resources toward silencing the senator?

Lila had to wonder if the Baron even existed. She'd always believed her mother when she claimed she didn't have to resort to hackers and bugs, that a well-placed spy could tell you everything you needed or wanted to know. What if it turned out that she was the same as any of them in the end? What if she had led her own daughter by the nose? It was the chairwoman who had told her La Roux's nickname. Perhaps she'd sent the article to them both, just so that Lila would fall into line as prime, just so she could get a troublesome senator removed from the senate in one shot. If she'd been the Baron all along, then she'd also controlled Reaper, which meant that she'd been responsible for Celeste and Patrick Wilson's downfall.

Oh gods, why didn't the whole plot seem far-fetched?

Whether or not her mother was behind it, La Roux would need protection. Moreover, Lila would have to find enough evidence linking her mother or another matron to the case. She'd also need to find evidence that the trap in the mental health registry had been faked. Lila had merely seen that the trap was crude and accepted the dates after a cursory scan, but she'd have to dig deeper now.

And if her mother was behind it?

What then?

Lila did not want to think about the consequences. If her mother really was behind the ruse and Lila gave the data to Chief Shaw, then she'd either have to take over as chairwoman of Wolf Industries or pick someone else to run it.

Neither idea appealed to her.

Who could she trust to take care of the family?

Her mother had posed the question thousands of times, over hundreds of cups of tea and glasses of wine. Now that the answer actually mattered, now that she would have to answer it, Lila balked.

That wasn't even the worst part. Not only would she have to appoint a new chairwoman, but she'd have to lead her matron to the gallows.

Could she do that to her own mother?

In that moment, Lila understood Alex so much better. It was one thing to turn in family for a slave's term. It was another thing altogether to turn them into the executioner.

But if her mother had done what Lila suspected, she deserved the noose, didn't she? She likely didn't even care if Lila figured out her plan. After all, Lila would have to take up her position, and they both knew how she felt about that. Perhaps she'd gambled that her daughter would merely trade the knowledge for her mark, so long as she could retain her relationship with the family and seal her mother from BullNet for good.

The only thing she knew was that La Roux wasn't the Baron. He didn't have enough time to moonlight as a hacker. Besides, he was a senator of Bullstow. That might have given him opportunity, but where would he have picked up the skills?

The doorknob rattled, and Lila tucked the senator's palm back into his pocket. She then picked up her wine glass and darted to the window, gazing out into the darkness as though she had been lost in thought.

La Roux didn't seem to mind. He grabbed her hand and led her back to the center of the room for another round of dancing, hand light upon her back. She rested her head against his shoulder, but this time it had little to do with her own exhaustion.

The senator wasn't a scoundrel after all. He wasn't a criminal. He was a good man, despite being naïve and misguided. He was also funny, blunt, attentive, ambitious, and dedicated to his work. If she had to take a lover this season, she could have picked far worse.

And she did need to take a lover. She needed to get Tristan out of her head. She'd known it from the first moment they'd started sleeping with one another.

Lila lifted her face, wound her arms around La Roux's neck, and joined her lips to his.

She felt a brush of skin at her side, felt a tug at her dress's zipper, heard the pull of each tooth slowly giving way to the next as he worked it down. He didn't pull it off in a rush. Instead, he slipped his hand inside and traced the planes of her back.

Lila responded in kind. She had always yanked off the clothes of highborn men in a rush, both her and her partners too hungry and too enflamed to waste time with button holes and bra hooks. Something had usually been ripped, bent, or broken. She'd never tried slow before.

Except with Tristan.

She'd learned that slow could be nice.

Apparently La Roux had learned the lesson too. He tugged off his cravat and slipped his button-down off his shoulders, letting it fall to the ground while Lila traced his chest and abdomen. He obviously spent time in the gym, even during his off-seasons, filling out his clothes to their best proportions. He wasn't so large as to impair the tailoring; he just was large enough to hold a woman in a firm grip and not look brutish.

He had the same sort of frame as Tristan, just a tad more muscular.

La Roux unpinned her bun. Her hair fell to her shoulders, tickling her skin. One strap of her dress slipped off her shoulder as she pulled back the blankets on her bed. A silk negligee peeked out from under the blanket, something that could only have come from Alex. She tossed it onto the floor, losing the remaining strap of her dress.

She let the dress fall, pooling around her feet, watching La Roux as he watched her.

La Roux's smile faltered, brows twisted. "What happened?" He gingerly touched her hip. Her bruises had already turned a dark red since the motorcycle accident.

It was something Tristan would have asked.

"It's the consequences of owning a Firefly," she lied, slightly embarrassed that his first thought after seeing her nude was concern rather than desire.

Perhaps she looked worse than she thought.

"Maybe we shouldn't tonight."

Lila looked up. That wasn't something Tristan would have said.

"The bruises don't bother me. I'm just worried that you're unwell."

Lila stared at the floor. That wasn't something Tristan would have said, either. He would have been too caught up in the moment, only realizing he'd hurt her when she gave a moan of protest.

Just like the day before.

It wasn't that he didn't take care of her. He just took care of someone else, some other Lila she'd never be. He didn't notice the one beside him—one who lived on a highborn estate.

One he hated, if he could ever be honest with himself.

"You're not used to someone saying something like that, are you? Perhaps it's time you spent the night with a different sort of man." La Roux placed a gentle kiss on her shoulder before returning to her lips.

Lila unbuttoned La Roux's breeches and slid her hand into the hunter-green boxer briefs, the color of Beaulac. He bit down on her lip gently, groaning at the contact as she traced his cock. It responded, hardening at her touch.

Lila lay back on the bed, watching him.

La Roux's breeches hit the floor, and he joined her, finding her lips once again, sucking gently while he tugged down one strap of her bra, and then the next. He abandoned her lips for her neck, managing to raise her desire at the first stroke of his tongue, her collarbone, her chest, and finally her breast.

Her body responded to him, and he unclasped her bra and tossed it aside.

The rest of her clothes joined it.

La Roux had not been lying when he claimed expertise in dallying. As he sucked her nipples, he let his hand roam, tracing her neck, her unattended breast, her belly, the inside of her thigh.

Lila gasped, then moaned as he stroked her clit, mouth not letting up on her breasts. The pressure built up with each passing second, and his fingers slid inside her.

There was no pain this time. She had healed from the surgery, after all.

Lila tugged at his boxers, hinting, and he complied.

"Who doesn't want to dally now?" he said, and kissed her eyebrow.

"I'm not rushing. I just thought you were overdressed for the party."

"Is that so." He kissed his way to her neck, to her breasts, down her chest, to her hips. Finally he reached her slit.

She needed this. Not the sex, of course; she just needed someone to banish Tristan from her thoughts, finally and completely.

Lila came soon after La Roux's warm tongue touched her clit. She called out…

Words. A long string of them, meaningless syllables rushing in a furious jumble.

La Roux did not stop. His busy tongue lapped and sucked at her clit until the pressure built and released in another inarticulate wave.

And then another.

She kept reaching for a headboard that didn't exist, for wooden dowels that hadn't been strong enough for her grip. But her headboard was a bare piece of wood, elegant in its plainness.

She wrapped her thighs around La Roux's shoulders. Seconds later, the senator's mouth fastened onto her lips. His cock slipped inside her, filling her differently than Tristan.

"Fuck," she moaned, back arching as he pushed inside. "Fuck me."

La Roux did as he was bid. He moved past gentle and cycled into harder strokes, but it wasn't enough. Lila grabbed hold of his ass and thrust him into her, angry and frustrated and unfulfilled, her eyes closed to the room and the bed.

The pressure rose anew. She moaned and came, calling out again in a fury.

He joined her seconds later.

Gasping, he collapsed in a sweat, rolling onto the bed beside her, gathering his breath.

Lila opened her eyes.

La Roux stared back at her.

"I needed that," she said.

"I think we both did," he replied, taking her mouth once more. Locked in a sweaty embrace, she sucked at his lips, at his neck, let her hands rove across his body.

He rose again.

Lila hopped atop him this time, straddled him, rode him, vowing to give back as good as she had gotten. He matched her stroke for stroke, barely keeping up as she drove him inside her again and again. She smelled the light scent of whiskey, felt a touch at her back, and then he caressed her breasts.

Neither reached for her hips. When they dropped to grip her, he lingered on her thighs.

She came as he finally moaned his last. She didn't pull away, though. She just flopped her head upon his chest, his cock still lost inside her.

The smell of whiskey was gone. She only smelled Sangre.

La Roux struggled to catch his breath. "That was…"

"Bad?" Lila panted.

"Just a little rougher than I'm used to. Different. Not different bad, just different."

Lila lay down beside him. "Sorry."

"I'm not complaining." La Roux chuckled, tugging her back to his chest. "I have to ask, though…who were you having sex with just now? Who were you thinking about?"

"I was thinking about you."

"No, you weren't." He pushed back a lock of her hair and kissed her forehead, his thumb trailing her cheek. "It's okay. I've spent entire seasons dreaming that the other person in my bed was someone different. I know how it is sometimes. You have your lovers, but sometimes duty lies in one direction while your heart strains in another. Some say it's the mark of immaturity, but I disagree."

"I don't know what you're talking about."

"Oh, really? Then who's Tristan?"

Shit.

Lila shut her mouth, realizing it had been open for several long seconds. "Tristan who?"

"I asked first. You called out his name the entire time. Tristan… Tristan… Tristan…" he mocked gently.

"Did not."

La Roux rolled on top of her, held her down, and laughed. "Tristan… Tristan… Tristan…" he called out, his thumb tickling her hip.

"Get off," she squealed, jerking in his grasp, twisting, trying to get free.

Trying not to laugh.

"I did get off—a number of times, to my delight. "Tristan… Tristan… Tristan…" he sang out, humping her playfully. "Tell me. Who is Tristan?"

Lila stopped struggling and turned her head away. "I am so sorry."

"Don't be. I was thinking of someone else here and there, too."

Lila looked up. "Really?"

La Roux nodded.

"Who?"

He shook his head. "You didn't tell me, so I'm not telling you. I think we both like our secrets." He let go of her wrists, and took her mouth in a powerful kiss. "We don't have to pretend like we're in love, you know. We can just be friends and have fun when we're together. If we forget who we're in bed with from time to time, we can forgive one another for it."

"Did I really say his name?"

"You didn't so much say it as shout it. It was kind of cute, actually. It's good that I'm not a jealous man."

"It wouldn't matter if you were. He drew a line, and I crossed it tonight. It's over. He'll never speak to me again."

"He wanted to keep you all to himself? How selfish. He's a fool to demand that of another highborn, much less an heir. We have our duties. My cousin never demanded that of your sister. Mentioned his interest, yes. Talked about his feelings, sure. But demanded? What was the idiot thinking, giving out ultimatums?"

"Perhaps he wasn't thinking, not with his mind, anyway."

"Not with his cock, either. He fell in love with you."

Lila shrugged.

"You're in love with him?"

Lila looked up and shook her head. "No, of course not."

"Ah, she blushes." La Roux chuckled and stroked her cheek. "Being a highborn is harder when your heart is turned on. Highborn like us are the lone wicks burning in darkened rooms. We're what keeps the rest of our kind in the light. You're not alone in that."

"You've been in love too?"

"Far more in love than I should have been, and I've fallen out again after. I'm done staying out of the game because of my heart. Our lives demand certain sacrifices. Perhaps the more you care, the more you have to give up, but perhaps the more you care, the more good you can accomplish. It sucks, but that's life."

Lila breathed out a long sigh, finally understanding why La Roux had taken whole seasons off. He'd been in love, bending his career to the whims of his heart or someone else's. He'd walked the path she might have gone down, and he'd regretted it.

She'd been right to turn away. If she'd left her family for Tristan, she would have been exiled with absolutely nothing to show for it, regretting it for the rest of her days after they inevitably fell apart.

She might not have wanted to be prime, but at least she still had her family.

She startled as La Roux jerked beside her. "Tristan? You don't mean Tristan St. James of the Unity High House, do you?"

"What?"

"Lila, that man is nearly sixty years—"

"Oracle's light, no, not him." Lila groaned, turning to face him. "Yours isn't Charlotte Weberly, is it?"

"Oracle's light, no, not her," he said, his chuckles infecting her. "It's not any other member of the Weberly family. Or the Randolphs either," he said, beginning another assault on her neck.

By accident or design, he hit the spot Tristan always found so easily.

Tristonia. Tristanopolis. Tristanville.

This time when he rose, neither of them were as serious as before. La Roux's fingers twisted at her knee. When she giggled, he pushed into her at once.

Lila gasped at the surprise, moaned for fullness of it.

As he rocked into her, Lila spied an opening. She countered, tracing a spot on his ribs that induced him to fits.

Their night continued, paused and interrupted often by laughter.

# 21

Fabric rustled.

Lila yawned in the dim bedroom and stretched under her soft cotton sheets. Though her muscles protested slightly at the movement, she relished the soreness and the lack of complications that came along with it.

She relished the restfulness, too. She'd not dreamt, not of oracles or the warehouse.

For the first time in ages, her sleep had been peaceful and deep.

She turned her head, anticipating Senator La Roux dozing next to her. Instead, she saw him standing in the middle of the room, chest bare, caught in the act of pulling on his breeches. She was quite fond of his breeches, having recently had her hands inside them, but she would rather his clothes remain off.

"You're awake," she said sleepily, propping her head on her arm.

"I apologize, Chief Randolph. I was trying not to wake you."

"You shouldn't have tried so hard before you put so many layers between us."

La Roux froze while zipping his breeches, wrestling with a decision. Quite a hard one, from the look of it.

Her eyes dropped to the clock beside the bed. "It's only half past seven, senator. Surely we could entertain one another a bit longer?"

La Roux shook his head. "I must apologize for leaving you so soon, but I brought a great deal of work back from Beaulac. I cannot neglect it today. I confess if I had known that I might wake up to such fine company this morning, I never would have left it so late."

He leaned across the mattress and bent down to kiss her.

Lila turned her head away.

"No good morning kiss?"

"Champagne after a few hours of sleep." It seemed an awful lot of bother to leave a warm bed just to brush her teeth and kiss the senator goodbye.

La Roux ignored her protests and conquered her mouth, pressing his chest against her bare breasts. The contact brought the night back to her, and seconds later, she pulled him closer with a happy moan, wondering if she might tempt him once again.

Certainly, his straining cock begged her to try.

Her hands wandered south and stroked it. It took only seconds for La Roux to give up and peel out of his breeches. His stubble raked at her neck as she curled her legs around his waist. His fingers traced between her legs.

"Gods, you're already wet." He laughed, his tongue sliding over hers as his cock entered her, thrusting slowly as he sucked on her lips. "I could get used to this."

Lila grabbed at her headboard, a headboard that had not been broken overnight.

Her body answered his strokes anyway, and the orgasm built.

Back arching, toes curling, her mouth opened as he pumped. He watched her like a cat as she finished, then moaned toward his own conclusion.

"You didn't yell for your lover this time," he said, kissing her forehead, his stubble tickling her skin. "Perhaps I have earned my own place in your esteem."

"Perhaps," she said, a bit sad that she had not called out.

La Roux's head flopped between her breasts, and he let out a sigh of frustration, his auburn hair tickling her chin. "I should have finished my work earlier. I promise I won't ever leave my work so late again." He stood reluctantly, fishing his clothes from the pile on the floor before stepping into his breeches.

Lila crawled atop her blankets in a sleepy, naked pile, studying La Roux's every muscle and ridge as he bent and searched. "I'm not some fifth or sixth heir with nothing better to do than pine for a man's touch, senator. I have an office to clear out and another to get in order."

"That's right," he said, finding his shirt. "I'd nearly forgotten that you'll have a brand-new office in the move. A much bigger one, I suspect. That should be fun, shouldn't it?"

"An office is an office. I didn't expect you to remember."

"You should expect more from your suitors, Chief Randolph. I must admit that I like the idea of you as prime. The Randolphs are one of the most conscientious highborn families in Saxony. I believe you'll continue the trend. You might not want to be prime, but I suspect it will be good for your family and for Saxony."

Lila chuckled.

"What?"

"It's as if you're trying to talk me into it."

"I didn't know you needed to be. I'm not trying to talk you into anything, though. There's a difference between talking someone into something and being supportive of her decision and taking an interest. I'm guessing your former lover wasn't—"

"I don't want to talk about him anymore. It seems unfair."

"All right."

"You're not even supposed to know about me becoming prime."

La Roux winked. "I'll keep your secret, madam, as long you promise to keep your bed warm for me." He wandered around the room, his shirt and breeches open, snatching up his cravat. "Are you going to do that today, then? Move offices?"

"I suspect it will take me longer than one day, but I'll at least start sorting out my office." She finally slipped out of bed, plucking a silk crimson robe from her bathroom door. Slipping it around her body, she left it open and untied. Her breasts exposed, she leaned back against the window, eyeing him from head to toe as he finished dressing.

The senator narrowed his eyes. "You are a horrible tease, Chief Randolph."

"Call me Lila. And I'm not teasing you, and you know it."

La Roux licked his lips. "No, you aren't, Lila. You're just making it exceedingly difficult for me to leave."

"Oh, and how am I doing that, senator?"

"Dorian."

He prowled toward her. Unzipping his breeches, he pulled his cock from the folds of his boxers.

Lila smirked. "Oh, so—"

Dorian didn't wait for her to finish her thought. He grabbed her thigh and lifted her leg, then thrust into her. His green eyes glowed. "You know very well what you're doing to do me, and you're doing it very well. Am I matching it?"

Before she could answer, he grabbed her ass and lifted her off the ground. Then he dove into her again. Her back smacked against the cold wall as he fucked her, but she didn't care.

For now, at least, nothing in the world existed but Dorian and his stiff cock. Tristan, her mother, the assassin—everything dropped away from her mind. She wrapped her legs around Dorian, gasping as he thrust again and again.

She lifted her chin, coming in panting moans.

After his last thrust, he let her down, then took her mouth as roughly as he'd taken her body.

"Gods, you're fun." He chuckled, zipping up his breeches once more.

"You're not so bad yourself."

"Have dinner with me."

Lila fiddled with his collar. "When?"

"Tonight."

Lila thought back to everything on her to-do list. Now that she knew her mother or another matron might be behind the Baron, she had a new point of investigation. She couldn't spend her whole day and night working on the case, though. She had to eat sometime.

Besides, Dorian kept her mind off other things. Or, more correctly, other people. She refused to waste another tear or thought on Tristan DeLauncey. Dorian had been right about a lot of things. Being with someone who understood her and supported her was a relief. "Why don't you join my family for dinner? I'm sure the chairwoman would enjoy meeting you."

Dorian's eyes crinkled. "I would love to have dinner with you," he said, then leaned in toward her ear. "I'd love having dessert as well. And breakfast. I'll sneak in a bottle of Sangre, and we'll fuck all night long and on into the morning. You'll have to shove me out of bed to get me to leave."

He kissed her once more, then gathered up his coat and slipped out the door.

Lila finally tied her robe. On the way to the shower, she paused to turn on her desk computer. Her hand brushed the metal casing as she turned to leave.

The metal heated her skin.

She pressed her hand to the casing once more, mouth slack at the heat radiating from it.

Someone had been on her desktop.

How on earth had she not heard it?

Logging on quickly, she immediately pulled up her snoop programs and left them to their work. Her eyes strayed to her palm, still innocently perched in its slot above the speakers.

Snatching it up, she walked around the room, letting it search for novel signals. When she came to her silver coat of arms, the screen flashed red, digital needle waving.

She leaned over the sculpture, searching the back. A tiny audio bug hid behind a wolf's head.

She frowned, leaving it where she found it, and continued on. La Roux had placed another bug behind her bedside table, another in her bathroom, and another underneath her desk.

Was La Roux listening? Was she on transcription mode while he tended to more important things?

Lila left the bugs alone and connected her palm and desk computer via a cable, letting the snoop programs evaluate the device. While they worked, Lila stepped into the bathtub. As the water poured over her, she smeared herself with a thick layer of apple-scented soap.

La Roux was the Baron after all. He'd fucked her merely to bug her bedroom and gain access to her computer. She'd been nothing more than a tool.

Lila was getting sick of feeling like that.

She had invited the man to her room so she could sneak a peek at his palm, but she wouldn't have slept with him for it. She wouldn't have pretended an interest she didn't have.

Lila lathered herself again, her skin turning pink as she scrubbed harder and harder. How had La Roux even managed to hack BullNet? He was a senator. Where had he learned the skills to penetrate government servers?

The answer came quickly. His matron was a Masson. He must have received a different sort of education among his kinsmen, one unlike the senators of Bullstow. And as a Masson, he'd had access to Xavier Masson's ID, likely taken on a visit to the family compound.

He'd stolen from a dead boy, his own cousin nonetheless.

Lila thought back to the files on her desktop. Luckily, she'd encrypted all of them. She'd also hidden the most important files on star drives, placing them in her desk's secret compartments. They were safe there, far safer than in her computer. You had to know where the compartments were to find the seams. You also had to know how to open them, else you'd end up frustrated, with sore fingers and bloody nails. And even if La Roux had managed to break into the desk and find the drives, he'd still have to unencrypt them.

Lila rinsed off and hopped out of the shower, donning little more than an old militia t-shirt and a fluffy robe. She quickly worked her way through the desk's compartments, finding that all her star drives were still secure.

As she replaced the last compartment, the results from her snoop programs flashed onto her screen. La Roux hadn't gotten far in his infiltration, but he'd left behind a tangle of snoop programs.

A window popped up, prompting Lila to delete them, offering to restore her computer to what it had been the night before.

Lila hit cancel and yanked the cable from her palm. He'd not hacked into it at all. He'd merely snuck a GPS sensor and an audio bug inside the casing.

She drummed her fingers on her desk, unsure how to use the sabotage to her advantage.

She'd figure something out on the way to the security office.

Lila hopped up and ventured to her closet. Now that she knew that La Roux was the Baron, her job had become much simpler. She couldn't believe that he had used his childhood nickname as an ID, but people often made such stupid mistakes.

Like sleeping with people when you should have known better.

Gods, everything he'd said the night before had likely been a lie.

She opened her closet, and a string of curses flooded from her mouth. As predicted, the insufferable, tartan-clad idiot from the night before had cleared out her entire closet. Every militia uniform had been tossed out, and a sea of monochromatic crimson surrounded her.

Lila fetched a pair of black trousers from her hidden compartment and added a crimson sweater and her old crimson woolen coat, clothes she might have worn a month before. Then she donned a pair of new boots, snatched up her palm, and bound her damp hair in a twist.

She gave a last glance to her abandoned wine glass. Biting her lip, she poured the dregs into a small vial and snapped the lid closed.

She'd walk the sample over to the security office, assassin be damned. She had more important things to do than remain locked inside the great house.

Shoving her Colt into her coat pocket, she fled from the room.

At the top of the stairs, she ducked behind a door as she spied Alex pacing along the base of the staircase, a duster poised in her hand. Waiting to be paged, waiting to be intercepted, waiting to hear Lila recount every detail from the night before.

Lila waited too.

The front door quietly chimed a few moments later.

The slave retreated.

Lila darted from her hiding spot, sneaking through the empty kitchen and into the scullery.

Exiting through the back of the great house, Lila avoided the patrols and jogged toward the security office. The fog hung so thick that she could barely make out the buildings on the street. She tied her coat more tightly, longing for the warmth of her blackcoat, so thick that the chill would not have touched her.

But the privilege of wearing her blackcoat had been taken away. She'd never be allowed to wear it again outside of her own bedroom.

Shoving open the still-broken metal door, she marched into the security office. As it was a couple of hours after shift change, few people scrambled about. She nodded to the man at the front desk and rode the elevator to her office, nodding to the receptionist, who had just poured cream into her morning coffee.

The pair exchanged brisk nods.

Sergeant Jenkins sat at his desk as she entered his office, already tackling a pile of work. He looked up at her in confusion and annoyance, then opened his mouth to speak.

"Sergeant Jenkins, I'll be in my office all morning. I'm not to be disturbed, do you hear me? No calls. No visitors. No interruptions. No exceptions."

"Yes, madam," he said, raising an eyebrow.

Lila shook her head, and he did not say another word. "Fetch me at a quarter to twelve if I'm not gone already. I have a lunch appointment with the chairwoman at Wolf Tower. You know how she hates to be kept waiting."

"Yes, chief. As you wish."

Lila stalked passed his desk and entered her office, scrolling through several programs on her palm. She found La Roux's playlist from the night before and set it on an endless loop, placing it innocently in the cradle of her speakers.

Jazz filtered through the room, this time overshadowed by a husky, crooning singer. Lila snickered at what La Roux would find in the transcription file. Sometimes the programs became confused when sorting through lyrics. It usually turned the file into word soup.

If he did realize what she'd been listening to? He'd think she was besotted.

She closed her office door, returning to Sergeant Jenkins.

"As you were."

"What in the world was that about, chief? No calls? No visitors? And when have you ever wished me a good morning?"

"I wish you a good morning all the time."

"No, you don't. You hate mornings. They're all bad to you. Good afternoon, yes. Good evening, yes. Good morning? Not on—"

"I'm dangling bait. Don't go into my office, and don't let anyone else in, either."

Jenkins nodded, eyes twinkling with confused mischief.

Gods, if she had to go to Wolf Tower, she'd take Jenkins with her.

"So the bait needs to stay put? If you recall, you were supposed to stay put, too."

"I'm armed."

"That's not going to help if the assassin—"

"I know, but I can't hide away. Not today." She jerked her chin at his computer. "Would you mind terribly if I commandeered your workstation for a few moments?"

"I could use a break."

"How about a mission? I need you to take a sample to the lab. Rush job, my eyes only. Tell the captain that her paperwork will be along shortly. After that, I need a new palm from the tech department, since mine is currently indisposed."

"Certainly, chief." Mr. Jenkins took the vial and slipped it into his pocket. Then he backed up his wheelchair and rolled around the desk, propelling himself forward with a quick, practiced shove on his wheels.

With no desk chair available, Lila knelt on the floor and placed a call to Falcon Home, sitting back on her heels, knowing her knees would not be happy when she stood up.

Her father's face appeared on the screen, VR glasses perched on his nose. A plate of half-eaten scrambled eggs sat before his place at the dinner table. "Lila girl, I saw your name and I just assumed." He chuckled, taking the glasses off. "Where are you?"

"At Sergeant Jenkins's desk. I sent him on an errand."

"You're at work? Are we playing games this morning?"

"Perhaps."

"I heard you went home with Senator La Roux last night even before I arrived at the ball." He leaned back in his chair, elbows propped on both armrests. He cocked his head to the side as he considered her reaction.

"How many told you?"

"All of them. Then more people called me after Marie and I came back to Falcon Home. You picked well, I suppose. Senator La Roux has potential, though he's a bit old to be stuck in a city senate."

"He's twenty-five, and Beaulac is only one step below New Bristol."

"It's still one step below. He's not working hard enough if he's still in Beaulac at his age."

"Is that all you have against him?"

"His eyes are weird. They're the color of snot. I'm torn between feeling glad that the fool is not anywhere near you and irritated that he left you alone so early in the morning. Why in the world would he do that? What possible excuse could the boy have?"

"The boy? A moment ago he was old. He had work, Father."

"Work? What sort of work could possibly be more important than his lover's bed?"

"A minute ago he was lazy for being stuck in Beaulac, now he's too focused on work?"

Lemaire shrugged.

"Father, do you really want to talk about Senator La Roux right now?"

"No, not in the slightest."

She smiled at his grumpiness, not wanting to spoil his fun for a few more hours, not wanting to talk about the asshole in that way again. "This might make you happier. I've found that spider you sent me to find a month ago."

Lemaire sat up. "That's good. It's a weight off my shoulders. The chief's too."

"Yes, well, the chief and I will speak very soon. I just need time to do a little more research. Don't message my palm. It's bugged. I'll send you details for my temp palm soon."

Her father frowned, clearly not happy at that development.

"I know what you're going to say, but I'm leaving it for now. I might be able to turn it to my advantage, perhaps more than I already have."

It was that thought that forced Lila to wonder again about La Roux's palm. Everything on it must have been bait, carefully designed to put her at ease, just like his words.

Just like Dubois's introduction, no doubt. She wondered again if La Roux had partnered with his cousin, if Dubois knew his cousin's true nature.

She'd thought Patrick Wilson was a pretty fool once. Perhaps Dubois had tricked her too.

Perhaps he wasn't ready to let go of his career.

Lemaire rubbed his nose and sighed. "You really are playing games, aren't you?"

"Yes, Father. Yes, I am."

# 22

Lila powered down her laptop and slipped it into her satchel, glad that Pax was too busy at Randolph General to question why she'd spent her entire morning working in the converted nursery. After she'd returned from the security office, she'd eaten breakfast at his book-laden table and dug through piles of data, receiving quite a few confused looks from Isabel and Alex.

Luckily, Jewel and her mother had left for Wolf Tower before anyone could tell them of her strange behavior.

At eleven, Lila hopped up from Pax's massive leather chair and ventured into her bedroom. She quietly dressed and hid her laptop in her closet's secret compartment, exchanging her black trousers for crimson ones and a matching red leather coat. Though overly fussy, it brushed her calves and mimicked the cut of her blackcoat. As she twirled in the mirror, she knew she'd have several more made up in white when she took over as prime. It seemed like such a small thing, but she welcomed the familiar pull of so much leather. Perhaps she needed it.

The boots she'd been wearing all morning suited her too. They were comfortable and practical. With only a slight heel, she nearly felt like she had donned her militia boots for the day, gone to patrol in some far-off section of the estate. The only thing that annoyed her was that she hadn't been able to slip her boot knife inside.

That would have to be amended. It wasn't just the lack of a boot knife that bothered her; she felt naked without the weight of her Colt on her hip, without her short sword wobbling on the other. She still owned them, but she wouldn't be allowed to wear them as heir, not even on the family estate. It wasn't illegal for non-militia members to carry weapons; it was just unseemly for an heir to do so, even to defend her own life.

After all, there were blackcoats for that.

Perhaps that would be her first act of rebellion. Fuck tradition. Too many people wanted her dead lately to go around without a weapon, and one of them was still on the loose.

Lila put that thought out of her mind as she left her room and jogged downstairs. Brushing past a young footman, she marched from the great house.

Near the wolf fountain, Sergeant Jenkins popped wheelies, his plastic front wheels clacking against the drive whenever he landed. He had a little black box in his lap, the size of a pair of shoes.

Jenkins winked as she approached and held out the box. Lila lifted the lid and fished out her bugged palm from the folds of a militia t-shirt.

*Thank you*, she mouthed.

*Lunch?* he mouthed back, his stomach grumbling so loudly that La Roux likely heard it on the other end.

She flicked a thumb toward the great house and returned the box. *Stuff your face.*

Grinning, Jenkins sprinted to the front door, his wheels carrying him away loudly on the stone. Chef had promised to feed Lila's admin well for his troubles, not that she would know what those troubles were exactly.

Turning away, Lila marched along the gravel path toward the north gate, nodding to a militia patrol who broke away from the great house to follow her. She increased her pace, not to lose them, but so that she would not be late for Wolf Tower. She didn't rush for her mother, though, for her matron had no idea that she'd be coming. She rushed for whomever La Roux would send to intercept her.

She had a pretty good idea who it would be.

Sliding her tainted palm into her pocket, she stopped before the mirrored skyscraper in the center of the estate, which rose forty-five stories into sky and dwarfed all other structures on the compound. Most people considered Wolf Tower imposing, with its jagged angles, mirrored sides, and steel beams that crisscrossed in sharp triangles up and down the structure.

Perhaps it was imposing, at least from the outside.

Lila opened the door and slipped inside. The warm interior had little in common with the exterior. Thick woolen rugs dyed to match the family's colors dotted the smoked oak floors. Lush green plants lined the side of every staircase and covered whole walls, filtering the air, providing a bit of calming greenery as though a garden had been cut from the world and nailed to the wall. Priceless works of abstract art hung in each room. Very little light was needed, for sunlight streamed through the glass walls.

Here and there members of the Randolph family, as well as some highly paid and contracted workborn, bustled throughout the building, dressed in crimson finery that crossed from formal business attire into fashion. There was no such thing as casual dress in a Randolph office building, much less the main tower.

As it was the Saturday after the senate's Closing Ball, attendance was sparse. Many highborn had likely not gotten out of bed yet, still tired from the night's activities. Lila's mother, on the other hand, would have been in her office by ten o'clock. She'd leave at six for dinner, returning for a few more hours before bed.

Six days a week and a half-day on Sunday.

That would be her life in a few days.

Leaning on the front desk, she smiled at the receptionist, Mr. Fitzgerald, who was engaged in redirecting a call on his computer. He nodded pleasantly to acknowledge her presence, but his eyes popped wide as soon as recognition hit. Shaking fingers hopped to the keyboard in his haste to pause the call, but Lila merely gestured for him to finish his work.

Before he could even end his conversation, the front doors to the building opened. Two blackcoats marched across the foyer, uniforms a collection of black and burgundy piping. Golden roses

had been stitched upon their chests, and empty holsters protruded
from their hips, tranq guns absent, short swords missing.

The Randolph militia had not escorted the pair inside.

"Inform Chairwoman Randolph that we need to speak with her,"
the first officer drawled with his highborn accent, ignoring the fact
that the receptionist was busy with a call. The man's deep voice
matched the body that went along with it. He had not bothered
to shave that morning. His silent colleague was slight of stature,
though equal to his partner's bearing.

Neither man betrayed any hint as to the reason for their visit.

"Actually, Mr. Fitzgerald, I will take care of them myself," Lila
said. "Send someone into the Red Lounge with a pot of chocolate
at your first opportunity."

The receptionist bobbed in his seat.

Lila led the two officers through a long hallway and ushered
them into a room that had been painted in Randolph red. It
was as though the designer had dipped it straight into the paint
bucket, shook it out, and shoved it deep inside the building away
from the windows. The little crimson couch and plush sofa chairs
inside matched the walls exactly, and had been cut several years
out of fashion, with frayed cushions and a few missing buttons.
The coffee table was missing a leg, but its designer had ensured the
family that it would remain perfectly balanced up to two hundred
kilograms. The room looked so shabby that most any highborn
would deem it an insult to step inside.

The Red Lounge had been designed to provoke such feelings.

Lila sat upon the couch and gestured for the men to sit on
the chairs across from her. Sergeant Muller, clearly the superior,
withdrew his palm and set it on the three-legged coffee table,
studying it uneasily.

"I am the chief of security for Wolf Industries," Lila told the men
as a slave entered in crimson breeches and a matching coat. A pot
of hot chocolate perched on a tray at his shoulder. He poured it
into china and served her guests. Lila did not reach for her own

cup. The hot chocolate served inside the Red Lounge would be thin, cheap, and cold.

The slave bowed his way out of the room.

"We are well aware of you who you are, Chief Randolph," Muller said curtly, and winced as he sipped the cold chocolate. He put down his cup, eyeing his partner, who did the same. "It's lucky we caught you en route to see your mother. You're much more suited to answering our questions than she is. I'm Muller. This is Davies."

"Good afternoon, Sergeant Muller and Sergeant Davies." Lila's eyes flicked to the lone star on each of their collars. "Is there something specifically that I could do for you today? Are you here about the logins? If so, you are wasting your time. I have not changed my mind, and this is borderline harassment."

"You are aware that we are recording?"

"Yes. I'm fine with it if you are."

Muller nearly picked up his hot chocolate again, then awkwardly slid back on the crimson sofa chair. "Very good, then. We've come by to ask you a few questions about your whereabouts two days ago."

"Two days ago?" Lila asked, crossing her legs. "Is this about Shiloh?"

"No, madam, it is not. Your whereabouts?"

"I visited my father."

"Do you mind if I ask what sort of visit you had, when you arrived, and what time you left the prime minister's presence?"

"Yes, I do, actually."

"Are you refusing to cooperate?"

"Are you refusing to tell me what you're really doing here?"

"We're here to search your property, your living quarters, and your offices, including every computer you've had access to in the last week, as well as your network log."

Lila forced a smile. "You thought that you could just waltz inside my home without a warrant and ask for such a thing?"

"Are you refusing?"

"Most people would."

"It's no matter. The warrant is coming," Sergeant Davies said. "We will begin in your living quarters, if you would care to lead the way."

"I would care." Lila intertwined her fingers in her lap, refusing to stand. "I will see the warrant first."

"You know how this works, chief. We do not need a physical copy of the warrant with us when we begin our search. It will come through on our palms before we are done."

The blackcoats stood. Muller gestured toward the door. "If you will lead the way? I'd hate to call for backup. If I had to arrest you, the media would have time to gather. Your story would probably kick the Holguín's scandal off the front page of the *New Bristol Times*."

Lila pulled out her tainted palm. "Tell me the case number for this investigation. I'll need to verify that much before I lead you around the compound."

"Your living quarters, chief, before we are forced to call Bullstow and make your life more difficult."

Lila did not move. "No, you should stop this ridiculous charade before I make *your* life more difficult. If you actually had a legal warrant, or if you were in the process of getting one, you would have brought more of your little friends to do the grunt work."

"How many men does it take to search a few rooms?"

Davies scowled at his partner. "How do you like that? We try to save her family from scandal, and she threatens us."

"Let me save *your* family from scandal, Sergeant Davies, for your family can hardly afford it right now. You have no warrant to search anything at all on the premises. It has been a very nice chat and very informative, but I must regretfully take my leave, as should you. The chairwoman is expecting me for lunch."

She straightened her coat and opened the door, motioning for them to exit, her grip tight upon the doorknob.

The men did not budge.

"Chief Randolph, are you declining your right to be present when your property is searched?" Muller asked. "We do not need you to be present. It's only a courtesy, after all."

"You should leave now, *Sergeant* Muller and *Sergeant* Davies. We both know what will happen if you do not." Anger boiled within her, perhaps too hot to keep back. She might have hung above a firepit with only a thin violin string to keep her from the conflagration below.

Muller locked gazes with Lila.

He looked away seconds later, his shoulders falling slightly.

"Muller?" Davies interrupted, annoyed by his partner's paralysis. "Take us to your office, Chief Randolph. Now."

His command and his grating voice pushed her too far.

The violin string snapped.

Slamming the door of the Red Lounge, Lila stalked to Sergeant Davies. "Did you even notice the sign above the reception desk? *Visitors should have no expectation of privacy within this building.* You gave your consent to both audio and video surveillance by continuing past the reception desk. Every room in this building is wired for it, including this one."

"Even if that's true, signs like that don't always hold up in court."

"No, occasionally, the courts are fussy, but you both agreed to the recording at the very beginning of this little charade. I think it will suffice."

"So?"

"Let me make this abundantly clear, you dim little boy. You are caught out, and your partner has been around long enough to know when someone's not bluffing. You should both be ashamed of yourselves, if not for your distinct lack of morals, then for your flaming ineptitude. If I take this tape to your superiors, do you think you'll have a career afterward?"

"We have done nothing wrong. We're just having a chat."

"A chat without identifying yourself as officers? You left off your titles when you introduced yourselves. You also neglected to bring your badges and guns to this little meeting. I've read the Bullstow militia guidelines, you idiots. They aren't so very different from our own. You can't have a tranq or your badge on your person unless you're on duty, but it's not your fault if someone doesn't realize that. You've been speaking to me as if you're on the job this entire time. It's sneaky, but I've seen that trick many times before, and I've seen it done much better."

Davies shrugged. "It's not our fault if you took something we said as—"

"Asking questions off duty without having a case number is one thing, but lying about having a warrant is in a different league altogether. You'll lose your badges, and you know it. Someone must have claimed I had something pretty damning in my possession to even try it. Someone you trusted not to steer you wrong. Someone not in the militia, since you wouldn't be able to use the evidence in court due to how you obtained it. I wonder who that could be?" Lila crossed her arms over her chest and stared at them expectantly.

"We're going to find out what you've done. Whether you take us before the captain or—"

"Your captain?" Lila chuckled. "Do you honestly think I would bother talking to him when I have the ear of your chief? I suppose your captain is on the payroll, too?"

Muller's eyes tracked to his partner.

"Someone picked you, claiming they were digging for evidence against the Randolph family. Did they claim the case would revitalize your partner's stalled career? Did they say it would make up for that nasty wreck you had after all those beers at dinner? I did my research long before you stopped by. I know your recent difficulties. All you had to do to make it all go away was play-act a little. Poke at me so that I would think that Bullstow had an ongoing case. Eventually, you'd get the evidence, or so your puppet master claimed. But he's either burned you before, or you decided to be clever this time. I'm not sure who is dumber, your master for trusting you so much or the pair of you for trying to double-cross him. I suppose you thought you had an out. If you were brought up on charges, then you'd simply hand over the evidence to your matrons, returning to your families as heroes. It must have sounded like a brilliant plan when you thought of it. Were you drunk at the time?"

Muller bit the side of his cheek, and Lila knew the answer. They didn't even have that excuse to fall back on.

"I suppose you thought that whatever evidence you found would make up for being cast out of Bullstow, but you didn't understand that you were being used. There's nothing here but one highborn batting at another, and you fell for it. You're nothing more than a cat's paw, spent in a game that you are not even a part of."

Davies's face twisted at the slight.

"I'm guessing that your lunch break will end soon, gentlemen, and you'll need to get back to work. The next time you come to this estate, make sure that you have a case number and Bullstow's blessing before you try to question me, or I'll have you both fired for gross stupidity and brought up on charges. I still might. Perhaps it will be the Park family who will kick the Holguíns off the front page."

Davies lunged.

His partner tugged him back.

Lila stepped away from the men, disguising her shock as best she could. "I would have expected nothing less from a man parading in his betters' clothes."

"We'll be in touch," Sergeant Muller said, all bravado deflated from his body. He pulled the still-fuming Davies from the room.

Lila sent a message to Chief Shaw on her tainted palm, knowing he would reply in the affirmative to anything she sent him, exactly as she'd directed him to do after she'd called her father. *Let us have lunch tomorrow. I have something to discuss.*

Let the Baron chew on that.

# 23

Leaves crinkled under Lila's boots as she marched down the gravel trail through the estate. The smell of damp leaves filled her nose, and the roses on either side of the path bowed in the wind. Even at half past twelve, fog still slipped around the buildings, obscuring much of the world around her. The people on the compound seemed nothing more than little bursts of red.

Lila entered the security office and abandoned the tainted palm on her desk before crossing into Sutton's office. The commander had never gotten around to decorating, choosing instead to let Lila's interior designer give her office the same treatment. The only difference was that Sutton had a dozen framed pictures of her husband, children, and grandchildren spread out along the tops of several filing cabinets. She'd also clogged every outlet in the room with electric scent diffusers. Sutton pipped in a new scent every day.

Today, the room smelled of vanilla.

"I trust our friends from Bullstow have been escorted out?" Lila said, after a curt hello.

"Yes, madam, though I do not understand why you wished to let them inside at all. Their paperwork was sketchy at best."

"It was in the best interests of the family. Where was our militia? I didn't see an escort."

"You've grown soft after your vacation. I had them stationed along the route in plain clothes."

"Clever. I had not thought of that."

"It's nice that I can still impress you from time to time."

"It's why I made you the new chief. So few do."

Sutton inclined her head at the compliment. "Should I contact you if they call back?"

"Trust me. They won't. Chief Shaw will be contacting you instead. You are to follow his instructions, whatever they are."

"Bullstow, madam?" Sutton asked in surprise. "I thought we were done with them."

"We're never done with Bullstow." Lila sighed as she left the commander's office.

She retrieved her tainted palm, then started back across the compound, immediately putting Muller and Davies out of her mind. She had parried La Roux's first attack, but she was not sure what his counter would be.

Lila had other pieces in play, though.

When she entered the great house moments later, she asked Isabel to bring up a plate of sandwiches and fruit as she "had been put off her lunch." She hoped the flimsy excuse was enough for La Roux. She had left Wolf Tower immediately after seeing the militia out, not pausing in her duties to have lunch with her mother. It was not as if the chairwoman had been expecting her, but she would have certainly found out that the Bullstow militia had been in Wolf Tower.

Lila was not looking forward to that conversation.

She nibbled on a sandwich in the study room, wishing she'd been able to plant a bug on Muller or Davies or in the men's cruiser. Such an act would be for entertainment, rather than for information, though. La Roux had likely been listening in on their interrogation, and he would have seen her text to Shaw. He wouldn't risk exposing himself by contacting them again soon.

Alex tried to engage her in conversation when she came to take her meal away, but Lila shrugged her off, eschewing all details from the previous night. "I know why you're so grumpy," the slave whispered slyly. "You think that horrible woman came by last night and took away all your clothes, but you're wrong."

Alex put her finger up to her mouth and backed out of the room. She emerged several moments later, struggling under the weight of two trash bags. "I offered to help, you see. Actually, I offered to do it for her. I even offered to burn all these horribly unfashionable rags. At least, that's what she called them. The woman was overjoyed to have a slave do her bidding for the evening."

Lila leapt from Pax's chair and hugged Alex harder than she ever had before. The scent of honeysuckle and her friend's arms overwhelmed her.

"You're the best," she said, kneeling over the bags, stroking all her old things, unsure where she'd put them. She couldn't exactly hang them in her closet, for Isabel or Ms. O'Malley would notice, and she had no more space in her secret compartment.

Alex bowed, then took the tray of sandwiches and scampered away.

Lila took a break from scheming and dragged the bags into her room. Unsure what else to do, she hung her uniformed blackcoats in the closet and folded the rest of her clothes, hiding most of them in her fairly empty dresser.

She then changed into a pair of trousers and a militia tank, the same clothes that she usually wore for combat training, the same clothes that had excited Tristan so often. Now that she was dressed comfortably, she returned to the study room and spent the rest of the afternoon on her spare laptop, struggling to tie La Roux and the Baron together.

She also dug into the people he'd trapped within his web, finding more compromised heirs and senators. It was no wonder she'd never found much evidence against Reaper. There was little to find. Reaper had never been the brains behind the operation. As she'd suspected, he was just a hacker La Roux had caught and bent to his will, forcing the man to turn against his clients.

How many highborn had La Roux compromised over the years through people like Reaper? How many had he fed false information? How many ears did he whisper helpful advice into, advice that might have been heeded time and time again, as he'd done with Celeste and Patrick Wilson? How many cat's paws did La Roux have among the heirs and the senate, using favors piled upon favors, layered under a blanket of blackmail to advance his career?

Was that how La Roux had been elected to Beaulac in the first place?

Was that how Dubois had stayed in New Bristol for so long?

Were they partners or not?

After several hours of combing through all the data, she couldn't put Dubois and La Roux together, at least not financially. It was a relief. She enjoyed her future brother-in-law too much to think of him as a criminal.

Her temp palm vibrated. *You were right. I found a mild sedative in the wine.*

Her lab director's words turned her stomach.

The asshole had drugged her.

A knock sounded upon the door.

"Come in."

Alex, in her great house maid uniform, had dressed better for the evening. She took one look at Lila and her mouth hung open. "You can't meet the senator like that for dinner! What are you thinking? He's downstairs right now. I didn't intend for you to actually wear those clothes I rescued, not at a time like this."

"Now is the best time for it," Lila said, powering down her laptop. "Bring him up. I'll be in my room."

Alex stamped her foot, her heel loud against the wooden floor. "Do you want this man for the season or not?"

Lila shrugged and slid her laptop into her satchel. "I told you that no man is going to fuck me because of the clothes I'm wearing. Perhaps we shall skip dinner tonight. Why bother getting into clothes that I'll take off again ten minutes later?"

Alex faltered. She rushed into Lila's room and returned a second later with the silken red robe, the same robe Lila had taunted La Roux with that morning. "Put this on then when you meet him, then. It's beautiful."

Lila merely shook her head and hitched the satchel's strap onto her shoulder.

"You look like you're ready for battle," her friend said as she followed Lila into the bedroom.

"Please, Ms. Wilson, go fetch Senator La Roux."

Alex hung the robe on a peg in the bathroom, then slipped from the room.

Moments later, Alex returned with wine glasses and Senator La Roux, who clutched a bottle of Sangre in a silk burgundy bag, tied with a golden ribbon. His hair cascaded down his back. His suit coat and rose-pink shirt were effortlessly formal, as though he had put them on five minutes before leaving Bullstow and they just happened to suit their plans. Now that it was between sessions, he no longer had to wear the colors of his city senate.

If he wished to censure Lila about her casual attire, he did not show it.

Her stomach turned at the thought of him drugging her, fucking her, and planning to use her for his own ends.

Tristan never would have done that.

"Would you like dinner brought up, madam?"

"We'll let you know."

Alex bowed and turned away, the uncertain frown still upon her face.

The door closed softly behind her.

"Senator La Roux," Lila began. She kissed his cheek as he bent over the desk to greet her, avoiding his lips. "It's good to see you again."

"Likewise." He grinned warmly, uncorking the wine with a loud pop. "Thanks for sending a car for me, by the way. It was a nice surprise."

"I merely assumed. Many senators don't have their own."

"Don't think too highly of us. Most senators drive a lover's car whenever they can." La Roux poured wine into the two glasses. "My cousin enjoys riding your sister's Firefly immensely."

"That he does."

He put a glass before Lila and leaned against her desk. "I hope you don't think this is too forward, but I must admit that I've been thinking about you all day. I never should have left you this morning."

"I spent most of my day thinking about you as well."

The senator took her words as a positive sign. He circled the desk like a lazy cat and leaned over her chair, his fingers light as he began to massage her shoulders. "I have no plans for the season. Is that why you wanted me to stay this morning? So that we could talk about spending the next few months together?"

"That's a little presumptuous, don't you think, senator?"

"Dorian."

"Senator."

La Roux's fingers stilled. "I could make you very happy this winter. We might not be a love match like my cousin and your sister, but there are other sorts of matches. Sexual matches. We had fun, didn't we? Don't tell me you didn't enjoy it. I saw your face. I heard your moans."

Lila's stomach rolled as she remembered how much she had enjoyed him, knowing what he must have been thinking while he fucked her. He'd probably had his eyes on her room the entire time, wondering where he would plant his bugs.

She had cast Tristan away for this man.

That wasn't right, was it? She had cast Tristan away for her family. She had cast him away for duty. Senator La Roux had merely been on the agenda for the day.

Besides, Tristan had cast himself away long before she ever met the senator.

"Is that what you're used to? Have the lowborn women you've bedded been so eager to produce an heir from a pretty senator that they engaged you for the season after one night, hardly bothering to talk between all the rutting?"

La Roux slipped a finger underneath the strap of her militia tank and tugged it down. His soft finger trailed across her naked shoulder. "Are these your talking clothes?"

Lila shivered and knocked his hand away.

"What? I thought you liked bluntness?" He sat upon her desk, facing her once more, but his amusement did not reach his eyes tonight. Clearly, she had flummoxed him.

At least she had that going for her.

"Tell me about your day," she said.

La Roux seemed amused by her question, though annoyance had begun to bubble under it. He methodically listed his activities, from how he had woken up in her agreeable company, to staying in his room at Bullstow all morning while closing out his files, to enjoying a long lunch with a group of senators from Beaulac while they discussed a few bills for the next legislative session. Afterward, he had engaged in another battle against his office files before getting ready for dinner with Lila.

She heard the words but didn't listen to them. Instead she studied the way his eyes washed over hers when he lied, then away when he told the truth. The way his fingers alternately tapped or stilled upon her desk. The way he shifted underneath his suit coat.

"In point of fact, my day was rather boring. I'm sorry that I had to leave you this morning. I would have rather stayed in bed with you all afternoon. Tell me, what did Chief Elizabeth Victoria Lemaire-Randolph do with her day?"

His smile was a little too broad and proud.

She chuckled at the use of her full name, though it sounded forced even to her own ears. "I worked at the security office this morning, then returned to my room after lunch to organize my own files. I had so many that it quite overwhelmed me. In the end, I just wiped my computer. I'll tell everyone my hard drive crashed."

La Roux nearly choked on the wine.

"I also had a very interesting visit from the Bullstow militia. They seemed to be investigating some sort of disturbance at Bullstow a few days ago."

"Is that so. Why would they come to you about it?"

"No idea. Did you hear of anything that might have happened on Wednesday?"

La Roux shook his head. "I didn't even return from Beaulac until yesterday morning."

"Oh, that's right, isn't it? I know this might surprise you, being from Bullstow yourself, but not all men from Bullstow are ethical. The militia lied to my face. Sometimes men betray their calling when they think they can get away with it."

"Women, too."

"Yes, of course. Don't look so upset, senator. I'm not that worried about it. I'm rather good at reading people. I suppose it's a gift from the prime minister or my mother."

"What did you learn from the militia?"

"That they had no idea why they'd been sent. Someone used them to prod a hornets' nest and see what might come out."

La Roux's lips twitched just a fraction.

It was that split second of pride that did it, the proof of how much he was enjoying himself, the idea that he considered it a game. She no longer cared how far he fell. In fact, she wanted to be the one who pushed him.

"Who sent them, Lila?" La Roux asked, putting down his wine glass. When she did not immediately respond, he crossed his arms over his chest and studied her face.

"You know, senator, I really don't like it when people play on my computer without permission. Your first night in my bedroom? Really? How crass can you be?"

"I don't know what you're talking about."

"Liar," she said lazily.

La Roux considered her, and all at once, as if a string had been cut away from the top of his head, his entire demeanor relaxed. "I wanted confirmation of some suspicions that I had. I wasn't sure that I'd get another night with you, so I acted while you slept."

"While I slept off the drugs you slipped me. Was it worth it? Did you get the confirmation you wanted?"

The senator drained his glass. "You bet your sweet ass I did. You've been a naughty girl. I had no idea Wolf Industries was so corrupt, and I've barely read through one percent of the files I pulled from your computer. It doesn't matter that you've deleted them. I have copies."

"Is that so?"

"Yes. Your snoop programs show promise, but they're quite crude. It only took me two hours to crack the password with my own programs. You should know better than to use simple encryption. I suppose you got lazy."

"You've been running the files? Studying them?"

"Of course I have. All day." He poured himself another glass of wine, then stood up and moved to the window, gazing out at his new kingdom. "We should talk after dinner about my future in the Saxony Senate. We're going to have a very busy season together."

"Is that so?"

"It's just the start, *President* Randolph. We'll talk more after I seed your heir, after I see if we are as good together as I believe. Do you know how rare we are, madam? Technologically advanced above the highborn masses? Willing and capable of playing them like a drum and fife? You even share certain sympathies with the poorer classes that I do. I've reviewed your votes in the High Council, and I must say that I agreed with most of your judgments. I just never thought you'd be so eager in bed."

"What if I say no to the season?"

"You won't," he said, turning away from the window. "If you say no, I turn everything I have over to Bullstow. I should warn you that I lifted quite a bit from your computer."

The corner of his mouth twisted into a lecherous grin. "It's all worked out much better than I dreamed. You're an intelligent, ambitious woman. Quite my match, I'd say, and for more than just the season. We're going to do wonderful things together, Lila."

He strolled to the desk and kissed her cheek.

# 24

Lila rubbed the wetness away, then crossed her boots on top of her desk. "That's your plan?"

"Yes." La Roux rescued the bottle of Sangre, which threatened to fall onto the floor, and set it on her bedside table.

"You know, senator, I'm surprised that you'd stoop to coupling with such a corrupt family and that you'd force me to take you for the season."

"You weren't complaining about the pairing last night. And as for your family's corruption, I shall make up for it with every piece of legislation that crosses my desk. But I cannot do that unless I am at the capitol. The Saxon Senate needs me. None of those men will do what is just. They're too busy bowing and preening for the heirs."

"So you posit that caring about your job will make up for the manner in which you obtained it? You've stained the honor of Bullstow, but you believe that everything washes in the end?"

"I have been a force for good in the senate. I have passed fair and just laws that benefited everyone, not just the rich, and I've taken no bribes that favored them."

"Is that so, Baron?"

He stiffened. His eyes shot to hers. "What did you call me?"

"Baron," she said, drawing out each syllable. "You shouldn't use childhood nicknames when creating fake IDs, senator, certainly not if you're going to snoop in BullNet. Can you believe I thought someone had set you up because it was such a stupid mistake? I was prepared to rush in and save you from some corrupt matron or heir. Perhaps you should have gone with something bland, like sexysenator or isuckathis69. It's disappointing, really."

"I have no idea what you're talking about."

"You keep silent, and yet you want to be partners?" Lila tsked. "You know, I still don't understand how Reaper hacked my Prolix ID so quickly. It's bugged me for weeks."

"Reaper?" La Roux scoffed, his annoyance overcoming his wariness. "Reaper couldn't have found his dick in the dark. I figured out who you were a few hours after the BIRD break-in. It wasn't the login that did you in. It was a camera outside a lowborn shop near the senate."

"There was no footage that day. All the cameras had been taken out."

"I didn't need that day's footage. I needed a few days before. Senator Dubois has a picture of your family on his desk. I know your face, and you weren't window shopping."

"So you put me and Prolix together."

"I tasked Reaper with hacking your fake ID. I needed the proof, but other work kept me busy. Of course, Reaper bugged me every few hours when he got stuck, but I helped him get there in the end."

"He posted the article to let you know he was done. That's how he communicated with you. Clever. Then you asked me for one hundred thousand credits in exchange for your silence. Why?"

La Roux leaned into her face. She smelled the wine on his breath. "An unexpected expense came up."

"You sent my matron the information anyway."

"I was always going to do that no matter what. I needed you in a position to be useful. How could I win you if you were still wasting your life in the security office? I know what your mother did for Prime Minister Lemaire. I want the same done for me. I had a much more involved plan for getting into your trousers. Apparently, I didn't need it."

He cocked his head and tugged at her fly.

Lila batted his hand away. "Every senator would spit in your face if he knew what you've done. Every heir, too."

"That's big talk coming from a thief. You're the worst sort of hypocrite. I'm surrounded by them. Hypocrites and useless men. Has Senator Serrano done as much as I have for Saxony?"

"We're not talking about Senator Serrano. We're talking about you."

"We're not talking. We're negotiating terms."

Lila's stomach turned. The man was enjoying himself. "Why should I help you? Why shouldn't I call Chief Shaw right now and tell him what's in BullNet? The whole network is filled with your little traps."

"Because you don't want to go to the auction house. I have everything, Prolix, all your naughty little truths."

"So you've said. What is your end game? The senate?"

"Prime minister."

"What if I say no?"

"Then I will secure my place with another woman. It might take a little longer, but you weren't the only woman I had in play for this season. You heirs and primes aren't as rare and special as you think. If you say no to this arrangement, then I'll hand over my evidence to the media and find another. If you aren't hanged within the month, then you'll spend the rest of your life working as a slave in the mines. What will the chairwoman do without you to produce an heir? My cousin told me of his troubles this morning. What will your mother do when she learns that she'll have to produce another daughter so late in life or lose everything to her sisters after she retires? Which company does your Aunt Georgina run, again?"

"Spring. The wedding planning boutique. It brings in nine figures a year," Lila replied, feeling strangely protective of Georgina's record.

The senator chuckled and sat on the edge of her desk. "Well, I'm sure that she works very hard. I'm also sure that her work hasn't prepared her for running a monstrosity like Wolf Industries, though I've heard how tricky brides and grooms can be." He put down his glass and pushed Lila's hair back from her face. "Would you be so tricky on our day?"

Lila knocked his hand away.

"Come on, let's avoid any unpleasantness. The best deal for me is to seed an heir for the Randolph family. I'll be elevated to New Bristol next session, and I'll have a respected highborn family behind me. It's what you had planned before we had this conversation, isn't it? Retain me for the season and many seasons thereafter. I know I've impressed you. What do you think the last few weeks have been about? I've shown you that I'm more than a worthy match. We could be good together."

"You don't know me well enough to make that call. Besides, this morning I respected you more than I do now. I thought you knew how to play your hand. I have to say, I'm a little disappointed."

"Is that so?"

"Yes. For starters, I don't think you have any of my files at all."

"They're on my personal computer."

"What you took, Dorian, was a folder claiming to be from the security office. You weren't even on my private login, and you didn't have access to anything remotely important. I made it just difficult enough for someone to believe they'd bested my security. Someone impatient and impulsive. Trust me, little boy, I secure my information much better than that."

"You're lying."

"Those doctored files can easily be proven false with the simplest of searches, which you obviously neglected to perform. You must not have gotten too far into them, either, otherwise you would have had the pleasure of reading quite a number of badly written erotica novels I pulled off the net years ago. Hot sex scenes, but fairly sparse in the plot. Kind of like you, come to think of it. It's a test I devised a very long time ago for those who have access to my room and my computer. I haven't even updated the files since last year. I suppose you didn't notice."

His superior grin faded.

"I'd tell you to go back and look at the files more carefully, but you also downloaded a handful of my very favorite viruses, including a Trojan horse inside my snoop programs." She snickered at his face, frozen and pale. "I can't believe you were dumb enough to run the damn thing before you tested it, much less fail to see its purpose. Not only do you not have any incriminating files left, Dorian, but you won't even have a computer the next time you boot up, just a very expensive paperweight."

"You're lying."

"No, I'm not. Again, I'm disappointed."

"I don't need what was on your computer. I have your trail, Prolix."

"Where? On your extra-crispy computer?"

"I can find it in the logs again."

"Can you? Are you sure the proof is there any longer?"

"You were with me all last night, and you didn't move from your compound all day. You didn't return to Bullstow."

"I wiped the trail that night, senator. There's nothing to find. You have nothing."

"I have plenty. You just confirmed that you broke into a government network and more." La Roux retreated into the center of the room. "Your entire room is bugged. I'm backing up—"

"Which bug in particular? The one behind my bedside table, the one under my desk, or the one on the coat of arms? Or perhaps the one in my palm? I crushed them all under my heel while you were waiting for mc downstairs. By the way, the one you planted in the bathroom was just poor form, Dorian. It's creepy. I've had to go across the hall all day. It's a good thing my brother has been at Randolph General, or I would have had to explain myself."

La Roux spun around Lila's room, his breaths coming in labored pants. After a long moment of silence, the disgraced senator spoke again. "I still know what you did. We have plenty of computer geniuses at Bullstow. Any number of them could find the data."

"Unlikely, but that's not the point. You don't get it, do you? You're talking to one now. Who do you think Prolix is? Some highborn hacker who uses the data she finds to get ahead? I wasn't a liar when I spoke to you the other night. I never wanted to be an heir. I've always felt a very different sort of responsibility to those who work and live on this estate, to those who live in New Bristol and Saxony. My father has been nurturing those feelings since I was a child, and when he became prime minister, he recognized me as a resource and used me. I never sought out information for myself or for my family, I've only ever worked for Prime Minister Lemaire, and before that, Governor Lemaire. I'm good at what I do, which is why he hired me a month ago to find out who has been blackmailing hackers and the highborn."

"You say that as if they aren't criminals."

"Oh, they are deeply flawed," Lila agreed. "Just like you, netting highborn in your traps so you can blackmail them for cash and favors, just as you did with Celeste Wilson and her son. It angered the prime minister when he found evidence that highborns had broken into government databases, but what pissed him off the most was that someone was watching it happen and using that knowledge to profit."

"I was cleaning house."

"If you were cleaning house, then you would have turned those people into Bullstow immediately. You would have turned me into Chief Shaw the moment you caught me, but you didn't, did you? You wanted to play with me. You wanted to use me. Did you order Peter Kruger to kill me, too?"

La Roux shook his head. "Reaper ordered that without my knowledge, thinking he'd get rid of a loose end. The fool hacker almost cost me the greatest prize of all."

Lila drained her glass of wine. At least she hadn't slept with her potential assassin. "Aren't you noble?"

"I can't be held responsible for every decision my subordinates make."

"You didn't turn him in after he made that decision, did you?"

"You don't throw out a hammer because you smashed your thumb. He was too valuable for that. I'm not a killer, Lila."

"No, you just steal from dead children."

La Roux looked away.

"What about Senator Dubois? What's his part in all this?"

"Louis? You think I need his help? How do you think he's kept his place for so many years? Because he's your sister's pet? You heirs are so arrogant, so blind to Bullstow's games. I kept him there. Me."

"I bet he's been oh so accommodating."

"He doesn't even know. You give him too much credit. He never would have made it to the Saxony High House without seeding an heir for your sister. That's the problem with the entire system. Men like Senator Serrano are promoted to places they are ill-equipped to handle, whereas men like me get stuck in the city senates."

"You faked his fertility results, then?"

"I didn't know he had a need."

"They said my morality was flexible." She kicked her feet off the desk. "Thanks for admitting you controlled Reaper, by the way."

"It doesn't matter what I admit. If you try to get the militia involved, then I'll go to the press. Everyone will demand your father's neck in a noose. Allowing an heir to infiltrate BullNet? Giving her a free pass into its systems? A hacker who will soon be prime to a major family? He'll be a disgrace! He'll be brought up on—"

"Charges? I suppose it's likely, but he's been prepared for that, as were all of us. You won't get out of your guilt by exposing us."

"I don't care. If I go down, everyone else goes down with me. Everyone!" He slammed his empty wine glass on her desk, nearly shattering it. "I knew I should never have touched you. You disgusted me, you know. Every moment last night when I—"

"Came?"

"I faked it. You meant nothing to me."

"Now, that's no way to talk. I'll be honest, I thought you were a beautiful man when I saw you at the Closing Ball. You're obviously intelligent, though ambitious and cocky and naïve to a fault. Misguided, certainly, but I was attracted to you before I knew who you were. That's where you erred, you know. You didn't bother to find out who you would be blackmailing when you targeted me. You found out a little information, like my wine preference and that I like to dance, but you learned nothing of importance, just enough to get me into bed. You certainly didn't learn enough about who I was to pull this off."

"Who are you, then?"

"Someone who cares about her family. Can I say the same about you? Do you love your children, Senator La Roux?"

"Of course I do."

"Did you ever stop to think about them?"

"Of course. I'm making the world better for them. Do you know how many votes I control in Beaulac? In Saxony? It's enough to pass whatever I like, as long as I don't get too greedy too often. The slave bills will pass, both of them, and I will be remembered forever as the one who brought freedom to the Allied Lands. Think of what else I'll pass by the end."

"Because you'll make the best decisions for everyone?"

"How is it any different than the dried-up hags in the councils ordering the country about, exchanging favor upon favor to keep the status quo, ordering their spies to dig into networks that should have been off-limits? This is the only way to make things change. It's not like anyone else is doing anything. No one ever makes the guilty pay, but I would make them pay for breaking into Bullstow. It's ours."

"That's where you are wrong. You're about to see very soon how the guilty pay for breaking into Bullstow. Firsthand. And now your children will suffer under your reputation. No matter what happens to my father and me, you will either be hanged or put into slavery for betraying your office. You're never going to see your children again."

La Roux's eyes darkened as they bored into her.

Lila couldn't resist one more knock. "That will be a good thing, since you have the morality and the logic of a fruit bat."

Those were the last words Lila said before La Roux lunged and clasped his hands around her throat.

# 25

It retrospect, Lila understood that she had dealt the man too many blows in too short a time. La Roux's own cousin had called him proud. Over the course of one day, he had been within reach of what he wanted most, a path to the Saxon High House, only to have it snatched away. This man who had never quite lived up to his own high expectations, who never achieved exactly what he wanted, had held power over the Randolph family. He could have chosen which path to push Lila down. Instead, he'd watched that power fizzle, and Lila had vowed to ruin him.

He'd snapped from shock and anger.

Lila saw it cross his face. The red cheeks, the scowl, the sweat forming on his brow, the vacant eyes. La Roux no longer existed. He might have been a boy on the beaches of Costa Sur, watching an older child who was just a little bit stronger, just a little bit more attractive, just a little bit smarter, knock down his sand castle and laugh at the boy's frustration.

Had Lila laughed at him?

She was not sure, but it was too late now to do anything about it. She couldn't even scream for help. La Roux's hands had already closed around her throat, choking her so completely that she could not breathe. It was as though she were being punched, one long, continuous strike to her neck, and she knew that her voice would never function properly again. She'd be like Dixon, forever writing notes.

But before she lost her voice and air, La Roux would break her neck.

Lila panicked at the thought.

Still sitting in her desk chair, she twisted in La Roux's grasp, frightened that she would do the job for him by bucking too wildly.

What else could she do? Where could she kick, where could she punch, where could she stab with her fingers?

In his eyes?

She stretched forward, but her arms were not long enough.

As La Roux's hands tightened, she felt all the more powerless, feeble, and vulnerable. She was all too aware that her fighting skills had never progressed beyond drawing and aiming a loaded tranq.

Where was her Colt now?

Put away in her desk drawer, along with her career.

She had no plan for how to get away. She always had a plan and an angle, usually several, but tonight she had nothing but a swelling fear.

Regrets, too. Regrets that she hadn't started taking more hand-to-hand training.

Regrets that she hadn't run away with Tristan.

This was Peter Kruger approaching her with a loaded gun.

This was Reaper with a knife to her throat.

This was a room full of Italian mercs pointing guns at her head.

This was her motorcycle out of control, slamming into a brick wall.

This was her last death.

Regrets filled her mind, the same stupid wants and desires she hadn't followed up on, acts she wished she could take back. She'd die, and Tristan would shrug it off, not caring. He wouldn't even mourn her loss.

He might even think she deserved it.

Perhaps she did.

She'd killed. Now it was her turn to die.

Lila squeezed her eyes shut. She punched La Roux's wrists, trying to free herself, but he would not relent. She tried to jerk toward the wine bottle, thinking someone might come if they heard it shatter upon the floor, but La Roux had moved it far away. She stretched her fingers to the desk drawer that contained her Colt, but she couldn't reach it.

Her bucking did manage to unbalance La Roux slightly. His grip slipped for an instant, allowing her to gulp air before he ratcheted his hands around her neck again. His arms bent at the elbows, face closer, teeth bared in a snarl.

She scratched at his eyes with her fingernails.

That netted a reaction, but not one she wanted. "Bitch," he sneered, rubbing at his face. Seconds later, blows struck her jaw, her cheek, her chest, and then her stomach.

A kick landed against her ribs.

Instinct brought up her knees. She bowed her head and covered the back of her neck as more strikes landed.

"Murderer," she yelled. The word came out in a hoarse gasp, and she nearly cried out for the pain.

La Roux stopped and unclenched his hands. His jaw slack, he stared at her face, dumbfounded at what he had done.

Or tried to do.

Lila planted both feet on his chest and kicked him halfway across the room. As he flailed backward, she yanked a drawer from her desk. The contents spilled out on the floor and clattered to the ground.

Snatching up her Colt, she crab-walked away from him, planting herself in the corner.

La Roux sat down on Lila's bed and stared.

One hand around her neck, one hand clasped around her gun, she leaned against the wall for support. Lila could hardly believe the cold metal was in her hand now, ready to be used. The wild beast had been brought to heel.

It seemed odd to see him so calm and composed, like what had happened had been some silly mistake, like maybe she had imagined it.

Had she?

Had he meant to kill her?

If so, she'd be dead, wouldn't she?

An image of dead mercs on a warehouse floor invaded her mind. She no longer regretted those people, just as she wouldn't have regretted killing La Roux if he still had his hands around her throat, but she couldn't shoot him now. He wasn't doing anything but staring back at her with an open mouth. Horrified.

The gun warmed her hand as if it wanted to be used.

Lila did not pull the trigger. Instead, she stayed crouched in the corner. If he tried again, if he lunged at her, she would aim for his head and those vacant eyes.

"You just made me so angry," he whispered. "I didn't know that I could get so angry, but you pushed me too much. I just needed…"

"To kill me?" she asked, voice straining.

The senator ran his fingers through his hair. His eyes reddened, but not from madness. "Don't do this to me," he pleaded, elbows propped up on his knees. "I'll be ruined. I'm a good man, Lila, you know that. I don't deserve this. I just made a mistake."

Lila did not know what to say, torn between wondering how anyone would think himself good after such an attack and wondering if he might have a point.

When he approached her, instinct took over. She raised the gun to his head, ready to shoot. "Back the fuck away from me, or I'll unload every single dart into you," she croaked, throat burning from just a few words.

He took several steps away.

"Chief Shaw is waiting for you downstairs. We're going to leave now and meet him outside."

"Lila, say nothing, and I'll say nothing. Let's make a deal, a mutually beneficial arrangement," he said, echoing a phrase he must have used in the senate a thousand times. "Name your terms. I have money. I could help your family while I'm in Beaulac. Your family's oil rigs—"

"This isn't a business deal," Lila said in disgust. Her need to talk was more than the pain it caused, and the roughness in her voice grated on her ears. "You've committed treason and attempted murder."

"It wasn't like that. Damn it, Lila. It's not like I used what I learned to profit in some business deal, not like the others. I didn't turn anything over to a foreign power. I'm like you. I punished those who broke into BullNet."

"Is that it?"

"I'm not some murdering psychopath. I wouldn't have even hurt you if you hadn't—"

"Caught you?"

Lila stood up with some effort and backed away to the door.

"Look, I can help—"

She cocked the gun, and the senator closed his mouth.

"My scarf," she ordered, her voice clawing at her throat.

While La Roux fetched a scarf from her closet, Lila retrieved her red woolen coat. She put it on, thrusting one arm and then the other into its sleeves, all while keeping her gun trained on the senator's head. After he tossed her the scarf, she wound it around her neck, hoping that all signs of their struggle were hidden from view.

The two scratches on the senator's face might give them away, as could her jaw and cheek, which had already begun to swell, but there was nothing she could do about it.

"What happens now?"

"I escort you out the same way you came in." Given the hour, her family probably still lurked in their rooms, dressing for dinner. The staff likely busied themselves with last-minute dinner preparations. If she was lucky, she might pass through the entire house and not be seen by anyone.

Lila pulled the gun into her sleeve, hiding it from view. "If you make any movements toward anyone in this house, I will shoot you. If you try to run, I will shoot you. Do you understand?"

"Don't worry. I won't run. I haven't done anything wrong, not when the prime minister and his lackeys have been up to the same things."

Lila ignored his words, gesturing for him to open the door. She slid into the hallway a few steps behind him, keeping her steps light and her shoulders loose, as though they were doing nothing so interesting as going down to dinner.

Alex met them at the bottom of the staircase. "Are you attending dinner with the family after all?" she asked, brow furrowed in confusion at the twin scratches above La Roux's eyes, and Lila's swelling lip.

"No. We're going on a stroll," the senator answered bitterly. Since Lila knew her voice would give her away, she smiled benignly and inclined her head.

Alex took the hint and bustled away.

The pair met no one else on their way to the door but a young footman who was so bent on pleasing the highborn couple with his speed and the shine of his shoes that he did not notice the air that had turned tense.

Lila breathed easier when they passed through the front door of the great house, even though La Roux stiffened when it closed behind them. Sunset had arrived, and the horizon dimmed.

Lila shoved the muzzle of her gun into La Roux's back, reminding him of her instructions.

La Roux did not budge. Contrary to his earlier promise, he cast about wildly, his legs bent slightly as though he might bolt.

A group clad in black caught his attention. Four sentries marched toward the couple from thirty meters away, their hands on their Colts.

It was only then that La Roux finally complied, once he recognized Chief Shaw and two of his officers, all three dressed in Randolph colors for the evening.

Shaw snapped a pair of handcuffs on the senator's wrists, pinning his hands behind him. The two officers flanked the prisoner, ensuring he would not run away.

Shaw winced, spying Lila's chin. "I'm sorry, madam. By the time I realized there was a struggle upstairs, you already had it well in hand." Out of the four patrolmen, he was the only one with an earpiece, the only one who had clearance to hear what had been said upstairs.

"It's fine."

Shaw flinched at the hoarseness in her voice. "Sounds worse out here than it did over the mic. What did he do to you?" he asked, noting the scratches on the senator's brow.

La Roux stared at the wet grass under his feet and did not answer.

Sutton reached out timidly and unwound the scarf around Lila's neck. The bruises had already begun to form, and even in the dim light, the others could see the handprints plainly, redder than the roses lining the trail through the compound.

Sutton's cheeks flushed. "I don't know what any of this is about, but I've never wanted to hurt anyone so much in all my life."

"Let the man's brothers decide his fate, commander. Don't let them decide yours," Shaw cautioned.

"I wasn't talking about Senator La Roux. Why on earth is she helping you arrest this man? You left him alone with her. She's an heir, damn it!"

Lila felt bad for Sutton. She was the only one on the estate who even knew the government militia was on the premises, having driven them through the front gates herself, but she had no idea why Lila had allowed it. "She could have been—"

"I was my own fault. I should have kept my gun close. I just didn't think."

"He'll get his punishment soon enough," Shaw said. "I assure you. He'll hang next to Celeste and Patrick Wilson."

Lila saw the future pass over La Roux's face, the understanding that an executioner would soon put a noose around his neck. He would not know who wore the hood, tied the knot, and pulled the lever to drop the trapdoor under his boots. All that he would know was that it would be a Masson who did the deed, someone sent by his matron to salvage the family's honor.

His own brothers would be the ones to condemn him to his fate, the men of the Saxony Senate that he had wanted to join so intensely. After he saw Sutton's reaction, after he saw Shaw's gaze fall on Lila's neck, he had no more illusions about how they would vote.

"A moment with the heir, please," he said.

Sutton gripped the senator's shoulder. "Not a chance. We're driving you back to Bullstow before anyone notices that your hands aren't behind your back by choice."

"You have one minute," Lila whispered, her voice still on fire. If she didn't humor him, she'd always wonder what he wanted to say.

The blackcoats drifted off several meters away, circling around the pair, watching every move the senator made with cold precision.

"Don't let them charge me with this. My children, my family, they can't know. Make something up. I won't tell them about you or your father, just spare—"

"Don't make things worse for yourself. Shaw heard everything. The senate disciplinary committee will see the evidence and hear an edited version of our conversation—your confession in your own words. Go quietly, cooperate, and no one else might know of your crimes but a few Saxon senators who judge your case."

"And my family?"

"Your matron will be informed. Chairwoman Masson will choose someone to finish the job. I doubt she'll want to tell anyone either. It would shame the family too much."

She couldn't have wounded him as much if she had pulled the Colt from her sleeve, loaded it with bullets rather than darts, and shot him point-blank in the chest. He merely nodded at her and tilted his head for Shaw to lead him away to the waiting car. There was an exchange between the pair of them, and he gave Lila one last parting glance before he crawled inside the backseat, the two Bullstow officers dwarfing him on either side.

Sutton offered Lila a wave, climbed into the front seat, and drove the vehicle to the south gate. No one would stop the estate's commander, not if she didn't stop first.

Sutton didn't stop.

Lila watched the car pull from the compound, bound for Bullstow.

She didn't return to the house for some time. Lila wrapped her scarf tighter and trudged through the compound, buttoning her red woolen coat to the neck. The air was colder than it had been all year, and the wind lashed the rosebushes, ripping away the new buds.

She stayed out until she no could longer feel her toes, then slipped back into the great house, through the scullery, and past the kitchens. No one met her on the staircase. The only sign that anyone had been around at all was a tray that had been left on her desk. It contained fruit and her favorite chocolate cookies, but Lila did not eat any of it. Her throat hurt too much, even to swallow a sip of wine.

Stripping off her scarf and coat, she poured the wine down her bathroom sink, then fell into bed early.

# 26

Lila fumbled the vibrating palm on her bedside table and glanced at the dark windows, drapes closed tightly. She tapped the screen, expecting Commander Sutton's voice on the other end, ready with an emergency.

"Hello," she said, then regretted it immediately. Her voice emerged in a hoarse croak, as if she had caught a cold overnight. The jagged, rough pain in her throat and her sore ribs brought everything back. Her new position, Tristan, La Roux, the arrest, her near murder. She buried her head under the pillow at the memories, cheek brushing against a plastic baggie filled with cool water. Sutton had forced it upon her after returning to the compound.

She shoved the makeshift icepack away.

"I apologize for the short notice, but I need you to come down to Bullstow as soon as you can," Chief Shaw said delicately. "I waited for as long as I could, but we have some things to discuss, and we need to get your side of the story."

"My side?"

"For the report. Senator La Roux told us his side. We need to file your side as well. It would also help to take a few pictures, and maybe even get the medical report from your doctor. I can call her for you. Which doctor did you see last night?"

Lila frowned. After the shock of La Roux's attack wore off, she had just wanted to be alone, to go to bed, to try for sleep and oblivion. She had never considered seeing a doctor, not even when Sutton suggested it. It was only a few punches and kicks from a madman, after all, a brief moment spent with someone's hands around her neck.

But it hadn't just been that, had it?

In a country where violence was an anathema, it had happened to her.

Again.

"Madam?" Shaw asked tentatively.

"One hour."

Lila hung up, wincing as she got out of bed, her ribs protesting every movement and breath.

After a quick shower, Lia opened her closet to a sea of crimson. She avoided the dresses and chose red trousers and a red sweater, donning her new red leather coat atop it. If she'd been truly free to wear whatever she wished, she would have chosen her militia uniform and blackcoat instead. She would have felt ready for battle, and she needed that feeling again. Someone else was still trying to kill her, after all, and it wasn't La Roux.

But she wasn't supposed to even own the coat anymore. It should have been ash.

Lila strapped her harness around her hips, sliding her Colt onto her side. Then she donned her militia boots and thrust her backup knife into her boot.

She'd never be without them again, especially since she'd likely see La Roux at the Bullstow security office. Perhaps it would be through one-way glass, but that didn't matter much to Lila. She'd be armed this time, and he'd not lay a finger on her.

No one would ever again.

Tristan had been right over the last few years. She needed hand-to-hand lessons. She needed to pay attention this time.

She *would* pay attention this time.

Before she left, Lila returned to the closet and plucked a red scarf from the sea of crimson, wrapping it around the hard bruises that had formed around her swollen neck. Luckily, a thick layer of makeup had lightened the bruises on her face. Her jaw and right eye bulged slightly, but no one would notice if they didn't already know what to look for.

At least, that was her hope. She'd gotten good at hiding bruises lately.

Who would believe that someone had hit her, anyway? Things like that didn't happen in Saxony. Not to heirs. People weren't violent in the commonwealth.

Lila added a pair of shades to her ensemble, then jogged downstairs. She dodged Alex's insistence of breakfast with a firm shake of her head and marched down the gravel path to the garage, the door opening with an off-putting, loud grumble.

A lone blackcoat looked up from his perch at the front of the garage. The sergeant had guarded the elevator during the estate's lockdown.

"Chief?"

Lila gave a stiff nod and stopped before a black Cruz sedan.

"I'm supposed to notify the lieutenant if you want to leave the compound." He switched on the radio perched on his shoulder and spoke into his mic.

Rather than answer with a hoarse voice, she bent over the bumper of the car, ignoring the answering static and murmuring conversation. She searched the sedan's exterior and interior thoroughly with her palm. Finding the GPS tracker and audio bug quickly, she tossed them deeper into the garage.

They hit the cement floor with a tiny, bouncing *pling* and skittered away.

"No one's messed with it," the sergeant assured her as she opened the garage door with a grating rumble. "Several of us have been stationed here since the lockdown. The others are taking a look around the garage right now."

Lila gave him a nod.

The sergeant bowed.

She bundled herself inside the sedan, and the sergeant leaned on her window. "I'll go—"

Lila pulled from the garage with a squeal.

The sergeant sprinted backward to avoid the wheels.

Lila peeled down Villanueva Lane, waving at Sergeant Nolan, who stood beside the gatehouse, her breath visible in thick white curls. The blackcoat moved to slap a button on the gatehouse control panel, locking her inside, but Lila hit the gas pedal and swerved around the gate's arm.

Assassin be damned.

Guards be damned.

She was probably safer at Bullstow than on the Randolph estate, anyway.

It only took her a few moments to reach Bullstow and pull through the gate, the area clear of early morning protestors. Chief Shaw met her on the first floor of his security office, his eyes bleary and his uniform wrinkled in the back and around his waist. His hands dwarfed a stainless steel coffee mug, and she wondered how many times he'd refilled it during the night.

Shaw's eyes wandered to her scarf and shades. Thankfully, he said nothing and led her to his office, filled with a large desk and two comfortable leather chairs. A map of Saxony hung across one whole wall, with little lights that oozed and flowed, detailing the crimes taking place on public lands throughout the state. A little computer whirled on the ceiling, collating the data.

He closed the door and pointed at her scarf. "Can I see it?" he asked gently, the tenor in his voice betraying the fact that he didn't want to but needed to.

Lila removed the cashmere scarf, triggering a worried hiss from the chief as he bent over his desk, white knuckles pressed into the desk.

"What did the doctor say?"

"I didn't go," she confessed.

Shaw cursed and snatched up his palm. "I'll have Dr. Booth here immediately. I want you checked out before—"

"No. I'll see my own doctor this morning."

"No, you're seeing Dr. Booth now. I should have ordered one of my men to drive you straight to Randolph General. I don't know what I was thinking."

"I'm fine."

"Your bruises tell a different story. They're darker than a Bullstow rose. What if your neck had swollen and closed off your windpipe?"

"It didn't. I'll see my doctor later, but right now we have a job to do. Stop treating me as if I'm a child," she said, her words spoiled by her hoarse voice.

"Fine. I'll get you something hot to drink." He hesitated at the door, as though worried about leaving her alone.

Eventually, he darted away.

Lila crossed a leg over her knee and watched the map light up, hundreds of little flashes like firecrackers bursting overhead. Hundreds of blackcoats keying in burglaries and car accidents and trespassers…

And assaults and attempted murders.

She'd been a flicker of light on Shaw's map the night before.

She'd been a flicker of light on Shaw's map for a very long time, one of the many blackcoats keying in crimes, oblivious to the clock ticking down her own time.

Lila bit her lip and watched the morning's story unfurl before her eyes.

She didn't realize that tears had begun running down her cheek until it was too late. She wiped them away with the cuff of her sweater and snatched up the remote from Shaw's desk, turning the whole map off.

A white wall stared back at her, blank now, with not even a framed picture to adorn it.

Slipping into the bathroom, she fixed her makeup as best she could and returned to her chair. It wouldn't do for anyone to know that an heir had shed a tear, a judge for the High Council, no less. Such women were supposed to know everything, to point the country in the right direction, to ensure everyone in their care had enough work and that their family made enough money for food, for healthcare, for shelter.

Leaders didn't cry. They were too busy leading.

Lila stared at the empty wall.

Shaw returned moments later with three lidded cups, all as large as her head. He said nothing about the map; a slight pause in his step was the only evidence he'd even noticed it.

"Tea? Coffee? Hot chocolate?" he asked. "I didn't know which one you might like, so I just got all of them."

Lila grabbed one at random and smiled as the warmth spread down her throat. Only milk had been added to the tea, which was how she liked it.

Shaw nodded, clearly pleased that he had done something help-ful. "When you're ready, I should take photos for the report." His eyes fell upon the camera on his desk.

"Let's get it over with," she replied, putting down her cup.

Shaw picked up the camera while Lila took off her coat and backed against the bare wall. He directed her how to turn so that he could get adequate coverage of the bruises on her neck and jaw, not that she needed the instructions. The camera emitted an obnoxious, dead click whenever it captured a shot. She'd done the same as Shaw before, asking someone to pose their broken body for the camera. She'd never thought much about it then. She'd never realized how much an intrusion it was, how much it pained her to know that La Roux's file would preserve the memory of the attack, long after her bruises had healed.

But the formalities had to be observed.

She knew that.

She even lifted her shirt so that he could photograph the bruises on her ribs and stomach, though the act was almost worse than receiving the blows themselves. At least the chief had not photo-graphed anything above her mouth.

No one would be able to tie the pictures to Elizabeth Victoria Lemaire-Randolph. As always, he had recorded her anonymously, and the report would live in his private records, rather than BullNet.

"I need your account of the evening's events," he said, with-drawing his palm. He tapped on the device's screen, then noted the date and time as well as his name and rank. It was a familiar routine when the pair debriefed after a job. Usually no one but the prime minister would see the report, but this time would be different. This time excerpts would be sent to a few key members of the senate's disciplinary committee.

The High Council of Judges would confirm their judgment. She'd have to recuse herself from that meeting, wouldn't she?

Of course she would. It wouldn't be right to rule on such a case.

Lila picked up her tea and ran through what had happened the night before. She didn't speak in much detail about La Roux's web of blackmail because she hadn't ferreted out all his victims yet. It would take her weeks to finish that. She spoke in broad strokes only, except when it came to the attack.

She was very precise when she got to that.

"You aren't listening as you usually do," she chided gently after she had finished her account. Her voice hurt worse than ever, as if scratched by burning embers as she spoke. She sipped her second cup of tea, hoping to ease it.

Shaw tapped on his screen, turning off the recording program. "It's not your usual story," he said, tucking his palm into a deep pocket in his blackcoat. "You're usually in and out, and no one's the wiser. This time was different. Such violence is usually committed by the mentally ill, by anarchists, by drunks, by people like that hacker or Peter Kruger. My oldest son played with Senator La Roux as a boy. I always believed that he was a moral man. He was a highborn, raised and educated in Bullstow. We all had something to do with it."

Lila could relate. She'd felt similarly when Patrick Wilson had been picked up for his crimes. She and Alex had taught him how to tie his shoes and ride a bike.

"You feel responsible for his actions?"

"Such behavior reflects on us all. We were his teachers. This was his milieu. We should have seen the defects within him long before he graduated."

"Do you also blame the citizens of Beaulac? He lived there for years."

"Only during the legislative session," he said, turning back to his coffee. "In truth, madam, I don't know what to think about it all. I don't know who's to blame."

"Perhaps you should blame Senator La Roux. People change. They don't always change for the better."

"Sometimes they don't change at all. Sometimes you never knew them to start with." He rubbed his eyes, which had turned red without sleep. "We're lucky that Senator La Roux never told anyone about your extracurricular activities. Your identity is still safe."

"He could still talk. He probably will talk before the end. Has he requested another deal? He was full of them last night."

Shaw fiddled with his coffee cup. "I don't know how to tell you this, and I don't know if it will make what happened last night better or worse, but Senator La Roux is dead."

Lila felt the punch in her stomach.

The senator had managed yet another blow.

"I don't understand. He was in a holding cell. How can he be dead?"

"I was with him when it happened. He wouldn't admit to any wrongdoing no matter how often I threatened him with truth serum. He did give me a list of those he had caught inside the network, though, several dozen highborn and hackers. He told me the evidence against them was stored on a backup drive in his suite, and since his computer was likely nothing more than 'an expensive paperweight,' if you were to be believed, we should start there. He said he'd be damned if he'd be thrown in a holding cell while they got off scot-free."

He passed her the list, and Lila shook her head. "He blackmailed far more than that."

"You'll find them all. I'm quite confident in your abilities."

"I don't understand where all the money was going."

"Favors? Votes? We'll look over his financials and bring every-one in for interrogation. It won't take long to see the pattern, to understand what he was trying to do. We already know the goal."

"Get elected in the Saxony Senate."

"Then Unity and beyond." Shaw rubbed at his mustache. "He didn't hold back with what he did to you. He called it an accident, said that he wasn't himself, but he admitted it. It's about the only thing he did admit to. Then he grabbed my gun when my back was turned. It was a rookie mistake."

Lila didn't believe it for a moment, especially when Shaw's eyes slid to the floor. "You carry a gun with bullets?"

"Of course. I'm the chief and ultimate authority on this compound. It is my burden."

"Bullshit. Senator La Roux asked for a gun, and you gave it to him."

Chief Shaw licked his lips, and his fingers ran across the supplies on his desk: pens, paperclips, a couple of stray booklets bound in plastic spirals. "You were right before when you asked if he had made a deal. I called the prime minister with the details, and he accepted. It killed your father to do it, madam. He wanted Senator La Roux to pay a steep price for his actions, for what he had done to you, but the needs of Bullstow must come before vengeance."

"What deal?"

Shaw shifted in his chair. It squeaked in the quiet room. "Senator La Roux told me that he didn't want his children to suffer for what he had done, and he knew that your father and I would not want Bullstow to suffer for it either. You understand our position, madam. The prime minister would rather this whole affair did not come out. What good would it do if the people of Saxony found out that a senator had tried to bribe his way into a better seat? That's not how the men of Bullstow are raised. Besides, if the idiots out there knew you were watching BullNet, they'd be harder to catch. It would also put you, me, and your father in danger."

"I don't understand."

Chief Shaw rubbed his mustache. "One of the cooks at Hotel Emeraude prepared a meal for him, and I left him my gun for dessert. One bullet."

"Just like that?"

"If it makes you feel any better, he needed two. I was slow to help him."

Lila stretched her hands out on Shaw's desk, uncomprehending. Her mind didn't call forth her last images of La Roux, with his face scowling and angry, his hands around her neck. No, her mind pulled deeper. Her mind reached for the La Roux she had met on the night of the ball, teasing her with his cocky smile.

The La Roux who had lain atop her, naked and hard, thrusting in and out of her body.

The La Roux who had ticked her ribs.

The La Roux who had needed her help.

"It's not as if this is the first time a deal like this has been struck. The senate interns are told about it by their mentors after they win their first nomination. The senate is not as clean as we'd like for people to believe. We wash away stains of dishonor with blood, just like the families."

"How often do you wash it with blood?"

"I've lost my gun three times in the last fifteen years. Two more senators didn't have the nerve. They went to trial."

Lila crossed her arms over her chest and leaned back in her seat. "Senators Hardwicke and Jackson."

"Yes, madam."

She remembered the two well. Their scandals and trials had been in the media for months, flooring the country.

"What will Saxony know?"

"Senator La Roux suffered a horrible car accident this morning, and Dr. Booth cremated the body soon after. He's signed off on the official report and classified the autopsy. No one will know the real story. If I'm not very much mistaken, it's already in the papers."

"And Commander Sutton?"

"Your father has spoken to her personally, not that she knows the truth. He claimed she'd listen to him."

"What about his family?"

"Senator Pierre La Roux spoke to his son last night and vowed to keep the secret. He's a Unity senator, so he knows the score. He won't tell anyone but Chairwoman Masson. It would bring shame on him, his children, and his son's children if the secret got out. It would render his son's sacrifice as pointless in the end."

"And his mother?"

"The senator promised to break the news if she questioned the report. She won't, though. Parents tend to know. She won't look too closely and spoil the fairytale image of her son."

Lila shook her head in disbelief. "Just like that, you've erased everything he's done."

"Nothing can erase it completely. You'll always remember, and it will be in my records. Some might guess, of course, after we arrest the highborn and hackers who infiltrated the government servers. But from what Senator La Roux told us, he was careful for them not to know who pulled the strings. The things he had them to do were subtle, much more subtle than his treatment of you, or he would have been in the Saxony Senate by now. In a few weeks, Bullstow will exile Sergeant Muller and Sergeant Davies. Things will sort themselves out."

"I don't know if this is right or if it's wrong."

"Maybe it was just the best end to a bad situation. Everyone benefited from the deal, and he knew it. He would have been hanged within the month. At least this way, his family's honor and the honor of High House are both upheld."

"Still doesn't seem right somehow."

"I think it was the thought of his children living with the scandal that sent him over the edge. If he didn't have them, he might not have cared what anyone thought. He wouldn't have taken the honorable way out. He would have gone to the press. You have no idea what a father would do for his children."

# 27

Lila drove past her reserved space near the entrance of Randolph General and parked in a spot behind the building. She felt vulnerable in the mostly empty lot. It wasn't the thought of her assassin that made her nervous. It was the thought of her visit showing up in the press that made her wary. She wouldn't be named, of course, not when she hadn't announced her role as prime, but it wouldn't take a genius to guess her identity based on a thinly disguised euphemism. *The heir who favors black. The favorite daughter of the wolves. The serpent's downfall.* Any of them would be easy to guess.

Before disembarking from the car, she checked her reflection in the rearview mirror. Her makeup still obscured the bruise upon her jaw. She slid her sunglasses over her eyes and quickly arranged her scarf around her neck, then darted through the back entrance, sans coat.

Her vibrating palm drew her attention as she scampered upstairs. *I've arrived at the clinic,* Helen had written.

*Me too,* Lila typed before sliding the device back into her pocket. She jogged up another flight of stairs and crossed the hall, ducking quickly through the double doors of the clinic. Only a teenager had spied her from the opposite end of the hall, but he'd been too focused on a row of snack machines to look up.

Luckily, the clinic's front desk was dark and empty. Lila fiddled with her sunglasses while she waited for Helen, careful to hide her family's coat of arms in case anyone peeked in and saw her.

"Come inside," Helen said, opening the door in the back. "No one should arrive for another hour. If we're lucky, no one will even know you were here."

Lila followed her into an exam room, the scent of cinnamon cleanser thick in the air. "If we're not lucky?"

"Then I'll sneak you out." Helen patted the exam table.

Lila didn't have the energy to resist. She removed her glasses and placed them on a chair in the corner, then folded her scarf and laid it on top. The paper on the exam table crinkled as she sat down.

Helen winced at Lila's neck. She asked a few questions about the attack that Lila didn't want to answer, but didn't pester her for details and didn't make Lila speak any more than was necessary. Indeed, she completed the exam as quickly as possible, though she insisted on pressing Lila's ribs to see if La Roux had broken them.

Lila shrank back too quickly for Helen's comfort.

The doctor took several X-rays and even a blood sample, ignoring Lila's protests. "I know you think you're fine, Lila, but you've been through a lot. Let me do my job," she admonished before capping the vial and promising to walk it to the lab herself.

"I don't want—"

"Your name is not on it. Just sit tight. I'll be back in a sec."

When the doctor's steps retreated from the clinic, Lila put on her sweater and retrieved her palm. She'd nearly sent a message to Tristan and Dixon the night before, letting them know that the Baron had finally been caught. But every time she'd tried to write the message, she couldn't progress past the first few words. Nothing sounded right, and she'd decided last night to write it later.

Later had come, and she still had the same problem.

Helen entered with her X-rays, latching them on to a lit screen on the back wall. Her finger traced over the translucent bones, and she cocked her head to the side to study them. "Nothing is broken, even though you're more bruise than person at this point. You've been through quite a trauma, Lila. You should go home and rest. Let your body heal."

"That's not possible. I start working for my mother tomorrow."

"Work can wait."

"Clearly, you haven't spent enough time with my mother."

"You forget, I grew up with her," Helen said, tossing her stethoscope over her neck. "You let me worry about your mother. I'll get you a few days' rest."

The doctor sat down on a rolling stool, which rattled dully as she moved closer. "Now on to the next order of business. Since the office was closed yesterday for the Closing Ball, I had time to look into Dr. Rubio. Actually, I've been looking into her for the last few days. I just hadn't found anything."

"You found something?"

Helen nodded. "I drove to Dr. Rodriguez's lab. I didn't think the trip would yield anything, but I couldn't get the idea out of my head. The good doctor has been doing some brilliant work in the last ten years, and she didn't mind spending the morning boasting to a colleague. I couldn't believe how much further she's taken her research since Dr. Rubio left the group. They've isolated the really nasty compounds in NAT, including the one that halts sperm production. They've been puzzling out exactly how it works, hoping that they might understand it well enough to produce a treatment for male infertility."

"Perhaps such a treatment might be used for Senator Dubois."

"They're decades away from anything like that. But while having lunch with Dr. Rodriguez, I mentioned Dr. Rubio's name. I wanted to get the doctor's impressions of her. Turns out that Dr. Rubio visited the lab almost a year ago. Some of their samples also went missing around that time."

"What sort of samples?"

"Well, they don't have a treatment for male infertility right now. What they do have is a very potent form of male birth control, birth control that doesn't seem to have the unpleasant side effects of NAT."

"Birth control?" Lila exclaimed, her brain spinning. "You think Dr. Rubio stole the samples and dosed Senator Dubois?"

"Yes, though I don't understand why or how she'd do it."

Lila's stomach twisted. She knew exactly why and how. "Does this drug need to be ingested or injected?"

"Ingested would suffice."

Lila stiffened on the exam table. Dubois had dined with the family several times a week for years. She'd eaten with him, watched him smile and laugh while another person at the table fed him an untested drug, changing the course of his career against his will. Had her mother studied his face all these months, reveling in the power she had over him?

Had she done the same with her daughters, thinking of them as her puppets?

Probably.

No wonder the chairwoman had sat with Jewel and Dubois all night long, crying with them, pretending to care. She had shaped their reaction, pushing them toward the one conclusion she wanted.

Lila pinched the bridge of her nose. She was the chief of security. She should have seen what was going on. She should have stopped it.

What if there were side effects?

"How long will it take for Senator Dubois to recover his seed?"

Helen's gaze fell to the floor. "Lila, from what Dr. Rodriguez has ascertained in the rodent trials, the effect is permanent. It's the reason they haven't tested it on human subjects yet. It's a vasectomy in powder form. Dr. Rodriguez's group is considering the market, but the fact that it's permanent..."

Lila pictured Dubois milling around the park in the middle of Bullstow, wearing nothing more formal than a t-shirt and jeans, he and his brothers surrounded by children. Dubois, teaching his nephews how to throw a curve ball. Dubois, scooping up crying toddlers and setting them to rights once again. Dubois, wandering on the outskirts of the park, taking care of other men's children, all the while dreaming of his own.

She recalled his list, a faded, yellowing strip of paper with all the names he had hoped to call his children one day, if only the mother would listen.

He'd bashfully shown it to her once, a very long time ago.

If she had just accepted her responsibility back then, he'd still have a chance to use it.

Helen's palm vibrated. She checked her display and slipped it back into her pocket.

"I have to go." Lila snatched up her scarf. "Thank you for the information."

"Wait. Sit down. There's something else we need to talk about."

Lila cocked her head and hopped back on the exam table. "What is it?"

"The results of your blood tests," Helen said with a contemplative frown. She rolled her stool closer. "Did you have sex with Senator La Roux?"

Lila shrugged, attempting to ignore the nervous twinge that erupted in her belly. "Why?"

Helen sighed heavily. "I warned you not to have sex with any of those men unless you wanted—"

Lila's throat burned as she gulped. This time her mind didn't call forth the charming La Roux. It brought up the brutal black-mailer. The same man who had punched and kicked and tried to murder her, with a red scowl and sweaty forehead and his fingers around her neck.

"I'm not pregnant," she said, shaking her head.

"Even virgins can get pregnant the first time."

"How do you even know? It hasn't been forty-eight hours."

"It takes forty hours to be sure of a no. It can take less time to detect the EPF in the blood for a yes. I thought I should test after—"

Lila hopped up from the exam table and paced throughout the room again, her stomach whirling. "Could it be a false positive?"

"Yes, but that's—"

"Is it a boy or a girl?"

"It's a collection of cells, and barely that. It'll be months before we know the baby's sex."

"Is it…"

"Calm down, child."

"No. Senator La Roux's dead. He died this morning," she confessed, not giving any further details than that. The man who had beaten her, the man who had tried to murder her, had left something of his behind.

Inside her.

It was more nauseating than a tranq dart.

"Do you want to keep the baby?" Helen asked gently. "You might lose it anyway. Many miscarriages happen in the first few weeks of pregnancy. Most women never even know they're pregnant before it's gone."

Lila stopped. "I don't know," she said, barely conscious of the words that had just come out of her mouth, for another thought had entered her mind.

La Roux hadn't been the only one who had been inside her lately. Tristan had gotten there first. They'd been having sex for weeks before she'd had the operation, including the night before. "What if someone else had been in the picture before Dr. Rubio reversed my CUT? I had a very long vacation."

"I didn't realize you had a lover."

"I don't. He didn't like the idea of sharing."

"I see. Sperm can live in a woman's body for up to five days. Light a match and toss it into a bucket of gasoline, Elizabeth. That's the equivalent of what Dr. Rubio did to you. Whether you had sex before or after the procedure, it makes little difference. The father is anyone's guess, at least until I can do a paternity test."

"Don't call me Elizabeth. That's what people call me when I've done something wrong."

Helen cupped her cheeks. "Child, you did nothing wrong. It's a baby."

Lila turned her head away.

"There are pills I could prescribe for you."

Lila ignored the doctor as she prattled on. She didn't think of the baby. She couldn't think of the baby. All she could think about was La Roux's hands around her throat, killing her as a baby had killed her grandmother while she pushed.

Helen touched her shoulder, startling her. "Lila, if you change your mind, I can prescribe something that will make this all go away. If you wait too late for pills, then I can schedule an abortion. I won't do any of that today, not when you're this upset, but I promise you, I will help you if that's what you decide. No one will never learn of it."

Lila nodded and pulled away, tugging her scarf around her neck. "Senator Dubois will never have the children he desperately wants, and I will have a child that I never wanted. At the risk of sounding, like a petulant little girl, life is not fair."

"It rarely is."

Lila eyed the darkened computer in the back of the room. Helen hadn't written a damn thing down during the entire visit.

"The lab has already lost your sample." Helen dropped the X-rays into the trash, the glossy photos unmarked by a patient number or her name.

Lila nodded, still too stunned to say much. "I'm grateful for any discretion you have to offer, though I'm sure someone else in the department will pick up the slack."

"Then they will not work here for long, not if I have anything to do with it."

Lila slid her sunglasses back onto her face. "I fear you'll be too short-staffed to make that decision easily. By the end of the day, Dr. Rubio will no longer work at this clinic—or anywhere else, if I can help it."

Helen smiled. "I'll try to temper my disappointment."

# 28

Lila braked inside her family's garage and slammed the sedan's door, nearly forgetting to adjust her scarf before disembarking. She ignored the two blackcoats in the garage, and neither tried to speak with her. They looked at her as one looks at a bomb about to explode.

Lila also ignored Sutton, who paced outside the garage, waiting for her as she brushed past. "Chief—"

"If you intend to yell, do it at another time."

Sutton frowned. "This afternoon, then, when you've had a chance to calm down."

"Keep your palm with you. I'll send you orders later."

The commander stopped at the great house's front door.

A young footman opened it. He didn't utter a single word as Lila hurried past.

She jogged upstairs and dropped her crimson coat on her bedroom floor before falling into her desk chair.

She'd had a bit more time to think on her way home from the hospital, and those thoughts had not led anywhere she wanted to go. After setting her computer to delete all of La Roux's snoops on her desktop and palm, she ran several searches.

It took only a few hours to confirm what she had feared.

Snatching up her palm, she called a familiar number.

While she waited, Isabel brought up a bottle of wine and placed it on her desk, then bowed and withdrew. The scent of Gregorie filled the room as Lila uncorked with bottle with a hollow pop. It wasn't until after she'd poured her first glass that she realized her mistake.

"Damn it," she hissed, knowing she'd have to get along without wine for a while. Nine months, to be specific, not unless she miscarried.

Not unless she took care of the baby in a different way.

Lila shook her head, not wanting to think about it.

Thumbing the Gregorie label, she left the bottle behind and moved to the center of the couch, not a single light turned on to expose her swollen jaw.

Jewel barged in moments later with barely a knock. Her hair had been styled into a few thick curls, which had been swept off her neck in a swishing ponytail. She wore her whitecoat, the Randolph coat of arms stitched in crimson on her breast, and stylish boots of the same hue. "Louis and I were about to leave for a walk. What is so important that—"

Lila kicked the coffee table away.

It smacked against the edge of her dresser.

Jewel startled, and she dropped the gloves she'd been twirling in her hand. They hit the floor with a dull flop.

Lila toed an ottoman before her. "Sit."

Jewel swallowed and shook her head. "Later. Louis is waiting."

"I said, sit down."

"Why are you so angry?" Jewel asked, sitting on the ottoman as though merely humoring her. "You sound sick. Did—"

"I blamed Mother first," Lila interrupted, crossing one leg over the other. "I always blame Mother for everything, but sometimes she just observes someone else's betrayal and does nothing if it benefits her agenda. I'm chief of the family's militia, Jewel. Did you think I wouldn't figure it out?"

Jewel's eyes widened slightly. "I don't know what you're talking about. What did Mother do now?"

"Nothing. She did absolutely nothing. That probably pisses me off the most. Why would you do it, Jewel? Why would you hurt the one you claim to love?"

"I would never hurt you."

"I'm not talking about me, and you know it. I was too quick to judge Mother. She had nothing to gain with this plan, except deniability. That's why she never said a word against it."

"What plan?"

"You never stopped taking your birth control. All those years with Senator Dubois and the men before him, and you never stopped taking it."

"Lila, what are you talking about? I haven't taken birth control in—"

"Of course, you couldn't get away with it forever. Mother would start making noise for you to see doctors, perhaps even give you a few fertility shots whether you needed them or not. Maybe she already had, or maybe the senator pushed you to see a doctor? Is that what gave you the idea? You saw a way out by turning him into the sick one? You wanted children too much to risk your own body, didn't you?"

This time, Jewel did not say a word. She merely cocked her head to the side as if silently asking Lila how much she had figured out.

"You had Cristina Rubio for a TA at Bokington. Freshman biology. You knew what she'd been working on as a graduate student. Maybe you even knew that she transferred to med school. You must have been surprised to see her on the estate last year."

"Yes, I was."

"Did you have a nice lunch catching up?"

"She's not even properly highborn. I never had lunch with—"

"I might not be able to prove that you both ate lunch at the same table, but your accounts were billed at the exact same time at the same restaurants, several times in one month nearly a year ago. You should have paid with cash."

"You hacked into my—"

"Sit down. I'm not finished."

"You're not the chief of security anymore. Stop pretending," Jewel said as she stood up and started toward the door, her curls bouncing.

Lila lunged, grabbed her sister's wrist, and dragged her back to the ottoman, ignoring her own sore knuckles and ribs. "You will sit down and you will answer every damn question I ask, or I swear to the oracles, I will drag you to Chief Shaw in a pair of shiny handcuffs. Do you understand me?"

"You're crazy," Jewel whispered, settling back onto the ottoman, her knees twisted to the side as though she might bolt.

"I'm crazy? Your name was attached to Dr. Rubio's application for Randolph General. You pushed her through the hiring committee. You have been cutting her an extra paycheck every month out of our family's discretionary fund, leaving a trail of breadcrumbs any idiot would be able to find. Dr. Rubio just had to do one small thing to earn the position and the money."

"What was that? You seem to have made up an entire story. How does it end?"

"With you poisoning the man you claim to love, ruining him so that he'll never have children. This isn't the first job you've helped Dr. Rubio get. She worked at Grace Medical during her breaks in med school at Alex's company. Did Mother impress upon you the need to groom underlings and spies? How many more do you have in various nooks and crannies?"

Jewel tried to stand up again, but Lila drew her Colt and placed it beside her thigh.

"You wouldn't."

"Nothing would make me smile more. I am still technically the chief of security. I have the power to arrest anyone on the estate, even the chairwoman. So you should sit the fuck down and close your mouth unless I have asked you to open it."

Jewel eyed the Colt, and her gaze cut to the door.

She chose the ottoman.

"Tell me why."

Jewel shook her head. "You don't know what you're talking about, Lila. It's not anything like you're making it out to be. It's just birth control. They can reverse it at any time."

"That's not true, and you know it."

"They'll figure it out. They're close to a breakthrough right now."

"He trusted you, and you poisoned him. But you don't even care."

"I do care. I had to do something."

"You could have quit."

"I couldn't have, and you know it. You know how Mother is. You know her intolerance of those who cannot handle their positions. It had to be Mother's idea, her conclusion. It was the only way."

"You could have poisoned yourself. You could have traded away your happiness if it was so damn important to you, but you didn't do that. You didn't even think about it, did you? You didn't want to be barren. You still want kids. For the experience. For your art."

Jewel worried her whitecoat's hem, ignoring the jab. "What are you going to do?"

"Me? I'm not going to do a damn thing. I'm going to relax right here, eat some lunch, and wait while you go next door and tell Senator Dubois all about what you've done. Then I'm going to speak with your ex-fiancé, and see how he would like for me to proceed."

"You can't do that, Lila. I'm sorry. I—"

"Don't waste your breath on me. Get your mercy from Senator Dubois."

"Can't we—"

"If you don't get out of my sight right now, you won't even have a shot at mercy. I will shove you in a holding cell and draw up charges for theft. You seem to forget, Jewel, that you used a hospital account for this little scheme, and I have plenty of evidence to put you away. So unless you wish to spend the next week before the disciplinary committee pleading your case, I suggest you get off your ass and go confess everything to Senator Dubois before I take that option away."

Jewel slunk out her bedroom, her face a parade of tears in waiting.

Lila put her boots up on the ottoman and considered a trek downstairs for lunch. But while Chef might not press her for details about her bruises, she would certainly forward the information to the chairwoman, considering it a duty from one mother to another.

Lila didn't want to have that conversation. In fact, she didn't want to have any conversation with her mother at all, not before she took Jewel down to the holding cells. The chairwoman would surely attempt some sort of deal for her sister's security, and Lila didn't want to listen to it. Or more correctly, she didn't want to risk it.

Instead she paged Isabel to replace the wine with a kettle of tea and bring her lunch. Then she sent a message to Sutton. *Find Dr. Cristina Rubio and detain her for questioning. Message me when she is in a holding cell.*

*As you wish,* the commander wrote back. *We will talk later of your little escape this morning.*

Lila slipped her palm into her pocket.

The dim room pressed in on her, the walls cloying and suffocating.

She wondered where Tristan was and what he and Dixon were doing. She'd escaped death once more, yet she was right back where she started, staying away from the person she longed to be with the most.

Tristan was who she wanted. No one else came close, not even after his ultimatum.

She stroked her belly, knowing that she wouldn't have come to that conclusion without La Roux. If his hands had not wrapped around her throat, if she hadn't been forced to think of her life in immediacies.

Death never listened to reason and duty. It listened to the deepest parts of one's heart.

Her heart had yearned for him again.

It had regretted him again.

Perhaps it wouldn't have gone there if La Roux hadn't told her what she'd said during sex. What she had whispered. Moaned. Screamed.

Ignored. Rejected. Dismissed. Refused.

It would be like that every time. Her body and her mind wanting Tristan, even if the part between her legs responded to someone else, doing what it had been made to do.

Even if her heart desired, missed, mourned…

Loved.

Yes, perhaps she did love him.

At least La Roux had been good for clarifying things. Not that it mattered if her feelings had been clarified. She rubbed her belly again, knowing that her situation had not changed. It had only become more complicated. She was still a highborn, and he was still a former slave. She had still rejected him, and he would believe she had cheated on him with La Roux.

He'd never forgive her, especially if she carried another man's child in her womb.

Perhaps it didn't matter much. She wasn't sure she wanted to share her bed with anyone for a while, not when the last man to share it had so nearly tossed her life aside in anger.

Had part of it been her fault? She'd pressed him, made him angry.

Perhaps it was her fault, at least a little.

Tristan often got angry at her, too.

The last time they spoke, he was even angrier than usual.

Isabel returned with a silver tray. Underneath lay a bowl of soup, which turned the air thick with the scent of chicken. Crackers lined a small plate beside it, and a kettle of tea perched in her other hand. She set the food down on the wayward coffee table, nudging it back in place with a few quick shoves.

"Have you seen the news, madam?" she asked with an awkward little bob.

It dawned on Lila at last. The staff believed she mourned for La Roux. "I already know. The news claims that we were linked?"

"Yes, madam. They aren't saying your name, but it's easy to figure out. I mentioned to Chef how horrible your voice sounded. She made this for you, rather than the lamb."

"It is appreciated. Thank you, Isabel. Both of you."

Isabel bowed and disappeared into the hall with a swish of her skirts.

Lila couldn't help but wonder where Alex had wondered off to.

She couldn't help but wonder about Tristan, too. Tristan, who now knew that she had taken a lover, though a doomed lover at that.

He even knew the man's name.

Lila poured a cup of tea and took a few spoonfuls of soup, then messaged her father. *I suppose my mess is cleaned up now.*

*I didn't believe it at first,* he wrote back immediately. *Did you visit Helen?*

*Yes, I'm fine.*

She looked up to see Dubois, leaning against her doorframe as though emerging from a battle. His unwrinkled coat seemed at odds with his expression, and his eyes were lost and red and raw. After seeing him happy and relaxed for so many years, it was tough to see the change, especially when she knew her family had caused it.

"She told you," Lila said in lieu of a greeting.

Dubois nodded and fell onto the couch beside her. "You sound horrible."

"It's just a cold. What did Jewel say?"

"She told me what she's been slipping into my coffee and why. She told me she loved me. She said she'd still marry me even if I couldn't have children. I almost hate her more for the last part."

"I'm so sorry, Louis," she whispered, using his given name for the first time in their long acquaintance. "I didn't figure it out until this morning. I should have caught it earlier. I should have paid more attention instead of relying on accountants and—"

"Stop," he said, wiping at his eyes. "Is it permanent? Is there really no way?"

"As far as I know, you will always be infertile."

Dubois slumped over his lap. She had never been good at playing the supportive role, so she did not try. Or rather, she did the only supportive thing she knew how to do.

She wrapped her arms around him and rested her chin upon his shoulder. "I have evidence of what she has done. Sister or not, she should be brought up on charges. If you're uncomfortable with others knowing about your condition, then I could get her five years for theft alone. It's more than she'd get for the poison. She might have meant to render you infertile, but I don't think anyone could prove she had any intention of harming you beyond that."

"She didn't, did she?" he asked hopefully.

"No, but that doesn't change what she did. I could charge her with more if you'd come forward, but her sentence doesn't really matter. She's a prime heir. A chairwoman's daughter. Many families will bid high for her mark at auction. She'll end up a slave for the rest of her life."

"I don't think your mother would appreciate any charges at all."

"Screw her. I don't really care what she might appreciate right now."

Dubois chuckled bitterly. "Yes, screw her. Screw your whole damn family."

"Everyone except Pax and Shiloh. They're good kids."

"Yes, they are. You're not so bad either when you aren't being prickly."

Lila nodded, uncertain of how to respond.

They sat in silence for several long moments.

"What do you want me to do?" Lila took her arms away and faced him, letting him recline into the couch.

"I don't know, to be honest. I never thought she'd do anything like that to me. I know she loves me. I saw the change in her months ago. She always looked at me like I was just some guy, but one day, it was like fairy dust had been blown into her eyes."

"She kept doing it anyway, Louis. Just because she's in love with you now, doesn't mean that she didn't hurt you. It doesn't mean she wouldn't hurt you again. Let me bring her up on charges, then leave, and never look back."

"It's not that simple, Lila."

"Why isn't it?"

"Because I love her," he said, a miserable smile pasted onto his face. "Even now. She knocked a hole in my stomach, but having her arrested? It won't fill it."

"What will?"

"Time."

Lila stared at him disbelievingly. "You can't be serious. You want to forgive her after what she's done? You want to work things out with her? She didn't wreck your car, Louis. She poisoned you. She turned you into a lab rat."

The senator winced. "Don't say it like that. She didn't know what she was doing. She thought it would be reversible. It was only supposed to be until your mother changed her mind about her being prime. Then later she'd stop giving me the powder. We'd have a miracle child and start a family."

"Does that sound as dumb and false to you as it does to me?"

"She's going to donate some funding to Dr. Rodriguez. She said the lab is close to—"

"They aren't close. She's lying."

"She's trying to make it right. Doesn't that count for anything?"

"No, she's trying to throw money at the problem because that's how our family solves everything. It's not my place, but I don't think you should want to work things out with her. That drug was completely untested on humans. It might have killed you or hurt you. She didn't ask you to take the risk. She decided for you. She betrayed your trust. She could have done something like that to herself, but she chose to do it to you. In the process, she stole your future."

"You're thinking of your security office. She betrayed you too. I understand why you'd want revenge for that, but—"

"It has nothing to do with revenge. I know this is strange coming from me, but a baby means so much more than a job. She took that from you. How do you know that she won't do it to you again? Or worse?"

"How do I know that the next one won't? How do I know that I won't regret pushing her out of my life before I gave her a chance to make amends? I need to think before I end things. I can't lose anyone else today."

And with that, Lila remembered that Dubois had no idea who La Roux truly was. To him, his cousin wasn't a monster. He was beloved.

Lila tried to bring up La Roux but couldn't. She couldn't pretend sympathy for the man who'd tried to murder her. "Will you return to the senate after this season?"

"Perhaps I might keep my senate seat if I sell my soul, but Jewel's probably already taken that from me as well. If you come forward with what you know, I don't have a chance. They'll know I'm seedless, and I'll never earn a place in any senate again. On the other hand, if Jewel and I merely part, they might elect me for another year, then perhaps shuttle me off to some city in the country for another session or two. After I don't produce an heir, they'll guess at my situation. I'll have to return to Bullstow, but at least I might do some good before I go."

"You already have done a great deal of good for Saxony. I've followed your career," she said, squeezing his arm. "Every senator who doesn't marry returns to Bullstow at some point for retraining. It's not a failing to find another occupation."

"I know. But I always thought I wouldn't be put out to pasture for another decade. Then I met Jewel, and I thought my course had been set on a different star, but now a storm has thrown me overboard." He shifted on the couch and studied her face. "Lila, I have to tell you something about my cousin—"

"I know. I'm sorry."

Jewel hadn't been the only one to take something precious from him. Lila had taken as well, just like with Alex, and she wasn't even sorry about it.

He pulled his wallet from his breeches and dug out a yellowed piece of paper. Lila didn't need to open it to know what it was. "Take this. I won't need it anymore. Maybe you'll get some use from it."

"Louis..."

He shook his head. The paper crinkled as she took it.

"Life is funny. You wake up in one world, and by lunch, you're swept up in a whole new one. I guess life is a nothing more than a series of adjustments."

"I guess we have to learn to adjust."

"We have to try." He stood and walked to the door. "Thank you for giving me the choice with Jewel, but I don't see what good it would do. Let it go, Lila. I can't figure this out if she's gone."

"Maybe you won't be able to figure it out *until* she's gone."

"Maybe it's just a question of what and how much I want to lose. You gave me the choice when she didn't. Please don't take it back because you don't agree with my answer."

Lila fought the urge to debate the issue once more, but she'd already said enough. "Okay. Let me know if you change your mind."

The senator nodded and turned the doorknob. "I don't know if I'll be back in this house."

"I won't look for you."

Dubois nodded and disappeared down the corridor.

# 29

Isabel brought up a fresh kettle of tea to ward off Lila's cold, the cold she was sure that Lila had caught at the ball due to her hoarse voice. Jewel's sobs bubbled through the walls intermittently. Neither of them wanted to get involved. Lila because she would be the target of Jewel's histrionics and rage if she could only stop crying for long enough. And Isabel because experience had taught her to avoid Jewel in such moods. Pax only ventured into the hallway once, peeking into Lila's room for an explanation.

"Don't seek out this gossip. If you can't study through the noise, then take a well-deserved afternoon off. It's the weekend."

"Maybe you should take that advice yourself. It sounds like you're getting sick."

"I'm fine."

"At least turn on a light, then. It's depressing, especially with all the crying."

Lila put up her arm, stopping Pax from turning on the lights. Dubois and Jewel had been too absorbed in their own drama that morning to spot her bruises, and Lila had stayed in the shadows whenever Isabel entered her room. Pax would spot her injuries instantly, though. He'd worked at the hospital too long to dismiss their placement or their shape.

He'd know, and he'd worry.

Pax finally returned to his sanctuary rather than lingering or taking the day off, just as she suspected. He had no one to spend the day with, and Lila did not have the energy to join him.

She was such a bad sister, she thought, stroking her belly.

Alex did not stay away for long either. The slave entered with yet another fresh kettle of tea from Isabel. Beside it lay a hastily scribbled message from the chairwoman.

Jewel wailed away in the next room.

It was strange not to see Alex actively digging for information. Lila thought her own expression must be very grim indeed.

"No sarcasm for me this afternoon?" Lila asked. "I suspect that I could use some. This is from my mother, after all."

"I'm sorry. I suppose I'm just tired. Do you need anything else? More tea for your throat?"

Lila didn't answer at first. Instead, she scanned the short letter, a summons downstairs for an early dinner. "Tell the chairwoman that I'll be down momentarily."

Her friend nodded and disappeared from the room.

Lila sipped on the mug of hot tea, hoping her voice would improve. She unwound her scarf and flipped through her wardrobe, finally settling on a high-necked crimson sweater that hid her bruises from view. She caked on more makeup, hoping to conceal the rest of the marks, then trudged downstairs.

Tugging her palm from her pocket, she skimmed a message from Sutton before sliding it back into her pocket. *Dr. Rubio is missing. We're searching her condo, but her wife is protesting. I'll message you when I know more.*

If the senator didn't want to press charges against Jewel, then Lila could at least punish Rubio for her part. She might not be able to arrest the doctor for the stolen drugs, but she could at least take them away so no one else would get hurt. They'd take care of things inside the family, forcing Rubio to resign her position at the hospital.

She'd never work in healthcare again. Lila would see to it.

Lila padded into the dining room. Pax sat at the table across from Jewel's empty seat. It didn't surprise Lila to find her sister missing. She glanced up at the ceiling in the direction of Jewel's room, wondering when she might actually make an appearance. No one would be able to hear it when she did, not for months.

"Sit, Lila," the chairwoman said gently.

The family dined on sea bass. Lila picked at hers and ignored her glass of wine, sipping several cups of tea. The group spoke of trivial things, all careful not to mention Jewel.

It was almost normal, just another day with an unpredictable, emotional sister.

But Lila knew that the chairwoman had not demanded her presence for no reason.

Pax excused himself as soon as he finished his meal, sensing the looming cloud between the two women.

"The lure of organic chemistry cannot be ignored," Lila said, her smile strained.

"*Lure* is not the correct word. There's not a bit of meat on the hook."

"I'm sure you'll do well. Study hard."

Pax nodded, and his thundering steps soon faded on the staircase. The women had been left alone at last.

"You sound ill, Lila."

"It's just a cold."

The chairwoman nodded. "It appears that Jewel had a dramatic morning. Would you happen to know what it was about?"

"No idea."

"Don't be difficult, Elizabeth. I have heard from the staff that she is upset, and Senator Dubois left without a word to me this afternoon. He's usually much more polite. I can only assume that the pair has had a lover's quarrel. I find it exceedingly odd that he kept his manners with his future sister-in-law but not with me."

"Fishing, Mother? That's not like you."

Lila wondered who had seen the senator slip into her bedroom. Most likely, the chairwoman had dug it out of Pax, though she doubted he had given it up willingly or knowingly. Did the chairwoman know more? Had anyone heard the conversation play out between Lila and her sister, between her sister and the senator? Lila had raised her voice a few times, that was for sure, but it was too broken to be heard in the hall. She had not heard Jewel's usual dramatics while she confessed to her fiancé, either. The hysterical crying had not occurred until after.

Perhaps the chairwoman had not been told what had happened. Perhaps Lila's reaction, as well as Dubois's, had conferred to Jewel the nature of her betrayal. She didn't want anyone to know what she had done. She knew that she would get no sympathy this time, only more looks of disgust.

But Lila didn't believe for a second that her mother was in the dark. "Let's stop dancing, Mother. You already know."

"You give me too much credit, Lila."

"No, I gave Jewel too much. I didn't really think about it until just now, but she's not devious enough to have engineered such a plot all by herself. She had help. You gave Jewel the idea, just a few hints she could connect, and then you waited for her to carry it out. You allowed her to harm her lover, her fiancé, a senator of New Bristol. For what? Just so you have me as prime again? You should be brought up on charges like Jewel."

Her mother intertwined her fingers. "Lila, am I the architect of every plot against you?"

Lila glanced at her mother with a bland expression.

"Perhaps I have authored a few, but I did not manage this one. Never, at any point, did I speak with your sister about poisoning her fiancé. Does that satisfy your sense of responsibility and honor?"

"Hardly."

"It is your sister with whom you should be angry, not me. She could have abdicated her position formally, just like you did once. She chose a different path."

"You knew the whole time."

"I'm surprised you didn't, but then again, you always have had a few blind spots. Not many, or I would never have approved your appointment as chief, but they are there, specifically when it comes to family and friends. I suppose you've been too busy lately to properly audit the hospital's accounts."

"Jewel has put the family at risk. You knew what she was planning to do before she even did it, and you didn't say a word, even for all those months while Senator Dubois was being drugged. That makes you an accomplice, Mother."

"So sanctimonious. Apparently you've forgotten that I also knew of your activities in BullNet. I didn't drag you to Chief Shaw, did I?"

"It's not the same."

"It seems like it to me. There's nothing to charge me with, Lila, and you know it."

"You profited by silence."

"Many people do. Pax will profit now. You will take care of him once you become prime. You will ensure that he—"

"I wouldn't do any more for Pax than you would. Stop pretending that you would sacrifice him just to spite me. You're a cold bitch, but you aren't that cold when it comes to him. Not yet, at least."

"A cold bitch?"

"Spare me the bullshit lines about how everything you do is for the greater good of Wolf Industries, how some sacrifices have to be made for the good of the family, how sometimes you have to make hard choices. There's a line, Mother, and you went too far over it this time."

"I'm not cold, nor am I a bitch," the chairwoman said stiffly. "If that's how you feel, then—"

"Of course that's how I feel. You even respect Jewel a little for this stunt, don't you? You think that maybe you were wrong, that maybe she has what it takes to be prime after all, since she's shown an ability to make a hard choice. Now you're second-guessing yourself, thinking I don't because I look at what she's done, at what you let happen, and I am appalled and want justice for your parts in it."

"You're half right. Jewel does have the will to succeed in business, but she lacks the intelligence, the foresight, the leadership, and, frankly, the stability to run a profitable empire. It only took a few months for me to confirm that. She'll never be a viable choice for prime. You have potential. She does not."

Lila poured herself another mug of tea and did not respond.

"When trouble surfaced, Jewel cheated to get her way, just to save face. I can't have a prime who would do that, Elizabeth. I can't respect it, either. But you're right. I do admire her for trying to find a way out of a difficult situation. Unfortunately, she was sloppy and criminal. Will charges be filed against her?"

"It depends on what Senator Dubois wants."

"So you won't charge her unless he presses it?"

"I don't know. I tried to talk him into it. She deserves it."

"Deserves it? You would condemn your own sister? You would condemn me for not turning her in even though I have also kept your secrets? If Bullstow examined your computer right now, what would they find? If they looked hard? If they knew what to look for?"

Lila shrugged.

"I suspect you did quite a bit of hacking to put Celeste Wilson and her son in a holding cell. Did you tell yourself it was for the good of the family? Perhaps the country? You've both acted in the family's best interests, and you both profit by my silence. Don't turn your nose up at your own sister or at me because you think yourself better. You're not."

Lila closed her eyes and looked away. Images of the warehouse filled her mind once more. She didn't think herself better. She knew she was much worse.

"You don't see anything wrong with a man losing his right to have a child?" Lila asked.

"Celeste and Patrick will lose their right to breathe."

"They dug their own graves."

"Yes, they did. Senator Dubois has not, but I'm not that fussed if the man can't breed, so long as it benefits my family, so long as it secures our future. I would take that right away from a hundred men. I'd even take it away from you."

"It must be nice to play with dolls all day."

"I could say the same about you. You're only a stickler for the rules when they work in your favor. I don't turn on blood. That is the appalling part in all this. You do. I thought I raised you better than that." Her mother gulped down her wine and poured herself another glass. "I have done absolutely nothing wrong. Get off your high horse, child. You're in the real world now. We all have choices to make."

"I can't respect yours."

"Then it's good I don't seek respect."

"You just seek money."

"Money is never the point. I seek security and stability for the family. The only way you get that is by cultivating money and power. I let you spend too much time with your father growing up. He brainwashed you, confused you in one of the most fundamental of ways."

"Oh, I remember all your lectures. I even believed them for a time. But you know what? Out of everything I was taught as a child, my father's morals are the only thing that I can respect."

"Yes, he was very moral when he tried to bribe me for Oskar Kruger. Jewel is your sister. Show some loyalty."

"I show no loyalty to criminals. Clearly, you misjudged me if you thought differently."

"What does that make you? If you can't show loyalty to blood, then at least show loyalty to the family. Right now you're more loyal to Bullstow than to the Randolphs. It's sickening."

"Will you intervene if Senator Dubois asks me to charge her?"

"I won't have to."

"You have something on him?"

"I have something on everyone."

"You'll use it, too, won't you? Maybe I should arrest her after all. I'd hate to see you take a turn on the senator. Our family has done enough to him."

"That's rich. You've cleaned up her behavior in the past. You didn't seem to have a problem with it back then."

"College indiscretions are hardly the same thing. She took a bunch of pills because she wanted to play the tortured artist that month. She drew a few pretty pictures afterwards and moved on to something else. It wasn't that hard to bury the story."

The chairwoman put down her wine. "Here's what I know. Two government blackcoats entered this estate yesterday and were allowed to pass through the gates. You wanted them to come inside, or you would have never allowed such a thing. You had a conversation with them in the Red Lounge, and all recordings of that meeting are absent from my records. The word from their superior is that they've been slated for exile in a few weeks."

Lila leaned back in her chair, vaguely annoyed that someone at Bullstow had let that slip, likely one of her cousins who thought the information was harmless enough. She would have questioned her mother further on that point, but she could not give her any indication that she was correct. From the way her mother studied her face, Lila believed that she was fishing.

"So what do I know? I know that you've finally cleaned up your mess. I don't know how Senator La Roux fits into it all, but I don't believe the reports of his car accident for a second. You picked him out of the crowd at the Closing Ball. You took him back here that night. Then you went out for a walk right before dinner yesterday, and he never came back. Instead, he conveniently got into a rather nasty accident on the way home. If the news hadn't come from Bullstow, if I didn't have the official report on my desk right now, if I didn't know you better, then I'd worry you murdered him."

"Really?"

"Blood squads are legal. You could have justified it to yourself by—"

"I didn't kill the senator."

"Your protest is comforting," the chairwoman said, and sipped her wine. "But I'd like to point out that you don't seem all that upset by his death. I haven't seen you shed a tear."

"I barely knew him."

"Who's the cold bitch now?"

Lila stilled her face.

"How much of one are you? I need to know, Elizabeth. If you harmed the senator—"

"I didn't. I'm not like Jewel."

Her mother licked her lips and nodded. "Good. Sutton told me you left this morning. Where did you go?"

"I had an errand."

"There's an assassin trying to put a bullet in your head, and you just left?"

"It was an important errand."

Her mother snorted. "I had hoped that when you became an adult we might be friends. I didn't have that with my mother. She died too early for us to be equals. Instead of fighting against me, insulting me, you should be learning from me. We should share this burden together."

"I can never be friends with someone I do not respect nor trust."

Lila almost felt sorry for her mother, the way her brow furrowed. "Trust? Everything I've ever done has been in your best interests."

"It's always been in your best interests, not necessarily mine, Mother. You and Jewel are too similar. If you want a friend, find someone else to be prime."

"I already know the purpose of your errand, child. I've been told you visited the clinic this morning. At least tell me the results from that. Let us celebrate some happy news."

Lila pushed back her chair. "I should have added that I could never be friends with someone who does not respect my privacy."

"It's my grandchild and my heir. I have a right to know." The chairwoman smacked her palms against the table.

"I didn't feel well, Mother. I have a cold." Lila stood at her place. "I also had surgery a few days ago. I might not feel so horrible if someone hadn't ordered my doctor to shoot me full of fertility drugs that I did not need. Drugs given without my knowledge or consent, I might add."

"You need an heir."

"No, you need an heir. I don't need anything at all."

"You'll have one, Lila, or—"

"Or what? We can't be friends? We can't be equals? I don't want to be your friend, and I'm damn glad I'm not your equal." Lila pushed her chair in and turned to leave the room.

"You might be the only reasonable choice to run Wolf Industries, but you'll never be as good as Ms. Wilson could have been."

Lila stopped and cocked her head to the side. "Sudden praise for Alex? Are you that desperate for my attention?"

A half-smile formed on the chairwoman's face. "You were right before when you said that Jewel wasn't smart enough to have come up with her plan on her own. It's a good lesson for you, maybe the last lesson I have to teach you, the one I've been trying to hammer into your head since you were a little girl, trying to fill in that blind spot. You can't trust people when you have as much power and money as we do, Lila. They always have an angle."

Lila studied her mother's taunting face. Or at least, she expected it to be taunting. Instead, her expression was merely worn and sad. For the first time her mother didn't look wise and fashionable. She looked...

Old.

"That was why I hoped that we could be equals. That was why I hoped that we could be friends. I can't remember when I've ever had one. A real one, one who I could trust."

"You'll always be trying to find an angle, Mother. That's why you're the first to see it and expect it in others. You don't want a friend. You want a lapdog who won't bite you back."

"Fine. If I can't have a friend, then I'll take a stubborn bitch who bites. As long as the family has its prime."

"You do have a prime. It just isn't me. You also have a chief of security who is more than a capable replacement. I'm leaving, Mother, and I'm taking my mark free and clear when I do. You'll let me, or I'll visit Chief Shaw, and he and I will have one very long chat."

"I could do the same."

"You could, but you won't. I understand now what Senator Dubois meant about needing time. I'm done with this family for a while. I don't want anything to do with any of you."

With that, Lila left the room.

# 30

Lila prowled through the great house, searching each floor, each room for Alex. It didn't take long to find her in the wine cellar, drifting from wooden rack to wooden rack. As a girl, Lila had never understood the layout of the place, row upon row of corks, labels hiding like skittish cats from their master's touch. How anyone ever found anything in the room had always been a mystery, for the light inside had always been far too dim. Alex did not seem to mind it. Perhaps as a slave, she had been forced to memorize the placement of the bottles.

She certainly hadn't known the layout when they were teenagers. They'd often snuck to the cellar and stolen wine on nights Alex slept over. One time, they'd hid under the table in the center when Ms. O'Malley had come to fetch Gregorie for the chairwoman, both fretting that the woman would turn them in. Ms. O'Malley had not even seen the pair, or more likely, had pretended not to, and they had laughed about it in a drunken glee for the rest of the night.

How things had changed.

How much they had stayed the same.

Had Alex ever snuck down into the cellar after bending Jewel's mind, uncorking an expensive bottle to celebrate? It would not to be too hard to misdirect one.

Lila tossed a crimson velvet bag onto the table, one she'd kept in her secret compartment since the day she'd made chief several years before. Something hard inside whacked against the oak, echoing in the room.

Alex jumped, nearly dropping the bottle in her grasp.

"You frightened me," she said, putting her hand up to her heart.

"I brought you something. A gift of sorts."

Alex's initial smile faltered after she noted her friend's expression. "Which bottle do you fancy these days?"

Alex shrugged, turning back to the racks. "I suppose I like Gregorie when you and I get a chance to relive the old days. I buy Masson whenever I have extra money from my slave's stipend. It's cheap, but it's a decent wine. I doubt the Massons ever drink it themselves."

Lila noted the small barb in Alex's voice. How long had it been there?

Months? Years?

Since the first day they'd become friends?

"Do you begrudge the Massons their success?"

Alex chuckled, though the mirth was forced. "Of course not," she said, replacing the wine she'd pulled from the rack.

"Do you begrudge my family for having what you no longer possess? Or me?"

"I'm not jealous. Why would I be? You are in a position that you do not want."

"So are you, but my position is so much higher. That has to be frustrating."

"If I had to choose between the two, I'd choose this. It's much less stressful." Alex turned back around and pulled out a few bottles, scanning the labels before moving on. "I told you. I tried that life, and I wasn't good at it. I'm happier here than I ever was there."

Lila leaned against a rack, blocking Alex's path. "That might be the biggest pile of bullshit I've ever heard. I might have swallowed it the other night, but don't expect me to swallow it now."

"I don't know what you mean. When? Which night?"

"That's a good question, actually. Who is the real Alexandra Craft-Wilson? The one who speaks to me or the one who whispers into my sister's ear?"

"I don't know what you mean."

"You claimed that you had some epiphany after you lost Grace Medical, that you were glad not to be the one who ruined your family, yet you dabble with mine. Did you hand Jewel the plan all at once, or did you feed it to her one part at a time?"

"I don't know what you're—"

"You betrayed this family after everything we've done for you and Simon. You betrayed me."

"I'd never betray you. Why are you saying these things? Did your mother accuse me of something? Did it ever occur to you that she's playing with your head again?"

"Not this time."

"Why is this time different?"

"Because my mother never does something unless it would benefit her more than it might cost her, and she risks a PR disaster if the media gets hold of what you've done."

"What have I done, exactly?"

Lila tossed a pair of handcuffs upon the table.

They fell upon the red velvet bag with a muffled thump.

"Stop being cute. It's tedious."

Alex's eyes narrowed, and her gaze returned to Lila's face. "You're not Chief Randolph anymore. You can't arrest me for anything. What would you even put in the report? I have done nothing."

"The idea came from somewhere."

"You can't arrest me for telling stories."

Lila pursed her lips. Her mother had been right. "It's called conspiracy, Alex. You're damn right I can arrest you for it."

"For telling stories? It's not my fault if someone acts on something I mentioned in passing."

"Are you planning on tipping off the media?"

The slave eyed the handcuffs. "Why on earth would I do that?"

"Because you believe it's your insurance policy. My mother only let it go this far because none of this was ever about you or Jewel or the senator. It wasn't even about making me prime. It was about teaching me a lesson. She was more than willing to sacrifice Jewel for that, just as Jewel was willing to sacrifice Senator Dubois to get her way. Just like you were willing to sacrifice us all to get what you want. Even me."

"What do I want?"

"Opportunity. I couldn't do much for you as chief. You wanted me in a position to help you, really help you, and this was the only way you knew that I'd accept becoming prime."

"You've been around your mother for too long. Too many plots have left you paranoid."

"I already knew that Dr. Rubio worked for you at Grace Medical, but I took another look at her accounts after dinner. Her financials showed a fairly large salary for an overglorified test tube washer. Why would a medical student get paid so handsomely?"

"I have no idea," Alex said, turning away again. She snatched up a bottle of Gregorie and dodged Lila's gaze.

Lila ripped the wine from her grasp. "Why did you pay her so much?"

"I had hundreds of employees. You can't expect me to remember every one, much less their salaries."

"Oh, I think you remember her quite well, and I think you told Jewel about her. About how you could depend on her if you need a tough job done as long as you rewarded her appropriately. How else would a girl from a poor family suddenly earn a full scholarship to medical school? What exactly were you paying her to do during all those vacations? What would I find if I dug a little deeper?"

Alex swallowed. "Don't."

"Why not?"

"Because sometimes secrets aren't for you to know. They're not always bad. Sometimes they're just private."

"Then tell me about this one."

Alex didn't speak for quite a while. She sat at the table and fiddled with the bag's strings. "If we were ever friends, you won't ask that of me."

"Were we ever friends?"

Alex's head snapped up. "What did you expect? That I would be happy as a maid in your house? That I would be happy at the thought of becoming the next Ms. O'Malley?"

"I thought you'd be happy not to work in the damn mines!"

"I was doing you a favor, Lila. You were never meant to walk around in a blackcoat and order your toy soldiers about. It's time to put away childish things and take up what you were born to do. Your mother would have forced the issue at some point. I only helped you come to it sooner."

"So that I would help you?"

"Yes! Can you blame me?"

Lila picked up her cuffs and slid them into her pocket. "I always wondered why my mother agreed to keep you in the great house. I suppose she knew it would only be a matter of time before you showed your true colors. She understood you far better than I ever did."

"My true colors? Don't pretend that you're perfect, Lila. I might not know the details of what you've been up to in your security office, but I know enough. You'd hack into my life right now, privacy be damned, laws be damned, so long as you'd decided that the cause was just. The only difference between us is that I saw you for what you were when we were growing up and I accepted it. I liked you for it. Don't pretend for a second that we're all that different."

Lila headed for the door, the bottle of wine still in her grasp.

"What are you going to do?"

"You ruined a good man, and because he is a good man, I can't do a damn thing about what you've done. But I'm done protecting you. What happens to you now is up to my mother."

"How do you know I won't go to the media?"

"That didn't take long, did it?"

"You've abandoned me. I have to look after myself." Alex snatched up the velvet bag.

"I think you've always been looking after yourself."

Alex pulled on the strings and withdrew a large silver coin. "My mark," she said, her thumb brushing the Saxony seal and her name, engraved on the back. "You've had it all this time, haven't you?"

"The chairwoman gave it to me the day I became chief. I can assure you that it's been a heavy burden, but not nearly so heavy as it is today. You keep it now. I don't want it anymore. And I wouldn't go to the media if I were you. I might dig further into that little secret of yours. I admit that I would hack your life right now if I thought the cause was just, and in this case, I suspect it would be."

"To protect your sister? What a joke. You'd—"

"To protect Senator Dubois, you ignorant little twat. You, my sister, and my mother have put him through enough. He doesn't deserve to have his career ruined and his life mocked in the press, to have the hurt rubbed in his face every time he turns on the news. To have everyone know. So you bet your ass that I'd dig up all your secrets to prevent that from happening. I'd tell them to the world."

Lila left the cellar and returned upstairs. It wasn't until she reached the kitchens that she remembered she couldn't drink the wine she'd taken.

She left the bottle on the counter and jogged upstairs to her room, snatching her riding jacket before slipping from the great house.

Night had fallen. Shadows loomed upon the grounds.

Lila didn't care if it might be dangerous. She just needed to get away from everything for a while. She needed to move. She needed to feel the wind arcing around her helmet and chilling her skin. She needed to see bluebonnets and a thousand crumbling buildings fly past her as she rode down a winding road. Like Dubois, she needed to think. She didn't even care that she had no destination in mind. She'd take her Firefly out tonight, assassin be damned.

She wouldn't let fear stop her.

Lila came upon the garage and gripped the door handle.

The second her fingers touched metal, a gun cocked behind her, lost somewhere amid the trees and shadows.

# 31

A thousand thoughts flew through Lila's mind, and she cursed herself for freezing, rather than spinning and reaching for her Colt.

"Put your hands up and turn around."

Lila paused, unwilling to give up her one chance to draw.

"Do it, now!" the woman snapped, breaking into Lila's panicked thoughts. "And do it slowly, or you'll be dead before you hit the ground."

Lila finally did as she was bid.

Cristina Rubio peeked out from around a tree, night-vision goggles perched on her head, a gun aimed at Lila's chest. A Weberly revolver, no less. Her hair was stringy, her eyes were wild, and her black coat matched the one Lila had seen on the security videos so many days ago.

"I waited too late, didn't I?" Rubio's words rushed together as though she had been drugged. "I should have returned yesterday to finish the job while I still had the chance."

"Is that so?" Lila crept forward slowly. Several cameras had been trained on the garage. If she could get Rubio into their path holding a gun, then whoever was watching the feeds would alert the nearest patrol.

"Stop. I told you. Don't move." The doctor stepped out from behind the tree, gaze flicking up to the roof of the garage, to the door behind Lila, to the darkness beyond. "The militia came to our condo. I saw them."

"Yes, you were to be detained for helping my sister poison her fiancé. I see now that you should be detained for other reasons entirely."

"Why couldn't you have asked me about Senator Dubois before you went under? I could have given you too much anesthesia. I could have made a mistake in my work. There are so many ways a person can die when they're in surgery. So many accidents can happen."

"It's never an accident when a prime dies in surgery," Lila pointed out, her fingers twitching. Rubio had not moved. She'd have to depend on her Colt to save her. Perhaps she could draw it before the doctor had a chance to get off a round. "Do you honestly think you would have survived an investigation? Killing me wouldn't have saved you."

"I would have risked it."

"Like you're risking it now? Commander Sutton already knows what you did. Do you think the charges are automatically—"

"I heard the militia talking over their radios. Commander Sutton doesn't know why she's detaining me. I have a chance to get away after you're gone."

"Your bullet will draw every militia—"

"It's not a bullet. It's a poisoned tranq. I learned my lesson last time. You'll be dead before anyone finds you, and I'll be gone."

Her hand kept shaking.

But she didn't pull the trigger.

Lila's fingers weren't any steadier. She was a fast draw and accurate, but the woman across from her didn't need to be faster or more accurate. She only needed one little prick upon her skin. Anywhere would do. Lila had moved far too close already, just trying to back Rubio into the path of a camera.

Even a poor shot like the good doctor could hit her with ease.

"Here I thought someone had tried to kill me for a good reason. But no, you were just trying to cover your own ass. Just like everyone else." Lila backed away slowly, trying to increase the distance between them as much as possible. She'd draw and chance it once Rubio got started talking, once the doctor stopped paying attention.

Just like Maria had done with the merc two weeks ago.

The doctor would be yet another body on a concrete floor. Something to dream about, but not regret.

Rubio bristled at Lila's irritated tone. "I'm not covering my ass. I'm protecting my life. I worked hard to get where I am. I have a wife, a good job—"

"Had. And you got them by lying."

"Everybody lies. Everybody makes deals. Just like your sister. I notice that you haven't arrested her yet."

"Last time I checked, she hadn't tried to kill me."

"That's not why you sicced your dogs on me. I didn't do anything except steal a drug and synthesize it. She's the one who poisoned her fiancé, not me. And yet here you are. You think I don't know the score just because my parents were—"

A shot rang out, cutting through Rubio's words.

The doctor jumped slightly as though startled, as though something had taken away her train of thought. Her Randolph pendant hopped at her neck, and her eyes lost their focus.

Lila startled as well, but she didn't feel the weight of a dart strike her neck. She didn't feel a needle burrowing into her, pumping poison throughout her blood.

What she didn't feel, she saw.

The thick puff of red mist at Cristina's temple.

The stream of crimson winding from the hole.

The meaningless shake of the doctor's body after the second bullet struck her.

Then a third puff of air.

Rubio's finger clenched on her trigger in shock or instinct or malice.

Lila grabbed her chest. Her body filled with a second rush of adrenaline, her heart pumping, pumping, pumping.

Lila looked down and spied the dart in her collar, caught in her leather jacket.

Rubio crumpled to the ground, staring at the black sky after one last, quiet gasp.

A dozen militia sprinted toward the garage from all sides, boots pounding in the gravel.

Someone grabbed Lila's shoulder, wrenching her around. Sutton panted in front of her, eyes roving over her body, weapon pointed at the ground. "Are you hit?"

Lila shook her head, her scarf too tight around her neck.

"I had to shoot her. A dart would have given her more time to fire before the sedative hit. I had to—"

"Yes. You had to."

Sutton licked her lips. Both women eyed the doctor on the ground, bleeding from the hole in her head and another through her neck. Sutton's aim had been good, so good that Rubio had likely been dead before she fell.

Lila could not look away. She wasn't a cloud this time as she stared at death, but an oozing pile of lava.

"How'd you know?" she asked, digging out the dart that still clung to her coat like an irritating scab. Sutton offered her a baggie, then sealed away what might have been.

"We found the wig and the remote for the plugs in the condo. Rubio also had the same approximate height and weight of the assassin. Oracle knows her wife's not that dainty. Captain McKinley looked through her net logs and found some interesting things in her search history, including research on motorcycle repair. Her last searches were on poisons."

Lila nodded, noticing that even the members of the militia could not look away from the body. They'd all seen plenty in their work, but none had been broken by a bullet.

"How'd you know Rubio was here?"

"I didn't. I just assumed she'd be coming for you again, so we contacted the great house. Ms. O'Malley saw you leave about five minutes ago. Captain McKinley was reviewing the camera footage, but I guessed where you'd run off to. You like to drive off on your own too much, just like this morning. We still need to talk about that, by the way."

"Later," Lila vowed.

"I guess she thought we wouldn't find her unless we turned on thermal imaging."

"I hope you were about to turn on thermal—"

"You're damn right we were."

"I owe you my life. All of you," Lila added, more loudly so that the militia heard her praise. The blackcoats bobbled their heads and turned back to mill around Rubio's corpse.

Sergeant Tripp had already crouched down before the body, checking the doctor's pulse. His pipe peeked from his front pocket.

"Sergeant Tripp, contact Captain McKinley at the security office and process the scene," Sutton ordered. "It's yours until she gets here."

Sutton patted Lila's back, leading her away from the body.

"If Tripp handles this well, I'm going to make him a lieutenant," Sutton said, their boots crunching on the gravel trail.

"He's due for it. Captain McKinley deserves praise for her part as well."

"She doesn't need the encouragement."

Lila shrugged, happy to see the lights of the great house. "Write up your statement and take tomorrow off."

"Everyone else gets praise, and I get punishment?"

"It's protocol. You just killed someone, Lucia. It wasn't a dart this time. That leaves a mark. It spins your head. You should be at home with your husband right now. I know you love him, regardless of how much you complain about him, so go to him. Write up your statement and go home."

"I know damn well what I did. That wasn't the first person I killed. Far from it."

"You're not on the front lines anymore. Go home."

"Is that an order?"

"Yes."

The chief snorted. "That's too bad that you already gave up your job, then."

"It's not yours yet," Lila pointed out, suddenly feeling very child-ish. She tugged on the ends of her jacket. "Look, if you want to ignore me and go in tomorrow, then fine, I can't stop you. I'm not about to get my mother involved, either. But at least for tonight, go home."

Sutton puffed out her chest. "Fine. After I get you back to the great house with a kettle of tea. Your voice sounds like shit."

This time, Lila did not contradict her.

# 32

Lila spun in her bedroom before the mirror, studying her new gray leather coat. It hit her ankles, and didn't look too far off from her blackcoat. She'd bought it earlier that morning at one of the shops across from the estate, ignoring the salesclerk's futile attempts to steer her into a "more appropriate color" befitting her family and station. Once purchased, she refused to allow the plump tailor to stitch the Randolph coat of arms on its breast. Instead, she carried it up to the great house in a red shopping bag with a half-dozen new scarves folded and wrapped in crimson tissue paper.

The coat might not have been tailored specifically for her, but it would do.

Besides, the familiar weight soothed her.

She wrapped a new scarf around her neck, some of her makeup already rubbing away. The bruises were brighter today, though her voice was less hoarse. It would take a while for the evidence of La Roux's attack to vanish, but at least it was hidden away.

A knock sounded upon the door.

"Ms. Gardner parked your car out front, just as you asked," Isabel said with a small bow.

"Thank you, Isabel."

"Are you going somewhere?" She fixed Lila with a curious, almost frightened look.

Lila felt sorry for her. Alex had disappeared from the servants' quarters overnight, and Ms. O'Malley had only told the staff that she had been transferred. None of them knew where she had been taken. Even Lila only had a vague suspicion about where she had ended up. One thing was for certain, though: Alex would fantasize about fetching trays for Jewel after her first day.

Unfortunately, Isabel had been left to deal with Jewel all alone, with only some small bit of relief from Ms. O'Malley. Jewel had ceased her crying, at least until she'd eaten breakfast with her mother. Something had started her up again, and Lila couldn't have cared less what it might have been.

She might have found out if she'd answered the summons to breakfast or the note that followed, but Lila had refused to open either of them. They lay on the floor next to her luggage. She didn't have much, for most of the clothes she liked belonged to a militia chief, and she wasn't that person anymore. She'd put the rest into a suitcase and her old canvas bag, along with her gadgets, her hard drives from her office and home computers, the paperwork for her mark, and a few pictures. She left behind the closet full of crimson coats and dresses and matching heels. She wouldn't have need of such colors for a while.

Luckily, she had plenty of money to buy new clothes, for she'd spread her credits into a dozen accounts throughout the commonwealth and Burgundy. She'd be far from broke when she moved into Hotel Emeraude, a temporary stop until she could decide on a new place to live, perhaps in a new city.

She didn't know where she'd go, but she knew where she didn't want to be.

She also knew a place she'd stop along the way. She owed someone a long conversation, regardless of how much they'd yell at one another. Her life was her own now, and she was tired of living with unfulfilled regrets.

"Yes, I'm going away for a little while. You'll take care of Pax and see that he takes care of himself?"

Isabel bowed again. "Of course, madam. He's my favorite," she answered with a rare, sly grin.

Lila grabbed her satchel and slipped it over her head. Both women snatched up a bag and trundled down the hall.

Pax did not come to see her off, still sulking after she'd said her goodbye that morning.

Lila would miss him, and he would miss her. But maybe, just maybe, her absence would nudge him back to school after the winter break.

After the suitcases were loaded into the Cruz sedan, Lila sped to Hotel Emeraude, located across from Bullstow.

Lila stared at the hotel when she reached it. No matter how many times she had seen Hotel Emeraude, her amusement with the place never ceased. It was as if a teenage architect had crossed the Parthenon with a doll's mansion. It wasn't just grand, it was grand taken one toe over the line. If one didn't look closely, one might miss the touches of whimsy, the windows shaped like gemstones, the trees trimmed in perfect circles, the little gargoyles peeking over the edge of the roof.

She parked in a back lot of the hotel, hiding the sedan among several large trucks, not that it needed much cover. She'd taken the most anonymous vehicle in her family's garage for a reason.

She didn't want to be found.

Lila jogged to the front of the hotel. The door opened as soon as she came near, and the owner of Hotel Emeraude stepped forward to greet her, awash in a cloud of vanilla fabric that contrasted with her ebony skin. The elegant woman extended her hand, her natural hair spiraling cheerfully around her face, like a goddess of the vine. "Prime Minister Lemaire waits for you in the café. We have a private booth for you there, Madame Randolph," she said in a thick French accent. The doorman reached for the satchel on Lila's shoulder. "My people will carry your bag to your room if you wish."

"That's okay," Lila said, eyeing the doorman, not trusting anyone around her laptop and drives. She hitched her satchel farther on her shoulder. "I will carry them all myself later, Madame Sauveterre."

"As you wish. I notice your family's colors. They are missing from your coat?" Madame Sauveterre inquired, tilting her head toward Lila's chest.

"I wear what I wear."

Madame Sauveterre's mouth crooked in a puzzled line as they stepped into the hotel lobby, which was far more exquisite than the exterior. The marble floors, a blend of white and gray geometric prints, were almost too immaculate to step on. Chiseled black pillars had been scattered throughout the space, reaching all way up into the ceiling, which spanned several floors. A crystal chandelier hung from the center of the ceiling. Bursts of silver flashed everywhere, from doorknobs to railings, to rods peeking out of the drapes, to the half-hidden lights nestled throughout the structure. Several ivory sculptures of fantastical beasts dotted the rooms, interspersed among the green sofas and pillows. One of Jewel's paintings had been hung behind the front counter, a bucking unicorn bought by Madame Sauveterre from her sister's second show.

Madame Sauveterre ushered Lila into the café and toward a row of doors at the back. She paused at the door to number three and handed over a key. "You are checked into Hotel Emeraude, Madame Randolph. I will take you to your room later if you wish?"

Lila nodded. "Thank you. As always, your hotel is one of the finest in all of Saxony."

"And the most discreet."

Madame Sauveterre bowed and drifted away, heels clicking on the tile.

Lila opened the door to the private booth, which could have fit a family of six with room to spare. A rug of the deepest green covered the space under a slick ebony table with two large benches on either side. At the table's center sat a trough of lilies.

Prime Minister Lemaire turned away from the window, which had been filled with one-way glass, composing an entire wall of the booth. "Lila, girl," he said, darting forward to lift her off the ground in a hug. Lila's coat caught the air as she twirled.

He let her slide to the ground eventually, but he did not let go.

"I always find them in the end," she said, not sure what else to say.

Lemaire put her down immediately and dragged her to the table. "For oracle's sake, you need tea. You voice sounds worse than Chief Shaw led me to believe."

"I've had buckets and bucket of tea."

"Well then, more won't hurt."

"You don't have to pee it out later."

He tugged down her scarf, squinting at her neck. "There's makeup on your scarf, and enough light in here for me to recognize bruises when—" He licked his thumb and rubbed it across her neck.

"Ew..." Lila batted his hand away. "I told you. I'm fine."

"You're not fine. You're just in one piece. At least when you're prime I won't have any sleepless nights. I had them all the time when..."

He trailed off as Lila darted around him, scanning the room with her palm. As it was not large and did not contain many furnishings, it did not take Lila all that long to finish. Finding nothing, she sank onto the bench across from her father and tossed her jammer near the lilies. The jammer was one of many gadgets she had taken with her when she left the Randolph estate.

"Being prime is dangerous too."

"There are different degrees of danger. And I already checked for bugs. I've made good use of your programs. You always have to check, though."

"I can't assume your palm hasn't been compromised."

"Well, it's good that I check as well. I can't assume yours hasn't been compromised either."

A waitress knocked on the door and entered, bearing a tray of sweet rolls and fruit. She poured hot chocolate from a kettle and turned to leave. "Green tea, please," Lemaire said as the woman skittered away.

"So how's being prime treating you, Lila girl?" he asked, and bit into a roll. His eyes flicked to her gray coat.

Unable to resist the hot chocolate, Lila sipped at her mug. "I imagine the same as the life of a councilman."

"You've cleaned up this mess as well as can be expected. I suppose I shouldn't complain."

"No, you shouldn't."

The waitress returned bearing a kettle of tea and placed it on the table. Then she scooted away, closing the door behind her.

The pair sat together, a bit awkwardly, staring out into the morning. Crowds walked by the hotel, many pointing at the beautiful windows or the gargoyles, taking pictures.

That could be a problem. It was only a matter of time before someone spied her and revealed her location to her mother.

If the chairwoman didn't know already where Lila had gone.

She'd have to move soon.

"How have you been handling the rest of your life, Lila?" her father asked, sensing her thoughts. "Madame Sauveterre walked you inside. That means you've checked in. Why would you stay here rather than your own home?"

"Because I don't live there anymore. Don't get involved."

"Why? Because it's women's business? Don't take that attitude with me. I taught you better than that."

"No, because you can't unhear the truth."

"Too late, your mother's already involved me," he said, popping a grape into his mouth. "Woke me up in a huff because you wouldn't come down to breakfast. I'm to do my fatherly duty and convince you to resume yours."

"You'll accept her command?"

"If I agree with it. Why did you leave, Lila?"

She tore off a little piece of a sweet roll and considered the question. Why had she left? It wasn't as though her mother's morals had been a new discovery. It wasn't as if she'd ever believed Jewel to be anything more than what she'd proven herself to be.

"I left because I need time to figure things out."

"You're twenty-eight years old. At your age, your mother—"

"Was already someone I could never respect."

"So don't be her."

Lila sipped at her hot chocolate. "At what point is forgiveness agreement?"

"I suspect your mother did not tell me the entire story." He crossed his arms over his chest. "Perhaps you'd like to share your side of things?"

"It's confidential even if it's—"

"It's your mother and you. It's always confidential."

"And Jewel. And Senator Dubois. And Ms. Wilson."

He quirked his eyebrows at the mention of Alex, especially when Lila referred to her so formally. "Somehow I feel like I'm going to regret getting in the middle of four women."

"I warned you. Turn back now."

Lila knew he wouldn't. Haltingly, she told him about Senator Dubois, about how her investigation into his condition had led her to Rubio and how it had eventually led to Jewel, to Alex, and to her mother. She studied every little twitch of his mouth, every line in his eyes, checking for outrage or apathy.

She hated her suspended anger, this need for his confirmation of her own feelings.

"I can't believe Jewel would do something so cruel. To take a man's chance at children—a senator, no less." He frowned and let out a heavy sigh. "Actually, I can believe it. I just don't want to. Has Senator Dubois contacted you?"

"No. I don't believe he'll want me to do anything. He's acting like those spouses, convinced the bruises don't matter because their lover apologized."

"You want to make his decision for him?"

"Are you implying that I'm like Jewel?"

"No, don't be so defensive. What happened to Senator Dubois is repugnant, but your mother was right. This is the real world. Life isn't always just, and even when it is, it isn't just equally."

"Jewel goes free, and Mother will get away with her part too. She had full knowledge of what would happen, and she didn't lift a finger to stop it."

"Can you prove it?"

Lila shook her head. "Ms. Wilson is probably in a mine somewhere, and Rubio is dead. How typical that the highborn go free when the lower classes—"

"Dr. Rubio wasn't punished for helping Jewel. She was killed because she tried to murder you. And as for Ms. Wilson, she proved herself unworthy of working in the great house. It is a position that requires trust, and she lost yours. She should have been sent away for violence against you last month, anyway. I'm glad she's gone. Is this why you've turned your back on the family?"

"I can't live among them anymore, knowing what they are capable of. Can you blame me?"

"Your mother was right, you know. You do have a blind spot. You always have. She thought it only applied to Ms. Wilson, but it didn't. You've always been blind to her and Jewel as well. You didn't know how far Jewel would go, or how much your mother would ignore, so long as the family came out better in the end. Her lesson backfired."

"How do you put up with her? You're a good man, you—"

"I have other responsibilities. I have to let go of the little things if I want to act on the big ones."

"Is Senator Dubois a little thing?"

"If he makes himself into one, then yes. You can't lend him your outrage, Lila. He has to act on it himself."

"That's ridiculous."

"That's the only way anything will ever come of it, which is why you didn't bring up charges against Jewel before you left." He sipped his hot chocolate and studied her face. "You're not going back there, are you?"

"Perhaps I should. I could do a great deal of good as prime. I could suck it up even if I hate it, even if I hate everyone in my whole damn family right now."

"Except for Pax and Shiloh."

Lila nodded.

"You know, there are a lot of ways that someone can do good. Things that don't include the Randolphs. Now that you have your mark, you have more options."

"What of the family?"

"You're not worried about the family, and this isn't about them. It never has been. It's about you. What do you want, Lila?"

"What I wanted is gone," Lila said, knowing she'd never be chief anymore, knowing she might never get Tristan back.

"Is it? Life is about what you want from it and what you can make of it. What can you make of your life now?"

"What a self-indulgent and irresponsible question. I can't believe that's coming out of your mouth."

"You can't make a difference if you don't agree with the manner in which you make that difference. That's what you'd have if you went back home. If you don't want to fight your battles that way, then find a new way."

"What battles?"

Lemaire traced a knot on the table. "I made a mistake with you, Lila. I freely admit that now. You were my first child, and I was just so excited by you, so fascinated, so in love with the idea of being the best sort of father I could be. I'd seen Senator Blanc's daughters make a mess of their family's finances for their own gains, and I overdid it. You were older and more responsible at ten than most senators, and I kept pushing you anyway."

He shook his head. "I did this to you, made you incapable of prioritizing yourself. You would have made a great senator, perhaps a far better prime minister than me, had you been born a man."

Lila spun her sapphire ring. "I hacked Liberté."

Lemaire's jaw dropped. It was one of the few times she'd ever seen him surprised.

"I did it for the case. Don't panic. Well, except for the first time, when I was a kid and I wanted to see if I could. My point is only that I would have made a lousy senator, just like I've made a lousy chief. We're not meant to prod and poke, and damn the means so long as the end result is useful. Alex and my mother were both right. I bend the rules when I feel the cause is just, or perhaps I just feel like I'm above them."

"You're thinking of Senator Dubois."

Lila didn't answer.

"If you had been born in the poorer classes, if you'd always owned your mark, what would you have done with yourself?"

"Private militia," she said immediately.

Lemaire leaned over the table, his brows raised and waiting.

Lila let out her breath. "I would have ended up like Max or Trudy Poole. There's not a doubt in my mind."

"You wouldn't have ended up like them. Ms. Poole hacked and spied for money, and her son does the same thing for the same reasons, but I think that's the most honest thing I've ever heard you say. I could make use of you, Lila. I need someone who understands both worlds, the games that the highborn play with one another, as well as the world of those who would steal from the masses. I need someone who can stay neutral in it all, someone I can trust, especially next year, when I ascend to the council. If you were from the poorer classes, I would have made you an offer long before now. I would have asked you to become a paid consultant. It's not unheard of for a woman to be absorbed into government if she has the skills we need. We could use you, Lila. Think about it."

Under the table, Lila rubbed her belly.

"We would have to talk about what happened with the oracles, though. You can't go off and make decisions on your own."

"Father…"

"Have you talked with the oracle yet?"

Lila shook her head. In point of fact, she had received a call from the oracle that very morning. She'd said that Lila was in danger. She'd seen it in a vision. She'd even promised to send a contingent of purplecoats to the south gate to escort Lila to safety.

The oracle didn't seem keen to tell Lila where that safety might be found.

"I've dealt with the assassin," she'd told the oracle, not in the mood for more bodyguards, and disconnected before the woman could say another word.

"Talk to the oracle soon, please. She won't stop calling, and I'm legally obligated to answer." His palm vibrated, and he checked the screen.

"Is that her?"

"No," he said, sucking in a breath.

Lila had never seen her father so startled. "Who, then?"

"Get your bag and get out of the hotel now."

"What? Why?"

He slid his palm across the table.

Lila saw a familiar article. This time, it wasn't in her inbox. It wasn't in her mother's, either. It had been posted on the front page of the *New Bristol Times's* website.

Tomorrow it would hit the papers, knocking aside any mention of the Holguíns and Oskar Kruger. The protestors would make brand-new signs with brand-new slogans, all about her.

"Mother did this?"

Maybe it was a joke.

Her fingers moved quickly across her father's palm as she scanned the page, eyeing the link below her story.

Another highborn revealed.

And another.

And another.

Not her mother, then. La Roux. He must have set it up as a dead man's switch. If he wasn't alive to prevent it, every piece of dirt on every highborn and lowborn he'd had in his clutches would be revealed and sent to the press.

The switch had been flipped.

Had he forgotten about it, or had he planned it all along, knowing that Bullstow wouldn't change their official story after it broke, knowing that his reputation would be safe? That his children wouldn't suffer under it?

He'd ended up with everything he'd wanted in the end, except his life and a place in the senate.

"Senator La Roux. He did this. He—"

"Yes, and you have to get out of here now," her father said, tugging her toward the door. "It's the only way I can keep you from a holding cell. I need to figure out how to handle this. I need to call Chief Shaw and find out what evidence has leaked. Go now."

Lila opened the door to the private booth and hurried from the hotel toward her car.

Slipping her key into the ignition, she faltered.

She had no idea where to go.

# Other Titles by the Author

# About the Author

Wren Weston grew up writing fantasy and science fiction stories, but one chance book club encounter with a romance novel changed her favorite genre forever.

She became addicted.

Not only can she not stop reading them, she can't stop injecting shades of the genre into everything she writes.

You have been warned, darlings.

*To contact Wren, visit www.wrenweston.com or drop her a line on Twitter or Facebook.*